MADDIE LEANED HER HEAD
AGAINST THE WINDOW

"Stupid, stupid girl," she muttered. "So what if he's handsome? So what if he can quote Shakespeare?"

Down in the garden, Quinlan turned around without warning and looked up at her.

"Damnation!" Maddie ducked backward. Perhaps he hadn't seen her. She counted to ten, took a breath, then stepped forward.

The marquis stood beneath her window, a white rose in one hand. With a smile, he held it up to her, then bowed with an absurdly grand flourish.

"Of all the nerve," she breathed. She stuck her tongue out at him.

He blew her a kiss.

Her heart pounding, Maddie unlatched the window and shoved it upward. "Don't you ruin my roses!" she shouted.

"'But soft,'" he called up to her with a deepening grin, "'what light through yonder window breaks? It is the east, and Juliet—'"

With a choked cry of outrage, she slammed the window shut.

Avon Books by
Suzanne Enoch

Historical Titles

BEFORE THE SCANDAL
AFTER THE KISS • TWICE THE TEMPTATION
SINS OF A DUKE • SOMETHING SINFUL
AN INVITATION TO SIN • SIN AND SENSIBILITY
ENGLAND'S PERFECT HERO
LONDON'S PERFECT SCOUNDREL
THE RAKE • A MATTER OF SCANDAL
MEET ME AT MIDNIGHT • REFORMING A RAKE
TAMING RAFE • BY LOVE UNDONE
STOLEN KISSES • LADY ROGUE

Contemporary Titles

A TOUCH OF MINX • BILLIONAIRES PREFER BLONDES
DON'T LOOK DOWN • FLIRTING WITH DANGER

By Love Undone

SUZANNE ENOCH

AVON

An Imprint of HarperCollins*Publishers*

This is a work of fiction. Names, characters, places, and incidents are products of the author's imagination or are used fictitiously and are not to be construed as real. Any resemblance to actual events, locales, organizations, or persons, living or dead, is entirely coincidental.

AVON BOOKS
An Imprint of HarperCollins*Publishers*
195 Broadway
New York, NY, 10007

Copyright © 1998 by Suzanne Enoch
ISBN 978-0-06-087525-1
www.avonromance.com

First Avon Books paperback printing: July 1998
First Avon Books revised paperback printing: October 2008

Avon Trademark Reg. U.S. Pat. Off. and in Other Countries, Marca Registrada, Hecho en U.S.A.
HarperCollins® is a registered trademark of HarperCollins Publishers.

Printed in the U.S.A.

10 9 8 7

For the world's best agent,
Nancy Yost, who took a chance
and has yet to admit regretting it

For Micki Nuding,
my editor extraordinaire,
who likes the funny parts, too

And for the ladies of TLT bb—
you know who you are—
thanks for your support (LOL)

Chapter 1

The yellow-red blossoms of the Lord Penzance rose-bush waved lazily in the light breeze. Humming a counterpoint to the robins singing in the trees behind her, Madeleine Willits snipped three of the perfect blooms and gently dropped them into her basket. And then she pricked her finger.

"Ouch! Blast it."

At the same time, a stentorian bellow rumbled from the master bedchamber window like a clap of thunder, and she jumped.

"Miss Maddie!" the housekeeper called frantically.

"Good Lord," Maddie muttered. Dropping her clippers into the basket, she gathered up her skirt and ran for the kitchen entry.

Mrs. Hudson pulled open the door as she reached it, and Maddie shoved the basket into the housekeeper's plump arms. "What happened?" she called over her shoulder, running through the main hall toward the stairs to the second floor. Curious servants hurried into the hallway, creating obstacles for her to dodge.

"I don't know, Miss Maddie," came from behind her. "Garrett was in with him!"

"Garrett!" she called.

The butler appeared at the top of the stairs. Red-faced, he wiped at the thick brown trails of gravy running down the front of his black coat. "It was just the post!" he protested.

Bill Tomkins, closely followed by a tea saucer, exited the bedchamber at high speed behind Garrett. "He nearly killed me that time," the footman panted, leaning against the bannister.

"You shouldn't have been in there," Maddie said unsympathetically, trying to regain her breath before she stepped into battle. She pulled the shawl from around her shoulders.

"What was I supposed to do, keep polishing the lamps while he's yowling like a Bedlamite? Scared the devil out of me," the footman exclaimed, shuddering.

The butler chuckled. "Then you should thank him."

Sending the servants a warning glance, Maddie fluttered the end of her shawl into the doorway. "We surrender, Mr. Bancroft. The household has been vanquished."

More rumbling issued from inside the room, followed by the thudding sound of a pillow hitting a wall. "Humph. Stop that nonsense and get your pretty face in here, girl," Malcolm Bancroft's irritated voice ordered.

Maddie entered the bedchamber. The remains of luncheon drippily decorated the near wall, while the pillows which had been propping Mr. Bancroft up in bed lay strewn about the floor, leaving her employer flat on his back amid a tangle of bed sheets.

"My, my. Such carnage." She clucked her tongue.

Awkwardly he lifted his head to pin her with a baleful, dark-eyed gaze. "Bah," he said, and lay flat again.

Stifling a grin, Maddie began gathering pillows in her arms. "Any interesting news in the post today?"

"I wouldn't be so blasted clever if I were you, Maddie. It's not news you'll relish, either. Damned stuffed shirts.''

An edge of uneasiness ran through her as she levered him into a sitting position with the help of the pillows. ''I see you've appropriated my favorite term for the nobility. The new king is coming to visit, I suppose. Shall I have the silver polished—or hidden? You know King George so much better than I.''

As she expected, the mention of George IV distracted her employer from whatever it was that had upset him. ''Mad King George, Fat King George. Who's next—Blind King George?''

Maddie chuckled, relieved as reluctant humor returned to his voice. ''Royalty are blind to everything but their purses, anyway.''

Mr. Bancroft snorted. ''So they are.'' With his weakened left hand he gestured at a badly crumpled paper resting on a slice of toasted bread. ''And that particular ailment infects most everyone in England who can lay claim to a title. Hand me that letter, my dear.''

She complied, shaking crumbs off and resisting the urge to read it herself. He would tell her the news. He always did.

Awkwardly he flattened the paper against his chest. ''Listen to this, Maddie. And brace yourself.'' Malcolm cleared his throat and lifted the wrinkled missive. '' 'Brother.' '' He stopped and looked up at her, obviously waiting for the significance of that single word to sink in.

Maddie's insides jolted unpleasantly, and the last pillow slipped from her fingers onto the floor. ''The Duke of Highbarrow has finally answered your letter,'' she muttered, sinking onto the comfortable chair beside his bed.

''It's been more than a fortnight since we wrote him. He was bound to answer eventually.'' He looked sideways at her. "I'd actually begun to wonder whether you'd burned the original letter."

Maddie straightened. "I told you I would send it," she said, wondering if he knew just how close she had come to 'accidently' misplacing the missive in her bedchamber fireplace.

"I know you did." Her employer smiled briefly, then returned his attention to the letter. " 'Brother,' " he began again. " 'I was away in York on business when news of your poorly timed illness arrived. I have sat to write you immediately upon my return to Highbarrow Castle.' "

"You were right," Maddie noted, as Mr. Bancroft paused to catch his breath. He tired so easily these days. "He always uses the word 'castle,' doesn't he?"

"At every opportunity. To continue, 'Victoria sends her wishes for a complete recovery, though as you know I really don't give a damn one way or the other.' "

"My word, he's awful."

" 'I am planting my crop at Highbarrow Castle at the moment. Otherwise, despite your past errors of judgment, I would make an effort to call upon you at Langley Hall.' "

"Of course," Maddie and Mr. Bancroft agreed in skeptical unison.

All she knew of the duke were tales of his monumental stuffiness and arrogance, and Maddie let out her breath in a silent sigh of relief. He wasn't coming. "So that's that, then," she said, rising. "Hardly enough to warrant frightening me half to death, though. Shame on you."

"That's the good news, I'm afraid."

Slowly Maddie sat down again. "Oh."

"Now please remain calm."

She nodded. "Just as you did," she teased.

"Hush. 'However,' " he resumed, " 'as getting the

crop in at Langley is of paramount importance, I have spoken with Quinlan. He has agreed to journey to Somerset to oversee planting and to tend to the estate during your recovery. He follows immediately upon this letter, and should arrive at Langley on the fifteenth of the month. Yours, Lewis.' ''

Maddie gazed out the window. The lovely spring morning, the first without rain in three days, had become a disaster. Worse than a disaster. She took a deep breath. ''I assume His Grace is referring to Quinlan Ulysses Bancroft?''

Her employer nodded, a sympathetic grimace touching his gaunt face. ''Afraid so. The Marquis of Warefield himself.''

Maddie cleared her throat. ''I see.''

He reached out and squeezed her fingers. ''I'm dreadfully sorry, my dear. You are acquainted with him, I suppose?''

She shook her head. ''Thankfully not. I believe he was in Spain during my . . . visit to London—if you could call it that.'' Maddie frowned at the memory.

''It wasn't your fault, my girl,'' Malcolm soothed.

She eyed him fondly, wondering who was supposed to be comforting whom. ''You're the only one who thinks so. None of them—not *one* of them—saw anything but that stupid kiss, and that stupid man trying to shove his hand down my dress. They didn't care that I wanted nothing to do with it, or with that awful scoundrel Spenser. And I want nothing to do with London society, ever again.''

''Well, Quinlan wasn't there, so don't worry yourself. He wouldn't say anything, anyway. Wouldn't be polite, you know.''

''I'm not worried.'' Maddie sat up straighter, pulling her fingers free from his comforting grip. ''Nor am I the least bit faint of heart, Mr. Bancroft.''

He chuckled. "I never said you were."

"It's merely that I'm . . . annoyed." Ready to throw a screaming fit would be closer to the truth, but she'd had the feeling lately that her peaceful days were numbered. Once the letter to Highbarrow Castle had gone out, someone had been bound to reply.

And even though she didn't know the Marquis of Warefield, she knew *of* him. Quinlan Ulysses Bancroft was the very pink of the *ton*, a favorite of the new king, the bluest of blue bloods, the epitome of propriety and dignity. She loathed him without ever having seen his pampered, spoiled, self-important visage. He was one of *them*.

"Nobility" might be what society called them, but from her experience, the word had nothing at all to do with their characters. "I thought we informed His Grace that you had someone tending to Langley during your illness."

"You didn't expect him to care about that, did you? He owns Langley Hall, my dear; I only manage it for him. And he will take whatever steps are necessary to preserve his considerable monetary well-being, with or without my consent. You know that."

She sighed. "Yes, I know that. Even so, he might have asked whether you wanted assistance before he foisted his son off on you."

Unexpectedly, Mr. Bancroft laughed again, rare color touching his pale cheeks. "I don't believe Quinlan allows himself to be 'foisted' on anyone."

"How noble he must be," Maddie said unenthusiastically.

Her employer narrowed his eyes, suspicion touching his expression. "Just remember, my dear, the less trouble you make for him, the shorter and less painful his visit is likely to be."

A flash of guilt ran through her. After all, this deuced

marquis was Mr. Bancroft's nephew, and it had been at least four years since they had seen one another. Even though she might detest him and the rest of the damned aristocracy, she knew all too well how lonely Malcolm must feel being cut off from his family.

So, little as she liked Warefield's coming, she had no intention of stamping her feet and throwing a tantrum. Not in front of her employer, anyway. "I shall behave," she assured him.

He smiled. "I have no doubt that you will."

"As long as he does," Maddie added.

"He will. I already told you, he's the epitome of good manners."

"I am bereft of words at the very idea of setting eyes upon his illustrious personage."

"Maddie," Bancroft warned with a slight grin. He pulled himself into a more upright position, grunting with effort as his still legs hampered the movement. "Best send Mrs. Iddings down to the village and have her spread the word."

"So the local folk can flee into the hills, I suppose?"

"Our neighbors will never forgive me if I don't give them advance notice that the Marquis of Warefield is coming to Langley. An actual title appearing in this part of Somerset is rarer than a camel passing through the eye of a needle."

She sighed. "They will be beside themselves with excitement. I daresay I have no idea how I will contain my feelings, myself."

"Do try, won't you?"

Maddie smiled. "Of course. But only for you."

He looked at her fondly, with an understanding her own father had never possessed. "Thank you."

"You're welcome." She stood. "I'll bring you up some more tea."

"And peach tarts, if you don't mind. My luncheon seems to have met with an accident."

She glanced over her shoulder and chuckled in amusement. "Lucky we kept some sweets in reserve, isn't it?"

"Bah."

Maddie apprised Mrs. Iddings of the Marquis of Warefield's imminent arrival and then sent the cook down to Harthgrove to purchase vegetables and gossip away the afternoon. After bringing Mr. Bancroft his replacement luncheon, Maddie escaped to the garden potting shed, where she could bang about and curse without being overheard. Stupid, stupid noblemen, always showing up where they weren't wanted! Or needed.

"Madeleine?"

"Dash it," Maddie muttered, wiping her hands against her pelisse. "In here, Mrs. Fowler," she called.

She'd hoped to have until tomorrow before the neighbors came prying for information. Apparently Mrs. Iddings's gossip was even more efficient than Mr. Bancroft had anticipated. Smoothing the annoyed expression from her face, she stepped out of the shed.

"Oh, there you are, Maddie." Jane Fowler was wearing her favorite visiting dress; no doubt she intended to carry her news to every home along the lane once she'd pried it out of Maddie.

"Good afternoon."

"I should say so." Mrs. Fowler sighed happily, her rounded cheeks dimpling. She plucked a stray leaf from Maddie's hair. "I hear that we're to have an important guest in Somerset. I am quite beside myself."

"Oh, well, you—"

"My goodness," Mrs. Fowler continued, clapping her hands together, "a marquis." She leaned forward and lowered her voice, even though there was no one about to hear them except for the finches. "And I hear that he's very handsome, and that he has *twenty thousand a year*. Can you imagine? Twenty thousand pounds a year!''

Swallowing her annoyance at such awestruck pointlessness, Maddie nodded and started back toward the house at a brisk pace. Bad enough she had to host Warefield without having to talk about him as well. ''You seem to know a great deal about him, Mrs. Fowler.''

''Mrs. Beauchamp does. Her cousin is Baron Montesse, you know.''

''Yes, I had heard that.'' *Endlessly and repeatedly.*

''How long will he be staying at Langley?''

''I really don't know. With the Season starting soon, I'm certain it can't be too long.''

Mrs. Fowler sighed reverently. ''Ah, yes, the Season.''

The worshipful look on her face made Maddie want to laugh. ''Have you told Lydia and Sally the news?''

''They were the ones who told *me*. Such good girls, they are. And Lydia has become quite proficient at the pianoforte, you know.''

''Yes, I d—''

''Oh, I know Sally isn't quite out yet, but she *is* seventeen. Here in the country, so very far from London, Lord Warefield couldn't expect us to stand on such strict ceremony, don't you think?''

From what she'd heard of the marquis, he stood upon strictest ceremony at all times. ''Of course not,'' she agreed, hiding her sly smile. If anything could encourage Warefield to shorten his stay at Langley, it would be the Fowler girls.

''Marvelous, marvelous.'' Mrs. Fowler continued on beside her, then stopped and lifted her handkerchief to her mouth, unsuccessfully stifling a rather giddy gale of giggles. ''I have just thought of the very thing!''

Maddie reluctantly halted her escape. ''Whatever might that be?''

"I will speak to Mr. Fowler, and we shall hold a country ball in honor of Lord Warefield. Won't that be spectacular? And I shall invite everyone—oh, everyone but the Dardinales. That Miss Dardinale is completely unacceptable."

By coincidence, Patricia Dardinale was also the prettiest young lady in the countryside. "I shouldn't think you would mind one more girl, Mrs. Fowler. I have heard Lydia's singing is much improved over last year. I believe if there is one thing to sway a gentleman's interest, it is a song well sung."

Mrs. Fowler clutched Maddie's arm. "Thank you, my dear. And you shall come as well, for I can't think that Mr. Bancroft would venture from Langley these days without you. Unless the marquis takes over his care, of course. How noble that would be. Oh, my, yes."

Maddie frowned. She hadn't considered that. It made sense that a meddling, busybody nobleman would think a woman incapable of her duties, however proficient she'd been with them over the past four years. "Yes, how noble, indeed."

For the forty-seventh time, Quinlan Ulysses Bancroft lost his place in *Ivanhoe*. He dropped the book onto the black leather seat beside him and, holding onto his hat with one hand, leaned his head out the window. "Really, Claymore, must we take a census of every wheel rut, rock, and puddle in Somerset?"

The groom's face appeared over the high corner of the coach. "Sorry, my lord," he said, and vanished again. "If you don't mind my saying," his voice drifted back, "it's my thinking that King George ain't traveled upon these roads lately."

Quin sat back and resumed reading, until another hard bump jolted him against the cushions. "Lucky George," he muttered.

Reluctantly he set the book aside again and stretched his long legs out to rest them on the opposite seat. With a sigh he settled back to watch southern Somerset County pass by outside. At least the weather had turned agreeable, and the green, tree-covered countryside smelled more of meadow grass than it did of cattle.

The marquis pulled his pocket watch out of his waistcoat and glanced down at it. By his estimation, another twenty minutes or so should finally put him at Langley Hall. Three damned days in a coach, with a perfectly good mount tethered behind. He might have left his luggage to follow and ridden on to Langley in half the time—except that the duke, his father, had written to indicate that he would arrive on the fifteenth.

Uncle Malcolm would undoubtedly take a hasty arrival as a threat against his management of Langley. And if there was one thing Quin did not wish to do, it was to further the antagonism between Lewis and Malcolm Bancroft. So he would not, under any circumstance, arrive before the fifteenth.

Little as he relished the idea of being his father's sacrificial lamb, the seven years of silence between the Bancroft brothers had long been a topic of jest and gossip in London's highest circles. Uncle Malcolm had always been his favorite relation, and even if it meant spending time with the rustics, he intended to do his damnedest to see that the wags were finally silenced. It looked very shabby and set a poor precedent before the rest of the nobility.

With any luck, he should be able to organize Langley's books and get the crop in the ground with little bother—which hopefully would make Uncle Malcolm look more favorably on making amends with his brother, which hopefully would leave His Grace feeling more amenable toward everyone in general.

And if events transpired as smoothly as he hoped, he

would even have time to return to Warefield for a few weeks before the Season began. Lord knew, the coming summer would leave him little time for himself. Once he arrived in London his first task would be to make wedding arrangements, and the remainder of his social engagements would stem from that.

Quin stretched, yawning. Eloise had been dropping more hints than usual in her letters lately, and their understanding needed to be formalized. At least marriage looked to be fairly painless—so the sooner, the better. The duke's grumbles about grandchildren had grown into bellows—as if he needed another excuse to bellow.

"My lord," Claymore called from his perch, "Langley, I believe."

Quin shifted to look out the opposite window. Sprawling at the top of a slight rise and overlooking a quaint wildflower garden and a small forest glade, Langley Hall rose red and white into the cloud-patched noon sky. Barely more than a cottage by London standards, the estate did offer some of the best fishing in Somerset—small recompense though that was for the journey.

"I'll have stew of you, ye blasted beast!"

A gargantuan cream-colored pig squealed and ran full tilt across the road. A farmer followed by another man and a red-faced woman, all brandishing pitchforks and rakes, headed at full speed after it. The high-spirited coach horses skittered sideways, nearly dumping the lot of them into the spiny hedge bordering the road.

"Whoa, lads!" Claymore bellowed, while Quin slammed into the side of the coach and lost his hat to the floor. "Apologies, my lord!" the groom called. "Damned country folk. No manners at all!"

The marquis leaned down and retrieved his chapeau. "Splendid," he sighed, dusting off his hat and resettling it on his head. "Country folk. Bloody marvelous."

Chapter 2

❦◦◦❦

"He's here! He's here!"
Madeleine jumped at the kitchen maid's excited pronouncement of the bad news. The Marquis of Warefield had arrived, and exactly on time. No doubt he considered it gauche to arrive late—though she'd been hoping he'd be delayed.

She wanted to run to the nearest window and look for herself, if only to confirm that the nightmare had begun. But she'd seen hundreds of carriages before, and more than her share of English lords. And the good Lord knew they weren't worth gawking at; in fact, they weren't worth much of anything at all.

She doggedly finished stitching the brim of last year's yellow spring bonnet. With a little luck it should last her through the summer, anyway. Out of necessity her sewing skills had greatly improved over the last few years, but she was still surprised when she turned the hat to view it and found that the repairs actually looked quite satisfactory.

"He's here, Miss Maddie! Come quickly!" Mrs. Hodges exclaimed.

"I know, I know," she said, though she doubted Bill Tomkins or the housekeeper heard her as they hurried past the open morning room door. Blowing out her breath, she set the bonnet aside and went to join the others.

"Oh, look at that, Mrs. Hodges! What a fine carriage!" Tomkins said. He craned his tall frame and peered out the foyer window over the other servants' heads. "I'd wager the King himself has none finer."

Even the normally impassive Garrett was fidgeting. His gaze traveled from the window to the grandfather clock in the hallway and back again, as though he were trying to judge the precise moment he should open the front door to achieve the greatest effect.

"Don't worry, Garrett," Maddie said encouragingly. "I imagine the marquis will caterwaul from time to time, but I'm certain he won't bite."

Garrett glanced at her. "You may be confident of that, but you've never encountered the rest of the Bancrofts. I've no intention of making a false step in Lord Warefield's presence."

"Oh, please. The only difference between a noble and a pauper is that one can afford to be rude, and the other can't."

From the annoyed looks and disapproving comments sent in her direction, none of the other servants was particularly interested in hearing further ruminations on the topic from her. Maddie rolled her eyes and purposely stayed back from the excited crowd at the window. They'd see soon enough how little their overstuffed hero resembled their worshipful imaginings.

The rumble of hoofbeats neared, to the accompaniment of the creaking clatter of a large carriage. Garrett tugged once more at his coat, nodded at the assembled servants, and flung open the double front doors. The procession of Langley employees, pulling at neckcloths and straightening apron ribbons, streamed out the door and down the shallow steps to line either side of the front walk.

Following them, Maddie stepped onto the short, wide marble portico where she could watch without being obvious about it.

The coach that rolled up the crushed stone drive was huge and black, with the Warefield crest emblazoned in bright yellow and red on the door panel. A superb quartet of matched black geldings came to an impatient stop before the gawking servants, while a striking bay hunter pranced to a halt at the rear of the vehicle. Maddie sniffed. The pompous boor had even brought his own mount, as if the contents of Langley's stables wouldn't be good enough for him.

Before Bill Tomkins could take more than a step forward to open the coach's door, a liveried servant clambered down from beside the driver's perch to perform the service. With practiced efficiency he flipped down the steps tucked beneath the door, and then with a bow stepped backward.

An elegant leg, sheathed in a polished Hessian boot of finest black leather, emerged from the dark coach. The second limb followed, revealing muscular thighs molded into a pair of fawn-colored buckskin trousers. Maddie's skeptical gaze touched on an elegant gray and blue waistcoat, a coat of dark blue superfine over a broad chest, and a snowy white cravat snuggled between impeccably stiff shirt-points. White kid-gloved fingers handed the footman a polished mahogany cane tipped in ivory-inlaid ebony wood.

The marquis looked down as he stepped from the coach, and a blue beaver hat, set at a rakish angle on wavy hair the rich color of bees' honey, obscured her view of his face. "Buffoon," she muttered, unimpressed. Fencing clubs and boxing halls might keep him lean and athletic, but they couldn't improve a bulbous nose or crooked teeth. Or mask the lines of idle dissipation.

He finally looked up. Twin pools of jade, green as the forest after rain, took in the drive, the excited servants, and the red stone walls of Langley Hall. Maddie's eyes took in a finely chiseled nose completely lacking in any sort of deformity, and a strong, lean jaw. Lips that could disquiet a maiden's heart murmured something to the footman, who immediately handed the cane back and motioned at the anxious Langley footmen to begin unloading the gargantuan mound of luggage atop the coach.

Then Lord Warefield strolled forward to meet Langley's servants.

Mrs. Hodges favored him with a deep curtsey. "Welcome to Langley, my lord," she said, her plump cheeks red with excitement and nervousness. "I am Mrs. Hodges, the housekeeper."

"Good afternoon." With a slight nod he dismissed her, moving on down the line. The jade eyes barely gave each servant so much as a glance. "Good afternoon. Greetings. Pleased." Each followed the other in succession as he made his way to the shallow steps.

The marquis stepped onto the portico, and his aloof gaze passed over young Ruth, Mrs. Iddings, and then Maddie. For a second, he met her eyes and paused, his forward progress arrested. Swiftly she caught herself and curtseyed, lowering her eyes. When she dared look up again, she found him already past her, handing his cane and hat to the butler. She had anticipated being ignored, so she was surprised by the strength of her sudden annoyance at his compelling look and swift dismissal.

"And how are you after all this time, Garrett?" the marquis asked, dropping his gloves one by one into the hat, his attention on the decor of the hall. No doubt he found his uncle's taste completely vulgar and rustic.

"Quite well, my lord, thank you. Shall I show you to your chambers, or would you rath—"

"I'd prefer to see my uncle," Lord Warefield interrupted. "Kindly direct my luggage to my chambers. My valet follows a short distance behind with the rest of my things."

Maddie looked at him in disbelief. They'd already unloaded enough baggage to see him through the summer. If anything more arrived, she'd have to believe he meant to set up permanent residence.

"Very good, my lord."

Garrett glanced at Maddie, and with a start she stepped forward. "I will take you to see Mr. Bancroft, if you please," she said, reminding herself again that she'd promised to behave.

Warefield turned to look at her. A curved eyebrow arched slightly, and then he inclined his head. With a graceful gesture of his long fingers, the marquis motioned her to precede him. "I do please."

She moved past him into the entryway and down the wide hall, the quiet tapping of his boots against the hardwood floor following her to the curving staircase at the far end. Trying not to rush or trip and draw any more attention to herself than necessary, Maddie gripped the smooth mahogany railing and kept her eyes on the stairs before her. The less of a stir she made, the less notice the marquis was likely to pay to her.

Yet she hadn't expected him to be so aggressively handsome that she couldn't help wanting to look at him and touch him. It somehow made the entire visit even more irritating. Over the past few years, she had envisioned all English noblemen as fat, pig-eyed, pompous dandies.

The Marquis of Warefield was not remotely fat, nor pig-eyed, and though his attire was surely the very latest style, she certainly couldn't call him a dandy. Dandies were quite a bit less . . . capable looking. But judging by his haughty greeting, her memories of Londoners' inflated self-importance were still quite accurate. She held onto that thought as she continued to the second floor.

"Are you my uncle's nurse?"

"I am his companion," she corrected him, keeping her eyes to the front as they reached the top of the stairs. Silence followed her remark, and belatedly she realized what he must be waiting for. "My lord." She scowled at her stupid omission.

"And how did you come to be in this . . . position?"

Curiosity touched his cultured voice, and she clenched her jaw. "I applied for it, my lord."

"I see."

Maddie wanted to argue, for obviously he did *not* see. From his tone, he thought her Mr. Bancroft's mistress or some such scandalous thing, but she didn't wish to prolong the conversation by correcting his idiotic misapprehension. He had no right to be prying into her affairs, anyway.

The door of Mr. Bancroft's bedchamber stood before her. Gritting her teeth, she kept a tight rein on her fraying temper. She was nearly rid of the marquis for now.

"What am I to call you, then?" His deep voice sounded smug and amused.

Maddie hesitated, but since Warefield traveled in such elevated circles, he'd have no reason to recognize her name. "I am Miss Willits, my lord."

"You know, Miss Willits, it's not considered improper to face someone while conversing with them," he pointed out.

Maddie blinked. *How dared he?* Embarrassment, mortification, and fury shot through her all in a rush. She would *drown* him in politeness if that was what he required!

Stifling a furious growl beneath a smile, she whirled

about in the doorway. "My apologies, my lord." She thrust her hand into the room. "Mr. Bancroft, my lord." As she glanced at him, his startled gaze caught hers. He opened his mouth to reply, but her legs swept her into swift, angry motion past him and back down the stairs. "If you'll excuse me, my lord."

Quin looked after his uncle's so-called companion as her slender form vanished down the stairs in a hurried blur of pink and white muslin. "Of course," he replied absently. *Odd chit.*

"Quinlan Ulysses Bancroft. Welcome to Langley Hall."

Quin shook himself and turned to face his uncle's bedchamber. "Uncle Malcolm, thank you."

With a smile he entered the room, taking in the colorful array of medicine bottles on the stand beside the bed, and the stack of books and cards and game pieces on the chest of drawers. Fresh flowers, set below the open window, waved gently in the soft spring breeze. Malcolm sat propped up by an enormous mound of pillows, his face pale and thin. Even so, his dark eyes twinkled as he smiled.

"Don't you look splendid, my boy."

Quin sketched a bow. "As do you. From Father's description I expected you to be already laid out in a coffin. You look quite well, I must say."

"No doubt my pending death was merely wishful thinking on Lewis's part." His uncle gestured at the chair beside the bed. "How was your journey?"

Refusing to take the bait and argue over his father's private ruminations, Quin instead took a seat. "Quite uneventful, thank you."

Malcolm shook his head and waved a finger energetically at his younger relation. "None of that, lad. You'll find I've become a regular gossip these days. You're to tell me who you passed on the road, what sort of weather you encountered, and how dismayed you were at being pulled away from Warefield before the Season.''

For a moment Quin eyed his uncle. Malcolm had previously been known for his stubborn independence rather than for eccentricity, but as the duke had mentioned several times, there was no telling what an apoplexy might have done to his cognitive abilities. ''Very well. I was not at all dismayed to come visit you, Uncle. It's been far too long, in fact. The sun shone periodically, though it rained once, and I passed two milk wagons, a mail stage, five farmers' wagons, and just a few minutes ago, a lone escaped pig with several angry persons in pursuit.''

Malcolm slapped the quilted bed covering, the corners of his eyes crinkling as he chuckled. The action winded him, and it was a moment before he could speak. ''That would be the infamous Miss Marguerite,'' he finally explained. ''I'll have to tell Maddie.''

''Maddie?''

''Miss Willits. Have you met her yet?''

Quin nodded slowly, still wondering at his initial, uncharacteristically heated reaction when he'd set eyes on her. ''I have. She is—''

''Lovely, isn't she? A true lifesaver, she's been. I thought she was going to show you up here.''

''She did.'' Apparently his assumption about Miss Willits's place in his uncle's household had been correct. ''And yes, she's quite attractive. A bit . . . unique in her manners, perhaps, but I imagine none of you are exactly pleased to have me here.''

Again his uncle grinned. ''Some of us more than others.''

Quin lifted an eyebrow, surprised at finding Malcolm in such good humor. ''Well, thank you very much, Uncle.''

"Excuse me, Mr. Bancroft, my lord."

Quinlan looked up. Miss Willits stood in the doorway. The high color in her unfashionably tanned cheeks and the tilt of her chin made it quite obvious that she had overheard his comment, and he stifled a scowl.

"Yes, Maddie?"

She stayed in the doorway, her light gray eyes averted from Quin. Irish blood, he decided admiringly, taking in her tall, slender figure and curling auburn hair, more slowly this time. By his guess, her unbound hair would hang to her waist, a far cry from the London fashion of daringly short curls. Nothing was so arousing in a woman as long, curling hair. His uncle had splendid taste in mistresses. Exquisite taste—as the rush of his pulse would indicate.

"Mr. Bancroft, Lord Warefield's luggage appears to be too substantial for the east room," she said stiffly. "If it's not too forward of me, perhaps his lordship might desire some of his things to be moved to the upstairs sitting room, so that he might utilize it as an office during his stay, especially if he should have need of reading or writing materials and space."

Her sensuous, full lips remained set in a stern, straight line, and his curiosity and interest rose another notch. Apparently she had a temper, this one. He'd corrected her behavior, and now she was angry at him for it.

"I've no wish to intrude," he offered easily, watching as her lovely eyes snapped in his direction and then away again. "I can read or write in the library."

"Nonsense. That's a splendid idea, my dear."

"I'll see to it at once." With a deep, formal curtsey, she left the doorway.

Quin returned his attention to Malcolm. "I want to assure you, Uncle, I am here only to be certain Langley runs smoothly until you are recovered. Father has no intention of turning you, or your staff," and he gestured in the direction Miss Willits had disappeared, ''out into the wilds of Somerset.''

Malcolm shifted the book lying across his lap. ''Heavens, no. I never thought so—wouldn't look at all proper, you know. And believe me, I'm well aware that the titled Bancrofts' prime objective is to appear proper at all times.''

Quin frowned. ''That's hardly fair, Un—''

''Once I've hopped the twig, though, no doubt you or Rafe will be calling Langley your own.''

''Rafe will be lucky to get a stick of furniture. And believe me, everything is still His Grace's.'' With a slight grin, Quin sat back in the chair. ''He makes quite certain everyone knows it, and it's far too late to expect him to change. If I had my way, Langley would've been deeded over to you a long time ago.''

His uncle glanced at him. ''It's not much by your standards, I imagine, but it has its attractions.''

''No doubt.'' Miss Maddie Willits seemed to be chief among them. He stood to leave. ''I'd best get myself situated. Unless you have a different idea, I'd thought to begin on the books this afternoon, and take a tour of the fields in the morning. If the weather looks likely to hold, I don't see any reason not to get the wheat and barley put in immediately.''

''No sense wasting time,'' his uncle agreed. ''Maddie knows where everything is.''

Quin nodded and turned for the door. ''Very good.''

''And Quinlan?''

He looked back again. ''Yes?''

''Take . . . care with Maddie. She's more than an old buffoon like me deserves.''

So he was being warned off already. It was easy to see why. In his incapacitated state, no doubt Malcolm hadn't been keeping her very occupied. If his brother had been the one sent to Langley, Rafael would likely have been more than willing to step into the void, as it were. Even for Quin, the thought was intriguing. "I shall take extreme care, Uncle."

Quin headed down the long portrait-lined hallway toward the east wing. Before the absurd quarrel between Lewis and Malcolm, he had spent several summers at Langley, and he had always regarded its generous wood beams and tall, wide windows with affection. The Hall seemed smaller than he remembered, but then he'd gained more than a foot in height and two decades in experience since his last visit.

He paused to gaze out one of the windows which overlooked the pond and the forest glade beyond. From his first brief view of Langley everything appeared to be fairly well organized, but he didn't look forward to delving into what must have become a chaos of bills and accounting over the past few weeks. Quin sighed.

"My lord?"

Starting, he turned around. Miss Willits and another servant stood in the hallway behind him, having apparently materialized out of thin air. "Yes?"

"Are you lost, my lord?"

"No, I'm not." He smiled. "But thank you for your concern."

Maddie nodded, then gestured at her companion. The older woman, though, flushed and backed away several steps. With an exasperated look, Miss Willits faced him again. "My most sincere apologies for disturbing you, my lord, but Mrs. Iddings, the cook, wishes to inquire whether you have any particular culinary preferences or dislikes. There was no time for us to inquire of your own cook at Warefield, my lord, and I believe the delicate constitutions of the nobility to be well documented."

"Oh." Quin nodded in what he hoped was an agreeable manner. "Of course. Thank you again." Now he was completely convinced; for some reason, Miss Willits strongly disliked him.

"Yes, my lord?"

Quin cleared his throat. "Well, I've no real love for blood pudding," he began, noting that Mrs. Iddings continued to keep her portly frame behind Miss Willits, while Maddie made no move at all. Not afraid of him either, then. He smiled in an attempt to placate the natives. "And I enjoy a nicely roasted pheasant, I suppose. All in all, I'm not very particular, despite any rumors to the contrary."

Maddie nodded coolly, no trace of a return smile in her gray eyes. "I am pleased to hear that, my lord." She turned to her companion. "Does that help you, Mrs. Iddings?" she asked, in a much warmer tone.

The cook curtsied. "Indeed it does. Thank you, Miss Maddie." She flushed again and bowed in the marquis's direction. "Thank—pleased—thank . . . God bless you, my lord." Mrs. Iddings hesitated, then hurried away down the hall.

"Thank you," he said to her back, though he doubted she heard him as she clumped down the back stairs. The servants at Langley seemed to be a rather odd bunch altogether. He looked back at Miss Willits, to find her glaring at him.

She swiftly wiped the look from her face and curtsied politely. "Thank you, my lord."

Before she could flee again, he stepped forward. "My uncle said you would show me where the account ledgers are, Miss Willits," he suggested. "Do you have a moment to do so?"

"I thought, my lord, that you said you weren't lost."

"I know exactly where I am. I simply don't know where my uncle keeps his ledgers these days."

"Very well, my lord," she answered smoothly, turning with a swirl of her pink muslin skirt. She stopped at

the head of the stairs, and pointedly faced him again.
"If you please, this way, my lord."

Quin shook his head and followed her down the stairs.
"How long have you been my uncle's companion, Miss
Willits?"

She stopped so suddenly he nearly ran into her. Quin
flung out a hand to catch his balance as she whirled on
the steep stairs to face him. His fingers lightly grazed
her cheek, and she flinched toward the railing. She took
a quick breath and smoothed her skirt. "Four years, my
lord."

Before he could apologize, or even open his mouth,
she'd reversed direction and begun descending the stairs
again. Torn between alarm and amusement, Quin continued after her. "Four years?" he repeated. "How old
are you, Miss Willits?"

As she halted and spun to face him again, he grabbed
onto the railing and stepped back. "I am twenty-three,
my lord." Her polite tone didn't nearly hide the furious
glint in her eyes.

Before she could begin spinning about again, Quin
put a hand on her arm. "If you please, Miss—"

She blanched and jerked away. "Don't—"

Genuine dismay touched her eyes. Swiftly he lowered
his hand, curiosity and surprise blazing through him as
the color left her delicate, high-boned cheeks. Maddie
Willits was primmer than any mistress he'd ever seen.
"Of course. My apologies. I wished only to know
whether you perform this unusual stairwell dance for all
of Langley's guests."

She pinched her lips together before she lifted her
chin in defiance again. "Only with those who order me
to face them when I speak, my lord."

"I did not order you . . . well, perhaps I did, but I
certainly didn't mean you should risk breaking your
neck every time I ask you a question."

She eyed him expectantly for a moment. "Forgive me, my lord," she finally ventured, "but I am now at a loss as to how to proceed."

Quin stopped his frown before it could more than half form, plagued by the muddy feeling that he'd just lost some sort of odd contest. "Please proceed down the stairs, Miss Willits."

"Of course, my lord."

Quin followed his escort into a small, tidy office tucked into the far east corner of the manor. Miss Willits went to the desk beneath the double windows and pulled open a drawer, exposing a stack of ledgers.

"Thank you, Miss Willits. That will do," he said quickly, stopping her before she could disturb the order of the ledgers and paperwork and render his task even more difficult. "I can manage from here."

She froze, her hands tightening around the books. Abruptly she released them, dumping them back into the drawer with a loud thud. This time he was expecting it when she spun to face him, her face a polite mask and her eyes glinting. "Of course, my lord. How presumptuous of me. Pray forgive my ill behavior."

"No apology is necessary." As she walked away, he sat at the desk and pulled out the first of the books.

"Thank you, my lord."

"Have some tea sent in, if you please," he said, distracted, as he flipped to the first page. His uncle's hand scrawled haphazardly across the paper, a series of loops and slashes and serrated lines. Quin groaned inwardly. Deciphering the figures would be difficult enough without translating each line of writing, as well.

"As you wish, my lord."

He looked up. "Miss Willits?"

She was nearly out the door. "My lord?"

"Do you have a stutter?"

She furrowed her brow, the sight both enchanting and

diverting despite the blatant hostility in the eyes beneath. "I don't believe so, my lord." She hesitated. "Why do you ask, my lord?"

"Generally one or two 'my lords' per conversation are enough to satisfy my pride," he said amiably, curious to see what her reaction would be. In most cases women didn't come to dislike him until *after* he'd explained that lovely as they were, he already had an understanding with Eloise Stokesley. "More than that begins to sound somewhat obsequious."

For the first time, her sensuous lips curved in a small smile as she curtsied and left the room. "Yes, my lord."

Chapter 3

Maddie liked the word "obsequious." It sounded unpleasant and haughty at the same time, the very sort of arrow she meant to aim at the Marquis of Warefield, however handsome and charming he seemed to think himself.

With luck he would concentrate on merely being attractive and pleasant. Otherwise, he might actually take enough time with the ledgers to ruin the year's book-keeping completely. As for the crops, if not for the last damned rain, she would already have had that business well begun. She could only pray Warefield would have as much aversion to dirtying his hands as the rest of the nobility, so she could organize the farm tenants before he deigned to set his lovely boots in a single field.

Once she had everything taken care of, Warefield would have absolutely no reason to hang about little Langley Hall in obscure Somerset County. He certainly wouldn't wish to prolong his stay just to visit, not with the rest of his kind beginning to prepare themselves for the ostentatious London Season.

"Twopence for your thoughts, Maddie."

Maddie shook herself and looked up at Mr. Bancroft. His amused expression deepened, and she wondered how long she'd been staring at her nicely roasted pheasant. Mrs. Iddings had certainly outdone herself, for she couldn't remember eating anything so delectable, damn it all. Not an undercooked or a burnt spot could be found. "Beg pardon?"

Malcolm chased a stray chunk of potato around his plate. "You had such a glare on your face. I merely wondered what you might be plotting—and against whom it might be aimed."

She narrowed her eyes. "I'm not plotting anything. I am merely wondering why your nephew decided to take his meal by himself in the formal dining room, rather than keeping company with his ailing uncle."

"Ah." He glanced up at her as she stabbed at her pheasant, imagining it to be a slice of Lord Warefield, well done. "Perhaps he's not comfortable with invalids. Many people aren't, you know."

She scowled. "I know that. But it's not as if you have the clap or something, for heaven's sake. A week ago you couldn't even move your hand, and now you're eating with it. You'll be out riding in a month, and the least he could do is—"

"Maddie," Mr. Bancroft interrupted.

At the same moment someone cleared his throat from the doorway. Flushing, Maddie added poor timing to Warefield's growing list of faults.

"Good evening, Quinlan," Malcolm said. "Have you dined?"

The marquis stepped into the room. He gave Maddie a quick, unreadable glance, then nodded at his uncle. "Indeed. Your cook is splendid, Uncle. That was quite possibly the most succulent pheasant I have ever tasted."

"I'll pass along the compliment. I'm certain Mrs. Iddings will be excessively pleased. Don't you think so, Maddie?"

Maddie kept her attention on her plate. "I'm certain she will be, Mr. Bancroft. She's quite delighted by his lordship's presence, as are the rest of us."

"Why, thank you, Miss Willits."

He hadn't even blinked at her considerable sarcasm. Perhaps she was too adept at it and he had thought her sincere. All the better, then; she could continue making a fool of him. "Not at all, my lord."

"I was wondering whom you might recommend as a guide when I tour the fields tomorrow," Lord Warefield continued, fiddling with the medicine bottles on the bed stand.

All of the dazzling bright colors were likely too tantalizing for him to resist, Maddie thought. Abruptly feeling cheery once more, she set aside her fork. "If I may be so bold, my lord," she said, "Sam Cardinal is quite knowledgeable. He's been a tenant here for more than fifty years, I believe."

The marquis nodded and smiled. "My thanks—"

"Nonsense, Maddie," Malcolm interrupted, with unusual obtuseness. "Sam Cardinal will talk poor Quinlan's ear off. Barley this, and barley that. I declare, the man's skull is stuffed with grain."

Lord Warefield chuckled, and glanced sideways at her again. "Do suggest someone else, then."

Maddie stifled her frown, wishing Mr. Bancroft would quit interfering. Then another, even more promising suggestion occurred to her, and she gleefully turned to the marquis. "Walter, the groom, grew up h—"

"Maddie," Mr. Bancroft scowled. "What in the blazes—"

"Actually, Miss Willits," Warefield interrupted, "I thought perhaps you might show me about, yourself."

"Me?" She felt his cool green gaze on her face, and looked pleadingly at Mr. Bancroft. "Surely your uncle needs my—"

"I think Maddie would be the logical choice, yes," Malcolm agreed, nodding. "She's familiar with all the local farms and tenants, and with what's grown well, and where, over the last few seasons."

Maddie's jaw clenched. *Traitor.* It seemed she was completely on her own in this. Well, so be it: one marquis could hardly be that much of a challenge. "Surely Lord Warefield doesn't wish to follow a female about Langley."

"I have no objection," the marquis countered. "And I could hardly hope to find a more attractive guide anywhere in Somerset."

She met his gaze. He found her attractive, did he? My, my, how very flattering. And he had no *objection* to her presence. He must be even more obtuse than she'd imagined. Maddie kept the strained smile fixed on her face and tried not to grind her teeth. "I'm quite the early riser." She wished she could take just one minute and tell him exactly what she thought of him and his sod-headed, gossip-mongering peers.

"Splendid. I'd hoped to make an early start of it. Shall we say first thing in the morning, then?"

Apparently nothing short of pummeling the marquis would convince him to change his mind. "Whatever pleases your lordship."

He looked at her, an odd expression on his face. Perhaps her sarcasm had finally penetrated—though it might merely have been gas. With a slight smile, the marquis turned back to his uncle. "I'm a bit tired tonight—too much sitting about in the coach, no doubt—but I thought we might have time to chat together tomorrow evening at dinner. I imagine I can fill your ears with enough London gossip to amuse you for a while."

Mr. Bancroft looked sideways at Maddie, and she cursed herself for having pricked the marquis's pride, thereby ruining tomorrow evening for all of them. Surprisingly, though, her employer smiled. "That would be grand, Quinlan. Maddie and I were just about to begin a game of piquet, if you've a mind."

This time Maddie couldn't help her strangled exclamation. "Mr. Bancroft!"

Both men looked at her. "Is something wrong, Maddie?"

She madly tried to think up an excuse for her outburst. "His lordship said he was tired," she ventured hastily. "Of course he doesn't wish to play cards."

"Perhaps another time." Lord Warefield nodded, then sketched a shallow, elegant bow in Maddie's direction. "Good evening, then."

"Good evening, Quinlan."

"My lord."

His quiet footsteps retreated down the hallway. As soon as he had passed out of earshot, Maddie snorted and set the remains of her dinner aside. "Me, show him about Langley, indeed."

"You said you would," her employer pointed out.

"*You* said I would. I have things to do tomorrow. I've been calling on Mrs. Collins every day with fresh flowers and the post since she came down with the gout, and John Ramsey wanted me to look at his new sluice gate and see if you might be interested in using the same design for the northern field. I'm certain your nephew can find someone else to follow about."

For a moment Malcolm gazed at her, his serious look a little unsettling. "You know, Maddie, I've been thinking: it might do you good to associate with those of your own station from time to time. You've been rusticating in Somerset for four years now."

She stood, her cheeks flushing. "He is not of my station, and no doubt he would be quite insulted to hear you say such a thing." Maddie took a slow, deep breath to calm herself down. "And being in the country," she continued in a more moderate tone, "is called rusticating only when you wish to be somewhere else. Which I do not."

"Well, Miss Willits," he returned, the fine lines around his eyes deepening as he smiled, "I must say I'm very pleased to have you here." He gestured at the dresser. "Now, get the cards, if you don't mind. I need to regain some of my losses."

A reluctant grin touched Maddie's lips. "Yes, you owe me four million pounds, don't you?"

He scowled. "Only temporarily, girl."

Warefield had said they were to meet first thing in the morning. Therefore, when Maddie crept down to the stable just after dawn, she decided it would be his own fault for missing her. He should have been more specific about the time. She would be well on her way to Harthgrove before Lord Warefield even dreamed of rising.

Most of the household staff was still to bed as she made her way out the rear entrance through the kitchen. The spring morning air had a bite to it, and she shivered despite her warm gray riding habit. Cold or not, though, Maddie smiled in amusement as she headed down the path to the stable. Hopefully the marquis would be forced to spend the day with Sam Cardinal or Walter after all, while she could sample the new berry pastries at the bakery and chat the morning away with Squire John Ramsey and his sister.

She strolled around to the front of the stable—and stopped in confusion. Her mare, Blossom, stood saddled and waiting for her, Walter holding the reins. "Walter, what—"

"Good morning, Miss Willits."

She jumped and spun around. The marquis was mounted upon the huge bay hunter he'd brought with him from Warefield. Maddie refused to admire the beast, and instead kept her annoyed attention focused on Langley's unwelcome guest. He sat easily, looking down at her with a slight smile on his blasted handsome face. The early morning sun lightened the jade of his eyes to emerald. The marquis leaned forward with a creak of leather, taking several moments to peruse quite thoroughly her attire. No doubt he thought it cheap—though even her completely unflatterable self couldn't help but notice the twinkle in his gaze and the responding flutter along her nerves.

Feeling distinctly outmaneuvered, she smiled and curtsied. "Good morning, my lord."

"I'd begun to wonder whether you'd forgotten our appointment." He wheeled the bay about as it pranced impatiently. "We did say first thing in the morning, did we not?"

"Yes, we did, my lord," she conceded airily, yanking the mare's reins from Walter's startled hands and stalking over so the groom could hand her up into the saddle. "I daresay I shall be the envy of the entire countryside today, being in your lordship's company."

"I daresay that's far too generous, but thank you for the compliment."

"You are quite welcome, my lord." She nudged Blossom into a trot. "Shall we begin, my lord?"

For just a moment he glanced at her dubiously, but before he could comment, she was off and moving toward the nearest of the tenant farms. Since he'd demanded her company, he would simply have to accept her "my lords" as well.

A light breeze set the new elm leaves dancing in the treetops. Clouds tumbled slowly toward the rising sun, and she wondered whether they were in for another bout of rain. She certainly hoped not, for that would prolong the marquis's stay at Langley.

"You sit well, Miss Willits." The bay cantered up

beside her, and again Warefield's eyes ran over her appraisingly.

Maddie flushed. He didn't need to sound so surprised, or to take so long gawking at her again. Once was quite enough to put her out of sorts. "You are far too kind, my lord," she returned, wanting to roll her eyes at his stuffiness. "I daresay I ride adequately for Somerset, but my goodness, I've never seen such a splendid mount as yours."

Predictably, his expression warmed at the *faux* praise. "Old Aristotle's a fine beast, indeed. I won him in a wager with my younger brother last year. If I don't take him everywhere with me, Rafe's been known to drop in at Warefield and attempt to make off with him."

"Only imagine, stealing a horse for amusement." Maddie chuckled and snapped the end of her reins against her thigh, harder than she intended. She flinched at the sting and blamed Warefield for that as well. "And to think that if common folk did such a thing, they could be hanged for it!"

He swung around to look at her, surprise and anger in his eyes. Perhaps he wasn't as obtuse as she'd thought—this time he'd actually noticed the insult. Before he could comment, though, a fortunate disaster caught her attention. She sat up straighter and pointed ahead of them.

"Oh, look, it's Miss Marguerite! Headed straight for Mrs. Whitmore's cabbage patch again, no doubt. We'd better head her off, or Langley will find itself in the middle of a tenant war."

The marquis regarded the pig trotting across the field in front of them. "She nearly sent my coach into a hedge yesterday. Several angry persons flailing farm implements were also involved."

Maddie grinned as she set Blossom into a canter behind the fleeing sow. "Yesterday? Miss Marguerite's be-

ing quite industrious. It's usually a week or more
between escapes.''

The marquis and Aristotle kept pace beside her. ''Ah.
This Miss Marguerite is a hardened criminal, then, I assume?''

''Most definitely.'' Abruptly, she remembered that
she detested Warefield. ''Though I daresay, my lord, that
compared to the fascinating amusements of London, a
marauding pig must be rather stale.''

He laughed in response, an unexpectedly warm, infectious sound. ''Not at all, Miss Willits. I don't spend
all my time in London, you know. And we do have pigs
at Warefield.''

''Not like this one, my lord.''

Granting him a smug glance, she took off across the
field in pursuit. As she'd predicted, Miss Marguerite had
angled along the stream bank, making straight for the
Whitmores' small tenant farm. In a moment Warefield
and Aristotle had flashed by her. He was a splendid
rider, rust-colored coattails flying out behind him as he
leaned low over the bay's back. However numerous his
other faults, she had to admit that he looked magnificent.
Maddie held Blossom back, curious to see how his lordship would handle this little adventure.

The marquis swept along the bank, swiftly closing the
distance between himself and the pig. Miss Marguerite
dodged sideways, and in response the marquis sent Aristotle forward in a sprint of speed, obviously trying to
trap the pig between the horse and the stream. The maneuver would have been a sterling one, if not for the
notorious mud at the edge of the water.

''Your lordship, be careful of. . . .'' Maddie trailed
off, grinning delightedly. This should be interesting.

Aristotle reached the edge of the water. Feeling the
ground give beneath his hooves, the bay balked and
scrambled sideways to regain his footing. The marquis,

his attention on the swerving pig in front of him, never saw it coming. With a startled yelp he went over the hunter's head, and, reins and hat flying, landed with a resounding splash in the stream.

"Damnation!"

The marquis swarmed to his feet, water cascading off his fine rust riding coat and filling his beautiful Hessian boots. Even with the spring melt, the water rose only as high as his hips, which she supposed was fortunate since he'd gone in head first. As he swept his wet blond hair out of his eyes, he issued several very colorful curses under his breath, which the morning breeze carried to Maddie's ears. They were quite imaginative, and he actually rose a notch or two in her estimation.

She took a deep breath, trying to stifle the laughter welling in her throat. "Oh, no, my lord! Are you unhurt?" she asked belatedly, coaxing Blossom closer to the stream.

He spun around to glare at her. "Yes. Quite."

"How dreadful! I cannot imagine . . . Is the water very cold?"

"Yes." Slowly he turned in a circle, then glowered up at her again. "Frightfully. Where is my hat?"

"I believe I saw it . . . floating downstream, my lord." A chuckle erupted from her chest, and she quickly covered it with a cough. "Do you wish me to fetch assistance, my lord?"

"Absolutely not."

He eyed her blank face suspiciously, then shook water from his honey-colored hair and waded toward the bank. In the slippery mud he lost his footing and nearly went down again, and Maddie swiftly turned away, biting her lip to keep from laughing aloud.

"I shall fetch Aristotle for you, my lord," she said, and wheeled Blossom toward the stand of tall grass where the bay stood looking embarrassed by the whole affair.

As soon as Miss Willits turned away to fetch his blasted horse, Quin scrambled ungracefully through the slick mud and made his way back up onto the stream bank. Water and mud squished coldly in his boots, and he sloshed over to a clear, sunny spot of field and sat down to pull them off.

The deuced pig was out of sight, but Miss Willits seemed to know where the beast was going. He'd be damned if he'd let Miss Marguerite escape after this. In fact, he fully intended to dine on ham for luncheon. He dumped the first boot out and put it aside while he yanked off the second. Maddie approached with the horses behind him, cutting off any further cursing. "My thanks, Miss—"

"Oh, my goodness!"

At her shocked exclamation he froze. Miss Willits had clearly viewed his tumble into the stream with no anxiety and a great deal of amusement, and he couldn't believe that the removal of his boots would overset her. He turned his head.

Beside Maddie, with nearly identical expressions of astonishment on their pale faces, two young women, a brunette and a blonde, sat upon a pair of chestnut mares. Maddie's intelligent gray eyes gazed at him steadily for a moment, something very much like amused triumph, and very little like shocked dismay, in her gaze.

Quin had already begun to regard Miss Willits with some suspicion. Now, as her lips trembled with the effort of not breaking into out-and-out laughter, he was nearly ready to think her capable of actual sabotage.

Abruptly she blinked and straightened. "Oh, pray forgive my momentary upset, my lord. I had no idea you were *en déshabille*. May I introduce the Misses Lydia

and Sally Fowler? Lydia, Sally, the Marquis of Warefield.''

Quin shook more water out of his hair and swiftly
climbed to his feet. ''Ladies,'' he intoned, feeling completely ridiculous standing there in his stockings and
with a sodden boot hanging from one hand, and even
more distracted by the discovery that his uncle's companion spoke French. ''Charmed.''

''My . . . lord,'' the brunette returned, blushing bright
red and thrusting one hand in his direction. ''What an
unexpected pleasure.''

Stifling a grimace, Quin dropped his boot into the
grass and stepped forward to grip her fingers.

''Lord Warefield, are you injured?'' the blond asked,
giggling nervously.

''Only my pride.''

''Surely not, my lord,'' Maddie said warmly. ''Not
when the venture was as noble as this one, and not when
your foe was so infamously and fiendishly clever.''

There it was again: that definite sarcasm even her
lovely innocent expression couldn't quite disguise. He'd
been intrigued enough by her apparent dislike of him to
suggest they spend the morning together. Obviously
he'd underestimated the degree of her antipathy—no
doubt because of the lust her mere appearance sparked
in him. Even the very cold water had only managed to
subdue his physical reaction to her.

''The venture was noble in thought, perhaps.'' He met
her gaze squarely. ''But I'm afraid that the poor cabbage
patch may be done for by now.''

Miss Willits's lips twitched, and she suddenly seemed
to feel the need to examine the skyline over her shoulder. The sunlight accented the red highlights in her hair,
and the gray riding habit, demure though it was, in no
way disguised the curving lines of her body. Quin didn't

realize how long he'd been staring at her until he heard the Misses Fowler whispering together.

"Lord Warefield," the older one said, "our home is just over the hill, if you'd care to dry your clothes."

"A splendid idea, Lydia," Miss Willits seconded.

An alarm bell immediately began ringing in Quin's skull. He was no fool, and it was rapidly becoming apparent that whatever Maddie favored had little to do with his own well-being. "My thanks, ladies, but Miss Willits and I have a great deal to do this morning. The sun is shining, and I daresay I'll dry soon enough."

Maddie looked disappointed, which convinced Quin that he'd made the correct decision. "Are you certain, my lord?" she pursued. "The Fowlers' cook makes a wonderful apple tart."

"Oh, yes!" Sally seconded, and actually reached down to put a hand on his arm. "Mama says Mrs. Plummer is the finest cook in Somerset. She's from Yorkshire, you know. It's because of Papa's sour stomach. He can't abide seasonings or spices of any kind, for they leave him with a terrible case of gas." She giggled.

Maddie made a sound in her throat, but when he glanced in her direction she had found a clump of grass to occupy her attention. "Are you well, Miss Willits?" he asked solicitously.

She started and glanced at him. "Quite, my lord. I was only thinking I should go see to Miss Marguerite before she completely decimates the cabbage crop."

She intended to abandon him to the Fowler sisters, then. "Yes, you're right," he said, hurriedly bending down to collect his boots and hobbling toward Aristotle. "We must be off."

"Are you certain you will not come to Renden Hall with us, my lord?" Lydia asked hopefully.

"My apologies, but I cannot." He pulled on one boot, his stockings squishing unpleasantly.

"Then you must call on us for tea tomorrow," Sally insisted.

Quin looked at her for a moment. Obviously she had no idea that only the head of the household was supposed to tender such an invitation, especially to a social superior. But he did not wish to appear as rude as she was. "Of course I shall," he answered, inwardly wincing. He glanced at Maddie and found sudden inspiration. "Would it be too forward of me to ask Miss Willits along as my guide? She does seem fond of Mrs. Plummer's tarts."

"What a grand idea!" Sally agreed. "Oh, Lydia, perhaps we could ask Squire John and his sister, and then we might play whist."

Quin watched Miss Willits from the corner of his eye. At the mention of this squire's name, her annoyed expression cleared.

"We shall see you tomorrow, then." Maddie clucked at her mare. "Come, Blossom, let's find Miss Marguerite."

Wondering if Uncle Malcolm was aware of Maddie's apparent fondness for the local squire, Quin quickly stomped into his other boot and grabbed Aristotle's dangling reins. "Ladies," he said absently, reaching up to touch the brim of his hat, only to remember that by now it must be on its way to Bristol Strait and the Atlantic Ocean. Drat it all, he'd been fond of that hat. "Until tomorrow."

"Until tomorrow, my lord."

"Yes, tomorrow, Lord Warefield."

A moment later he caught up to Miss Willits, who'd abandoned him without a backward glance. "What have I to look forward to with the Fowlers?"

"I could not say, my lord," she answered. The prickly annoyed female had returned, as though she hadn't found the previous encounter even the least bit amusing.

"I don't believe they have ever entertained a member of the nobility, my lord."

Something in her tone, in her insistence on continually referring to him as "my lord," began to make him wonder whether her dislike was personal, or something more. "Have you ever entertained a member of the nobility?"

She glanced at him. "I have no household and no standing, my lord."

Neither had she answered the question. "Would they feel more comfortable if Uncle Malcolm accompanied us as well?"

"Mr. Bancroft cannot walk, my lord. Nor can he yet tolerate sitting upright for any length of time." Again she looked briefly in his direction, her expression unreadable but her eyes snapping. "I'm certain, though, that the Fowlers appreciate your concern over their comfort. And Mr. Bancroft as well, of course."

This time the cut wasn't even veiled. Although no one besides his brother had ever insulted him so bluntly before, he was far more curious than offended. "My, my, Miss Willits," he said mildly, "has your tongue ever caused anyone bodily harm?"

The muscles of her fine jaw clenched. "Not that I'm aware of, my lord. My most sincere apologies if I have in any way offended you."

"No apology necessary." A small farmhouse and a pig rooting through a cabbage patch came into view ahead of them. "I wish to ask, though, if I have in any way offended *you*."

She kicked out of the stirrup and with easy grace hopped to the ground. "Oh, my lord, do not tease," she said, with obviously exaggerated alarm.

For a brief moment Quin had the impression that if she'd been a man, they would have been selecting dueling pistols. "Do not think me a fool," he returned, dismounting and heading after Miss Marguerite before she could increase her cabbage carnage.

"Begging your lordship's pardon," Maddie said, moving swiftly to the far side of the cabbage patch to turn the determined pig back in his direction, "but why should you care what I think of you?"

"Why should I not?"

Maddie hesitated, an arrested expression on her face. Just then the sow charged by him, squealing, and Quin nearly went down on his backside. "Dash it!"

Turning, he sprinted after the beast, abruptly angry at it—not for getting him tossed into the stream and nearly trampling him, but for interrupting the first genuine conversation he'd managed with Miss Willits.

Dirt and bits of grass and cabbage clung to Quin's damp breeches as he ran, but the blasted pig was *not* going to elude him again. He dodged after the animal, swearing under his breath. When Maddie called out behind him, she was quite a bit farther away than he'd realized.

"No, Mr. Whitmore!" she shouted. "Lord Warefield! Duck!"

At her alarmed tone, Quin threw himself forward into the muddy grass without hesitation. Before he'd hit the ground, he remembered her tendency to disregard his best interests, though, and cursed at his continued stupidity. An instant later, a musket thundered and a ball whistled over his head.

Breathing hard, Quin lurched to his feet and whipped around to see Miss Willits forcefully wrench a musket out of an older man's hands—one of the angry farmers he'd seen in pursuit of Miss Marguerite just the day before.

"Are you all right, Miss Willits?" he called, running back to the cabbage garden.

She quickly turned in his direction. "Yes, quite. And you, my lord?"

"No holes, thanks to you." At least she appeared not to want him dead, which was a relief. He stopped in front of the red-faced farmer. "You would be Mr. Whitmore, I presume?"

Maddie cleared her throat and returned the musket to its owner. "My lord, may I present Mr. Whitmore, one of your uncle's tenants? Mr. Whitmore, the Marquis of Warefield."

"The Mar—oh, good holy God, I'm sorry, my lord." Mr. Whitmore stumbled, blanching. "Terribly sorry."

He jabbed his free hand out at Quin, who lifted an eyebrow as he shook it. "Mr. Whitmore."

"I wasn't aiming for you, my lord, oh, no. It's just that blasted devil-spawned pig! That's the third time this month the beast has gotten into my vegetables!"

The marquis slapped at the mud and vegetation which continued to cling to him. "I'm none too fond of the animal, myself. What say we help ourselves to a side of pork, eh?"

The farmer grinned and hefted the musket. "Aye, my lord."

Miss Willits stepped forward and put her hand on the farmer's shoulder. "If I might make an alternate suggestion, my lord," she said hurriedly, "there will be piglets by May, and I'm certain no one would object if Mr. Whitmore chose the pick of Miss Marguerite's litter for himself."

The farmer scowled. "And what's to keep her from taking the rest of my crop before then?"

"The new fence Mr. Bancroft will see that the Hartleburys put up, to keep her where she belongs."

Mr. Whitmore eyed Maddie pleadingly, while Quin watched her with a great deal of interest. Langley didn't at all look like a holding in dire need of aid and repair, and he'd already begun to have a very strong suspicion why. Miss Willits spoke for his uncle readily enough, and the farmer accepted it as a matter of fact. And when, in frustration, Quin had skimmed ahead in the ledgers yesterday, the last few pages hadn't been in his uncle's indecipherable scrawl, but in a much neater, distinctly feminine hand. Maddie Willits was turning out to be quite an unusual mistress indeed.

"All right, Miss Maddie. I'll agree—if there ain't any more escapes."

Maddie smiled. "There won't be."

Considering that Miss Marguerite still wandered about in the wilds somewhere, it was an exceedingly bold statement. But the farmer bowed to Quin and turned away to examine the damage done to his cabbages.

She looked up at Quin. "Shall we continue your inspection, my lord?"

"Yes, of course. Though I'd like to return to Langley for a change of clothes first."

"I thought you might, my lord," she said mildly, perusing his water-, mud-, and grass-covered form with amusement, then turned to find Blossom.

Before she could ask the farmer for assistance in mounting, Quin stepped up behind her. Remembering her previous reaction to his touch, he cleared his throat. "If I may, Miss Willits."

She faced him, and then, with an exaggerated sigh of annoyance that didn't quite hide her discomfort, she nodded. "Thank you, my lord."

Quin slowly reached out to place his hands on her slender waist. Though his gloves were as dirty as the rest of him, for once Miss Willits had nothing disparaging to say. He looked down into her eyes and slowly lifted her up into the saddle. As she met his gaze evenly, he caught himself wishing she would smile just once at him.

Reluctantly he released her and retrieved Aristotle. As he swung up onto the hunter, he glanced in her direction. She was watching him, but swiftly turned her face away as he met her gaze.

"That was well done, Miss Willits," he complimented her, as they headed back down the road toward Langley. "You've granted Miss Marguerite a stay of execution."

"She is the Hartleburys' prize sow," she replied. "Without the income from her offspring, they'd not be able to make a go of it."

He waited for the omnipresent "my lord" to make an appearance. When it didn't, he smiled at her back. Apparently she'd made enough of a fool of him this morning that she felt them to be on more even ground—which Quin somehow didn't find insulting at all.

Chapter 4

Maddie shook her head and glared at her employer. "I had nothing to do with it," she protested.

"He's been here for one day, Maddie," Mr. Bancroft returned, his expression equally exasperated. "Whatever you might think of the nobility, he is from a well-respected family. In addition, I happen to be rather fond of him. I cannot—I *will* not—have him drowned or shot! Is that clear?"

"How was I to know that Miss Marguerite had escaped again? Lord Warefield was the one who wanted to continue the pursuit, not me. And *I* didn't fire the musket, either!"

He eyed her. "I'd not wager on any of that, girl."

"I—"

"Under the circumstances, I won't ask you to apologize. But I do think you might exert yourself to be polite tonight at dinner and when you call on the Fowlers tomorrow!"

Maddie halted her sharp retort. In the four years she'd lived at Langley, this was the first time he'd vented anything more than good-humored frustration on her. And she was abruptly worried that he might bring another

attack upon himself if he continued shouting at her, or
that he might just decide he'd been charitable enough
with her and ask her to leave. It had happened before,
in other households, and for much less cause.

"I apologize to you, then, Mr. Bancroft," she said
with as much dignity as she could muster, and turned to
leave. She'd never liked losing, though, especially to a
spoiled marquis, so she stopped in the doorway. "But I
still think he was just trying to show off and ended up
looking foolish. And *that* is certainly not my fault."

"Perhaps not," he sighed. "But do try not to kill him,
won't you, my dear? Please?"

She turned and curtsied, immensely relieved at the
reluctant amusement returning to his voice. "I shall
try," she agreed solemnly, and headed downstairs.

Lord Warefield, accompanied by Walter, the groom,
had left better than two hours ago to continue the Grand
Tour of the surrounding fields. He hadn't asked her to
continue as his guide, thank goodness, and in fact had
barely said a word to her on the ride back to the manor,
despite her solicitous concern. His jade eyes, the only
part of him that didn't seem to be covered with grass
and mud and water, had looked in her direction more
than once, but she'd pretended not to notice. It really
wasn't her fault, for heaven's sake—though she couldn't
have asked for a more perfect way to reintroduce him
to Langley.

Maddie chuckled. If she were the Marquis of Warefield, she would be packing by now to leave. After an
afternoon spent with Walter, she doubted he'd even want
to stay the night.

Mr. Bancroft typically napped in the early afternoon,
so she slipped downstairs into the library to read for an
hour or so. Far from being its usual quiet haven, though,
the room reverberated with excited rattlings from the
nearby kitchen and dining room. With the determination

of a conquering army, Mrs. Iddings, Garrett, and the other servants went about preparing dinner and polishing the contents of the silver closet. They'd already done that, and only four days ago, but no doubt Warefield had found a spot on some utensil or other.

Maddie glared at the wall, then sighed and settled deeper into the comfortable chair. Entirely too much fuss and upheaval and upset, for no blasted reason. For heaven's sake, covered in mud, the Marquis of Warefield looked just as ridiculous as any commoner, if not more so.

Still, the rest of the staff insisted on looking upon him as though he were Apollo himself. If only he'd thrown some sort of tantrum, her morning would have been complete. But she supposed that becoming hysterical in front of social inferiors would be beneath his dignity. Perhaps he'd wept in private when he'd gone to change his clothes.

She smiled at the image, though given how calmly Warefield had accepted both the dunking and being shot at, she had to admit that his distress was more likely fantasy than fact. But if he thought he'd survived the worst Langley and Maddie Willits had to offer, he was in for a surprise. Several, in fact. As the American John Paul Jones had said some forty years ago during the war with the Colonies, she had not yet begun to fight.

"I'll take care of it myself."

Maddie started at the marquis's voice. Immediately following that, the library door opened, and the man himself strolled into the library.

"My thanks, Garrett," he continued, looking back over his shoulder. "And please let me know when the post comes."

"With pleasure, my lord."

Warefield closed the door and turned around. And froze. "Miss Willits," he said, clearly surprised to see her there. Jade eyes took her in as she sat curled up in Mr. Bancroft's favorite chair, the unopened book still sitting across her lap.

"My lord," she answered, straightening self-consciously and annoyed at the interruption. Of course he was surprised to see her. Servants did not drape themselves all over their employer's furniture. No doubt he expected her to be in the kitchen or assisting with the silver polishing, or mopping some floor before his boots could tread upon it.

He nodded and turned back for the door. "My apologies. I didn't realize the library was occupied."

Quickly she stood and set the book aside. "Oh, please, my lord. Do not let me keep you from your literary pursuits. Your uncle must be awake by now; I'll take him his tea."

"It's not necess—"

"Don't trouble yourself, my lord, I beg of you." Pasting another smile on her face, Maddie stepped past him. Dash it, she'd thought to be free of him until dinner, at least.

"Miss Willits, stop!"

Reaching for any remaining restraint, she stopped and turned to face him again. "Yes, my lord?" she ground out, though quite a few more colorful epithets came readily to mind.

"Do not leave the library on my account," he said slowly, enunciating each word. "I came only to find some paper. I neglected to bring any with me, and I need to catch up on my correspondence."

Of course he intended to report immediately to the Duke of Highbarrow on the poor state of Langley. "Oh, my lord!" she said, hurrying over to the small writing desk. "You should have told me! Allow me to fetch it for you. Pray do not exert yourself any further after the horror of this morning."

The marquis narrowed his eyes. "I would hardly describe being outwitted by a pig as a horror," he said dryly. "An embarrassment, perhaps." He paused. "And a tale my brother would be delighted to hear. I shall have to determine whom to bribe to prevent that from happening."

Of course, pompous peer that he was, he would think he could solve all his troubles—such as they were—with money. No doubt he always had. Maddie pulled a stack of paper from a drawer. As attractive as he looked, she knew what lay beneath his skin. And she would *never* like him—devilish captivating smile and pseudocompassion or not.

"That was a joke, Miss Willits," he prompted.

Surprised, she looked up as she approached him with the paper. His eyes met hers, his expression amused.

"Yes, my lord."

"You may laugh if you wish, but I leave that wholly to your discretion."

"Thank you, my lord." So now he thought himself amusing and charming, as well. She might laugh *at* him, but she would never laugh *with* him. Ever. "I trust your tour of the fields went well?"

He lifted an eyebrow, his humor deepening. "Yes, quite. You know, I'd meant to ask you about that. My uncle's groom is . . . rather unique."

She nodded coolly. "Yes, we find him so, my lord."

"Quite knowledgeable about southern Somerset County, but I admit I hadn't anticipated his singular perspective on the nobility."

Maddie pinched her lips together and looked out the window. "Yes, my lord." She could feel his gaze on her, warm and discomfiting and unwelcome. *Don't laugh,* she reminded herself sternly. *He's not amusing.* "Apparently Walter was kicked in the head by a horse several years ago, and now believes himself to be a prince in hiding.''

''So I gathered.'' The marquis took a step closer. ''A son of the mad king, no less.'' He reached out and took the paper gently from her fingers. ''And I thought the residents of Somerset were unused to nobles.''

''Yes, we. . . .'' She trailed off. Now she was prolonging conversations with him for absolutely no good reason. ''May I go now, my lord?''

''I said you needn't leave, Miss Willits.''

''Yes, my lord, but I *wish* to go.''

His searching gaze made her want to turn away, or better yet, to spit in his eye. Or kiss him.

''Then go,'' he said finally.

She blinked, stunned that she would think such a thing. ''Thank you, my lord.''

Quin checked his appearance in the mirror one last time, while Bernard put away his day coat. No trace of the morning's fiasco remained, other than the filthy pile of clothes Bernard had sent down to be washed, or failing that, destroyed. Even so, Quin couldn't rid himself of the feeling that something was out of place.

''Is there anything else, my lord?'' Bernard asked, closing the portmanteau.

''Hm?'' Quin shook himself and turned to find his valet. ''Beg pardon?''

''Was there anything else you required, my lord?''

''No. Thank you.'' Quin scowled back at his reflection. ''Bernard?''

The valet stopped his retreat. ''My lord?''

''Do I have that beige coat with me? The one with the brown buttons?''

''No, my lord. My apologies. As your initial reaction to it was not entirely favorable, I did not realize you wished it packed. I shall send for it at once.''

The marquis nodded absently. "Very good. And another pair of boots, while you're at it. I'm not convinced my riding boots are salvageable."

"Of course, my lord."

The valet slipped out of the room, and Quin took one last look at himself. Perhaps all the swimming and mucking about in the mud had addled his brain. All of his buttons were fastened correctly; he looked fine. Not too ostentatious, not too plain. Quin scowled at his reflection and turned away. He was acting like a damned dandy.

He headed for the west wing and his uncle's bedchamber. Voices came from the half-open door, and he paused in mid-knock, his attention snared.

"Mr. Bancroft," Maddie was saying, "I ordered it all the way from Surrey."

Quin leaned against the wall, unused to hearing the genuine and infectious amusement in Miss Willits's voice.

"It looks ridiculous."

"It does not. It's modern. If you just try it, you'll see how much easier a time you'll—"

"I'll break my neck!"

Maddie laughed. "I'll show you how easy it is."

Intrigued, Quin peered around the doorway. Miss Willits sat in a wheeled wooden chair, which she moved back and forward erratically by pulling two overly large wheels on either side.

"A wheelchair," he said, strolling into the room. "Mrs. Balfour uses one to get about now."

Miss Willits stopped rolling and shot to her feet. The good humor in her gray eyes vanished as she glared up at him and took several quick breaths, the bosom of her green muslin dress rising and falling enticingly in response. "Good evening, my lord."

"Uncle, Miss Willits." He nodded, disappointed. Maddie still hated him, apparently.

"Did someone die, my lord?" she asked politely.

He furrowed his brow. "Die?"

"Yes. Your coat, and. . . ." She stopped and put one hand over her full, sensuous mouth. "Oh, my! My apologies. I have done it again, I fear. Black evening wear is quite the thing in London, no doubt."

Quin realized what had been nagging at him earlier. Miss Willits's sharp tongue. He glanced down at his garb and then met her eyes again. "It is, as a matter of fact."

"And you look splendid in it, my boy." Uncle Malcolm motioned for Quin to take one of the seats at the small table set beside the bed. "We may not be formal here, but there's no reason to ignore custom."

Quin caught his frown in time to force it into a smile. "Thank you, Uncle."

He made his way to the table. At that moment, however, Miss Willits found an urgent need to rearrange the vase of flowers by the window. Patiently he stood, waiting for her to take her seat first. With the same apparent patience, Maddie turned a red rose this way and that, pausing between adjustments to lean back and view her work. Out of the corner of her eye she sneaked a look at him, then continued with her arranging.

Then he realized he'd been correct all along. Maddie Willits was purposely taunting him, teasing him, and attempting to embarrass, frustrate, and humiliate him. And so far, she'd done a sterling job of it. Why, he had no idea, but he intended to find out.

With a glance at his uncle, who pretended to be absorbed in studying the plate of roast game hen set across his lap, Quin moved around the table and pulled out her chair. "Miss Willits?"

She turned around. "Oh, dear. Were you waiting for me, my lord?"

He smiled. "I was admiring two of the fairest blooms in Somerset," he corrected softly. "Waiting is my pleasure, I assure you."

For the space of several seconds she stared at him. "Thank you, my lord," she said slowly.

Quin sent another quick glance at his uncle, but Malcolm merely appeared amused at his mistress's antics. "Shall we?"

She reluctantly allowed him to seat her. Brushing her elbow with his hand, he took his own chair opposite her. By that time she'd rallied for another attack.

"Please forgive my being so forward as to have dinner served before your arrival, but there is so little room for footmen in here, and we did wait several minutes for you, my lord."

"Maddie," Malcolm grunted.

Quin took a sip of wine to cover his amusement. Sharp-witted, sharp-tongued, and sharp-mannered. It was a wonder he hadn't been killed already. "I'm afraid *I* must be the one to apologize for my tardiness. Unforgivably rude of me."

Miss Willits glared at him over her roast game hen. "Not at all, my lord," she said sweetly.

"Quinlan, you had some gossip for us, I believe?" his uncle broke in, making a bald attempt to turn the conversation.

"I do, though now that I've experienced the daily routine of Langley, I'm not certain anything I have to say could be as exciting."

"I'm just glad you didn't break your neck. You were damned lucky, my boy."

Miss Willits nodded at Malcolm. "Indeed. Thank heavens it's been raining, or Lord Warefield might have been seriously injured."

"And so might have Miss Marguerite," Quin added.

Maddie lifted an eyebrow, again the picture of beautiful disdain. "And the Hartleburys would have lost their best source of income over a muddied marquis." Even her chuckle sounded scornful. "What a jest."

"Or a joust," Quin muttered under his breath.

"Beg pardon, my lord?"

He looked up. "Hm? Oh, I was only saying that this morning's incident reminded me of my last encounter with the Earl of Westerly."

For the next hour, Quin regaled his audience with tales of his last sojourn to London. Uncle Malcolm seemed both relieved and amused at the change of subject, but then, he was acquainted with most of the participants. Miss Willits might as well have been regarding stones, for all the interest and enthusiasm she showed.

She pointedly retrieved a book from the chest of drawers, though Quin noted that either she was an exceptionally slow reader or she was paying more attention to his tales than to Walter Scott's. He had to consider that a small victory.

"Well, what do you think of the fields?" Malcolm asked finally.

Quin sipped the port Garrett had brought in earlier. "I noticed that the seed has already been prepared," he commented, glancing sideways at Miss Willits.

"No sense wasting valuable time," his uncle returned, "as you pointed out yesterday."

Quin was fairly sure Maddie had organized the crop. Everything was divided too fairly for the decision to have come from one of the tenant farmers. "I thought we might begin tilling tomorrow, on the three southernmost fields, anyway. They seem to be drier than the rest." Again he looked over at Maddie. "And I think Mr. Whitmore might appreciate a little preferential treatment after his cabbages were decimated this morning."

Malcolm nodded. "I agree."

"I assume you utilize all your tenants for joint planting and harvesting duties?"

"That is the fastest way to get the crop put in, my lord," Maddie said under her breath.

Quin had the distinct feeling he'd just been insulted again. "I'd hoped you would say that," he said, enjoying her disgruntled expression. "And perhaps you might assist me in assigning duties to the farmers, as you know their habits and character better than I?"

She narrowed her eyes. "I must see to Mr. Bancroft, my lord. And we have a luncheon which you engaged us to attend tomorrow."

"Maddie, Quin's quite correct. You might save us more than a day by doing the organizing." Malcolm held her indignant gaze. "And you will still have time for your luncheon with the Fowlers."

"Oh, very well." She stood, dropping her unread book on her chair. She leaned over to kiss Malcolm on the cheek, then coldly nodded at the marquis. "Good night, Mr. Bancroft, my lord."

"Good night, Maddie."

"Miss Willits."

Quin was surprised to see her leave, though he supposed he shouldn't be. In his unwell condition, Uncle Malcolm would probably have little use for her companionship. Even so, sharp-tempered and strong-willed as she was, he hadn't expected her to bother with making a show of going elsewhere to sleep. She certainly didn't seem interested in impressing him, at any rate—unless it was to kill him with kindness.

"Well, Quinlan, other than the stream and Miss Marguerite, how did you find Langley?"

"Quite exceptional, Uncle. Truth be told, it's hardly what I expected." Nothing here was—Miss Maddie Willits least of all.

"Hardly what Lewis expected, you mean. No burnt-out tenant houses, no floods or famine in Somerset without a Bancroft to oversee the land. I imagine he'll be quite disappointed."

"I shan't speculate." To avoid another family argument, Quin made a show of stretching. "Well, I'm off to bed myself. Shall I send your valet in for you?"

Malcolm shook his head. "Maddie will have seen to it. Good luck in the morning."

Quin grinned. "Thank you. I suspect I'll need it."

The Marquis of Warefield was up to something.

Maddie had watched him all morning: watched him chatting and being friendly with the awestruck farmers, and watched him actually pick a stone or two out of the soil and toss it out of the path of the plow.

She frowned at his lean, tanned profile and the curl of golden blond hair caressing his collar, and had to admit that he wasn't quite as dim as she had anticipated. Nobles didn't act nearly so amiable, she knew very well. Therefore, his affable demeanor toward the commoners was for some purpose. And she would find out what that was, before he could do any lasting damage to the good people of Somerset.

She'd instructed Bill Tomkins and the other footmen to erect a canopy at one edge of the Whitmores' field so that the marquis could take refuge from the sun when it should become too warm for him. Warefield had taken one look at the thing and the cushioned chair beneath, thanked her for her thoughtful attention to his health, and retreated to the far end of the field. There he'd stayed for the rest of the morning. She couldn't even hear him prattling on about whatever nonsense it was that had the farmers so interested.

"Coward," she muttered under her breath, glaring at him.

The workers' worshipful attention to him and his every command left her feeling practically useless, so she had to surmise that he'd insisted on her accompanying him merely to ensure himself an audience for his bloated, self-important conduct. Maddie plunked herself down on one of the shaded chairs and folded her arms. She was certainly not impressed by his efficiency. She could have done just as well—better, as a matter of fact—without him coming around at all.

"Miss Willits," he said, finally making his way around the plow horses toward her, "I believe we should return to Langley if we're not to be late to the Fowlers'."

Maddie stood and curtsied. "Of course, my lord. But who in the world will supervise while you're away?"

They walked toward Blossom and Aristotle, waiting in the shade of a stand of oaks. "I placed Sam Cardinal in charge. He seems to know a great deal about grain."

She concentrated on keeping the bland expression on her face. "I am aware of that, my lord."

"I know, Miss Willits. It was another attempt at humor. Pray forgive my ineptness."

He was making set-downs exceedingly difficult. It had to be deliberate. "Yes, my lord."

Unabashed at her lack of sympathy, he smiled and stepped toward her. "If you'll allow me," he murmured.

He slid his hands around her waist. She'd expected it, but even so, her breath caught at the warm strength of him. He hesitated, looking down into her eyes, and then lifted her easily up into the sidesaddle.

It was beastly awful, being a warm-blooded female helplessly attracted to a finely put together man, however pompous and useless she knew he must be. Maddie took a moment to fiddle with Blossom's reins before she looked at the marquis again and smiled stiffly. "My thanks, my lord."

"Again, a pleasure."

The marquis swung up onto Aristotle, and with a half wave at the farmers, who had already stopped their work to chatter about the noble in their midst, he led her back to Langley. Maddie glared at his back. There was no denying it any longer: he'd caught onto her game and was trying to make her feel guilty about making fun of him. That's why he was being nice to everyone. It wouldn't work, of course, because she knew all too well what his kind was really like. She'd have to modify her strategy a little.

Back at Langley she changed into her yellow and white sprig muslin gown. It had barely been fashionable two years ago and by now was hopelessly *passé,* but the Fowlers would hardly notice. And she certainly had no one else to impress.

Warefield had suggested they take his uncle's curricle. Not wanting to give him the opportunity to go lifting her yet again, Maddie hurried out to the stable, where Walter had the carriage waiting. He handed her up onto the narrow seat.

"I must say, Miss Maddie," the groom said, "it's terribly nice to have another blue blood in Somerset for a change. And a true gentleman, he is—promised right off not to let old Georgie know I was hereabouts."

Maddie nodded. "A true gentleman. No doubt he'll be the first to stand beside you if you decide to take your rightful place at court."

"My thanks for your vote of confidence, Miss Willits," the marquis's dry voice came from behind her. "I certainly shall."

Drat him for always sneaking up on her, and for the way his voice speeded her pulse. "I have great faith in. . . ." Maddie trailed off as he climbed up beside her. She'd expected more overly formal black attire, and even had a comment ready for it. She had not expected a simple gray day jacket and buckskin breeches tucked into his mud-dimmed Hessian boots, nor the amused smile that warmed his face as he took the seat next to her.

" 'Faith in. . . .' " he prompted.

"The nobility," she finished.

He lifted an eyebrow as he accepted the reins from Walter. "That surprises me."

"And why is that?"

He snapped the reins, and the matching bays took off at a smart trot. "I have sensed a slight criticism in your tone from time to time."

"You are quite mistaken, my lord," she returned quickly, putting a shocked expression on her face. "I would never dream of such a thing, my lord, I assure you! Who am I to criticize the Marquis of Warefield?"

"Yes, Miss Willits, who *are* you?"

At first she thought he was agreeing with her *faux* humility, and opened her mouth to make an equally cutting remark. When she glared at him, though, his expression showed nothing but curiosity. "I am your uncle's companion," she said, amending the extremely insulting comment she'd been about to make.

"Yes, for four years, because you applied for the position. But what did you do before that?"

Maddie could only stare at him, disconcerted. "You remembered. . . ."

"You do make something of an impression, you know," he returned dryly.

She swallowed, all of the insinuations and insults she'd planned for the ride vanishing in an instant. Blast him and his compliments. She neither needed nor wanted them. Maddie shook herself. She did know what to do *with* them: counterattack—immediately, before he realized he'd scored a hit. "Why do you bother with flattering me?"

"Is it flattery to ask a question?"

"It is flattery to feign interest for the sake of politeness, my lord."

"Ah," he nodded. "Then I am merely being polite?"

"Yes, of course."

"I see."

He made no other comment, and she dared to hope that she'd completely confused him with her dazzling logic. Pointedly ignoring him, she made a show of admiring the various wildflowers coming into bloom along the side of the road, and the robins and swallows building nests in the budding trees.

"You didn't answer my question."

Maddie shut her eyes for a moment. "Which question, my lord?"

"What did you do before you applied for the position with my uncle?"

"I . . . worked as a governess in several households," she answered slowly, wondering why she was so reluctant to lie to him. She owed him nothing. Yet she supposed she had no wish to be seen in the same light in which she saw him and his kind.

"Where?"

"Do you intend to check my references, my lord?"

He looked over at her again. "No. Of course not."

Maddie pointed down a rutted dirt track to the west. "Over there, my lord. About half a mile down."

Warefield turned the carriage in that direction. "You know," he said quietly, "I admire the job you've done here at Langley. I'm here only because my father wished it. I don't intend to turn you away."

She'd heard promises of integrity before. "Thank you for your assurances, my lord," Maddie said stiffly, "but they are completely unnecessary."

"And why is that?"

She turned to look directly at him. "*You* did not hire me, my lord."

He met her eyes, then pursed his lips and faced the road again. "True enough. Thank you for putting me in my place, Miss Willits."

Maddie pressed her advantage. "You are quite wel—"

"Oh, good God," he muttered.

"What is it?"

As they came around the bordering hedge, she saw what had prompted his curse. The entire Fowler household, nearly as substantial as Langley's, stood lined up at full attention along the curving drive leading all the way up the steps to the front door. A chuckle tickled up Maddie's chest and burst out of her throat before she could stop it.

"Are you laughing, Miss Willits?"

She clapped a hand over her mouth and coughed. "No, my lord," she managed. "'Twould not be seemly."

He scowled. "No, it wouldn't."

Much more enthusiastic than she had been a moment earlier, Maddie smiled at the Fowlers' butler as he came forward to help her to the ground. "My thanks, Mason."

"Miss Maddie."

Warefield came around to her side of the curricle, and she led him forward to where the Fowler family stood waiting at the end of the line. "My lord, may I present Mr. Fowler and Mrs. Fowler? Mr. and Mrs. Fowler, the Marquis of Warefield."

Tall James Fowler bent himself almost double in a bow, his normally dour expression stretched into a rather alarming-looking smile. Beside him, Jane Fowler sank so far to the ground in her curtsey that Sally had to help her upright again. "My lord," they breathed, echoing one another.

"It is an honor to have you at Renden Hall," Mrs. Fowler continued reverently. "You have met our dear daughters Lydia and Sally, I believe."

"Yes, I have." The marquis stepped forward to shake Mr. Fowler's hand. "You've a lovely family, sir."

"Thank you, my lord." Mr. Fowler gestured toward the house. "Allow me to show you inside."

Quite delighted to be ignored, Maddie followed behind the Fowlers and Lord Warefield as they passed the retinue of servants. They had nearly reached the front door when the marquis made a show of turning around and coming back to collect her.

"Can't have you getting lost, Miss Willits, can we, now?" He tucked her hand around his arm and held it against him.

"I know my way around, my lord," she muttered, trying unsuccessfully to free her hand, and surprised at his iron strength.

"That is precisely what I am afraid of," he murmured, nodding at the wide-eyed procession of footmen and maids who swarmed up the steps and into the house behind them.

"This way to the dining room, my lord," Mrs. Fowler announced regally, scattering servants out of her way and thrusting her daughters ahead of her. "Mrs. Plummer has outdone herself today, if I do say so myself. You have inspired her."

"Glad to be of some use," he said, glancing about but keeping Maddie pinioned securely at his side.

They entered the dining room to find it stuffed practically to the rafters with fresh-baked bread, puddings, ham, and chicken. Maddie simply stared for a moment. She hadn't seen this much food even at the Fowlers' annual Christmas pageant, famous throughout southern Somerset. For a country luncheon, unless they intended to feed all the farmers out plowing the fields, it was absurdly overwrought.

"Do let me go," she whispered, tugging again at the marquis's hand warmly covering hers as they toured the repast on the table and the sideboards.

He looked down at her, and at the unexpected humor in his gaze, she stopped struggling. Damnation, he was ruining everything. He wasn't supposed to be amused at the Fowlers's toadying; he was supposed to accept it as his due.

"I've no intention of letting you out of my sight," he whispered back. "This was *your* idea."

"They wouldn't have invited *me*," she pointed out, more disconcerted by his attention to her than she cared to admit. "*You* are the Marquis of Warefield, my lord. This is all for you."

"And I'm supposed to be honored?"

She glared at him. Maddie wasn't particularly fond of the Fowlers, either, but there was no reason to be cruel. She yanked her hand free. "I'm certain you're used to much better, my lord," she retorted in a hushed voice, "but this is their ideal of highest elegance."

He looked at her for a long moment, his expression serious and unreadable. "I see."

Maddie intentionally seated herself between Lydia and Sally, keeping as far from the marquis as she could manage. He'd goaded her into being directly rude again, when she'd decided to stay with the more subtle approach of victory through flattery. From the occasional looks he sent in her direction he hadn't welcomed her last comment, but it served him right.

"Lord Warefield, please tell us about London," Sally begged, giggling. "Have you been to Almack's?"

"Of course he's been to Almack's," Lydia countered in an exasperated tone. "He's dined with the King."

"Is His Majesty as fat as they say?"

"Sally!" Mrs. Fowler fanned her napkin in front of her face. "For heaven's sake, mind your manners!"

"But Mama, King George *is* fat. Everyone says so."

"Sally! Silence!" Jane Fowler leaned across the table to capture the marquis's hand, nearly causing him to drop his forkful of sliced ham. "Pray forgive my daughter, my lord. She's a little high strung, perhaps, but quite proficient in all the gentler arts. We had tutors for both girls, all the way from Surrey."

Lord Warefield glanced at Maddie, then set his fork back on his plate. "I have no doubts on that count, Mrs. Fowler. Miss Sally, I do occasionally go hunting with His Majesty, and he is a rather . . . well-rounded individual. If you ever meet him, though, I suggest you not mention it. He's rather sensitive about the subject."

"You see?" Sally said gleefully, and took another biscuit from the bowl in the center of the table.

"Please, my lord, eat."

The marquis retrieved his utensil and obligingly took a bite. The entire family watched as he chewed and swallowed. Maddie decided she didn't feel the least bit sorry for him.

"It's quite good," he said after a moment, taking a sip of wine.

"And not a grain of salt used," Mr. Fowler said proudly. "No spices at all."

The butler stepped into the dining room and came to attention. "Mr. and Mrs. Fowler, Lord Warefield, I am instructed to inform you that Mrs. Beauchamp has arrived."

"What? What is she doing—"

Mrs. Beauchamp, wearing a low-cut gown two sizes too small for her ample bosom and two decades out of style, swept into the room. Warefield automatically came to his feet, though he looked somewhat startled. Mr.

Fowler reluctantly rose a moment later, and Mrs. Beauchamp sank into a deep curtsey.

"My lord," she breathed, rising.

For several seconds Maddie sat where she was, dumbfounded at her tremendous luck, before she roused herself enough to stand. "Lord Warefield, another of Langley's esteemed neighbors, Mrs. Beauchamp."

The marquis nodded. "Mrs. Beauchamp. Charmed."

The lady came forward to clutch Lord Warefield's proffered hand and curtsied again. "I am delighted to meet you, my lord."

Mrs. Fowler leaned over to examine her neighbor's face. "Evelyn, whatever is that black spot on your cheek?"

"Oh, you silly thing," Mrs. Beauchamp tittered, fingering the small spot. "It's a patch. They're all the rage in London." She lifted her heavy jowled face toward the marquis's ear, still refusing to relinquish her grip on his hand. "My cousin is Baron Montesse," she whispered conspiratorially. "You may know him."

The marquis's lip twitched, and he cleared his throat. "Baron Montesse," he mused. "Of Berkshire?"

"Oh, no. Of Herefordshire, my lord."

"Ah. No, I don't believe we are acquainted, then. But I don't spend all that much time in London."

She frowned as Warefield finally managed to free his hand without pulling her over. "That's odd," she continued loudly, no doubt hoping the servants were listening. "I wrote that you were coming to Somerset, and he seemed familiar with you. Though he said something about your having a scar. But you don't, do you? Hmm. Perhaps he was mis—"

"A scar?" the marquis interrupted, and then smiled. "That explains it. He must be acquainted with my younger brother, Rafael. He was wounded at Waterloo. We do look something alike."

Mrs. Beauchamp's expression brightened. "Yes, that must be it, then." She gestured imperiously at one of the footmen to bring another chair forward. While Mrs. Fowler fumed, her neighbor sat on the far side of the marquis. "I knew we had mutual acquaintances. All of the nobility seems to know one another."

"Mother," Lydia hissed in protest, as Mrs. Beauchamp usurped her place of honor.

"Now, now, Lydia," her mother soothed, resuming her own seat. "You'll have your chance later, when you play for Lord Warefield."

Maddie cleared her throat and spread butter on her toasted bread. Again she felt the marquis's gaze on her face, but she refused to look. Let him suffer. At least she was enjoying herself . . .

Another footman brought a plate out for Mrs. Beauchamp, and she set to eating with her usual enthusiasm. Lord Warefield was barely able to touch his own plate, with all of the questions and absurd flattery sent in his direction. Maddie was amazed that the Fowlers and Mrs. Beauchamp were so eager to fawn over him. In all fairness, though, she'd grown up amid such nonsense and was used to it.

Sally leaned over the table to point her knife at Mrs. Beauchamp's soup. "I say, Mrs. Beauchamp, your patch has fallen off."

Laughter burst from Maddie's lips before she could stop it. Holding her napkin to her face and coughing to cover it as well as she could, she pushed to her feet. "Excuse me for a moment," she managed, and fled across the hall into the morning room. Pacing briskly, she tried to imagine something—anything—dull and somber.

"Miss Willits, are you quite all right?"

Still holding her hand over her mouth, Maddie whipped around. The marquis stood in the doorway gazing at her, while the dining room erupted in argument behind him. Attempting to cover her surprise, she leaned back against the couch. "Yes, I'm fine."

"I told them you had a bit of a cold, and that I wanted to make certain you were all right."

"Thank you. Though I don't need you to make my excu—" She stopped, her heart skittering with unexpected disquiet as he stepped into the room and shut the door behind him. An unbidden image of Benjamin Spenser entered her mind, but she sternly pushed it aside. She was not the stupid girl she once had been, and she knew quite well how to deal with men. "My lord?"

He took a deep breath and leaned back against the door. "Please, please, please tell me I may laugh at that," he muttered.

She stared at him and belatedly lowered the napkin from her lips. She'd half-expected an assault—not a conspiracy. "You . . . certainly don't need my permission, my lord."

Warefield folded his arms. "I certainly don't wish to give you another reason to scowl at me."

"I don't scowl at you," she shot back, trying to rally her anger again.

"Yes, you do." He pushed upright and took a step closer.

She backed away. "You awe and amaze me with your presence," she improvised weakly.

"Liar."

"Please, my lord, do not chastise me. I could not bear it."

"Yes, you could." He moved toward her again. "And how did *you* know the luncheon in there is not the height of elegance?"

Damnation. "I don't, my lord. I was simply judging by your reaction to—"

"Lord Warefield, are you going to return to the dining room?" Sally called, rapping at the door.

He didn't even glance behind him. "In a moment. Miss Willits is having difficulty catching her breath."

"I am not!" Maddie swerved around the couch and made for the door. "Don't use me to make excuses for your poor behavior, my lord. We should not be in here alone togeth—"

With unexpected swiftness the marquis dodged sideways and cut off her escape. "You said this luncheon was *the Fowlers'* ideal of elegance. Not yours."

She stopped, barely avoiding colliding with him. "I have been a governess in a variety of households, my lord. And your uncle is brother to the Duke of Highbarrow." She took a breath, reaching for her scattered wits and anger as she looked up at his heated expression. He was practically accosting her, after all. "Do you assume everyone you encounter in the country to be ignorant of the finer ways, Lord Warefield?"

He opened his mouth, then shut it again. "No. I do not." For a long moment he looked at her. "May I tell you something you will undoubtedly find shocking and annoying?"

Even more unsettled, Maddie swallowed. "Whatever pleases you, my lord."

"Sometimes—right at this moment, in fact—I have a rather strong urge to . . . kiss you."

Maddie flushed, her pulse suddenly pounding. "I— please restrain yourself, then, my lord," was the best she could manage. What she really wanted to do was flee back to Langley and lock all the doors before he could realize that she also had the recurring desire to fall upon him, damn him.

A slight, sensuous smile curved his mouth, and he nodded. "I shall attempt to do so." His long, elegant fingers gestured at the door. "If you please, Miss Willits."

Maddie smoothed her skirt, then approached. "Thank you, my lord."

"But I do intend to find out why you dislike me so much, Maddie."

She hesitated, then pulled open the door and hurried through. Sally eyed her with bald curiosity, but she pretended not to notice. Warefield followed close behind and resumed his seat and the luncheon conversation as though he'd never left the table.

Maddie glanced at him once. He was gazing directly at her, and she immediately looked away. The frustrated inquisitiveness in his eyes surprised and dismayed her. She'd expected anger—not this intense, extremely disconcerting curiosity. Nor had she expected him to be attracted to her, or her to him.

She was going to have to be more careful. Driving him away from Langley was one thing—but having the Marquis of Warefield discover her true identity was completely another.

Chapter 5

After luncheon, the afternoon spiraled downward from merely painful to excruciating. They all crowded into the tiny drawing room, where Lydia Fowler sat at the pianoforte to regale them with a completely hideous interpretation of Beethoven's *"Für Elise."*

Quin found himself sandwiched between Mrs. Fowler and Mrs. Beauchamp, while Maddie sat in the corner gazing peacefully out the window. Closer to fidgeting than since he had been a boy in church, he lasted in his chair until the piece ended. Then, still applauding, he stood.

"Excuse me, ladies," he said pleasantly, "but the fire is a bit too warm for me."

Immediately Mrs. Fowler jumped to her feet and grabbed for the servants' bell. "I shall see to it at once, my lord!"

"No need. I'll just sit by the window for a bit." He turned to the elder Fowler daughter. "Miss Fowler, please play us another."

Mrs. Fowler beamed delightedly, and Lydia obligingly began another piece. He had no idea what she might be rendering this time, but she seemed enthusiastic enough. Quin strolled over to where Maddie sat and took the seat beside her before she could escape.

Something he'd said earlier—most likely his idiotic confession about wanting to kiss her—had her on the run, and he was intrigued enough to pursue his advantage. Since he'd arrived, he'd been defending himself against a myriad of attacks on his honor, his nobility, and his person, and he still had no real idea why.

"Enjoying yourself, Miss Willits?" he asked quietly.

She continued looking out the window. "Of course. I love Haydn."

So that's what it was. He wondered how she happened to know that. If she had been a governess, she was a very well-educated one. For a country landlord's mistress, she was simply extraordinary. His gaze lowered to the curving line of her throat, and the minute throbbing of her pulse beneath. Kissing her was only the beginning of what he wanted of Maddie Willits.

Quin took a breath. "You're aware that Mrs. Fowler has been planning a ball in my honor?"

Finally she faced forward again. "She mentioned it to me a few days ago, yes."

"It would be a grand opportunity for Uncle Malcolm to make an appearance in his wheeled chair, don't you think?"

"If he feels up to it, yes, I suppose," she answered grudgingly.

"And you shall join us then, I presume?"

She glanced at him, then away again. "I am Mr. Bancroft's companion. If he wishes me to join him, I shall."

Quin would personally see to it that Malcolm did wish it. She hadn't uttered one "my lord" yet, a good indication that she was still in full retreat. "And will you dance with me there?" he asked, pressing his advantage.

"You are better aware of propriety than I am, my lord."

He scowled before he could cover it. Miss Willits, it seemed, regrouped quickly.

"If you think it proper for a marquis to dance with his uncle's companion, then I will do as you say," she continued.

Quin looked at her. "I would hardly order you to dance."

"Thank you, my lord."

They were back on even ground, it seemed. "But I would like to."

She faced him again, her gray eyes lit by the afternoon sun through the window. "To what, my lord?"

"To dance with you." He glanced at Mr. Fowler and Sally, but they were busily chatting and ignoring Lydia's play. Quin edged closer to Maddie so that his knee brushed her skirt, and lowered his voice. "You have forbidden a kiss, and you seem to regard me as something of a monster, Miss Willits. I would like a chance to prove to you that I am nothing of the kind."

"I think nothing of you at all, my lord. It is not my place to do so."

He sighed. "Relentless, aren't you?" he muttered.

Her lips twitched, and she faced the pianoforte. "I'd like to think so, my lord."

She was amused at his expense—again. And somehow, though he'd never received such abuse in his life, he remained far more intrigued and diverted than angry. He'd always loved a good puzzle, and Maddie Willits was a virtual Sphinx's Riddle.

Yet he had no excuse whatsoever for his own very odd behavior. He was practically engaged to a perfectly lovely woman he'd known for twenty-three years, and at the same time he was lusting after a woman—his uncle's mistress, yet—he'd known for only three days.

As soon as he could politely do so, he made their excuses and they returned to Langley. Maddie was back to her previous hostile self, but Quin thought he detected more amusement in her demeanor than before. He hoped so, anyway. She vanished into the house as soon as he drove the curricle into the stable yard, so he really couldn't ask her.

Quin headed inside to change. He wanted to see how the plowing was progressing, and he needed to escape from Maddie's intoxicating, infuriating presence. Before he could do anything, though, Garrett intercepted him at the foot of the stairs.

"My lord, a letter arrived for you with the post." The butler held up for Quin's examination the silver tray containing the missive. "You said you wished to be notified."

"My thanks, Garrett." Quin took the letter upstairs with him. He immediately recognized the neat, ornate script of the address. Eloise Stokesley hadn't wasted any time in corresponding, but then she was always very prompt in such matters.

He summoned his valet and opened the one-page missive.

Dearest Quinlan,

I was heartbroken to read in your last letter that you've been banished to Somerset. I had hoped you would be able to visit us at Stafford Green, as we had planned.

"So had I," he muttered, though the stay at Langley had been much less of an annoyance than he had anticipated.

I know I shouldn't say so, but I miss you, Quinlan. I count the days until we shall be together in London, and even more the days until we shall be

*married. Please, tell me of your adventures in
Somerset. I await your return letter with greatest
anticipation.*

> *Yours forever,*
> *Eloise*

Bernard entered, and Quin set the letter on his dressing table. The best service he could do for Eloise was to get the planting and the ledgers finished and return to Warefield—hopefully by way of Stafford Green.

He had no intention of asking Maddie to accompany him out to the fields again. But if he allowed her to escape completely, she would have time to regroup and mount another attack.

If she was bored here at Langley, since her full services were no longer required by Malcolm, perhaps he had happened along just in time to capture her wandering attention. That theory didn't quite fit, since her actions were certainly not those of a woman trying to lure a man to her bed, but anything was worth a try.

Quin paused, frowning. Good God, now he was contemplating stealing another man's—his uncle's—lady. Perhaps it was Somerset itself making him mad. It seemed to have had that effect on several of the locals.

He went downstairs and out to the stable, stopping at the sound of voices coming from the garden.

"No, Bill, you're doing it all wrong."

"I am not, Miss Maddie."

"Yes, you are. You'll dump him on the ground."

"I will not!"

Quin leaned around the corner of the house. Bill Tomkins stood at the edge of the garden path. Malcolm, bundled in enough blankets to keep the entire Third Regiment warm in the middle of a Prussian winter, sat in the wheeled chair in front of the footman. Maddie stood beside them, scowling furiously.

"Maddie, it's all right."

"It is not, Mr. Bancroft. You need sunlight, not a dunking in the fish pond. Bill, leave off. I shall push him."

Malcolm chuckled. "You'd best do as she says, Bill."

The footman sighed heavily and relinquished his grip on the back of the chair. "Yes, Mr. Bancroft. Give me a yell when you want back up the stairs."

"Thank you, Bill." The footman strolled off back to the house, and Maddie took over the steering of the chair. "You should keep to the path, my dear."

"Nonsense. I want to show you the new roses. And did you bring the book?"

"The one thing that still works on me is my lap, Maddie."

She pushed him onto the soft grass, and they came to an abrupt halt. "Drat," she muttered.

"I think I'm sinking," Malcolm noted calmly.

Quin pushed away from the wall to perform a rescue.

Maddie shoved harder against the back of the chair, and with a sucking sound it came free of the mud. "See?" she said, moving him toward the roses at the far end of the garden. "Now, where were we?"

Malcolm produced a small book from the mountain of blankets surrounding him and opened it. "Let's see. Beatrice was telling Benedick that scratching up his face wouldn't make it look any worse."

She smiled. "Ah. And Benedick says, 'Well, you are a rare parrot-teacher.' " She released the chair and pranced in front of Malcolm, putting her hands on her hips. "And Beatrice rightly replies, 'A bird of my tongue is better than a beast of yours.' " As Malcolm awkwardly applauded, she turned about again and assumed a more masculine stance and voice. " 'I would my horse had the speed of your tongue, and . . .' ''

Quin cursed as she caught sight of him. Immediately she ceased her recitation and went back to pushing his uncle toward the rosebushes. Quin strode after them. '' 'I would my horse had the speed of your tongue, and so good a continuer,' '' he finished.

''Ah, Quinlan. Good afternoon.'' Malcolm twisted around to greet his nephew.

''Miss Willits, I didn't know you enjoyed Shakespeare.'' He wanted to ask her where in blazes she'd learned to quote the bard by heart.

She turned to face him, her face flushed. ''Of course you didn't know, my lord,'' she snapped, obviously embarrassed. ''No doubt you also were unaware that your uncle enjoys it as well, or that he was quite looking forward to seeing you after four years—or you might have spent more than two hours speaking with him over the past three days.''

''Maddie, that's enough,'' Malcolm said sharply. ''I can fend for myself, thank you very much. You should not speak to Quinlan in that manner.''

''Well, obviously no one else does.'' She turned to Quin. ''Will you see your uncle safely back to his bed-chamber?''

''Yes.'' He wondered why her words made him feel so completely . . . inadequate.

''Thank you. Mr. Bancroft, I'm going to see Squire John.'' With a flounce of her skirts, she stalked off around the side of the manor.

Quin looked down at Malcolm, who had an expression of mixed amusement and exasperation on his face. ''I hadn't realized I'd been slighting you,'' he said quietly, crouching at his uncle's side.

Malcolm glanced at him, then smiled and patted his nephew on the cheek. ''You didn't come here to be my nursemaid. You came to see that Langley remains a profitable holding.''

"Yes, we must keep up appearances.'' He stood again and gripped the handles of the chair. "Do you wish to go inside, or see the roses?''

"I thought you'd be headed out to the fields to oversee the plowing.''

"I changed my mind. Which direction?''

Malcolm's shoulders relaxed a little. "The roses, then, if you don't mind. I haven't been out of doors in nearly two months. And Maddie seems to have a unique understanding of the plants.''

Quin resumed their trek. "Must be all the thorns.''

His uncle laughed. "You may be right.'' He sobered and turned his head to look up at Quin. "Just remember how beautiful is the flower they protect.''

"You don't mind her going off to visit this squire?''

"John Ramsey? No, he's a good fellow. I've known him and his sister since they were born.'' They stopped beside the nearest bush. "In fact, you used to play with him when you came to visit, as I recall.''

Quin closed one eye, searching his memory. "John Ramsey . . . wasn't he the one who liked frogs?''

"No, that was Rafe. John was the one always building boats.''

"Oh, I remember. Quiet little fellow.''

"Yes, that's him. He's got a new irrigation system. He and some mathematician from Edinburgh came up with it. Maddie's been itching to try it on our north field.''

"Why didn't she say anything to me about it?''

"I assume she didn't think you'd be interested. It'd add at least another week to your stay. We'll put it in next year. I should be up and about by then.''

There it was again, that criticism, the assumption that he'd rather be elsewhere. The assumption that he was only doing his duty. "Perhaps I'll invite this squire up to the far field in the morning."

Malcolm smiled in pleased surprise. "Splendid."

In the morning, when Lord Warefield invited her to accompany him out to the fields again, Maddie wasn't certain she'd be able to keep her temper even for the short carriage ride to the crossroads. He must realize by now how much she detested him, yet it hadn't discouraged him one bit. That he'd sat with his uncle for most of the evening, playing piquet and being generally agreeable, didn't mean anything.

She hadn't mentioned his visit to Squire John or Lucy when she'd gone visiting, and though they must have known of his presence at Langley, they had been tactful enough not to bring it up. As she and the marquis came in view of the crossroads, she was therefore surprised to see the squire seated on his gelding, Dullard, apparently waiting for them.

"Good morning," Warefield said brightly, leaning from the curricle and holding out his hand. "John Ramsey. I believe I owe you an apology for sinking a boat several years ago."

"No apology necessary—though as I recall, it was nearly an entire fleet." The squire shook the marquis's hand. "Thank you for asking me out here. I was beginning to believe Maddie was the only one interested in modernizing hereabouts."

They rode over to John's holding to view the new irrigation system, and despite her skepticism, Maddie had to concede that the marquis's interest seemed genuine. Even more surprising, when she tried to make an escape into Harthgrove later, Lord Warefield volunteered to accompany her.

"I'd like to put in an order immediately for the planking we'll need to go about putting that system in at Langley,'' he said.

"But I'm only going to bring bread and vegetables to some of the tenants,'' she protested, as Walter helped her lift baskets into the back of the curricle.

"I'll go with you as my uncle's representative,'' he offered, loading another basket.

"*I* am your uncle's representative,'' she snapped.

He lifted his hands in surrender. "Very well, Miss Willits. May I accompany you to Harthgrove as no one at all?''

She clenched her jaw. "As you wish, my lord.''

Maddie clambered onto the seat first and took the reins, clucking to the team as soon as she was settled. Still climbing up on the other side, the marquis nearly ended on his backside in the stable yard, but he managed to hang on and make his way onto the seat beside her. "Remind me not to turn my back on you, Maddie,'' he said.

She stifled an unexpected smile and concentrated on picking the most rutted part of the road all the way into Harthgrove. The vegetables no doubt got a little bruised, and so did her backside, but at least the marquis was too occupied with hanging on to try to converse.

When they reached the village, she pulled up the carriage. "The mercantile shop is over there,'' she said, pointing, "and the cottages I visit are further down the lane. Shall we meet here in an hour, my lord?''

He hopped to the ground and stepped around to offer her his hand. "I'm in no hurry, Miss Willits. And I'd like to meet more of Langley's tenants.''

Reluctantly she gripped his fingers, and he helped her to the ground. "Why?''

Warefield shrugged. "I thought that by carrying a few baskets I might be of some use to you.''

"Why would a marquis wish to be of use to me, of

all people?'' she asked, trying to ignore his tall, compelling warmth beside her as she gathered up baskets.

"Why wouldn't I?" he replied, taking the rest of the load himself.

She strode off down the lane, her green muslin skirts raising a light dust. A moment later, the marquis appeared beside her, his long legs taking the fast pace much more easily than her own. "Don't you have better things to do, my lord?" she suggested desperately. "The planting? The irrigation construction?"

He looked down at her and grinned. "Trying to get rid of me?"

Maddie sniffed and continued on her way. The other pedestrians stopped and stared as the Marquis of Warefield strolled down their dusty avenue. The bowing and curtseying that followed in their wake made Maddie feel as if she were leading some sort of parade, though of course everyone ignored her. At the Simmonds cottage she stopped and rapped on the door.

Usually one of the children rushed to the door and pulled it open. This morning, though, all she received was a muffled, "Come in, if ye please."

With a slight frown Maddie pulled the latch and pushed the door open—and stopped. With the exception of Mr. Simmonds, who was in Dorsetshire tending his sick mother, the entire Simmonds clan stood in a line along one wall of the cottage. The seven children, with Mrs. Simmonds in the middle, all bowed in ragged unison as the marquis stepped into the dark room beside her.

"My lord," they mumbled.

With renewed glee, Maddie set about introducing each of them to Lord Warefield as she set the basket on the small stone hearth and retrieved the emptied one from the week before. The children, especially the youngest of them, regarded the marquis with complete awe. He looked like a lean, tawny lion in a cage filled with squeaking mice as they leapt around him. Even after the performance was repeated twelve more times as they went from cottage to cottage, though, Warefield appeared only slightly embarrassed by the whole worshipful crowd, and not at all out of sorts.

"What shall I do with all the flowers they've given me?" he asked, as they returned to the curricle.

"I always make them up into a bouquet for your uncle's room," she said, dumping the empty baskets back into the carriage.

He examined the substantial handful of spring wildflowers for a moment, then met her eyes. "These are usually meant for you, then," he said, and held them out to her.

"Don't be silly," she said, embarrassed, and turned for the mercantile shop. No man had ever given her flowers before. Not even Charles. And she certainly had no intention of accepting a gift from the Marquis of Warefield. "We'd best put in an order for those planks."

"But I want you to have them," he insisted, not moving.

Maddie sighed heavily to cover her sudden discomfiture. *Damn him for unsettling her so.* Making a show of annoyance, she turned back around and took the bouquet from his fingers. "Thank you." She placed them in one of the baskets and faced him again. "May we go now?"

He smiled at her, though she couldn't see what in the world he was so pleased about. She'd only give them to Mr. Bancroft once they returned to Langley.

"By all means," he said, gesturing her to precede him. "Let's order those planks."

The next morning Malcolm had fresh roses in his bedchamber, which meant that Maddie either had kept the wildflowers for herself, or thrown them away. But she had accepted them from him, and without a negative comment.

Considering the opposition she'd been putting up, Quin felt a bit like Wellington at Waterloo. Perhaps the victory wasn't as definitive, nor as spectacular, but nevertheless he whistled as he rode out to the fields. She'd been in hiding all morning and had failed to appear for breakfast altogether. Most likely she was licking her wounds and readying for another attack—but Quin had been doing some battle planning of his own.

There was something about her—something he needed to pursue. He didn't quite know whether it was out of curiosity, or because he was, after all, a male and she was lovely. But the more skeptically she viewed him, the more determined he became to erase that look from her face.

He dismounted, leaving Aristotle to graze in the meadow while he headed for the group of farmers. Better yet, he wanted the opportunity to show Maddie Willits that not all of the nobility were as pompous as she apparently thought. And he knew just where he'd like to prove that to her, as well. In his bed, with her long auburn hair swept out across the white pillows, and. . . .

"Look out, my lord!"

Quin blinked and stepped back just in time to avoid being run down by a very large plow horse. The nearest of the farmers eyed him, but immediately went back to clearing the field when he looked in their direction. He shook himself and bent down to clear a few of the last stones out of the plowed earth.

He was helping unload sacks of seed when he realized he'd forgotten about Eloise's correspondence. Rarely did he answer her letters on the same day he received them;

he was often extremely busy, and besides, it seemed somewhat weak-kneed of him to do so. After all, he was not a dewy-eyed romantic, and he had had an understanding with Eloise since they were children. But forgetting completely was entirely uncharacteristic.

Remembering Maddie's harsh words about his concern over his uncle, Quin made a point of returning to the manor for luncheon with Malcolm. Again Maddie was nowhere in sight. "Where is Miss Willits this afternoon?" he asked offhandedly.

"Potting."

Quin looked up. "Beg pardon?"

"In the garden shed," Malcolm explained. "Maddie's roses have become quite popular in Somerset. They're in great demand in the spring, so she roots cuttings and sends them to the neighbors."

So she didn't hate everyone, then. Just marquises— or just the Marquis of Warefield. Quin pursed his lips, trying to decide how much he could ask Malcolm without giving away his own growing interest. "Malcolm, might I ask you a question?"

"Certainly."

"Why does Miss Willits seem to . . . dislike me so intensely? I haven't done anything to offend her, have I?"

Malcolm grinned. "You'll have to ask her. It's not for me to say."

Quin sighed and climbed to his feet. "You warned me to be careful with her. You might have warned me to bring a suit of armor along, as well."

His uncle only laughed.

Seeing Eloise's letter propped up on his dressing table reminded him once more that he hadn't written since he'd set out for Langley. With an impatient glance out the window toward the garden, he sat and pulled out a pen and some ink.

Dearest Eloise,

Uncle Malcolm is doing well. Unfortunately, it appears that I'll be staying here longer than we'd planned—in addition to the crops and accounts, a new irrigation system is needed at Langley. No real adventures to speak of. . . .

Quin sat back. That last part wasn't exactly true, but he didn't wish to relate the near-drowning or near-shooting incidents, and he doubted Eloise would find his war with Miss Marguerite amusing. Nor was she likely to appreciate his odd battle of wits with Miss Willits.

He dipped the pen again.

. . . but Langley is rather rustic. I still plan to visit you at Stafford Green before the Season. Please give my regards to your father.

> *Yours,*
> *Quinlan*

It wasn't very long, but it would have to do for now. He'd give her more details in the next missive, when he knew how much longer he'd be staying. He sealed the letter, scrawled Eloise's address on the outside, and left it for Garrett to send out with the post.

He restlessly wandered about the house for a while, hoping Maddie would return from her seclusion before he had to return to the fields. Exasperated, he looked through the morning room window just in time to see her green skirt disappearing into the garden shed. Quin started outside, then stopped. If he appeared, she'd only accuse him of following her and neglecting his duty to Malcolm, and to Langley—and he'd damned well heard enough of that rubbish. So he'd have to be certain he wasn't neglecting anything.

Inspiration hit. "Aha," he muttered, grinning, and headed into the office at the far end of the hallway. Lifting the last ledger book out of its drawer, he flipped to the page where the handwriting changed.

With the book tucked under his arm, he marched into battle. "Miss Willits?" he called, making a show of looking about the grounds for her. "Miss Willits, are you here?"

For several moments she neglected to answer, but just as he was beginning to think he'd have to "accidentally" discover her in the potting shed, she emerged.

"Yes, my lord?" she said, brushing a stray lock of auburn hair back behind her ear.

"Ah, Miss Willits. I've a question for you."

Distrust entered her gray eyes as she watched him open the ledger. He stepped over next to her, holding the book so she could see it, too. She smelled of earth and lavender, and dirt smudged her fingers and one cheek. And the heat that began coursing along his veins had absolutely nothing to do with simple curiosity.

Attempting to return his attention to the accounts, Quin pointed at one of the last entries, dated only two days before. She'd been sneaking in and doing the accounts while he was out working—after he'd asked her to refrain from touching them. "What is this?"

She leaned a little closer to him to look at the page, then glanced up at his face. "How should I know, my lord?"

"Do you think me a complete idiot, Miss Willits?" He stifled a smile as she opened her mouth to respond. "No, don't answer that. Allow me to explain. Here," and he turned back several pages, "is my uncle's writing. The only Bancroft with worse writing is my brother." He pointed at another, much later entry. "This is my writing. Not much better, but at least you can tell the t's from the w's." He returned to the indicated page and its rows of neat entries. "And this writing, I believe, is yours."

She gave the page a sour look. "All right, my lord, I confess. I know how to do arithmetic." She pointed at one of the lines. "But if you'll note, my lord, nowhere did I allow my writing to touch yours."

Ignoring that, he lowered the book to look at her. "Why didn't you say you'd been tending Langley?"

"We wrote as much to your father." Maddie met his gaze. "You didn't seem to be interested."

Actually, he was more interested than he cared to admit. "Why don't we say that I was ignorant of the facts? You've done a great deal of good here, both for my uncle and for the Bancrofts."

"I do what I am employed to do," she answered shortly, and turned back to the shed. "Was that all you required, my lord?"

"I just wanted to thank you for tending my uncle."

She looked over her shoulder at him. "Someone needed to be here, my lord."

After yesterday, that same thought had occurred to him. If Maddie hadn't been Uncle Malcolm's companion, both the situation at Langley and Malcolm himself might have been in much worse condition than even the duke had surmised. He followed her, angry at the prick to his pride. "Ah. Now you are criticizing me for not coming to Langley sooner."

"It is not my place to criticize you for your shortcomings, my lord."

"Merely to point them out to me."

She curtsied. "As you wish, my lord."

That was too much. "Just a moment!" he growled, striding after her.

Maddie stopped and faced him. "Yes, my lord?" she asked, only the slightest hesitation showing in her eyes.

"Miss Willits, what in God's name. . . ." He stopped,

not because she lifted her chin at him defiantly, but because her hands shook before she moved them behind her back. "What," he began again, revising his choice of words, "have I done to distress you?"

She looked at him for a long moment. "Nothing, my lord," she said slowly. "And I wish to keep it that way."

Finally. "What if I were to assure you that I have nothing but the best intentions where you, my uncle, and Langley are concerned?" Quin put his hand over his heart. "I swear not to harm any of you. Including Miss Marguerite."

Maddie narrowed her eyes, her expression so clearly suspicious that Quin couldn't help smiling. She weighed what he'd said against whatever it was she thought she knew about him. For a moment he couldn't tell which side had won. Then she lifted her chin.

"If you had come here to help Mr. Bancroft," she said slowly, "I would have much less objection to you."

"I *did* come here to help him," Quin protested. "What do you think—"

She raised a dirt-smudged finger at him. "You came here to help your father. To see to the crops, and keep up the ledgers. And you didn't come for three weeks, and then arrived precisely on the fifteenth."

Quin took a deep breath. By God, this woman was infuriating. "I was at Warefield," he snapped. "I didn't know anything had happened to Malcolm until my father sent for me." He leaned toward her, closer to losing his temper than he'd been in years. "Why didn't *you* write sooner?" he accused hotly.

Maddie glared at him. "He wouldn't let me, at first. Mr. Bancroft doesn't like your side of the family." She folded her arms over her chest. "And now that I think about it, neither do I."

Quin leaned closer still, his face only inches from

hers. And then his eyes focused on her lips. The anger in his veins became something else entirely—something equally hot and equally disturbing. "You don't know me," he murmured, meeting her gaze again.

She held his eyes, still fearless. "And you don't know me."

"I would like to," he said, in a low voice.

Her mouth opened, and then shut again. "You—I—" Maddie swallowed. "Bah," she finally snapped, and turned her back on him.

Quin watched her stalk back to the house. A slow smile touched his lips. This was becoming very interesting indeed.

Chapter 6

"**W**onderful," Maddie snarled, shutting her door with a thud and plunking herself down on her bed. "Wonderful. Now he really *does* want to seduce me."

She jumped to her feet again and strode to the window. He was still out there in the garden—she could see one leg and part of his arm if she craned her head against the cool glass. With all the insults she'd handed him, Lord Warefield still thought he could win her good favor simply by looking at her with those beguiling eyes and by talking nicely.

"Ha, ha, ha," she said to his elbow down below. "I've heard nice words before. Nicer than that." What she should have done—what she *would* have done, if he hadn't temporarily surprised her out of her wits—was tell him to go to Jericho and leave her in peace.

Maddie scowled. In point of fact, she'd had ample opportunity to tell him exactly that, and she hadn't done it. She'd gawked at him like some stupid, doe-eyed half-wit, and then even worse, had turned tail and run.

She banged her head against the glass. "Stupid, stupid girl," she muttered. "So what if he's handsome? So what if he can quote Shakespeare? I'm sure most everyone can. And so what if he doesn't mind chasing pigs through the mud and ruining a perfectly splendid set of clothes? And. . . ."

Down in the garden, he turned around without warning and looked up at her.

"Drat!" Maddie ducked backward. She stayed hidden behind the curtains for a long moment, smacking her hands together in agitation. With the light outside, he might not have seen her gaping at him through the window. She counted to ten, took a breath, and then stepped forward again.

The marquis stood beneath her window, a white rose in one hand. With a smile, he held it up to her, then bowed with an absurdly grand flourish.

"Of all the nerve," she breathed. Her clever game had crumbled into a shambles, and he thought he had beaten her. The marquis had a surprise coming. She stuck out her tongue at him.

He blew her a kiss.

Her heart pounding, Maddie unlatched the window and shoved it open. "Don't you ruin my roses!" she shouted at him.

" 'But soft,' " he called up to her with a deepening grin, " 'what light through yonder window breaks? It is the east, and Juliet—' "

With a choked cry of outrage, she slammed the window shut again. No more speaking to him, or looking at him, or assisting him with anything. That would show him! She stomped to her door and threw it open. And she certainly wasn't going to the Fowlers' ball and dance with that arrogant, self-centered *aristocrat*.

She turned down the hallway and was nearly run over by Mr. Bancroft as he scooted around the corner in his wheeled chair. "Mr. Bancroft!" she said, trying to swallow her annoyance at his evil, seductive nephew. "How wonderful!"

"Perhaps this contraption isn't so bad, after all," he admitted. "Though I do seem to go in circles quite a bit."

"I told you that you'd like it." She cleared her throat. "Mr. Bancroft, I don't think I need to go—"

"And since I've been getting about so well," he interrupted happily, "I thought the Fowlers' ball on Friday would be a splendid opportunity for me to make my public debut."

Maddie closed her mouth again.

He reached out and took her hand. "Would you be my escort, Maddie?"

"I haven't anything to wear," she hedged, wondering if he could hear the reluctance in her voice.

"Nonsense. What about the gown you had made for the Dardinales' Christmas soiree? That was lovely."

"But it was for winter," she protested, "two years ago."

"No one here will notice."

Someone *would* notice, and she was unsettled to realize it was Lord Warefield's reaction she'd been thinking of. "I . . . suppose not."

"There you go. I'm not much for dancing at the moment, but I do quite a handy job at holding glasses of punch."

She laughed halfheartedly. "Yes, Mr. Bancroft. I would be delighted to accompany you."

But saying she would attend and actually preparing for the ball were two very different things. As soon as Warefield returned to his planting, she began rooting through her scanty wardrobe. When Maddie tried the gown on, it still fit, though the burgundy pelisse hardly seemed appropriate for a spring soiree, and the looser waist was hopelessly dated. And her shoes were the same black slippers she'd worn to every formal and semi-formal gathering since she'd come to Langley.

Maddie frowned. She had three days. It was time to begin sewing.

"Miss Maddie?"

"Come in, Mrs. Hodges," she called, twisting in front of the mirror to eye her hemline skeptically. Using every ounce of skill and patience she possessed, she'd taken in the waist and adjusted the length a total of four times, and was still able to concede only that she looked passable. Barely.

"Oh, that's lovely," the housekeeper said approvingly, as she opened the door. "You'll have that Squire John mooning after you for certain."

Maddie smiled. "John Ramsey is a friend, Mrs. Hodges, nothing more."

"Hm. All the same, those Fowler girls'll be lucky to be noticed enough at their own party to keep from being bumped into." She laid a silver hair ribbon on the dressing table. "And I wager his lordship'll have no complaints, either."

A sudden nervous tremor shook Maddie's fingers, and she picked up the ribbon to cover it. Apparently she'd frightened him off, for he had barely spoken to her at all in the past three days. Of course, he would likely claim that he'd been occupied with the planting, but she knew better—the coward. "My thanks for the hair ribbon. I hadn't realized all of mine were so worn."

"That's because you never go into Harthgrove with us to look at the catalogs of London fashions."

"Who has time for London fashions so far from London?" Maddie returned, unable to keep an edge of disdain out of her voice.

"Well, at least *I* have a new hair ribbon to lend to other people who don't care about fashion," Mrs. Hodges sniffed with exaggerated haughtiness, turning for the door.

Maddie grinned. "Thank you very, very much for the loan, Mrs. Hodges."

The housekeeper returned to Maddie's side and kissed her on the cheek. "My pleasure, Miss Maddie."

Garrett clumsily rolled the wheeled chair down the stairs, while Bill Tomkins carried Mr. Bancroft to the ground floor. Maddie followed behind, still fiddling with her hair and muttering a prayer that an April snowstorm would sweep through Somerset before they reached the coach, and cause them to miss the soiree.

"You look ravishing, Maddie," Mr. Bancroft said appreciatively, smiling.

She looked back up the stairs, another nervous flutter running along her skin. "How long do you think we'll have to wait for Lord Warefield? If we arrive as fashionably late as they do in London, the ball will be over before we get there."

"I'm certain he'll be along before Michaelmas. And Maddie, try not to criticize his attire tonight, if you don't mind. You'll have the poor fellow weeping."

She chuckled reluctantly. "How else is he supposed to learn?"

Only a moment later, unhurried bootsteps sounded in the hall upstairs. Maddie leaned back against the wall and folded her arms. Affixing a look of bored disdain on her face, she kept her gaze on the grandfather clock. He might have caught her off guard once or twice, but the war was by no means over.

"Ah, good evening, Quinlan." Mr. Bancroft rolled to the foot of the stairs to greet his nephew.

"Good evening, Uncle. I trust I'm not too tardy?"

"Not at all."

Maddie waited for seven seconds to tick off the clock before she turned around. She'd intended to wait for ten, but she couldn't quite manage it. "Good evening, my lord,'' she said, curtseying. As she lifted her eyes to his, she nearly lost her balance.

''Miss Willits.''

Quinlan stood looking down at her, a slight, amused expression on his lean, handsome face. She'd expected him to be wearing his black too-formal attire, but apparently he'd learned his lesson. Instead, a rich brown coat cut in a jaunty style cloaked his broad shoulders, while a cream-colored waistcoat and black breeches drew her helplessly attracted gaze once more to his well-muscled thighs.

For the first time in days, his Hessian boots were completely free of mud, and were shiny enough to reflect her own unwillingly mesmerized expression back at her. ''My goodness, my lord. However will anyone be able to concentrate on dancing with such a splendid sight before them? I am quite ready to faint myself.''

''Maddie,'' Mr. Bancroft warned.

''I think they'll be distracted enough by you to forget about me,'' the marquis said softly. ''At least, all the men will be.'' He came forward and took her hand, lifting it to his lips. His gaze traveled down the length of her gown and back up again, pausing at her low-cut neckline. ''You are lovely.''

Maddie swallowed and swiftly retrieved her hand as a warm, pleasant flush crept from her toes all the way to her face. She took a quick breath, trying to gather her melting, scattering wits back into cohesion. ''Not nearly as lovely as you, my lord.''

Mr. Bancroft snorted. ''Well, someone compliment me, so we can be on our way.''

Immediately Maddie hurried over and kissed her employer on the cheek. ''I can't tell you how happy I am to see you getting about so well.'' She smiled at him, taking his hand in hers. ''Next month, *you* will be dancing.''

When she straightened, Quinlan was looking from one to the other of them, his expression unreadable. "I don't think I can say it better than that," he murmured, his gaze stopping on Maddie. "Shall we be off?"

The wheeled chair was strapped to the back of Lord Warefield's coach, and the marquis lifted his uncle and placed him on the soft leather seat inside. As the coach started off, Maddie caught Quinlan looking at her from the opposite seat yet again, and far too smugly for her peace of mind.

"My lord," she began in her most deferential voice, "whyever didn't you wear this magnificent coat to dinner the other night? No one in the world could have found fault with such perfection."

The marquis glanced away for a moment, his expression distinctly uncomfortable. Barely able to keep from chortling gleefully, she leaned forward and gestured at his boots. "And your valet must truly be a marvel! It's taken him—what, eight days—to remove the last of the mud from those boots. How in the world did he manage it?"

"Aye," Mr. Bancroft agreed. "It would be a handy secret to have in Somerset, no doubt about that."

"Well . . . it will simply have to remain a secret," the marquis said rather brusquely, and looked out the window.

Maddie and Malcolm glanced at one another. "Excuse me, my lord," she said with carefully hidden amusement, "but do you mean your coat and boots are truly some sort of secret?"

He glared at her. "Yes. They are."

Before Maddie could pursue her interrogation any further, they arrived at the Fowlers' residence. Light shone from every window and from the lanterns scattered along the drive, which was already crowded with carriages and wagons. Apparently Mrs. Fowler had been as good as her word and had invited every landowner in the area to attend the marquis's grand unveiling.

A footman arrived to help Maddie to the ground and then assist the marquis with untying the chair. Once they had Mr. Bancroft settled, Maddie stepped behind the chair and took the handles.

"I'll do that, Miss Willits," the marquis said.

"Oh, I wouldn't hear of it, my lord!" she gasped with mock horror. "However will everyone be able to shake your hand if you are pushing Mr. Bancroft about?"

"Miss Willits, it is not seemly for you—"

"I know perfectly well what is seemly and what is not," she countered, unable to keep the abrupt anger out of her voice. "Far better—"

"Maddie," Mr. Bancroft said quietly.

She stopped. "Mr. Bancroft is my employer," she continued more evenly. "Allow me to do my duty by him."

His eyes studying hers, Quinlan slowly nodded and stepped back. "Of course."

The uneven drive didn't make things any easier, but stubborn determination could do wonders, and Maddie managed to maneuver the chair up to the stairs. Two footmen who'd obviously been primed regarding their duties then took over, lifting Mr. Bancroft and the contraption into the manor house, and then all the way upstairs to the second floor. The marquis fell into step beside her as she followed, and she could feel his gaze on her again.

"I didn't intend to offend you, Maddie," he said.

"It would be an honor to be offended by such a gentleman as yourself," she replied coolly, hoping the trio of trumpeters she spied at the entrance to the ballroom was there to announce the marquis's arrival.

"Good God," he muttered as he, too, noticed them.

"Did you have something to do with this, Miss Willits?"

She put a hand to her breast. "Me, my lord? I would never presume."

Quin's eyes followed the gesture, then returned to her face. He slowly reached out to straighten her sleeve, his fingers brushing her bare arm. "What a shame."

Maddie narrowed her eyes. "What—"

Before she could complete the sentence, the trilling fanfare began. Quinlan looked completely appalled, and Maddie was forced to clap a hand over her mouth to contain her amusement.

Apparently they'd been expected to arrive late. The entire assemblage, dressed in the finest attire Maddie had ever seen them wear, stood lining either side of the doorway. As their party entered, the guests, the footmen, and the musicians in the back of the room bowed almost in unison. Mrs. Fowler came forward, her arms outstretched in a gracious greeting, while her husband followed behind.

"My lord," she breathed, curtseying deeply. "You honor us again with your presence."

He smiled dazzlingly as he took her hand. "Thank you, Mrs. Fowler. I'm happy to be here."

"Please, my lord, allow me to introduce you."

With that the crowd swept forward, surrounding them and making a rather alarming racket. Maddie leaned forward over the back of Malcolm's chair as they waited, abandoned, in the entryway. "Would you care for some punch, Mr. Bancroft?"

"Thank you, my dear, yes, I would."

She wheeled him to the refreshment table. "You'd think they could at least be bothered to welcome *you*," she commented, glancing back at the multitude. "You've done more for them than Warefield would ever dream of."

"Perhaps, but Quinlan is a novelty. I'm merely an antique hereabouts."

"You're quite a bit more than that." She glanced at the marquis again to see him showing off his warm smile and jade eyes to anyone bold enough to speak to him. He played the role of gentleman marquis with absolute perfection. But no one was that nice—especially not a titled nobleman. "My, he does make a magnificent centerpiece, though, doesn't he?"

Mr. Bancroft accepted a glass of punch. "Are you certain, my dear, that this little game you've concocted is going as you think?"

She looked at him. "What game?"

"Come, Madeleine, we've known one another for four years. Do you think I can't tell that you're attempting to kill him with kindness?"

Maddie put a hand over her heart, aware that she'd already spent an inordinate amount of time this evening proclaiming her innocence. "I assure you, I have no idea—"

"Does he look like he's ready to be driven away, Maddie?" he said quietly.

She looked once more at the marquis. He was gazing over Mr. Fitzroy's head, directly at her. And then he grinned.

"Oh, damnation!" she hissed, turning away and feeling warmth creep up her cheeks again. And all he'd done this time was show her his teeth, for heaven's sake.

"Quinlan's used to getting his way, but he's no fool. What's he supposed to think, with you attacking him at every turn for no good reason?"

"I have a very good reason," she snapped. "And I'm certainly not trying to attract his interest."

"Perhaps you'd best tell him that."

She folded her arms indignantly, unable to slow the fast beating of her heart. "I'll be happy to."

The orchestra struck up a country dance, and Maddie jumped. The marquis was escorting Miss Fowler onto the narrow, polished dance floor, while her younger sister scowled and Jane Fowler simply glowed. Realizing how tensely she'd been holding herself, Maddie let her shoulders relax a little. Of course he wouldn't dance with her. There might be no other nobility about, but there were daughters of propertied gentlemen. She was only a companion.

"Maddie, may I have the honor?"

She looked up at Squire John Ramsey as he stopped before her. "Of course, John." Before she took his hand, though, she turned to Mr. Bancroft. "Do you wish me to stay?"

"Heavens, no. Go dance, girl."

Luckily the only open spot on the floor was halfway across the room from the marquis, so she wouldn't have to dance with him for more than a few seconds as they passed one another. She smiled at John, grateful that at least one person hadn't ignored her this evening.

"Lord Warefield seems to be enjoying himself," he said, as they stepped around one another.

"Even better, Langley will be adopting your watering system," she said. "Mr. Bancroft is quite pleased."

"I'm gratified," John admitted. "When Warefield asked me to meet him the other morning, I half thought he meant to tell me to mind my own business and let the Bancrofts take care of their own."

"You don't like the marquis, then?"

John grinned. "I don't know him well enough to say, either way."

"But you knew one another as children, didn't you?"

He shrugged and took her hand to step forward. "He visited Malcolm a few times during the summer, years ago. We played together, I suppose, though it mostly seemed to consist of him and his brother ambushing and sinking the toy boats I used to make.''

She sniffed. "How typical."

"I haven't seen him since I was eight, Maddie. I doubt he stones frigates out on the Thames." He stopped speaking as they circled past Sally Fowler and James Preston, then took her hand again. "I take it you don't share the community's delight over our guest?"

"He's a bit stuffy for me."

"Well, he did come to help Malcolm."

Some help. "Yes, I suppose he did," she said reluctantly.

John moved past her, and Maddie wound around James Preston, Mr. Fowler, Mr. Dardinale, and then Lord Warefield. He kept hold of her fingers a moment longer than he should have. "You know John Ramsey quite well, don't you?" he murmured.

She looked straight at him and pulled her fingers free. "Yes."

It was completely ridiculous, but now that even Mr. Bancroft had noticed Quinlan's apparent interest, the marquis did sound almost jealous. Perhaps, though, he was only chastising her for dancing with one of her betters. That made more sense than anything else.

When he took Sally out for a quadrille, and James Preston danced with her, she decided she must have been right. She had only offended his overdeveloped sense of propriety, and he had been unable to resist pointing out her *faux pas* to her.

The butler announced that dinner was ready, and unmindful of any propriety at all, the entire female contingent present, minus one, herded around the marquis, undoubtedly hoping to be the one he chose to escort into the dining room. The chattering, giggling din was deafening. Lord Warefield didn't forget his own manners, though, and deftly he picked Mrs. Fowler out of the crowd, wrapped her arm around his, and led the way out of the ballroom.

With great ceremony Mr. Fowler pushed Mr. Bancroft's chair to the foot of the table. The marquis, of course, sat at the head. Maddie rolled her eyes and took the seat next to her employer. "I've lost my appetite, I think," she muttered.

He smiled, but didn't say anything. His face had become rather pale, only a few shades darker than his starched cravat. Immediately forgetting her annoyance, Maddie leaned close to him.

"Are you well?" she whispered.

"I'm fine," he returned. "Just a bit tired."

"You shouldn't have exerted yourself so soon. We'll go." She started to her feet, but he shook his head and put his hand over hers.

"No worries, my dear. I may fall asleep in my chair, but I shall survive the evening." He smiled. "I promise."

A warm hand slid down Maddie's shoulder to rest on her arm. "Uncle?"

Startled, Maddie looked up at Quinlan. He leaned over her shoulder, gazing at his uncle with the same concern in his eyes that she felt herself.

"You two are making me feel old," Malcolm grumbled. "Go back and sit down, boy, before you begin a riot."

Quinlan glanced down at her. "Keep an eye on him," he murmured.

She lifted her chin. "I always do."

He paused, his eyes holding hers. "I know."

He returned to his seat, and after innumerable toasts and speeches in his honor, the footmen finally brought out the food. Maddie did keep a close watch on Mr. Bancroft, but his appetite hadn't diminished, and she decided that he'd been telling the truth when he said he was only tired. All the same, she'd been so consumed with disdaining Warefield that she'd nearly forgotten her duties.

"Ladies and gentlemen?"

Quinlan stood at the head of the table, a glass of wine in his hand, and Maddie groaned. She'd already drunk a thousand toasts this evening, and now Warefield had to think of something clever to make everyone else look shabby.

"If I may," the marquis continued, as every eye looked at him, "I know there've been quite a few toasts already this evening, but I would feel remiss if I didn't add one more."

"Please do, my lord," Mrs. Fowler begged.

"This is a double toast, actually." He raised his glass. "To my uncle, Malcolm Bancroft, for his courage and strength and for his unflagging concern for the well-being of the people of Somerset."

"To Malcolm Bancroft," everyone echoed. For once Maddie was pleased to join in, and she smiled down at her employer.

"And to Madeleine Willits, for the great care she has taken with my uncle, and for her tolerance in putting up with a very annoying interloper at Langley." He grinned at her.

"To Maddie," came the second echo. Quinlan tipped his glass, his eyes still holding hers as he drank.

"Oh, dear," Maddie whispered, heat sliding along her veins.

Apparently Mr. Bancroft had been correct, after all. She'd never thought that the son of the Duke of Highbarrow Castle would take her antagonism to mean interest. If she'd encouraged him, it hadn't been done intentionally. She didn't think so, anyway—but from the way her body continued to react to his every look and expression, anything was possible.

Maddie looked at Quin, wondering when precisely she'd ceased hating him. And what precisely she was going to do about it now.

Chapter 7

⟨⟨◦⟩⟩

Quin couldn't keep his eyes off her.

Somerset featured a pleasant enough selection of eligible young ladies, he supposed; daughters of squires and knights and second sons of second sons of barons. Some of them wore the latest fashions of London and Paris and actually looked quite pretty in them. Bobbed and curled haircuts in the style encouraged by Beau Brummell's followers seemed to be the order of the day, even here.

And then there was Maddie Willits: long auburn hair with wispy tendrils escaping from silver ribbon and a dark burgundy dress easily two years out of fashion—yet which brought out the gray of her eyes. The elegant, practiced ease with which she danced made him yearn to take her in his arms. She fit in with these rustics as well as a plow horse would fit into Highbarrow Castle's stables. As well as he fit in at Langley. Or at least as well as she *wanted* him to think he fit in at Langley.

By the time dinner ended, he was becoming quite tired of everyone pointing out the graceful tilt of his hand as he brought a fork to his mouth, and the cultured turn of his wrist when he took a sip of wine. Being dissected in a physician school's anatomy class would have been less trying. At least he would have been dead, and wouldn't have had to listen to the ridiculous commentary.

After dinner he stood for a quadrille with Patricia Dardinale, mainly because Mrs. Fowler had been attempting to keep the two of them apart all evening. "You dance quite well," he said approvingly. The Fowler daughters had already assured him of bruised ankles by morning, and he'd had his toes stepped on twice.

Blue eyes beneath dark, curling lashes looked up at him, and she smiled. "Thank you, my lord. My governess came directly from London."

"You do her good credit."

He looked about for his reluctant house mate, and finally spied her in one of the other groups of dancers. Maddie hadn't lacked for a partner all evening and had always managed to be either in a different set, or at the far end of the line from him. The quadrille was her second dance with John Ramsey.

"How long do you plan to stay in Somerset, my lord?" Miss Dardinale asked, as he approached her again.

"I had planned to leave at the end of the week, but I may stay a bit longer, to see the new irrigation system finished."

"Oh, yes," she nodded. "Papa, Squire John, and Maddie have been trying to find a way to bring water to our east pasture for a year now. I think they've finally figured it out."

He glanced over at the blasted annoying female again. "Miss Willits seems quite adept at mathematics." Apparently she was the Leonardo da Vinci of Somerset.

"Mama tried to hire her away from Mr. Bancroft to be my governess," Patricia admitted. "She wouldn't go, but she has been coming over twice a week to teach me Latin." The alabaster brow wrinkled for a moment, then smoothed itself out again. "It's very difficult." She smiled. "I prefer French. It seems much more romantic, don't you think?"

Quin looked at her absently. "Yes, quite."

So his uncle's companion spoke French and wrote in Latin, knew Shakespeare well enough to quote the bard from memory, and could both keep estate account ledgers and engineer irrigation plans. "Do they ever play waltzes in Somerset?" he asked his partner.

"Oh, yes." She glanced about, then leaned a little closer as they linked elbows. "I doubt Mrs. Fowler will request one for tonight. Lydia's terrible at the waltz." She giggled.

He didn't plan to waltz with Lydia.

As soon as the quadrille ended, he strolled over to his hostess. "Mrs. Fowler, might I make a request of the orchestra?"

"Of course, my lord. They know all of the latest tunes and dances. We long to hear something that's popular right now in London."

"Splendid." He turned to face the dozen musicians. "Might we have a waltz?"

The violinist nodded. "Our pleasure, my lord. Any waltz in particular?"

"No. Anything at all." Quin turned around again as a score of females began heading in his direction. "Miss Willits?" he called, hoping she hadn't heard the request and bolted.

After a moment she came out from behind Uncle Malcolm's chair. "Yes, my lord?"

"You promised to show me a waltz, as I recall," he lied, not feeling the least bit guilty about it. "Will you do so now?"

She glared at him with thinly veiled annoyance, clearly realizing that if she argued, the crowd would turn against her faster than the villagers had against Frankenstein's monster. "Of course, my lord. It would be my greatest honor."

"Thank you."

He strolled up and took her hand. Behind her annoyance he sensed confusion and uncertainty, which was better than outright hostility. Beneath his thumb, the pulse at her wrist beat fast and hard, the one measure of her feelings she was unable to control. The music began, and he led her out to the middle of the floor.

"Shall we?" he murmured.

"I hate you," she whispered back, fitting her hand into his and allowing him to slide his arm about her waist.

He smiled. "And why is that?"

They glided into the waltz. As he had suspected, she danced superbly—which, added to her other accomplishments and abilities, made her the most talented, as well as most lovely, governess, companion, and mistress he could ever remember encountering. She glanced about the room, and following her gaze, he belatedly realized that they were the only couple on the dance floor. Undoubtedly the other guests had taken his request for a waltz to be a royal command. Well, that was perfectly fine with him.

"You shouldn't be dancing with me, my lord," she said, avoiding his gaze.

Quin wondered how far he could push her before she renewed her attempt to do him bodily harm. "I can dance with whomever I wish," he returned. "I'm the Marquis of Warefield."

She narrowed her eyes. "Not by any accomplishment of your own. Do you expect me to be impressed simply because you can afford to wear splendid clothes and drive fine carriages?"

He wished she would stop mentioning his damned suit. If she ever found out he'd actually sent to Warefield for it, he'd never hear the end of it. ''No.''

''And don't think I haven't heard that you sent all the way to Warefield for your magnificent attire. A four-day journey for a coat and a pair of boots.''

Damnation. ''If you weren't so hard to please, I wouldn't have had to do it,'' he countered.

''I am not hard to please. And you did it to please your own vanity.''

''I did it out of a sense of self-preservation.'' Distracted and on the attack, Maddie seemed to forget just how many people were watching them. Shamelessly taking advantage, he pulled her lithe body closer. ''So, Maddie, why do you hate me?''

She looked down at his cravat. ''You needn't concern yourself with my feelings, my lord.''

''So you keep repeating. But tell me, anyway.''

''Because you are the Marquis of Warefield, I suppose,'' she said finally, in a voice so quiet and reluctant he could barely make it out, even with only inches between them.

''But you've already said I can't claim responsibility for the fact of my birth,'' he said softly. ''If that's true, how can you blame me for it?''

He thought he'd cornered her, but she lifted her chin and met his gaze squarely. ''Because I choose to.''

''Now, that's hardly fair. I've been trying to play by your rules, but you keep changing them. Makes it rather difficult, you know.''

Maddie hesitated. ''Makes *what* rather difficult?''

Quin let his eyes drift to where they'd been wanting to go all evening. He focused on her soft, full lips. ''Winning you over,'' he murmured. She jerked her hand, but he held her fingers and kept her close to him. ''We couldn't possibly have met before, since you have only been employed as a governess, and I generally don't visit houses with young children. So is it my family?'' He shook his head before she could answer. ''No, because you work for my uncle.''

''Don't let it disturb you, my lord. No doubt your mind is used to contemplating far loftier issues.''

''Sweet Lucifer,'' he swore softly, wondering where he had gained such a great tolerance for insolence. He'd never had it before. ''What do I have to do to earn a civil response from you?''

''I have been quite civil, I think.''

Quin looked down at her, dancing calmly and gracefully in his arms while she flayed him alive with her tongue. And he wanted to kiss her only a little more than he wanted to wring her neck. ''Miss Willits, I surrender. You are the victor. I am helpless before you. Have pity.''

Her lips twitched. ''No.''

''How about a bargain?'' he pursued. Behind him, at the edges of the dance floor, he could hear murmurs of conversation, but he dismissed them. Tonight, he was dancing with Maddie. And enjoying himself more than he could remember in a long time. ''I will pretend I am not the Marquis of Warefield, and you will pretend you don't hate me.''

''I don't . . .'' She stopped. ''Why do you insist on my liking you?'' Maddie revised, her eyes meeting his.

''Because I like *you,* Maddie. My uncle regards you very highly. Your opinion is listened to and respected. And yet this beautiful, forthright woman,'' he continued, trying very hard not to kiss her right in the middle of the waltz, ''apparently hates me. I just want to know what it is that I've done to you. Whatever it was, believe me, it was not intentional.''

For a long moment she held his gaze. Finally she sighed, a little unsteadily. ''All right. A truce. Until you leave. Not one second longer.''

Ah, victory. Of a sort, anyway. ''So I no longer need

to check my bed sheets every evening for thorns or poisonous spiders?''

Unexpectedly, she chuckled. "I hadn't thought of that."

He liked her laugh. "Thank God."

By the time the evening ended, Quin felt as tired as Malcolm looked. Maddie stayed quiet during the carriage ride back to Langley, and even when he intentionally left her several good openings for an insult, she didn't take the bait. Apparently she meant to honor the truce. He glanced at Malcolm. Honor had little to do with any of this: he was supposed to be aiding his uncle, and all he could think about was how he would go about maneuvering Maddie into his bed. It was pure madness—and he had never thought he'd enjoy madness quite so much.

It just didn't make sense that the one titled gentleman she'd spoken to in four years would be the one man able to look beyond his title, the one noble who could simply be . . . nice. Even so, Maddie was willing to concede that perhaps she'd been a little hard on Quinlan. If Charles Dunfrey had fallen into some stream, he probably would have drowned rather than surface to face ridicule.

Maddie paused in mid-snip and regarded the white rose before her. It had been a long time since she'd thought about Charles Dunfrey without either flinching or wanting to hit something badly. Good. As a fiancé he had been handsome enough, but he'd been severely lacking in the qualities of trust and loyalty. He'd also lacked the vision to see beyond the obvious, as had her own supposed friends and acquaintances. She'd assumed that every other person of his station was therefore the same. Apparently, she hadn't been entirely correct.

"Maddie?"

She jumped and turned around. Quinlan strolled

through the garden toward her, his coat missing and his shirtsleeves rolled halfway up to his elbows. He looked like a Grecian statue of a mythical hero. "Yes, my lord?"

"Blasted hot this morning, isn't it?" he said, stopping before her. "I just returned from Harthgrove. It looks as though the last load of lumber may be in by this afternoon." He stepped closer, leaning down to lift one of the roses out of her arm basket. "Exquisite," he murmured, running a finger along the delicate edge of the white petals.

Maddie swallowed and continued choosing her bouquet. "That's good news. You'll be finished here by the end of the week." And that, to her surprise, didn't please her very much at all.

Quinlan grinned. "So now that you're bound to a truce, you only want me gone, hm?"

She met his gaze, hoping she looked more composed than she felt. But however amusing he might think himself, however handsome he might be, she'd agreed to the truce because what he'd said last evening had made sense. Not because he'd convinced her to surrender. Just one hint that he intended to act like—well, like a noble, and she would renew her attack. "I only wanted you gone before." She snipped another bloom.

"And you weren't exactly subtle about it." For a moment he was quiet, and then sun-warmed petals brushed against her cheek.

Unsettled, she stepped over to the next bush, crimson buds waving in the warm breeze. "Have you told Mr. Bancroft the news?"

He followed her. "Not yet."

"You should let him know. He's been anxious about it."

The rose and then his fingertips brushed across the back of her neck. "I will."

She shivered. "Stop it."

"How is it that a lady as lovely and intelligent as you is still unmarried?" he asked softly, ignoring her demand.

Maddie shut her eyes for a moment and tried to slow her breathing. "Because I choose to be," she lied.

"You know," he continued in the same quiet voice, "I think you never really disliked me at all." His fingers trailed down her arm to her wrist, and slowly he pulled her around to face him.

"Yes, I did."

Jade eyes caught and held hers. "Oh, I think you wanted to," he conceded, only his soft murmur separating his mouth from hers.

Quinlan was right. He was right, and this was wrong—and Maddie leaned up toward him and closed her eyes. His lips ever so gently touched hers. He tasted of tea and honey, and warm spring mornings and everything that had ever made her smile.

In helpless response she lifted her arms around his neck and pressed herself closer against him. Quinlan made a sound in his throat as he deepened the embrace of their mouths, and she trembled in answer. She hadn't been kissed in so long, and the last time. . . .

"Quinlan!"

White-hot mortification shot through her at the sound of Mr. Bancroft's furious bellow. Gasping in horror, Maddie tore her mouth from the marquis's, and without looking at him or at her employer, she bolted around the back of the house.

"Oh, my God, oh, my God," she sobbed, holding her hands over her face and weeping as she slammed open the door to the servants' stairs and hurried up to her bedchamber.

She'd done it again. Even worse, this time she had known perfectly well what Quinlan's intention was, and she'd let him kiss her anyway. She'd even encouraged it! Everyone in London was right. She was stupid, fast, and loose.

Yelling began in the office downstairs, the words muffled, but the emotion behind them clear. First came Mr. Bancroft's low, angry rumble, and then Quinlan's sharper-voiced response. Maddie wiped her eyes and returned to the door. Everything had slipped out of control without anyone realizing it until it was too late. It had been an accident.

She took a deep breath and opened the door. An accident. Mr. Bancroft needed his nephew right now more than he needed her, and she would just explain that she'd been the stupid one and was completely at fault. She was ruined anyway, so it didn't really matter.

Quin paced angrily before the window of his uncle's office. "Look," he snapped, "I'll apologize for overstepping my bounds, if you want, but I won't have you bellowing at me as if I were some idiotic schoolboy!"

Malcolm kept the wheelchair moving to face his nephew. "I'll bellow at you in whatever manner I damned well please," he growled. "By God, Quinlan, I thought better of you than that!"

Attempting to rein in his temper, Quin took a deep breath. "It was just a bloody kiss," he grated, not mentioning that he'd been wanting to kiss her for days, or that he had hoped the kiss would be a prelude to something much more intimate. "And she didn't exactly try to turn me away."

"Quinlan—"

The marquis flung out his arm, furious and frustrated, half his thoughts still on how very good it had felt to have her in his arms, until his damned uncle had appeared and ruined everything. "You're no good to her now, anyway. Why not let someone else have a go at her?''

''*What?* You bas—''

''Excuse me.''

Quin whipped around to face the doorway. Maddie stood there, white-faced, tears trailing down her cheeks. He blanched, hoping she hadn't heard what he'd just said. God, he was an idiot. ''Maddie, I didn't—''

''I just wanted to say that it was a misunderstanding and an accident,'' she said in a subdued voice, avoiding Quin's gaze. ''Lord Warefield is not to blame. I'm sorry, Mr. Bancroft. You deserve better.''

Malcolm, his face paling, wheeled forward. ''Maddie, don't—''

She turned around and disappeared.

''Damnation! Now you've done it, boy!'' The resemblance between Malcolm and the Duke of Highbarrow suddenly became more obvious.

''I have not done anything. It was a kiss, Uncle.''

Malcolm glared at him for a long moment. ''Close the door,'' he finally commanded, in a more controlled voice.

Quinlan complied, but refused to take the seat his uncle indicated. ''Now what?'' he demanded, crossing his arms over his chest.

''Just who do you think she is?''

''What do you mean, who do I think she—''

''You think she's my bedamned mistress, don't you, Quinlan?''

Quin narrowed his eyes. Something was going on. ''Well, what else was I supposed to think? A beautiful, intelligent woman, out here in the middle of Somerset, tending . . . you?''

''Tending an old cripple, you mean?''

''No.''

''Madeleine Willits is the oldest daughter of Viscount

Halverston," Malcolm said, obviously reluctant to utter the words, "and she is not my mistress. Nor is she anyone else's."

Quin sat down. All the questions, all the intriguing hints he'd picked up about Maddie, and he'd never suspected she might be nobility. "What in Lucifer's name is she doing here with you?"

"She was engaged, five years ago. Apparently one of her betrothed's friends got drunk and kissed her, among other things. The wrong person saw it, and she was ruined."

"Over a. . . ." Quin sat back. "Over a kiss," he said, half to himself. No wonder she'd looked so horrified.

"Yes. Maddie's a bit . . . spirited, and according to her, she left London and her family rather than listen to their stupid accusations when she hadn't done anything wrong."

Quin gazed at his uncle for a moment. "And so, five years later, she's become self-sufficient and found employment completely without references or assistance from her family or friends."

"Yes."

He shook his head. "Bloody remarkable."

Malcolm sighed. "She is a remarkable young woman."

"Why didn't you tell me?"

"It wasn't my story to tell. I thought I knew who she was, but it still took her three years to tell me. And *I'm* not titled. Thank God."

"So. What would you have me do, Uncle?"

The door opened. Maddie entered again, this time looking much more composed. And laden with two large valises.

Quin stood quickly, dismay tightening his chest. "Miss Willits."

"Excuse me again. I only wanted to say good-bye to Mr. Bancroft."

"I'd have you do what's right," Malcolm snapped, glaring at Quin.

"Do what's. . . ." Quin closed his mouth, stunned out of any remaining composure. "You mean, *marry* her?"

"Absolutely not!" Maddie dumped her bags onto the floor, her face a mask of hurt and wounded fury. "Don't be ridiculous!"

"Now, Maddie, that's—"

"I'm already ruined, Mr. Bancroft," she interrupted hotly. "It doesn't matter."

"Then why are you leaving?" he barked at her.

She faltered, looking at her employer. Quin studied her face, fascinated at the play of emotions across her sensitive features. There was more to her than he'd begun to imagine. If not for Eloise—or his father—the idea of marrying Madeleine Willits wouldn't have been all that preposterous. Or, surprisingly, all that unwelcome.

"Maddie," he said softly, and her eyes darted in his direction, "it was my fault. Not yours." He hesitated, holding her gaze. "And I'm engaged already. Or just about. Otherwise. . . ."

"I can take responsibility for my own stupidity, thank you very much," she said stiffly. "And you're a noble already. You don't need to pretend to be possessed of the quality."

Quin narrowed his eyes. Marriage to the spitfire might not have been preposterous, but it would have been dangerous. "I don't believe *you* have the right to question *my* nobil—"

"Please!" Malcolm bellowed.

Quin started and looked in his uncle's direction. He'd forgotten the older man's presence. From Maddie's reaction, she had as well.

"Thank you," Malcolm resumed, in a more even tone. "I am quite aware of your . . . arrangement with Eloise, Quinlan. I had something else in mind."

"Something else? What?" Maddie asked suspiciously.

"I've actually been considering this for several days now." Malcolm faced his nephew. "If you and the rest of the titled Bancrofts were to reintroduce Maddie to society, it could—"

"No!" Maddie gasped, paling.

"—It could undo the harm done to her reputation and enable her to secure a husband," he continued, undaunted. He looked over at her again. "It would set your life back the way it was before the scandal, my dear."

"Absolutely not!" she returned at high volume. "I am *never* going back to London. And certainly not with *him!*"

Quin smiled wryly. Apparently he'd broken the truce. "You liked me for a moment, I believe."

"You agree, then, Quinlan? Your ill behavior could turn this into something positive."

"It was *my* ill behavior, blast it!" Maddie argued. "Don't try to solve my problems. Please! Just let me leave in peace."

Quin frowned. His Grace would be beyond furious, but Malcolm was correct. Whatever Maddie might think, and whatever insanity had overcome him in the garden— and since he'd set eyes on her—he considered himself to be a man of honor. "I agree."

She turned on him. "It is not your decision."

He lifted an eyebrow. "I believe it is."

Maddie stomped her foot. "This is absurd! I am leaving!"

Quin strode forward and lifted her luggage before she could. "Yes, you are. I'll have to inform my father. We need to leave for Highbarrow Castle immediately." He turned to his uncle, plans and strategy already forming in his mind, and surprising elation running through him. Apparently, he and Maddie Willits weren't quite finished with one another yet, after all. "I'll go see John Ramsey and arrange to have him supervise the remainder of the irrigation work. The planting will be finished today."

Maddie grabbed for the bags, but he evaded her easily. "Give those to me at once!" she shouted.

"Maddie, listen to Quinlan. It's for the best."

"Do you always solve your problems by running away?" Quin said, taunting her. "I hadn't thought you a coward."

"I am not a coward!"

Malcolm lifted a hand to his forehead and sank back in his chair. Concerned, Quin dropped the valises and came forward. "Uncle?"

Maddie pushed him out of the way and knelt in front of her employer. "I'm sorry," she murmured, putting her hands on his knee and looking earnestly at Malcolm's face. "It's all right. Just take a deep breath."

"Stop arguing. Please," Malcolm muttered, rubbing at his temple.

"We have. Shh. You must be calm."

Maddie lowered her head, and Malcolm caught Quin's eye. Then he winked. Quin gaped at him for a moment, torn between astonishment and amusement at the old man's duplicity, and then he bent to take Maddie's shoulders. "We'll do as he says," he murmured. "It will be all right."

His uncle put his fingers under Maddie's chin so she had to look up at him. "Make me a promise, my dear. Do as Quinlan and his family say, just until you can be presented again at Almack's. If they accept you there, you will have no troubles anywhere in London."

"Mr. Bancroft," she pleaded, tears welling again in her gray eyes.

"After that, if you still don't wish to remain with your family and your friends, you may return to Langley."

She looked over her shoulder at Quin. Attempting to ignore the queer mix of anticipation and compassion she seemed to be stirring in him, he kept a solemn expression on his face and nodded. "I would like the chance to redeem myself. And to help you, if I may."

Maddie shut her eyes for a long moment. "All right. Just until Almack's."

"I just don't understand how you could simply hire someone from Harthgrove and expect them to be able to care for your uncle," Maddie snapped.

"I did not 'just hire' someone. Both Malcolm and your squire highly recommended him."

"John Ramsey is not *my* squire. And I don't care who recommended that man. It's *my* duty to care for Mr. Bancroft."

Maddie sat back in the carriage, attempting to ignore both the pretty wooded country outside and the handsome, annoying man seated opposite her. She should never have given in—and in any case, she should never have agreed to travel to Highbarrow Castle alone with him. Well, alone except for a second coach carrying their luggage, two drivers, his valet, and two footmen.

He'd called her a coward again, though, and then he'd flung her argument back in her face when she'd protested. If she was already ruined, what did it matter how she got to Highbarrow? Now, three days later, she could answer that it mattered a great deal, because she couldn't stop thinking about the stupid kiss, and how it had melted like fire along her veins.

"Miss Willits, for the eight thousand, nine hundred and thirty-second time, Uncle Malcolm will do quite well without you. He said so himself. Please, let it be. Whining about it will certainly not make me turn the coach around and take you back, or believe me, I would have done it already.''

She folded her arms across her chest. ''I am not whining.''

He glanced out the window, the fourth time he'd done so over the last ten minutes, and then looked at her again. ''You know, if I wasn't in dire fear of the consequences, I'd say I liked it better when you were fawning.''

Maddie sniffed. ''No doubt you did. I'm surprised you even noticed anything was out of the ordinary.''

''You are hardly of the ordinary,'' he returned.

He'd been doing that to her for the past three days, giving her offhand compliments that could just as easily be taken as insults. He hadn't tried to kiss her again, and in fact had made it clear that he was doing what he saw as his duty, to compensate her for an unfortunate mistake. She tried to see it the same way, but dismissing the embrace—and her reaction to it—as a simple mistaken moment of madness took more effort than she expected.

When he glanced outside yet again, the butterflies which had begun dancing in her stomach turned into very large crows. Quinlan cleared his throat. ''Well, have a look.''

Taking a steadying breath, Maddie leaned forward. Immediately she saw why Highbarrow Castle was always referred to by its full title. She'd grown up at Halverston Hall, but it was nothing like this. Gray spires rose into the blue sky from an immense estate sprawled in the center of a vast clearing. A birch and oak forest bordered the grounds on three sides, with a glassy lake behind.

''It's . . . very nice,'' she offered, swallowing her sudden nervousness.

Unexpectedly, the marquis chuckled. ''Don't let His

Grace hear you say that. He wouldn't appreciate a four-hundred-and-thirty-eight-year-old symbol of Saxon resilience being called 'nice.' ''

"Oh, I know," she said absently, continuing to gaze at the gray stones of Highbarrow Castle. It was beyond magnificent, by its very design meant to be overpowering and intimidating. But she did not intend to be intimidated. "Mr. Bancroft told me all about the duke."

He looked sideways at her. "Wonderful."

It took twenty more minutes for the coach to pass through the wooded glade, up the gradual slope, around the winding way, and across the moat bridge up to the front drive of Highbarrow Castle. Fleetingly she wondered what lay in the dark, still waters that flowed from the lake in a ring around the grounds.

Though she'd never seen him so much as ruffled before, she thought Quinlan seemed rather edgy. For once she couldn't blame him. She'd heard enough about the Duke of Highbarrow to know that he would not take the news of her arrival well. Not that she felt sorry for the marquis. She'd tried to leave, and he and Mr. Bancroft had insisted she stay. This was because of their stubbornness, not hers.

The coach rocked to a stop. Quinlan sat for a moment, looking at her. "I won't tell you to behave, because I know you wouldn't do as I tell you to save your life," he said.

"I might, to save my life," Maddie countered. "I'm not an idiot. But this has nothing to do with that."

"It has to do with your honor. Isn't that the same thing?"

She returned his curious gaze. "I used to think so."

The latch turned, and a meticulously dressed footman pulled open the carriage door. "Lord Warefield, welcome," he intoned, bowing.

The marquis gestured for her to precede him. "Thank you."

The footman helped Maddie to the ground, glancing at her curiously, and then moved back to let Quinlan step down on his own. She looked up. The huge dwelling looked even grander up close, with endless rows of windows gazing out imperiously over lush Suffolk County.

"Is His Grace home?"

"Yes, my lord. The duke and the duchess are taking tea in the south drawing room."

"Splendid."

The butler stood holding the front door and also greeted the marquis with the deference. Quinlan handed over Maddie's shawl and his hat and gloves, then took her by the elbow to lead her down a very long hallway with a high, arched ceiling. Portrait upon portrait lined one wall from floor to ceiling, the subjects ranging from men and women in current fashion to fierce-eyed, armor-clad Saxon chieftains.

Where Langley had been open and warm, Highbarrow seemed entirely designed to make Maddie more nervous than she already was. Servants appeared and disappeared through doorways, silent except for the quiet "Good day, my lord"'s they murmured in Lord Warefield's direction.

At the end of the hallway, the marquis stopped. He released Maddie's elbow and looked down at her. "Do you wish me to explain you first, or would you rather accompany me into the lion's den?"

"Are you asking me for my sake, or for your own, my lord?" she returned coolly, somewhat bolstered by his tense demeanor.

He gave a brief grin. "You'd dance on my grave, too, wouldn't you?" He knocked on the door.

She shrugged. "If I ever visited it."

"Enter," a soft female voice called.

If she'd had any doubts about Mr. Bancroft's description of his older brother, they vanished as the marquis ushered her into the south drawing room. The Duke of Highbarrow Castle sat beneath the window, the afternoon sun silvering the gray in his dark hair. Cool brown eyes beneath straight black brows lifted from the *London Times* to rest on his son, and a moment later flicked over to assess her.

Maddie was suddenly acutely aware of the cheap fabric of her traveling gown, and of the thrice-mended yellow bonnet on her head. And she had no intention of letting any of them know it. With a slight lift of her chin she stopped beside Quinlan, turning her gaze to take in the rest of the room. Each piece of silver, from the candlesticks to the spoon sitting on the tea tray, shone brighter than starlight. Not one particle of dust showed on anything, and the polish of the mahogany furniture gave the smooth red wood an almost mirror-like appearance.

"Back so soon?" a low, cold voice rumbled. Maddie's eyes returned to the duke.

"Pleased to see you again as well, Father," Quinlan returned in the same cool tone. Maddie glanced at him curiously, because she never heard him sound so much, well, like a noble before.

"Welcome, Quin," a much warmer female voice said, and a small woman rose from one of the small chairs by the fireplace to grasp the marquis's hands. He smiled and kissed her on the cheek.

Silvery blond hair was coiled on top of her head, and her slender figure was draped in a beautiful muslin gown of green and white. The duchess's eyes were the same jade color as her son's, though their warmth cooled considerably as she turned to view Maddie.

"And who have we here?" she asked, only the slightest surprise entering her voice.

"Allow me to introduce Miss Willits. Maddie, the Duke and Duchess of Highbarrow."

"Your Graces," Maddie said, curtseying and bending her head, keenly aware of how very far she was from Somerset and any friends, or even acquaintances. She glanced at Quinlan. He was the closest to an ally she had here, and she could hardly rely on him. She wouldn't allow herself to rely on him, Maddie amended silently. No one but herself, ever again.

"Where did she come from?" The duke remained seated, and in fact, far from coming to his feet to greet either her or his son, crossed his ankles and flipped to the next page.

"Langley." Quinlan smiled at her, his eyes warning her to behave. "She was Uncle Malcolm's companion."

"I *am* Mr. Bancroft's companion," Maddie corrected politely, trying not to glare at the duke for his rudeness. After all, farfetched as the idea was, he might simply be shy. She'd give him the benefit of the doubt, for the sake of Mr. Bancroft. She'd given her word to make a go of this stupidity, and so she would—as long as the rest of the illustrious Bancrofts kept up their side of the agreement.

The duke snapped the paper and resumed reading. "Malcolm's whore, you mean."

Maddie flushed, while the marquis stirred beside her. "No, his companion," she corrected evenly, before Quinlan could do so. "And he's feeling much better. The doctor has even said he doesn't believe the paralysis will be permanent. Thank you for your concern."

The surprised expression the duchess wore deepened, and the *London Times* abruptly folded over and dropped to the floor. "Insolent thing, aren't you?"

The duke stood. Quinlan was the taller of the two, but

Lewis Bancroft looked broader than his lean son. Maddie shifted a little closer to the marquis.

"What's she doing here, Quinlan?"

The marquis hesitated for just a moment, obviously searching for the least inflammatory words he could find. "She is the eldest daughter of Viscount Halverston. You may recall some—"

"You're the one Charles Dunfrey cast off when he found you lifting your heels for one of his friends." Highbarrow sneered. "Stupid mistake. And now you've had to settle for poor, crippled Malcolm." He glanced at Quinlan. "Or is it my son you've got your claws into now?"

"Father," Quin said sharply, his annoyed, wary expression deepening.

This was what Maddie was used to from the nobility. And somehow, it made her feel more comfortable to know that some of her memories and suppositions had been correct all along. She began to fume. "I do not, Your Grace."

"Actually, I am the one at fault," Quinlan offered in a calmer voice. "I had no idea who Miss Willits was, and I. . . . " He looked at her again. "I behaved improperly toward her. Malcolm suggested I might be able to right two wrongs by bringing her here."

"She's not carrying your brat, is she? Good God, Quinlan! A shrew-mouthed whore, and three months before you're to marry Eloise."

"Lord Warefield *kissed* me," Maddie said sharply. "That is all. And I did not wish to come here. That was all his and Mr. Bancroft's idea. I would just as soon leave immediately."

"Good."

"Insufferable snob," Maddie muttered, and gathered her skirts. "Good day, Your Graces." Not even looking at the marquis, she turned and headed out the door and back down the long hall.

Quin strode after her and grabbed her arm to turn her about to face him. "For God's sake, give me a moment to explain," he whispered.

"In another few moments I will be forced to call your father out and shoot him," Maddie hissed back. "He's far worse than you are."

His lips twitched. Quin nodded, his fingers still hard and warm and tight around her arm. "Yes, he is. But I made a promise. Give me another damned minute, Maddie."

She jabbed a finger at him and wrenched her arm free. "One."

Quin took a deep breath and ushered her back inside. The duke had already seated himself again. The duchess, though, stood by the door and watched them approach. "Father," the marquis began over again, "I did wrong by Miss Willits. She is a properly bred young lady, falsely accused of wrongdoing. I wished to make amends. Uncle Malcolm thought that with the help of our family, she might be reintroduced into society. I agreed."

"Oh. *You* agreed."

"Yes. I did. And she stays, until we can all repair to London. I can't very well take her to Warefield without completing the damage, so she will stay here, as our guest."

The duke stood again. "You know, I might have expected this nonsense from Rafael, but until this morning I was not aware that *you* were an idiot. Pay her off and send her away." Highbarrow strode forward, stopping a few feet short of Maddie so that she had to look up at him. "What will it take, *Miss* Willits? Ten pounds? A hundred? Name the price it will take you to keep from wagging your tongue about my son's indiscretions, and be gone.''

Maddie glanced over at the mantel clock. Fifty-eight seconds, fifty-nine, one minute was up. She'd kept her word. ''Your Grace,'' she began, so angry her voice shook, ''if I chose to wag my tongue about your son's misbehavior, every penny you own wouldn't be enough to keep me silent.''

''Then wha—''

''I didn't come here for money,'' she interrupted. ''I came here because Mr. Bancroft felt I had been wronged, and he took this silliness as a chance to set things right for me. I will tell you what I told him: I am perfectly happy with the way my life is. And I have no desire to spend another moment in your arrogant, self-centered, pompous company. Good day.''

''Quin, did you agree to this?'' the duchess asked, putting a hand on Maddie's arm before she could depart, ruining another chance at an effectively dramatic exit.

He nodded. ''When I arrived at Langley, Miss Willits had done such a fine job of estate managing that I scarcely had anything to do. If nothing else, I intend to help her out of gratitude.''

''No, you won't,'' the duke snarled, his face flushed. ''I want her out of this house! Now!''

''Just a moment, Lewis,'' the duchess countered. For a second she looked at Maddie, then returned her gaze to her husband. ''Quin gave his word. I won't have him break it because you feel inconvenienced.''

''Victoria! I will not—''

''It's settled, Lewis,'' Lady Highbarrow said firmly. Her fingers twitched on Maddie's arm, but she continued to eye the duke coolly.

Highbarrow clenched his fist as though he wanted to hit one of them. Abruptly he turned on his heel. ''Bah.

Do what you will. I'm going to London. You may join me when this . . . *girl* is gone.''

"Lewis!"

"Enough, wife!" The duke's roaring retreated with him down the hallway and abruptly cut off as a door distantly slammed.

Quinlan looked after his vanished father. "That went well," he muttered.

"He was planning on leaving for London at the end of the week anyway. Some new trade agreement." The duchess removed her hand from Maddie's arm and placed it on her son's. "Excuse us for a moment, Miss Willits," she said, and walked with Quin to the door.

"Don't go anywhere," the marquis instructed Maddie, looking back at her.

Maddie tried to manufacture a scowl, but had to settle for nodding. He'd stood up for her when she hadn't needed or wanted him to—or so she thought, until he briefly grinned at her, and she suddenly felt as though everything would be all right. And Maddie wondered when, exactly, she'd begun to think of Quin Bancroft as an ally.

Upstairs the duke continued to bellow and slam things about as he stirred up the Highbarrow household in preparation for his departure. Quin listened, mostly to be certain His Grace didn't go back to the south drawing room and continue his argument with Maddie. She'd made his father genuinely angry, something people didn't dare do very often. And she'd done it in a rather spectacular manner. Quin couldn't recall anyone ever calling his father pompous before—certainly not to his face. Likely the duke couldn't recall it, either.

"I received a letter from Rafael a few days ago," the duchess said, stopping before one of the tall windows overlooking the gardens.

Quin leaned against the wall beside her. "And what's the scoundrel up to this time?"

"Apparently he's spent the past six months in Africa, as a special envoy for King George."

"Africa?" Quin repeated, surprised. "He's supposed to be guarding the Tower or something, isn't he?"

"I believe he volunteered for Africa, just as he did for Wellington's regiment at Waterloo. Anyway, he's been granted a leave, finally. He hopes to join us in London before the end of the Season, unless the local tribesmen begin their rebellion again."

"Do you think he's ready to sell out his commission?" Quin was very aware that his mother's attention was on the girl in the drawing room, but she'd get around to asking about Maddie when she was ready.

"Perhaps. He really didn't say." She smiled. "He did ask after Aristotle."

"Yes, well, I've a few things to tell him about the damned animal, too."

"Why did you kiss this Miss Willits?" She turned from the view to look at him. "And why did you feel the need to make amends for it?"

He shrugged. "I thought Malcolm might suffer another apoplexy if I didn't agree to do something. I practically expected him to horsewhip me."

"Does he care for her?"

"He's very fond of her. She's more like a daughter than anything else, though, I think."

"Why did you kiss her?"

Quin looked down for a moment, unable and unwilling to explain the turmoil of emotions Maddie Willits had awakened in him from the moment he'd first viewed her. "You know, I'm not really certain. She . . . she has a very bad opinion of the nobility, and she damned well says what's on her mind. And I suppose I wanted to prove to her afterward that not everyone is like this

Charles Dunfrey who turned her away, or the bastard who ruined her before.''

''Which I believe he did by kissing her when he had no business being anywhere near her.''

''Yes, Mother, I see the parallel, thank you very much,'' he returned dryly.

She looked at him for a moment. ''Did you argue with Eloise?''

''No, of course not. Why?''

''You haven't been known for dallying before, Quin. At least you've never felt the need to inform your father or me about it if you have.'' She turned back to the garden view. ''Though I'd assume if you'd dallied, the ladies would have been of more solid standing in society than Miss Willits—or of no standing at all.''

That had occurred to him as well. ''I know.'' He started back for the drawing room. ''At any rate, I gave my word. And as I said, I couldn't very well take her to Warefield and still expect her to have any chance of returning to society. So I thought you . . . might be persuaded to assist me.''

''Your father doesn't want anything to do with it.''

''Yes, but he won't be here.'' He strolled back to her side and took her hand in his. ''Will you help me redeem myself, Mother?''

Her eyes twinkled. ''She called Lewis arrogant and self-centered.''

''And pompous.''

She chuckled. ''If you feel it's that important, of course I'll help.'' The duchess's smile faded. ''But only to a point, Quin. I won't allow the Bancroft name to be sullied any more than your father would. If society continues to frown on her when she returns, she must be sent away. Agreed?''

He took a deep breath, far more relieved than he expected. He had Maddie for another few weeks, anyway. ''Agreed.''

Chapter 8

〜〜〜○Gᗧ〜〜〜

"I do not need a dressmaker. I can sew my own clothes."

Maddie glared at Quinlan, who stood in the doorway of her borrowed bedchamber and glared back at her. The maid standing just inside the door looked as though she desperately wanted to flee, but she couldn't do so without going past the marquis.

"Making you presentable to London society is part of my promise to Uncle Malcolm," Quin returned sternly. "In two weeks' time you will not be able to sew enough clothes to last you more than a day or two in London. The dressmaker will be here this afternoon."

"No."

"Yes."

She wanted to throw something at him, but instead plunked herself down on the soft bed. "I refuse to end up owing you anything." She'd decided that from the beginning: being in his debt would be worse than being ruined in the first place. That's why she'd left home. She, and no one else, would be responsible for her welfare and her well-being. And if she was being stubborn and impractical, it was her right.

"Is that why you insisted on paying for you own

room at the inns on the way here?'' he asked. Far from becoming angry, he looked only curious. Apparently he was almost constantly curious about her, for he was always asking questions she'd rather not answer. And he had an oddly compelling way of making her want to answer at the same time.

After a moment he seemed to notice the maid, and absently gestured her to leave. The girl scurried out so fast, her apron might have been on fire.

''Yes. That is exactly why I paid my own way.''

He strolled over to lean against the bed's tall footboard. ''Maddie, I am *extremely* wealthy. When I become Duke of Highbarrow, I will be obscenely so. You can't match me.''

''I'm very aware of that, my lord,'' she said stiffly. ''You don't need to point it out.''

Quin shook his head. ''No, no, no. What I mean is, my uncle's idea was for you to be reintroduced in such a manner that no one could gainsay you. *I* can afford to do that without even noticing the loss. You've worked hard for what you've earned. Save it for something . . . for yourself.''

She looked up at him, trying to summon the anger at him that had been absent since the night of the Fowler ball. Without the anger there, she kept noticing the slight, amused smiles that touched his mouth, and the lean line of his jaw, and the way the sunlight turned his honey-colored hair to gold. ''If you cared about what I wanted,'' she answered finally, ''you would never have dragged me away from Langley.''

''Uncle Malcolm cares about what you want. And despite having nearly been drowned and shot in your presence, I do as well.''

Maddie looked down at her hands. ''I gave my word to go with you only for your uncle's sake. So please don't expect me to go to the gallows with a smile on my face.''

To her surprise, he sat on the bed beside her. ''The gallows? I can't say I've ever heard London referred to in quite that way before.''

She smiled briefly, trying not to smell his light cologne or notice that a lock of hair had fallen across his forehead. ''It was certainly the scene of my social execution.''

''Don't you miss it, even a little?''

She shook her head vehemently. ''No.''

He fiddled with the edge of her skirt, the cheap muslin rustling against her legs and making her nerves tingle pleasantly. Good Lord, now she was thinking about kissing him again.

''But—''

''You have no idea what it's like, do you?'' she interrupted, trying to rally her indignation again. ''No one would dare cut you, whatever you did. Both you and your father are too wealthy and too powerful for anyone even to consider it. I'm only the daughter of a second generation viscount.'' She stopped, but he continued looking at her with his intense jade eyes, and she found herself continuing when she had meant not to.

''I was invited everywhere, especially once I became engaged. And after that . . . stupid, stupid night, not even my so-called friends would visit me, or even look at me. My parents locked me in my room for three days. I think they intended to send me to a convent. Ha! Can you imagine? Me, in a convent?''

''No, I can't.'' He lifted his hand and tucked a straying strand of hair behind her ear. ''How did you get away?''

An unexpected shiver ran down Maddie's spine at his gentle touch. ''I waited for bad weather, then packed a valise, threw it out my window, and climbed down the rose trellis. I walked to Charing Cross Road, and then took the stage to Brighton. I intended to set sail for America, but I didn't have enough money.''

"By damn," he murmured, studying her face closely.

His scrutiny unsettled her, but he didn't seem to be laughing at her, so she shrugged. "So I hired on as a governess in Brighton. I lasted a fortnight, until the news over the scandal broke there, and my employer figured out who I must be. He gave me four shillings and set me out onto the street." She scowled. "*After* he offered to keep my tale quiet in exchange for certain . . . favors." Maddie flushed. Spenser pawing at her had been bad enough.

"Who was it?" Quin asked.

"It doesn't matter. They're all the same."

"No, we're not."

No, they didn't seem to be, and that was somehow hard to accept. "You kissed me," she pointed out, more to remind herself than him. "Was that just because you thought I was Mr. Bancroft's mistress, and of no account?"

He shot to his feet. "No! Absolutely not." Agitated, he strode to her window and then turned around again. "That kiss was . . . something else entirely."

"What, then?" She wanted to know. And not simply to confirm that it hadn't meant anything to him.

"A mistake. Of sorts."

She lowered her eyes, hurt. "Of what sort?"

"Of the sort that I really can't regret, but wouldn't dare to repeat."

"No?"

He held her gaze for a moment. "No," he said softly, then took a quick breath, as though he had only just realized they were alone in her bedchamber. "Mrs. . . . the dressmaker will be here at two. Don't—"

"You don't remember the poor woman's name?" she teased.

"Damnation. It rhymes with sunflower." His lips quirked.

"Hm. That's something, anyway."

"She's my mother's dressmaker. Not mine."

Before she could summon an insulting response to that, he was gone, whistling down the hallway. Maddie gazed after him for a long time.

She felt at a distinct disadvantage at Highbarrow. At Langley she'd been comfortable, on good terms with all the servants and the neighbors, and familiar with the routines and minute details.

Except for a few hours spent in the Marquis of Tewksbury's ballroom five years before, she'd never experienced such pomp and circumstance and wealth as she saw at Highbarrow Castle. It was unnerving—yet still nothing compared to what she would be going through the moment she set foot in London.

The duke thankfully departed with his two coaches and a retinue of servants before noon. She wouldn't have minded arguing with him some more, but as she was woefully short of allies, she didn't want to risk angering the duchess over something as foolish as His Grace.

Maddie took luncheon alone, sitting at a huge, polished oak dining table that could easily have seated the entire household staff at Langley. Quinlan had ridden off to visit some neighbors, and apparently the duchess, despite her earlier support, wasn't ready actually to socialize with the interloper.

Mrs. Neubauer arrived at two in the afternoon. The dressmaker was tall and thin, with an impossibly pointed chin that Maddie couldn't help staring at—especially after the woman spent a full minute walking around her, fingering her muslin gown and sniffing.

"No wonder the duchess wanted new clothes for

you,'' she muttered, examining the hem of Maddie's sleeve. ''Well below *my* standards, that's for certain. But then, my standards are why Her Grace sent for me.''

''How fortunate for me.'' Maddie tried to decide whether she was annoyed or amused.

''Hm.'' Mrs. Neubauer finally stopped her circling and crossed her arms over her chest. ''What am I to measure you for, then?''

Maddie folded her own arms, leaning decidedly toward annoyance. ''I have no idea, I'm sure.''

''Gowns, for morning, afternoon, and evening.'' The Duchess of Highbarrow glided into Maddie's bedchamber, one of her maids in tow. ''Suitable for London society.''

The maid pulled out the dressing table chair, and the duchess seated herself. Maddie looked at her for a moment, more uncomfortable than she had ever been in Quin's presence, then belatedly curtsied. ''Your Grace.''

''Quin says you have no manners. I see you do remember something of your upbringing.''

Maddie clenched her jaw. ''More than I care to, my lady,'' she answered as politely as she could.

The duchess looked at her for a moment, then sat back and waved her hand at the dressmaker. ''Get on with it, Mrs. Neubauer.''

''Of course, Your Grace.''

After a thorough measuring session, Maddie had to stand and watch as Her Grace and the dressmaker decided on color and fabric and style. Neither of them asked her opinion, though they did spend some moments debating how best to showcase her bosom.

''I don't wish to be showcased,'' Maddie said stiffly. She'd been stared at enough the night of the disaster. Just the idea of going through something like that again left her feeling queasy. ''And I won't wear blue, for heaven's sake. It makes me look tallow-faced.''

The duchess glanced at her, then continued conversing with her dressmaker. "Substitute a gray and green silk for the blue. With gray slippers."

"Thank you, Your Grace," Maddie said, offering a slight smile.

"We certainly don't want you to look tallow-faced," the duchess said dryly.

Finally Mrs. Neubauer gathered her things together and left. Her Grace, though, remained seated in Maddie's chair.

"Do you have anything nicer than what you're wearing now, so you may dress for dinner?"

Again Maddie kept a rein on her flashing temper. If it had been Quinlan asking the question, she would have given him a sound set-down for it. But this haughty woman had stood up for her. She would take an insult or two in return. "A little nicer," she admitted. "We are—were—less formal at Langley."

"No doubt." The duchess stood with an elegant swirl of lavender. "We are more formal here. I expect you to comply with that." She headed out the door.

"If you didn't want me here, then why did you speak up for me?" Maddie said to her back.

The duchess stopped and turned around. "I spoke up for my son. We have all learned that the best way to maintain peace in the family is to concede to my husband's wishes. This time Quin chose not to do so." Lady Highbarrow spent another moment looking at Maddie, her expression the speculative one Maddie had seen Quinlan wear. "And I really can't think of a good reason why he should risk his father's temper over a foul-tempered flirt of inconsequential family." She shrugged and walked away down the hall. "We shall see."

Victoria Bancroft paused at the downstairs landing to listen. The girl's door had closed quietly, without any of the outburst or angry hysterics she'd half expected to hear. She waited a moment longer, then continued down to the first floor.

The whole affair was extremely odd. Quin chasing another female so close to his own engagement was not all that surprising, poorly as it must be regarded. Given his general levelheadedness and keen measure of common sense, his bringing that same woman to his parents' home and practically demanding that she be taken in and cared for was surprising in the extreme.

His Grace had, of course, chosen to view the entire incident as an affront to his dignity and stomped off to London, leaving her to sort out the absurd mess before the Bancrofts became the topic of the new Season's gossip. Just a whisper that the Marquis of Warefield had taken up with his estranged uncle's castoff would be enough to set the town ablaze.

Quin unexpectedly came in the front door as she started down the hallway. Since he rarely got the chance to amuse himself, when he went fishing with Jack Dunsmoore he always stayed out until well after nightfall. And it was barely past teatime. Victoria stopped and waited for him to catch up. "How was Lord Dunsmoore?"

"Quite well. I left him fishing. Not a damned thing biting this afternoon. How did the fitting go?" He slapped at the thin layer of dust covering his buckskin breeches.

"Miss Willits will have suitable attire beginning the day after tomorrow."

"She didn't try to throw anyone out a window, or go about stabbing old what's-her-name with pins?" The marquis chuckled.

Victoria stopped and faced her elder son. "Do you find it amusing that a supposedly well-bred young lady would throw a tantrum every few moments?"

Quin leaned back against the wall. "She's not some rabid wolf, Mother. She's merely been on her own for quite a—"

"She's merely been living off the good graces of your uncle, you mean," she interrupted.

Quin's smile faded. "I wasn't joking when I said she'd been tending to Langley, you know. And as well as any estate manager I've come across. Better than some."

"And?"

"And as for living off Malcolm's good graces, she purchased him a wheeled chair so he could begin to get about. I looked through the ledgers, and there was no notation of it. She finally admitted yesterday that the blunt had come out of her own salary—and she hadn't told Malcolm. She wanted it to be a gift."

"So she bought him a chair. It wasn't a diamond watch fob. You're being ridiculous, and it's not like you."

The marquis gave her another look and then straightened. "*We* didn't get him anything," he said quietly, and turned down the hallway. "Father even decided not to notice Malcolm was ill until there became a danger that Langley's crop wouldn't get put down in time."

"We sent *you*," she reminded him, but he'd already turned the corner. Victoria looked after him until the sound of his boots against the marble floor faded away, and then she continued on to the west drawing room. Two things were becoming clear. This kiss apparently hadn't been as much of an accident as Quin had claimed—and Lewis should never have sent him to Somerset in the first place.

"I thought perhaps you intended a hunger strike," Quin said mildly, watching Maddie take her seat at the dining table. He seated himself and gestured to the footmen to begin serving dinner.

"*I* thought perhaps I'd be dining alone again," she said demurely, folding her hands in her lap. "Is your mother going to join us, my lord?" She smiled at one of the servants as he offered her a selection from the platter of roast chicken.

"Uh-oh. What've I done this time?" Quin asked, noting that the pretty smile she gave the footman vanished as she met his gaze.

"Nothing, my lord. Why do you ask?"

"I'm being 'my lord'ed again. In your vocabulary I believe that to be an insult." He lifted an eyebrow. "Or do I err?"

"It is the proper way to address you, Quin," the duchess said from the doorway. "Don't fault her for it."

He stood again as Lady Highbarrow entered the dining room. Her customary place to the right of the duke's chair had been set, but disregarding that, she took the seat beside Maddie. As the head footman scurried to move her utensils, alarm bells began going off in Quin's head. Victoria Bancroft, though she was far more levelheaded than her husband, had as deep a sense of pride about the Bancroft line and standing as did the duke. Perhaps she wasn't as volatile as Maddie, but he'd seen her scar more than one upstart with her sharp tongue.

She'd made it fairly obvious that she had strong reservations about Maddie, and she rarely amended her opinion once it had been given. Quin was surprised to realize that he wanted his mother to like their reluctant houseguest—now eyeing him from beyond the duchess with accusing fury in her eyes—and that he didn't want to see Maddie turned away by his family, as she had been by her own.

"I'm not faulting Miss Willits for anything," he corrected innocently. "I am merely curious as to whether she is enjoying being at Highbarrow."

"How could I not enjoy it, my lord?" Maddie asked sweetly, her teeth clenched.

Quin stifled a grin as he locked eyes with her, abruptly deciding he'd best begin checking his bed sheets for poisonous spiders again. "My thought exactly."

The duchess leaned forward for her glass of wine, blocking Maddie from his view. Quin blinked.

"I meant to ask you, Quin," she said. "Do you have any word from Eloise?"

Eloise. Damnation, he'd forgotten to write her again. She thought him still at Langley. He shook his head. "I doubt her correspondence has had time to catch up to me," he hedged. "The last I heard from her, she was doing well and was looking forward to seeing you in London."

"Do you still plan to wait until autumn for the wedding? As I've said before, you'll have a much better turnout if you marry in June or July."

"Oh, I agree, Your Grace," Maddie said brightly, as Victoria sipped her wine.

The duchess lifted an eyebrow. "You do?"

"Most definitely. Once hunting season has begun, bringing everyone back together, even for such a prestigious event as the Marquis of Warefield's wedding, will be a monstrous headache."

Quin looked at her suspiciously. Maddie at her most solicitous was invariably Maddie at her most devious. "Why so helpful now?"

"*Now*, my lord?" she repeated, gazing at him quizzically. "Have I been unhelpful to you previously? I can't recall."

"No," he returned slowly, his deep suspicion growing. "I don't suppose you have been."

Lady Highbarrow continued to regard Maddie with

cool green eyes. "You are in favor of this marriage, then?"

Maddie smiled engagingly. "I could hardly oppose it, even were it my place to do so. I barely know one of the participants, and I am not acquainted with the other at all."

The duchess looked at her for another moment. "Do you often kiss men with whom you are barely acquainted, then?"

Maddie compressed her lips, the only outward sign she gave of being angry. "I suppose that would depend on whose gossip you listen to, Your Grace."

"But you did kiss him," Lady Highbarrow pursued.

"It was a morning Byron would have admired," Quin interrupted. "Quite overwhelmingly romantic. And as it gives me the opportunity to repay Miss Willits for her kindness to Malcolm, I can't help but look upon the kiss as a fortunate . . . accident."

Behind his mother, Maddie glared at Quin. He returned her gaze coolly, wondering that this clever, witty woman had ever fooled him for even one second with her dim sycophantic veneer.

Maddie lifted her fork. "I have to admit," she said smoothly, "I have wondered why it is *my* poor character everyone is concerned with, when Lord Warefield keeps insisting he was the one at fault."

He rested his chin on his hand and regarded her. "Because you liked it?" he suggested.

Immediately he regretted the jibe, for, clearly embarrassed, Maddie paled and slammed her fork back down onto the table. "You big, arrogant—"

"Quin!" his mother snapped, even as he sought an apology. "Whatever feelings were involved, if you insist on reminding Miss Willits of her indiscretion, she will have no chance of redeeming her character."

"*My* indiscretion," Maddie repeated. "His lips, but

my indiscretion.'' She looked at Quin. ''I see now why you prize your nobility so highly. Apparently it automatically absolves you from any hint of wrongdoing, at the expense of the nearest social inferior.'' She stood. ''Excuse me. I've lost my appetite.''

''Maddie,'' Quin muttered, scowling.

Lady Highbarrow caught her hand before she could escape. ''Miss Willits, at the risk of being blunt, Quin is the future Duke of Highbarrow. In comparison, you *are* a social inferior.''

''My lady, I have never been more proud to be called so.''

The duchess's patronizing smile froze in place.

Quin realized his jaw had dropped, and he snapped it shut before the surprised chuckle that began deep in his chest could make itself heard. He cleared his throat and shot to his feet.

''Mother, if you'll excuse me for just a moment,'' he said hurriedly, striding around the table to grab Maddie's hand away. ''Apparently there are several things I did not make clear to our guest.'' He yanked Maddie toward the door. ''Miss Willits, if you please,'' he continued sternly.

As soon as they were out of earshot, Maddie pulled her hand free from his. ''I will not be dragged about like a mewling infant,'' she hissed, her gray eyes snapping with fury. ''Next you'll be trying to take me over your knee!''

The image her words instantly conjured likely had little in common with what she was describing. This woman had just soundly insulted his mother, and he had no business daydreaming about having her seated naked on his lap, her long auburn hair tumbling down her shoulders past her bare breasts—

''Lord Warefield!'' Maddie was growling, ''I said, I am leaving!''

Quin grabbed hold of her arm again and spun her back around to face him. "No, you're not!" The sudden anger blazing through his veins surprised him—not because she hadn't said enough to make him angry, but because he absolutely did not want her to go.

"No one but you wants me here!" she snapped, coiling her delicate hand into a fist. "You pompous ass!"

He ducked backward as she swung at him. "Don't think I'm so refined that I wouldn't set you on your pretty ass if you hit me," he snarled, shaking her by the arm. "You're not making me break my word to Uncle Malcolm, and you are keeping your promise as well. Is that clear?"

For a long moment she glared at him, her bosom heaving with her fast, furious breathing. "I hate you, you bully," she muttered, wrenching her arm free again.

"Is that clear?" he repeated.

"Yes. Very clear."

Quin watched her stomp upstairs to her bedchamber. When her door finally slammed, he let out the breath he'd been holding and leaned back against the wall. Whatever it was he felt toward Madeleine Willits, it damned well wasn't hatred. And that scared him more than the blackest fit of anger ever could.

By the time Quin declared their absurd little group ready for London, Maddie possessed more gowns in more fabrics and colors than she'd ever owned in her life. She'd learned every waltz, country dance, and quadrille invented over the past five years, and been tested on all the ones in style before that time and since the beginning of history. Most painful of all, she'd been forced to read back issues of the *London Times* to refamiliarize herself with who had been married, buried, and welcomed into society's highest circles.

After her argument with the marquis, she had made

every possible attempt to avoid him, and except for the annoying lessons and instructions, he had seemed to do the same. In a house as huge as Highbarrow Castle, it wasn't all that difficult. From time to time she actually felt bad about saying she hated him, but he'd deserved it, shaking her and ordering her about like that when she'd begun to think of him as an ally—and as a friend, if one could call a man one thought about kissing and touching and holding all the time as merely a friend.

She desperately wanted to avoid going to London, but she didn't want to prolong her stay at Highbarrow, either. She hadn't felt so trapped since her parents had locked her in her bedchamber five years ago, and she endured it only because she would be able to leave it all behind her again after Almack's.

They'd even hired a maid for her, and Maddie watched, her arms crossed, as poor Mary finished stuffing another portmanteau full of ballgowns. "We could always leave one behind by accident," she suggested with a smile.

Mary wiped her hand across her forehead. "It would be the one that Her Grace was especially counting on your wearing, Miss Maddie."

"No doubt. Are you certain you don't want my help?" At least Mary had a sense of humor, and she wondered fleetingly whether Quin had hired her, or whether he or the duchess had assigned the task of finding a maid to the head housekeeper.

"Oh, no, ma'am. It wouldn't be seemly, you know."

Maddie sighed. "Yes, I know."

A throat cleared from the open doorway. Immediately recognizing the sound, Maddie stiffened and turned around. "My lord," she acknowledged, echoing Mary's curtsey.

"Nearly packed?" Quin asked smoothly.

"Yes, thank you," she answered politely. He'd

avoided speaking to her for almost a fortnight, so his seeking her out now couldn't bode well.

"Splendid. We're all set to leave in the morning, then."

"Splendid," she echoed unenthusiastically. He stayed in the doorway, and after a moment Maddie looked over at him again. "Was there something else, my lord?"

"Yes. Do you have a minute?"

Immediately Mary ducked her head and scurried for the doorway. Maddie put out a hand to stop the maid's retreat. "It's quite all right, Mary. My legs work as well as yours."

"Yes, Miss Maddie."

Quin straightened and opened his mouth. "Miss Wil—"

"My lord, shall we?" Maddie interrupted, and stepped past him into the hallway.

He followed her. "Why do you insist on the servants calling you Miss Maddie?"

She lifted her chin. "I don't. I ask them to call me Maddie, and then we compromise."

"It's not your proper address. You're a viscount's eldest daughter. Once we get to London, you will be addressed as Miss Willits."

Talking about her family still had the ability to upset Maddie. She shook her head and started back to her bedchamber. "You may wish to consult with my parents about that. I believe I may have been disowned."

He stood behind her, silent, for a long moment. "Maddie?"

She whirled back around. "Oh, my apologies, my lord. I'm supposed to face you when I speak to you. I'd forgotten." The words sounded brittle to her, but she tucked her arms behind her back defiantly, daring him to comment.

"Why didn't you tell me about your parents?" he asked instead.

"Does this change your mind? Should I leave now?"

He frowned. "No, of course not. It would have been helpful to know, though. I might have written Lord Halverston and—"

"No!" She strode back to him, dismay and dread tightening her throat. "You will *not* write my family about anything!"

"What do you suggest I do, then? We can't very well pretend you're someone else. You will be recognized, you know." He stepped closer, his jade eyes serious. "And it's *you* I promised to restore to society—not some mystery lady with no past."

Maddie turned away. "As I've told you all along, my lord, none of this is necessary. Nor is it going to be as simple and easy as you seem to think."

"Do you have any idea what I think, Maddie?"

She had no intention of being intimidated by his supreme kindness, or whatever it was he thought he'd bestowed upon her, and she looked up at him again. "I think that you kissed me to see what I would do, and once you discovered I wasn't a whore and wouldn't be your mistress, you were so embarrassed that you trapped yourself into going to ridiculous lengths to ease your own mind. Or do I err, my lord?"

Eyes glinting, he glared at her for a long moment. Slowly, though, and to her growing consternation, his expression eased. "Don't let your anger at a few idiots color the way you see the rest of the world, Miss Willits." He reached out and softly ran his finger along her cheek. "Perhaps I kissed you because I was attracted to you. And perhaps you kissed me back because you were attracted to me."

Her pulse skittering at his caress, Maddie pulled away before he could realize he'd scored a hit. Only a conceited buffoon would throw her own unfortunate weakness back in her face. "You are in error, my lord," she said stiffly. "The only thing I've enjoyed where you are concerned was seeing you face down in the mud." Before he could reply, she hurried back to her bedchamber and slammed the door.

"That arrogant, pompous. . . ." she muttered.

"Excuse me, Miss Maddie?" Mary straightened from stuffing a mountain of undergarments into a trunk.

"Oh, nothing." Scowling, Maddie sat at her dressing table and wrote Mr. Bancroft another very nice letter about how well everything was going and how well she and the titled Bancrofts were getting along, and how much she was looking forward to seeing London again. She wondered if he'd believe a word of it.

"Well, what does it say?"

Malcolm looked up from Maddie's letter. Chin in one hand, Squire John Ramsey sat glaring at him from the far side of their chess game. A leaf sailed down from the garden tree they sat beneath, and Malcolm brushed it off the board.

"Lewis—my brother—fled to London after five minutes with her, and she's apparently declared war on the rest of the family. I wouldn't be surprised if they had to clap her in irons to get her inside the coach to London."

"What's so amusing about that?" John challenged. "She must be absolutely miserable."

Malcolm couldn't explain that he was able to judge Maddie's spirits just from the mild tone of her letter. Langley seemed more quiet and calm than it had been for years, since the defiant beauty had first arrived and dared him to hire her. He missed her terribly, but from the moment he'd taken her up on the challenge, he'd known she wouldn't stay forever. He shook his head at his companion.

"Maddie's a fighter. She needs a challenge—something to push against. If my illustrious relations had greeted her with honey and cake, they'd never have been able to drag her to London, because she'd have them twisted around her little finger by now."

"As she does every male in Somerset," John sighed.

Malcolm looked at the letter once more, then set it aside to resume the game. "Yes, she does." And Quinlan had better be taking proper care of her, or there would be hell to pay.

"Maddie, please come down from the carriage," Quin pleaded soothingly, while he attempted to ignore the curious gawking of the butler and the scores of footmen needed to unload the Bancroft party's luggage.

"No," came her tense voice from inside the darkened coach.

"What nonsense." The Duchess of Highbarrow rolled her eyes, snapped her fan shut, and headed up the front steps into Bancroft House amid a sea of bowing servants.

Quin leaned against the open door of the coach. He should have ridden the last few miles with her—but then his mother or her maid would have had to join them, and he'd never have been able to talk to her. Not that they'd done much talking the last few times he'd made the attempt. Whenever he saw her, he immediately became seized with the desire either to bellow at her or kiss her. It had become quite irritating.

"Maddie, Bancroft House is surrounded by a very healthy border of oak trees, with a hedge of blooming pink rhododendrums beneath. In addition to its being quite picturesque, I assure you that the drive cannot be seen from the street."

"I want to go home," she stated.

The loneliness in her voice made him pause. "And where would that be, precisely?" he prompted quietly.

Given her keen sense of the practical, he thought that would get her attention. And indeed, a moment later her hand emerged from the dark. Swiftly he clasped it in his own. She was shaking, and he realized how unnerved she must be by the whole experience. Even before they'd entered the suburbs of London, she'd pulled the curtains shut in the carriage's small windows. From Aristotle's back he'd tried repeatedly to lure her to peek outside, but she wouldn't even answer him.

Slowly he drew her out of the coach. Her eyes were shut tight, and she stopped when her feet touched the drive. "Eventually you *will* run into something that way," he murmured, amused and sympathetic at the same time.

"I know," she said through clenched teeth. "Just give me a moment."

"Take several."

She continued to clasp his fingers tightly. Apparently she detested the rest of London more than she disliked him. Quin hadn't anticipated being elevated from enemy to ally, but the circumstance wasn't unwelcome. He gazed at her wan face. Good God, she was beautiful.

Finally, with a slow, deep breath, she opened her vulnerable gray eyes. She took in the huge house, the drive, the scattering of curious servants, and then Quin. "It's lovely," she said woodenly.

"Hm. I'll consider that high praise, coming from you. Shall we?" He gestured toward the open front door.

Maddie didn't budge, or loosen her grip on his hand. "Will you be staying here?"

Quin hadn't intended to. During the Season he typically stayed at Whiting House on Grosvenor Street, which had at one time belonged to his grandmother's

family. Spending the entire summer at Bancroft House—
with his parents—was a torture he hadn't had to endure
since he turned eighteen and was admitted to Oxford.
"Of course I'm staying here. Until you're settled, anyway."

The poisonous look Maddie shot at him was easy to
read—she would never be settled in London.

"I am to be married sometime this summer, you
know," he said in answer. "I can't very well have Eloise living here as well."

"Then perhaps you shouldn't have found me attractive," she said smoothly, a hint of color returning to her
cheeks. "Though I suppose it's not uncommon for
someone of your rank to promise yourself to someone
and then throw yourself at someone else."

Apparently she'd recovered from her fit of nerves. "I
did not *throw* myself at you. I believe it was a mutual
collision."

A swiftly stifled grin touched her lips. "Don't flatter
yourself," she said haughtily, as she freed her fingers
from his and flounced past Beeks, the butler, and into
the house.

"How can I possibly flatter myself, with you about?"
Quin muttered at her back, before he followed her inside.

Chapter 9

O n her first and only stay in London, Maddie had
been ecstatic. She had finally been able to see the
famous places like Hyde Park, Bond Street, and the dark
Tower of London—places she'd only heard about. Fab-
ulous balls had been full of exciting, famous people who
had treated her as an equal and claimed to be pleased to
meet her.

And she had no desire to see any of those places or
any of those people ever again.

"Miss Maddie, do you wish to change for luncheon?"

Maddie let the bedchamber curtains slide shut through
her fingers, closing her off from the quiet view of elegant King Street. "I suppose I should."

She was still unused to having someone to help her
dress and do her hair, but neither did she want to refuse
Mary's help and cause the poor girl to be let go—no
doubt exactly what Lord Warefield had anticipated.
When she'd donned her new green and yellow silk
gown, she glanced at the mantel clock and then reluctantly emerged from her bedchamber. Half a dozen servants nodded politely at her as she made her way
downstairs to the dining room—where she stopped
short.

The Duke of Highbarrow looked up from slicing a peach. "You're still about?" he asked gruffly, and returned to his luncheon.

"Good afternoon, Your Grace."

A footman hurried forward to pull out a chair, and rather than have the duke think her a coward, Maddie sat. His Grace rudely continued to ignore her, and she glanced about the room impatiently. Quin had said repeatedly that while in town the Bancrofts sat for luncheon precisely at one. So here she was, precisely at five minutes after one, when everyone else should have been there.

Another footman offered her a platter of fresh fruit, and with a grateful smile she selected a peach. Like everything else she'd seen in the house, it was perfect, round and golden. Maddie narrowed her eyes, imagining Quin's perfect smile and his handsome and very late backside, and sliced the fruit in two.

She glanced sideways at Lewis Bancroft again. Now that he wasn't bellowing at her and insulting her, she noticed that he was more heavyset than Malcolm, and that his dark brown hair was more generously tinged with silver about the temples. His complexion was ruddier, though Mr. Bancroft had been so pale over the past few weeks she'd been at Langley that she tended to think of that pallor as his natural coloring. And though she admitted that she might be prejudiced, she thought the duke's expression much less kind than Malcolm's.

"What are you staring at, girl?"

Maddie blinked. "I was looking for the resemblance between you and your brother, Your Grace."

"Bah. Malcolm's fortunate I still claim him as kin."

"Perhaps, Your Grace, it is *you* who is fortun—"

Quin skidded into the doorway. "Good afternoon, Father, Miss Willits," he said hurriedly, straightening his cravat and taking the seat opposite Maddie. "Apologies.

I was catching up on some correspondence and lost track of the time.''

The duke pinned him with annoyed brown eyes. ''You're staying here now, as well? What in damnation's wrong with Whiting House?''

The marquis motioned for a cup of tea. ''Nothing at all. I've merely decided to stay here for a few weeks.''

His Grace lowered his brow. ''Why?''

''He's keeping his word, as he was raised to do.'' The duchess glided into the room to sit opposite her husband. ''He can't very well have Miss Willits at Whiting House. She needs a chaperon. And that would be me.''

''Absolute nonsense. She's ruined already.''

Well, that was enough of that. ''I did not—''

''Perhaps so,'' the marquis said mildly, glancing warningly at Maddie, ''but I will proceed, with or without your assistance.''

''Without, I assure you.'' The duke pushed away from the table and stood. ''At the first sign of trouble, it will be without your mother's assistance as well. And I don't want the girl getting in my way. With you here, Quinlan, it's too damned crowded already.''

You could fit the entire Fifth Regiment in this house and still have room for a cannon. Seething, Maddie smiled brightly. ''I will avoid you at every opportunity, Your Grace. You may be assured of that.''

Lord Highbarrow paused on his way out the door. ''Absolute nonsense,'' he repeated, and continued on his way.

''Please try to avoid antagonizing him,'' Quin asked, looking at Maddie.

''He antagonizes me,'' she protested.

''Still, it would be much easier if he was on our side, don't you think?''

''Why should he be, my lord? There is nothing in this

to benefit him. Restoring me to society gains him absolutely nothing.''

"Let's not begin this argument again, Maddie," Quin grumbled.

"I agree," the duchess contributed unexpectedly. "Lewis is not known for his patience. We must begin plans for your return to society without delay." She drummed her fingers on the table. "Nothing formal to start with, of course," she mused, eyeing Maddie with an uncomfortable intensity. "You should first be seen with me, so your coincidental connection to Quin doesn't become the gossips' primary focus."

"I have no connection with Quin—Lord Warefield," Maddie countered, the color rising in her cheeks.

"Shopping, I think," the duchess continued, as though she hadn't heard Maddie's protest. "Very good. Yes. Bond Street, tomorrow morning."

"But . . . I don't need anything." A wave of anguished nervousness suddenly made her fingers shake. People would see her. People who knew her.

" 'Need' is not the reason one goes shopping on Bond Street. Being seen is the point of shopping on Bond Street. And so you shall be."

"But—"

"My mother is correct," Quin cut in. "This has to begin somewhere." He reached for a slice of fresh bread. "Besides, everyone will be addressing their conversation to Her Grace, with this being her first time out in public since her return to London. I doubt you'll have to say a word." He glanced up at her, his green eyes dancing. "That may be the most difficult thing for you."

"Oh, ha, ha," Maddie smirked, nevertheless bolstered by his comments. He was undoubtedly correct, after all, for he knew much more about snobbery and etiquette than she ever cared to learn. "And what important task will be occupying your day then, my lord?"

"I have to see that Whiting House is opened."

"My," she said, opening her eyes wide in awe. "Really?"

He sternly pointed a finger at her. "Yes, it means I shall stand about all day ordering servants hither and thither. No doubt I shall be quite exhausted by evening."

Lady Highbarrow cleared her throat delicately. "Not so exhausted that you can't attend dinner with us at Lady Finch's, I hope."

The duchess eyed her son, then flicked her gaze back over to Maddie, who quickly wiped the look of horror from her face. "Oh, my. Dinner?"

"I wrote Evelyn last week and asked her to put together an intimate gathering for a few select friends."

"Well, thank you, Mother," Quin said, his tone surprised. A moment later he kicked Maddie under the table.

She jumped. "Yes, thank you, Your Grace," she echoed, and kicked him back.

The Duke of Highbarrow skipped dinner that night, and instead went off to White's to smoke cigars and play cards. Actually, he could probably stand to miss a few dinners, for recently he'd become rather gouty, which left him even more ill-tempered than usual.

Quin would have liked to visit one of his clubs as well, but Maddie, of course, couldn't go anywhere, which also trapped his mother inside. So instead, the three of them played whist for several hours. Maddie had a natural cutthroat instinct for cards, which wasn't surprising in the least. The real surprise of the evening was the duchess smiling—not once, but twice—at things Maddie said.

In the morning, Quin rode off to Whiting House as he'd said he would. Once there, he instructed Baker, his butler, to open the house, with the explanation that he would be staying there from time to time, and would undoubtedly make use of it later in the Season. That accomplished, he swung back up on Aristotle and turned east for Bond Street.

His mother had been correct; if Maddie's purportedly wronged and injured character was to be redeemed, it would never do for him—or any man—to be seen with her on her first day back among the London *ton*. But nothing said he couldn't hang about in the shadows and make certain everything went well.

He left Aristotle and ten pence in the care of a young street urchin, and strolled up the crowded street in search of a new walking cane, which seemed the most logical thing for him to be looking for. It took nearly half an hour of aimless wandering before he spied the two women. The duchess emerged from a store, followed in succession by Maddie, four clerks carrying boxes, and Lady DeReese and Mrs. Oster. Quin dodged behind a parked barouche and peered over the top at them.

As he'd suspected, Maddie seemed to be of little interest to the two ladies in comparison with the esteemed Duchess of Highbarrow. Miss Willits stood a little to one side, clearly trying to look interested in the conversation, though just as clearly not. With her auburn hair glinting red in the sunlight, and her yellow silk gown showing off her lithe, slender figure, she was easily the most attractive lady on the street, if not in all of London.

He couldn't believe her parents would attempt to lock such a sprite away, much less consider sending her to a convent! What a wasted life that would have been for such a vibrant creature. Nor did he think she could have been completely happy at Langley. As much as Uncle Malcolm thought of her and she of him, he would never have been able to convince her to leave if she hadn't somehow truly wished it.

"Warefield!"

Quin started and looked up the street. "Danson," he replied, nodding. "Didn't know you were in London, yet."

"Yes, well my creditors think I'm still in Cornwall," Thomas Danson answered, clasping Quin's hand. "It's a bit early in the Season for you as well, isn't it?"

Quin shrugged, hoping the ladies across the busy lane hadn't noticed him or heard the conversation. "A bit. Had some business to attend to."

Danson turned away to toy with his dark hair in the reflection of the bakery window. "I say, why don't you buy me some luncheon at the Navy Club?"

With difficulty Quin kept from looking in Maddie's direction. "Why not?" he said, hoping his reluctance didn't show in his voice. He linked his arm through Thomas's, keeping his companion between him and the ladies. He was far too old to be acting like a schoolboy, and far too close to being engaged to be mooning after Maddie Willits. That was what had gotten him into such trouble in the first place.

"When is Eloise due back in town?" Danson asked.

Quin risked one glance at Maddie, to find her staring at him, barely contained fury in her gray eyes. Quickly he looked away again, cursing to himself. "Tomorrow, I should think," he answered, wondering how in the world he was going to explain himself this time.

Maddie would accuse him of spying, and she would be right. And he couldn't very well say that he'd only been gawking at her, not spying, because then she would accuse him of finding her attractive again. Next she would throw his near-engagement to Eloise back in his face as a *coup de grâce*. "Eloise said her father intended to be here by the twelfth."

"Have you made your declaration official yet?" Danson chuckled. "No, I don't suppose you have. Hasn't been a full-page announcement in the *London Times* yet.''

''Please, nothing so tasteless as that. Half a page, at most.''

Belatedly it occurred to him that he owed someone else an explanation for his rather ramshackle behavior. Eloise Stokesley probably wouldn't mind a stray kiss with a pretty, ruined girl in Somerset. Not nearly so much, anyway, as she would mind whatever madness had prompted him to take it upon himself to reintroduce Madeleine Willits into society. And he wasn't certain he could explain it adequately anyway.

Quin sighed. As much damned trouble as Maddie was causing him, he supposed he shouldn't be enjoying the entire debacle nearly as much as he was.

Maddie stood as close to the Duchess of Highbarrow as she could without tromping on the older woman's gown, and looked about Lady Finch's drawing room. Her Grace had declared their shopping expedition a success, leaving Maddie no excuses or protests to avoid the evening's dinner soiree.

Actually, walking about and shopping had been easy compared with tonight. She'd never been privileged to travel in such high circles. Tonight she would be expected to behave like a meek, demure young lady who would never have done such a thing as allow a gentleman to kiss her or fondle her front in public. And yet, she'd made that same mistake twice, now. Maddie smiled politely as Lady Finch nodded at her.

The first time truly hadn't been her fault, for she'd been caught by surprise by that snake Spenser. Slimy, wet, and cold—her first thought, before she realized she'd just been ruined, had been that she'd rather be kissed by a fish.

It was the second kiss that was becoming more troublesome by the moment, particularly as Quin refused to abandon her. She'd known that morning exactly what was going to happen—blast it all, she'd even encouraged it, wanted it, and relished it.

Maddie glanced across the room. Tall and handsome, Quinlan stood chatting with a few friends. He looked completely at ease, completely in his element, charming and witty and not a bit self-conscious. She hadn't been so close to hating him since he'd first appeared at Langley.

All afternoon she'd been looking for a chance to confront him on following her about like a spy. But all afternoon, obviously knowing he was in for a severe tongue lashing, he'd avoided her. And she couldn't very well have brought it up during the coach ride to Lady Finch's—not with the duchess there, reciting what she should and shouldn't do during the soiree.

Staring at Quin was one of the things she'd been directly told to avoid, but she was completely unable to resist several scowls and a glower. Shouting and hitting would have been much more satisfying. Almost as satisfying as kissing him again.

"Come, my dear," the duchess said, in the warm tone she seemed able to adopt the instant they were in public. "I wish to sit by the fire, where it's warmer."

She offered her arm, and Maddie hurriedly took it. "Of course, Your Grace."

Even before they'd settled themselves in, they were surrounded by a dozen other ladies, all inquiring after Lady Highbarrow's health, and that of her husband and two sons. No one inquired about Malcolm Bancroft's health, or about Maddie's, but at least it meant she didn't have to answer any questions. Instead, Maddie smiled and nodded agreement to the duchess's conversation at all the proper times, and offered no independent opinion or commentary—much as some of the ladies' silly gossip deserved it.

The duchess had warned her that while everyone would be looking at her and judging her comportment, no one was likely to speak to her at her first formal gathering. According to Her Grace, no one would approach her until she'd been deemed harmless. Maddie thought it more likely that no one wanted to be the first to acknowledge her.

"Mother, Miss Willits, may I fetch you a glass of Madeira?" Quin asked, stopping before them.

"Yes, thank you," the duchess answered, and nudged Maddie in the ribs.

"If you please, my lord," she blurted, glancing up at him and then away.

He vanished, then reappeared shortly with their drinks. As he handed Maddie hers, he leaned closer. "How are you doing?"

"I very much wish to spit at you, but I'm attempting to behave," she whispered back. "Go away."

He bowed, a smile tugging at his lips. "Yes, my lady."

"Quin, go away," the duchess repeated, glaring at him imperiously.

"I am, I am," he chuckled and wandered off.

"Miss Willits?"

Startled, Maddie looked up at the small, white-haired lady standing beside the fireplace. "Yes?" she said hesitantly, uncertain whether she should be ready to fight or to flee.

"Anne," the duchess said warmly, as she turned to look as well. "I didn't expect you in London yet."

"Neither did I." The lady smiled. "Ashton insisted."

"Anne, may I present Miss Willits? Maddie, Lady Ashton."

Then Maddie remembered her. "You were at the Tewksbury ball," she stated.

"Yes, I—"

"You called Spenser a drunken lout."

Lady Ashton nodded. "I should have said it louder. Would you and Her Grace join me for tea on Thursday?"

"We'd be delighted," the duchess answered.

"Oh, yes," Maddie seconded, smiling. Perhaps Quin was right, after all—some warmth and decency did survive in London.

Finally the duchess declared that they might depart, and Maddie practically bolted for the door and the coach. Quin joined them a moment later.

"That went quite well, don't you think?" he asked, leaning back in the seat opposite her.

"The soiree isn't what counts," Maddie said succinctly, gazing out the window until they passed Curzon Street—where Willits House stood. The conversation inside the coach suddenly became much more interesting.

"It's not? Then what, pray tell, were we doing there? And why did I spend twenty minutes conversing with that rattlebrain Lord Avery?"

She eyed him, amused by his pretend exasperation—though of course she'd never let him know it. "It's what everyone will say about me now that we're gone that counts. People rarely insult you to your face, as you have just demonstrated regarding Lord Avery."

"Now, Maddie—"

"She's correct, Quin," the duchess interrupted. "And you weren't helping things, hovering about like a footman."

"I was *not* hovering," he protested indignantly. "I was being a dutiful son and host."

"Well, do it less obtrusively next time, won't you, dear?"

Quin folded his arms. "I'll certainly try. Do I still accompany you to the opera tomorrow, or have you managed to recruit Father?"

"The opera?" Maddie gasped, her heart pounding in dismay. "Oh, no. Not yet."

"Yes, you will escort us," the duchess answered, ignoring their guest's protest. Unexpectedly, she reached over and took Maddie's hand. "Whatever they may mutter among themselves, they would do it whether you were there or not. Whatever they would say to you in my presence, they had best be polite about it."

"If I'm accepted only in your company, Your Grace, there seems little point in any of this," Maddie said shakily, thankful nevertheless for the duchess's unexpected support. *Everyone* went to the opera at the beginning of the Season, with no grand balls or soirees organized yet. Everyone who was in town would be there, not just the select acquaintances of the duchess.

"It's a beginning, Maddie," Quin said. "One step at a time."

"That's easy for you to say, Lord Warefield. You're not the one on the edge of the abyss."

"Neither are you."

"And what am I to do if I come across Charles Dunfrey?" She swallowed. "Or my parents?"

"Your parents are not in town yet," Quin answered calmly. "I already inquired. As for Dunfrey, my friend Danson tells me he sold his box last Season. I very much doubt he'll be at the opera tomorrow night."

"Yes, but what about—"

"Maddie," he interrupted. "Don't worry. I will keep my word to you. Whatever else happens, you'll end the Season well."

The duchess looked from one to the other, and settled back in her seat. Quin had told her the two of them fought every time they saw each other. To her, it didn't look nearly as much like fighting as it did flirting. And she wondered what would happen when they realized that as well.

The duke claimed a meeting, while the duchess and Maddie, not quite so unwilling as yesterday, undertook another preliminary shopping excursion. If Napoleon had planned his campaign as well as the Duchess of Highbarrow had planned Maddie's, he wouldn't be rotting on Saint Helena.

Quin, grateful for a few hours' reprieve, spent most of the morning pacing about the Bancroft library. Eloise would be in London by the afternoon, and what he hadn't been able to disclose in his correspondence he felt even less able to tell her in person—at least without making it sound as though he had some ulterior motive for bringing Maddie Willits to London. Which he didn't, of course.

"Like hell I don't," he muttered aloud, dropping the book he carried onto a chair. "Well, Eloise," he began, "I felt sorry for the girl, stuck rusticating in Somerset with my stodgy old uncle." He paused by the library window, then shook his head and began circling the room again, feeling rather like a bird searching for a safe roost before two very lovely nightingales could peck his eyes out.

He cleared his throat and tried again. "You see, my dear, Uncle Malcolm pleaded with me to assist Miss Willits, and sickly as he was, I could hardly refuse." Quin rubbed at his temples. "Ahem." He dropped into a chair. "Good God, I'm a dreadful liar."

"Might I suggest 'I tried tumbling the chit, and she threatened to cry rape unless I took her to London and foisted her off on my parents'?"

Quin looked up, scowling, as his father stopped in the doorway. "I did not try to tumble her," he snapped, wishing he'd remembered to close the door. For God's sake, Maddie might have heard him. He'd never have lived it down.

Lord Highbarrow scowled and folded his arms. "Oh, really?" he said, cynicism dripping from his voice.

"Yes, really. And I practically had to drag her by her hair to get her to come to London. And please keep your voice down, Your Grace. Someone might hear you."

"No one who matters. I always thought Rafael was my idiot son. She's abusing your generosity. You don't actually think she intends to storm back to Malcolm if she can drag the future Duke of Highbarrow before the archbishop, do you? Sweet Lucifer, boy, stop using your balls for brains!"

Quin shot to his feet, anger tearing through him. "I am marrying Eloise, as *you* require. I—"

"I didn't ask for a recital of the obvious, Quinlan. That's what my accountants are for. You'd best not forget that you *are* marrying Eloise, *if* you want to remain the Marquis of Warefield. It's my damned title, yours to use by my leave only!"

"I know that. I haven't done anything except feel pity for a—"

"That isn't pity I see in your eyes when you look at her, boy," the duke cut in. "If you want to rut with her, that's fine. But get your damned whore out from under my roof!"

His face flushing, Quin clenched his fist. "Maddie Willits is not a damned—"

"Bah!"

His Grace stomped out the door and down the hall, bellowing at the butler for a glass of port as he went. Incensed both at the accusation and at how close some of it was to the truth, Quin grabbed the brandy decanter and hurled it into the fireplace. It shattered against the hot bricks, the brandy exploding in a satisfying hiss of blue flames. "Bloody, pompous—"

"Should I pack, then?" Maddie's voice came from the doorway.

Quin whipped around, paling. "Damn . . . I didn't know you'd returned. Excuse my language, Maddie."

Shaking her head, she backed up into the hallway. "No need, my lord. And you don't have to be so polite, you know." She brushed at her eyes as a single tear ran down her cheek. "It's what they're all saying, I'm certain."

Quin followed her into the hall and grabbed her hand. "Wait," he said, pulling her back into the library and closing the door. "None of that was meant for you to hear."

She looked away, her lower lip trembling. Her slim wrist, clenched tightly in his fingers, shook a little. "It doesn't matter."

"Of course it does. His Grace just likes to roar and intimidate the rest of the pack. He's nothing but wind."

"That was . . . quite rude of him," she said unsteadily, obviously very hurt and making a heroic effort to stop crying. "No wonder Mr. Bancroft doesn't like him. I don't, either."

"Neither do I, at the moment," he said. "Please don't cry."

"I'm not crying. I'm very angry."

Slowly Quin drew her closer. "I'm sorry," he murmured, wanting to hold her in his arms. "And don't think you need to leave. I'll speak to him again—in a more civil tone. I promise."

He was rather surprised he'd made the offer: begging to His Grace on bended knee was not something he did on a frequent basis. In fact, he couldn't recall either one of them ever backing down after an argument. But if he didn't apologize, Maddie would leave. And he didn't want her to leave.

"This is ridiculous, anyway. If my parents or . . . or Charles—if they should see me, everything would be ruined. Especially me."

Quin reached down and lifted her chin with his fingers. "And what makes you think I don't enjoy a little bit of the ridiculous every now and then?"

He wanted to kiss her. He wanted to feel her lips against his—he wanted to feel her body against his.

Maddie met his gaze. "Oh, no," she whispered. "Not again."

"Should I not?"

"Yes. No. Oh, blast." She lifted up on her toes, and twined her arms about his neck. As she pulled herself up against him, he leaned down and brushed his lips against hers. The touch was electric. Unable to help himself, he kissed her again, more roughly, sliding his hands down her hips and pulling her against him.

"Quin?" the duchess called. "Quin, I need to talk to you."

With a strangled sound, Maddie wrenched away from him. "Stop it," she said sharply, shoving at his chest. "Stop it!"

He stared at her for a moment, stunned at his own reaction to her, and exceedingly frustrated at having been interrupted. "You started it. And don't go anywhere," he ordered, taking a last look at her and then slipping through the library door.

Maddie sighed and plunked herself down in one of the chairs. "I started it? Oh, I suppose I did. Drat." Slowly she reached up and traced her lips with her fingertips. Only a kiss, and it had gone through her like lightning—worse than before, and it left her with a raw, aching yearning for him.

A few moments later Quin came back into the room.

His face was somber, and her heart began pounding again, this time with dread. "I have to leave, don't I?" And the duke would probably see to it that she couldn't go back to Langley now. Which narrowed down her choices to none. "Don't I?"

"No, you don't." He cleared his throat. "Unfortunately, though, there has been a complication."

She rallied enough to lift an eyebrow. "Only one?"

"So to speak. His Grace has forbidden my mother to assist you. Her compromise was that you be allowed to remain here until arrangements can be made to send you back to Langley. And she will still accompany us to the opera tonight, as she gave her word. My family is very big on honoring their word."

"I've noticed." She wondered for a wrenching moment what would have happened between them if she'd been able to stay. "It's over, then."

"No, it's not. Tonight will go a long way toward repairing the damage. And I have a few ideas."

"Just let me go back, my lord. You've done more than your part."

He tilted his head at her. "Call me Quin."

"I don't want to."

"Why not? We've kissed twice now."

She couldn't tell him that it meant there was some sort of connection between them, that she had a difficult enough time with distancing herself from him already, that over the past few weeks she had begun to regard him with a great deal more affection than she thought possible. "It's not proper."

The marquis actually laughed. "Call me Quin," he repeated.

Maddie took a deep breath. "Just let me leave, Quin."

"No."

She didn't know precisely why he was continuing to argue, for he was nearly engaged. Still, for a bare, exhilarating moment she was relieved that he insisted on pursuing this stubborn course of action. For whatever reason, he wanted her there.

"Now, if you'll excuse me, I need to go change."

Maddie blinked, reluctantly floating down from her daydream. "Why?"

Quin grimaced, edging for the door. "I'm meeting someone this afternoon."

At the sight of his sheepish expression, she immediately realized to whom he was referring. "Of course. Lady Stokesley arrives in London today." The remains of her fantasy sank with a thud into a very deep mud puddle.

"Yes." He paused. "Which could be quite opportune for you."

She looked at him skeptically. "For *me?*"

He strode forward to clasp her hands in his. "Of course. Father might be able to forbid my mother from assisting us, but he can't very well order Eloise around. She's only a second cousin."

Humiliation flushed Maddie's cheeks. "No, Quin. That's a terrible idea. I'm sure she'll want nothing to do with me. How would you ever explain me to her, anyway?"

His smile faltered a little. "Eloise is very understanding."

Maddie nodded, pulling her hands free. "Even so," she returned, trying to sound cynical and amused instead of heartbroken, "if I were you, I wouldn't mention that you kissed me. Twice."

"Maddie," he began, closing the distance between them again.

She backed away. "Don't try to explain. We'll just put it to the general weakness of men."

His eyes searched hers. "I'd rather you didn't," he

said, "but I don't think it would be wise to pursue an explanation any further at the moment."

Looking at the slight smile curving his mouth, and the jade eyes studying her face, Maddie abruptly agreed with him. This was becoming extremely complicated. "Well? You'd best be off, then."

"Don't go anywhere while I'm away," he warned.

She put a hand to her chest. "Me?"

"Miss Willits, don't make me lock you—"

"All right, all right," she surrendered. "I won't go anywhere while you're off visiting."

He nodded. "Good."

"Quin!" Eloise, Lady Stokesley, hurried downstairs in a fashionable swirl of blue silk.

She'd cut her hair since last autumn, her long blond tresses now a short, daring cascade of curls framing her perfect alabaster features. Her blue eyes reflected the fine material of her gown as she stopped before him. They'd known one another for so long that Quin sometimes forgot how lovely she was—until he set eyes on her after a few months of being apart. He took her hands and drew them to his lips.

"Eloise," he said with a smile. She stood a few inches above Maddie's height—though he'd never thought of her as being overly tall before. "You are a vision, my dear, as always."

She curled up a delicate fist and hit him on the shoulder. "I'm very angry at you."

There was no heat in either the blow or her voice, and he lifted an eyebrow. "Whatever for?"

"I've had a terrible time keeping track of you, you beast. First you're at Warefield, and then you go off to Somerset, of all places. You hardly correspond with me, and then, when I finally think my letters have caught up to you, your uncle writes to inform me you're at Highbarrow Castle. Then you go off to London without a word. And without coming to Stafford Green first.''

Quin led her into the Stokesley House morning room. ''Yes, well, that's one of the reasons I wanted to see you right away. I've had ... something of an adventure.''

Eloise seated herself on the couch, beckoning him to join her. ''Do tell me what's kept you so occupied.''

He heard the slight censure in her voice but ignored it. He *had* been less than communicative over the past few weeks. ''It's a rather long story.''

''I should imagine so. Tell me.''

Quin settled back against the cushions. ''Well, you know Uncle Malcolm had an apoplexy, and that Father sent me to Langley to help with the planting.''

She nodded. ''Yes, you did manage to write me about that, and about how inconvenient it would be to your schedule.''

It had been inconvenient only until he'd set eyes on Maddie. ''It turned out that Uncle Malcolm already had an assistant who was quite proficient at estate management,'' he continued.

''Then why didn't you take your leave early and visit me, as we'd planned?''

''I'm getting to that. This assistant of my uncle's was a female.''

Eloise's eyes widened, and she put a hand over her mouth. ''Oh, my,'' she said slyly. ''How wicked of your uncle. And such a shame that the best gossip is always within one's family, so one can't spread it about.''

Quin frowned, then wiped the expression from his face when she looked at him curiously. Funny, he'd never taken notice of gossip before. But then, he'd never seen the effects of it—until Maddie. ''I don't think it was like that at all,'' he countered, a little stiffly. ''She was more like a daughter to him, I believe. And it turned out that she was the eldest daughter of Viscount Halverston.''

''The . . . we came out the same Season. She's the one who ran off after half the *ton* discovered her lifting her skirts for that awful Benjamin Spenser, isn't she?''

''I'm not convinced that was her fault.''

Eloise looked up at his sharp tone. ''Oh, really?''

Charging to Maddie's defense would only make things worse. And Maddie certainly wouldn't appreciate it. ''As you said,'' he continued, ''Spenser doesn't have the best reputation as a gentleman. At any rate, my uncle believed her to be innocent of any wrongdoing. He . . . he asked me to reintroduce her to London society.''

''He did what?'' Eloise stood. ''You had that . . . lightskirt with you when you traveled to Highbarrow?''

''Eloise, please,'' he cut in, before she could say something worse about Maddie. ''My mother has been helping her. She's very sweet.''

Her eyes narrowed suspiciously. *''Sweet?''*

It wasn't exactly the perfect word to describe Maddie, but he couldn't very well tell Eloise that he was half addle-brained over the wild-hearted chit. ''Yes. Except that now Father's on a rampage about how she'll somehow tarnish the Bancroft name, and you know Mother won't directly defy him, so . . . so I need your help, Eloise.''

''My help?''

Quin shrugged. ''Well, yes. I promised Malcolm I'd see her able to marry any gentleman in London. I can't very well chaperon her myself.''

For a long moment she looked at him. Finally, she sat again and took his hand in hers. ''Of course I'll help, my marquis.'' Eloise moved closer, leaning her head against his shoulder. ''Poor dear, she'd be all alone if not for us.''

"Well, she's not exactly helpless. In fact, I believe her to be quite capable."

"Capable?" Eloise chuckled. "Oh, my. You make her sound like a milkmaid. I can't wait to meet her."

"You said you came out together."

She shook her head. "No, I said we came out the same Season. I imagine we attended a few of the same soirees, but Halverston's a very small holding, you know."

He knew what she meant—that Maddie hadn't been privileged to travel in the same high circles into which he and Eloise had been born. "Yes, I know. Mother's last official duty is to chaperon her to the opera tonight. I'll bring her by tomorrow, if that's all right."

"Oh, yes! I'm quite looking forward to helping her now. We shall be like sisters."

Quin smiled, relieved, and kissed Eloise on the cheek. "Thank you."

"Come by at one, and we'll have luncheon in the garden."

With a nod, Quin collected his hat and went outside to retrieve Aristotle. That hadn't been nearly as sticky as he'd anticipated. Perhaps there was a chance he would escape the Season in one piece.

With Mary's assistance, Maddie dressed in her dark green and gray gown with a scooped neck and short puffy sleeves. The flowing silk was easily the most lovely thing she'd worn in years, if not ever. It was a gown fit for a prime box at the opera, and as she twisted in front of the full-length mirror, she was terrified. "This is so stupid."

"You look beautiful, Miss Maddie," Mary protested, reaching out to adjust one last out-of-place curl.

"Well, thank you, but that's not quite what I meant." She'd made Quin promise four different times that her parents weren't in town yet, and another three times that Charles Dunfrey wouldn't be attending *The Magic Flute*. Which left only a thousand other people to stare at her and laugh that she would think of returning to London society—even in the company of the Bancrofts.

Her door rattled with Quin's confident knock. "Ready, Maddie?"

"I really don't think we should upset your father any further," she told the door. "You go. I'll begin packing for Langley."

The bedchamber door opened. "No excuses. . . ." the marquis began, then closed his mouth as he ran his gaze over her. " 'My prime request,' " he said softly, " 'Which I do last pronounce, is, oh, you wonder, if you be maid or no?' "

She couldn't help the smile that touched her lips. " 'No wonder, sir, but certainly a maid.' "

He stepped closer, apparently oblivious of Mary's presence. "Then you know *The Tempest*, as well."

"I've recently had a great deal of time to read." Belatedly she backed away from him. "And you shouldn't be in here."

He lifted an eyebrow. "Don't want you escaping out the window, you know. The coach is waiting. Shall we?"

Maddie shook her head. "No, I don't think so."

"After tonight it will be much easier. Come on."

He was entirely too high-spirited, which made her even more nervous than she had been a few minutes earlier. Reluctantly she followed him downstairs. "You've never been cut, have you, my lord?"

He looked sideways at her.

"Quin," she corrected.

"No, I haven't. Except by you, of course."

"Well, as I imagine you'll find out tonight," she said,

while the butler helped her on with her shawl, "*I* don't matter, Quin. And thank you, Beeks."

"You could be a little more positive about this, Maddie." He gestured her to precede him out the door.

Reluctantly, Maddie complied.

Shrugging, she stepped up into the coach to sit beside the duchess. He didn't understand—and he wouldn't understand, because it had never happened to him.

Once they exited the coach at the front of the opera house, however, she thought perhaps he'd been right, after all. She received several startled second looks and heard the murmured commentary going about the huge lobby, but no one actually turned his back on her. She held tightly onto Quin's arm, grateful for his tall, strong presence, and tried to look relaxed. The marquis, with Her Grace on his other arm, smiled and greeted their friends and acquaintances as though nothing out of the ordinary was occurring.

"See?" Quin murmured at her, as they started up the long, winding staircase leading to the balcony and the exclusive boxes.

"They can't cut me without cutting you and the duchess," she muttered back, through teeth clenched in a determinedly amused smile.

"It was five years ago, Maddie. Probably no one so much as remembers the specifics. If you comport yourself well, they'll have no reason to cut you."

She had her doubts about that. Even so, as she stepped through the curtains at the back of the Bancroft box and took the forward seat beside the duchess, as she'd been instructed, she couldn't help a moment of optimism. So far, the nightmare she'd imagined hadn't materialized. Perhaps Quin was right, and no one remembered her at all.

A few pairs of opera glasses, then more, turned in her direction at the beginning of the first act, but she thought they might just as easily have been aimed at the illustrious Bancrofts. She hadn't been to the opera in a long time, and once everyone settled down to watch, she allowed herself to be absorbed in the comedy unfolding on the stage below.

She hardly realized intermission had arrived until the massive curtains swung shut and the house lights brightened. A wave of uneasiness ran through her again, even stronger than before. *Everyone* mingled at intermission.

"Shall we?" Quin said, rising and stretching.

"Polite nods and one- or two-word answers. For anything more, defer to me—is that clear, Maddie?" the duchess said, motioning her toward the back of the box.

She nodded, hoping no one could hear her knees knocking together. "Don't worry about that."

It was like remembering, like something she had done before, but not exactly in the same way. The French phrase for it—*déjà vu*—that was what it felt like, to emerge from a theater box into a crowd of glittering nobility, but at the same time to know with absolute certainty that she did not belong.

"Your Grace. How splendid to see you back in London." A short, very broad woman whose neck sparkled with diamonds appeared from one side of the wide hallway. She clasped the duchess's hand.

"Lady Hatton," the duchess returned. "I was so sorry to hear of your cousin's death. My condolences to you and your family."

"Oh, thank you, Your Grace. One would have thought India more civilized by now." The white-haired woman looked at Quin and curtsied, then turned her attention to Maddie. "I don't believe I've met your companion, Your Grace."

"Ah, of course. Lady Hatton, I should like to introduce Miss Willits, an old family friend. Madeleine, Lady Hatton of Staffordshire."

Maddie nodded politely, self-consciously taking Quin's arm again. "Pleased to meet you." It was actually four words, but she couldn't think how to limit it to less and not sound like a halfwit.

"And you as well, my dear." Lady Hatton smiled. "What a lovely girl you are."

"Thank you, my lady."

A moment later three other grand ladies had approached, all of them thankfully more interested in learning the state of the duke's health and wealth than in being introduced to Maddie. Relieved, she turned away—only to find herself being stared at intently by a very beautiful, tall woman with a profusion of short blond ringlets framing her face.

She looked familiar, and as she parted from her companions and came forward, Maddie remembered who she was. Her heart and her courage sank.

"Eloise," Quin said warmly, and Maddie belatedly released her grip on his arm. She'd likely left bruises, but he didn't give any indication of being in dire pain. Instead, he smiled again. "Why didn't you say you would be attending this evening?"

"It was something of a last minute decision," Lady Stokesley answered, and stopped before Maddie. "You must be Miss Willits. Your face is somewhat familiar, but I don't think we've ever been formally introduced."

"Then allow me," Quin said. "Eloise, Miss Willits. Maddie, Lady Stokesley."

"How do you do?" Maddie said, trying not to stare. This was the woman who held Quin's heart, and she wasn't certain she was ready to like her at all.

"Quin's told me all about you," Eloise replied. "I do hope we can be friends."

Maddie forced a smile. "So do I."

Lady Stokesley wrapped her arm around Quin's. "May I borrow Lord Warefield for just a moment?"

"Of course."

They stepped away, and Maddie abruptly realized that she was alone. Very alone. She turned to find the duchess, but Her Grace was nowhere in sight. And then neither was Quin, nor Lady Stokesley.

"Miss Willits?"

With a start, Maddie turned again. The stocky gentleman gazing at her looked somewhat familiar, but so did half of the London nobility, and she couldn't place him.

"I say, it *is* you. Maddie, isn't it?"

He came closer and took her hand, bringing it to his lips.

"Have we met?" she asked stiffly, trying to free her hand while he kissed her knuckles again.

"We have mutual friends, I think. I'm Edward Lumley."

"I'm afraid I don't—"

"By gum, the time away from London hasn't damaged you a spot," he said admiringly, taking in her gown, and particularly its low neckline.

"Thank you. If you'll excuse—"

"I'd wager you're a real goer," he continued, stepping still closer. "What'd it take to steal you away from Warefield?" He grinned, running his fingers up her arm. "He makes a bit of a stodgy ride, no doubt. I've been to the Spice Islands, you know. Learned all sorts of techniques."

For a moment Maddie stared at him, hardly following what he was saying, and even less able to believe that he would dare say it to her face. "I believe," she said coldly, narrowing her eyes as his gaze dropped to her bosom again, "you are mistaken about me."

"What, you don't belong to the duke, do you?"

Maddie belted him.

Chapter 10

⟨○○⟩

Quin looked up as Edward Lumley hit the polished floor.

"My goodness!" Eloise exclaimed.

Lumley scrambled back to his feet. Red-faced, he strode up to the young woman eyeing him with wounded fury, her fists clenched before her.

Quin swiftly reached out to grab Lumley's arm and wrenched him around. "Terribly sorry there, Lumley," he said, brushing at the idiot's coat with his free hand. "Didn't see you standing there. Not a pleasant thing, to get an elbow in the eye like that."

Lumley glared at him, the scarlet of his face deepening to crimson. He jutted a finger at Maddie. "She—"

"Yes, she is lovely, but I think you'd best recover yourself a little before I introduce you to my mother's companion, Lumley. Perhaps a breath of fresh air is what you need."

The iron grip on his arm and the angry glint in Quin's eyes was apparently enough to convince Mr. Lumley to make himself scarce, and with a parting sneer at Maddie, he collected his dented hat and wounded pride and departed.

Quin shrugged as he looked after the gentleman, and

a polite round of chuckles answered the motion. Silently he counted to five, then turned back to Maddie, who stood staring at him, white-faced.

"I believe Her Grace is looking for you, Miss Willits." He smiled, forcibly unbending her clenched fingers and tucking them over his arm.

"Thank you, Lord Warefield," she returned gamely, smiling despite the hurt and anger still in her eyes.

They walked to the fringes of the crowd, with Maddie clinging ferociously to his forearm. When they finally reached the top of the stairs, he stopped and made a show of checking the elbow of his coat for damage. "What in damnation happened?" he murmured, looking at her sideways.

"He—that—that Edward Lumley person wanted me to be his mistress!" she sputtered, clearly still furious.

"Calm down," he said, glancing back at the noisy crowd.

"Calm down?" she repeated. "*Calm down*? He said you were too dull, and that he'd learned all sorts of things in the Spice Islands!"

"I'm too dull, am I?" Quin narrowed his eyes, abruptly liking Lumley even less now. "Maddie, whatever he said, you can't go about hitting people when they insult you. It's not at all *comme il faut*."

"No?" she replied indignantly, her color beginning to return. "This was *your* fault, Warefield."

"And why is that, pray tell?"

"You're a Bancroft: the great, grand Marquis of Warefield. Your name would protect me from all insult and innuendo, remember? Wasn't that what you said?"

"Maddie, I—"

"*No* one's forgotten what happened," she cut in. "They all think I'm some sort of whore. What am I supposed . . . supposed to do when someone says that to me?'' Her defiance melted and tears began to form in her eyes.

"Give them a set-down," he returned more quietly, wanting to kiss the tears from her eyes. "Just don't set them down on the floor."

"That's easy for you to say. No one would dare utter something like that in *your* presence. *You* don't have to deal with it."

Quin sighed. She was right—and he had been too arrogant in his assumption about the protection his name would provide her. "That's still no excuse."

"I don't care. I want to leave."

"We can't leave after that little show of yours. We have to stay and act as if nothing happened. Come on, we'd better find my mother."

She put her hands on her hips and he tensed, ready for another of her uniquely spectacular scenes. "What about my honor?"

"What do you mean, 'your honor'?"

"That man insulted me, and all you're worried about is whether anyone noticed. You're exactly what I thought you were."

Quin didn't know exactly what that was, but he didn't like the implication. Especially since she was probably right. "I'm sorry," he murmured. "I should not have left you alone. I won't abandon you again, Maddie. I promise."

If he hadn't been so relieved that her first meeting with Eloise had gone so smoothly, he would have realized how idiotic it had been to leave her side. Quin touched her chin, tilting her face up, then hurriedly lowered his hand as Lady Granville passed by. "I'm sorry," he repeated.

She held his gaze for a long moment, then nodded. "All right?"

She nodded again, and then abruptly grasped his arm again, holding him tightly.

He headed them back toward the box. "My, my, Maddie Willits, speechless," he teased softly. Something he'd said had finally been the right thing, though he had no idea which something it had been.

The duchess was already seated and waiting expectantly for them, but when he shook his head she refrained from inquiring about what had happened. As the opera began again, Quin sat back and studied Maddie's profile. Obviously she was nowhere near ready to be set loose into society, if she allowed herself to be so hurt by any comment about her past. And volatile and emotional as she was, convincing her to ignore the insults would be next to impossible.

He needed to come up with some other way to help her get past the innuendos and propositions of the less-principled members of society—though he could hardly blame them for desiring her companionship. The sooner he and Eloise could find her some nice, quiet, unassuming gentleman, the better off he'd be. Quin frowned. The better off *Maddie* would be.

Eloise Stokesley sat beside her mother, Lady Stafford, and looked down at the opera glasses in her lap. She and Quin Bancroft had been promised to one another since her birth. The idea had never bothered her. Quite the contrary, actually—the Marquis of Warefield was highly esteemed, very wealthy, and handsome as a Greek sun god. Her friends all knew she was to marry him, and they envied and admired her for it.

So when he'd asked last year if she would mind one year's delay before he made an official declaration, she had agreed. The Bancroft properties were so vast, a few months would be necessary just for his father and their horde of solicitors to decide which additional lands and funds should come to him upon his marriage. And it gave her another Season to flirt with her myriad male admirers and gloat about her coming nuptials.

She looked up, across the orchestra and the throng of the less wealthy below. The Bancroft box was nearly opposite the Stokesleys', and in the near darkness she could just make out the three of them sitting there. The duchess, Quin, and *her*. Eloise lifted the opera glasses.

Madeleine Willits. Eloise remembered her as a determined flirt with a smile for anyone who amused her, no matter how base they might have been. No wonder she'd earned such a fast reputation. And pretty as she was, no wonder she had snared Quin's attention. Eloise turned the glasses to view her nearly betrothed. She narrowed her eyes.

He sat in the shadows, his attention not on the stage, but on the woman seated in front of him. His expression as he studied her was amused, but it was also keenly interested. The moment Quin had approached her to ask her assistance in introducing Miss Willits back into society, she'd suspected his motive was more than simple compassion. Now she had no doubt of it.

But women had been unsuccessfully throwing themselves at the Marquis of Warefield for years. She knew he'd taken several mistresses in the past, but they hadn't been of any quality to threaten her own status, and he'd certainly never been overly attached to any of them. This one was different. He'd never taken any of the others to the opera, or bothered having them chaperoned by his mother.

Eloise lowered the glasses again before anyone could notice her discomfiture. Something would have to be done to set things back into their proper order. As the future Duchess of Highbarrow, she had a stake in the doings of the Bancroft family. And Maddie Willits did not belong there.

*   *   *

Maddie looked up the Bancroft House drive, and with a curse, ducked behind the duchess's roses. Quin and Aristotle rode by, returning to the stable from their morning ride in Hyde Park. Quin had barely spoken to her after the opera, but from the way he'd kept looking at her, he had something in mind. She just didn't want to hear it. They'd tried and failed.

She'd been away from this nonsense for too long, and she couldn't adapt to it again. She didn't *want* to adapt to it again. Only now, even the idea of returning to Langley Hall had its drawbacks: Quin wouldn't be there. Last night, when he'd promised not to abandon her, she had wanted so much to throw her arms around him and kiss him, even though he couldn't possibly have known how much those words meant to her.

She bent down to yank another weed out of the ground, shredding the offending plant into the bucket hanging off her arm, and grateful that the duchess had let her putter about in the garden. At least it kept her from feeling completely useless.

A terrible commotion erupted from the direction of the stables, and she whipped around, wondering with some alarm whether Quin had been trampled by his independent-minded mount.

Hefting the heavy bucket, she hurried down the carriage path toward the noise. As she rounded the hedge, a man all in black flashed out of the stable doors, mounted on Aristotle. Quin emerged right behind them, covered in straw and with a pitchfork in one hand.

''Stop him!'' he bellowed.

The rider dodged around one of the stable hands and thundered down the path toward Maddie and the street beyond. Reacting instinctively, she swung the wooden bucket up as hard as she could. It caught the rider in the shoulder, and with a grunt he canted sideways out of the saddle and tumbled to the ground.

He rolled a short distance, then immediately returned to his feet to shake himself and stride angrily in her direction. Alarmed, Maddie backed away and raised the bucket menacingly.

"Blast it, that hurt!" he said, rubbing his left shoulder.

"Don't come any closer unless you want worse," she warned. She heard Quin coming up behind her and shifted sideways, hoping he was still armed.

"Where's my damned horse?" the marquis asked with surprising composure, leaning on the pitchfork and breathing hard.

"*My* damned horse, you mean," the other replied, and put two fingers to his mouth. The sharp two-toned whistle surprised Maddie. Even more surprising was the sight of Aristotle trotting back up the drive and coming to a stop beside his abductor.

"Show-off," Quin muttered.

The lean, sandy-haired man patted the gelding's neck and received a nuzzle in the shoulder in return. "Who's your trained assassin, Warefield?" he asked, looking at Maddie and grinning. A long, narrow white scar ran from high on his left cheekbone almost to his jaw, giving him a vaguely piratical air.

"You're Rafael," Maddie whispered, blanching. Now she'd nearly killed the marquis's brother. Good Lord, the Bancrofts would be lucky if she didn't do them all in.

He swept a bow, his light green eyes dancing. "I see my reputation as a horse thief precedes me. But it *is* my animal."

"Rafe, Miss Willits." Quin supplied with a reluctant grin. "Maddie, my idiot brother Rafael."

Rafael Bancroft did look a great deal like his older

brother, though his face was thinner than Quin's, and darkened by much time spent out-of-doors. He lacked an inch or so of the marquis's height, but they shared the appearance of lean, contained strength.

She set down the bucket and stuck out her hand. "Pleased to make your acquaintance."

He shook her hand, his grip firm and friendly. "You're lethal, you know," he chuckled, rubbing at his shoulder again.

"I'm sorry. I heard Quin yell, and—"

"No need to explain," he said, glancing at his brother. "And where did you meet *Quin*?"

She heard his emphasis on the name and blushed. "It's a very long story," she offered, hesitating to explain her presence to another of the unpredictable Bancrofts.

"She was staying at Langley as Malcolm's companion," Quin said, reaching around his brother to grab Aristotle's bridle. "Help me put my damned horse up, and I'll tell you the whole story."

"*My* damned horse, Warefield."

Maddie watched the two of them stroll back to the stable, knowing she was being excluded, and wondering what sort of tale the marquis intended to spin about her presence. He'd best fill her in later if there was a lie involved, so she wouldn't trip over it by accident.

"She *what*?" Rafe asked, leaning over the stall door.

"She hit him," Quin repeated, hanging up Aristotle's bridle. "Laid him out flat."

"That's extraordinary."

"It's a deuced lot of trouble." The marquis glanced up at his younger brother and shook his head. "*She's* a deuced lot of trouble."

"Then you probably shouldn't have kissed her." Rafe

grinned. "Not that I blame you. She's a diamond of the first water."

"Which doesn't help me any."

"From what you've said, she seems to know what she wants, Quin. Are you so certain Langley's not the best place for her?"

He'd asked himself the same question over and over. And he kept coming up with the same answer. Or at least, the answer he was willing to voice aloud. "She was wronged. If she wants to go back, that's fine. But she should have a choice about it. I won't have some loudmouthed jackanapes driving her off."

"Fair enough, but if she goes about hitting every rake who insults her, she won't last long here, anyway."

The beginning of an idea tickled at Quin's mind. He needed to think it through a little further, though, before he dared bring it up with Maddie. "How was Africa?"

"Full of angry Dutch settlers." Rafe shrugged. "And hot as Hades." He backed up as his brother exited the stall. "Is she the reason you're not at Whiting? I laid in wait for two hours there this morning, until I finally accosted your groom and he said you were here."

"I'm trying to be the buffer between Maddie and Father. Does he know you're back yet?"

"No." Rafael paused, letting Quin leave the stable ahead of him. "Warefield, you haven't set a date for you and Eloise yet, have you? Because although it's not really my place to say, have you considered another reason you might have Maddie staying h—"

"You're right," Quin said sharply. "It really *isn't* your place to say. And no, I haven't spoken to Eloise about our marriage yet."

"That's a fine welcome home, brother," Rafe said, unruffled. "I imagine I'll receive more of the same from Father."

"He wants you to resign your commission," Quin

informed him, grateful they'd returned to a safer topic. "The idea of your being accepted into the Coldstream Guards was that you'd be stationed in London—not in Africa."

"That was Prinny's idea. I think he got tired of my being more carefully protected than he was."

"Nonsense," Quin countered. "You volunteered. You as much as said you wanted to go to Africa."

"His Grace didn't want me in Belgium, either. I got a nice, shiny medal for that."

"You nearly got yourself killed." Quin gestured at his brother's face. "And His Grace doesn't want you risking your hide."

"What would I do here?"

"I don't know," Quin answered, slowing as Maddie reappeared from behind the line of rosebushes. His heartbeat quickened at the sight of her, as it had every time since he'd first set eyes on her. "Something less dangerous."

"Yes, I can see myself in the priesthood," Rafe returned. "Miss Willits, surely you've not been assigned the task of gardening in return for your room and board at Bancroft House?"

"I like to garden," she said defensively.

"You are a rose among toadstools," he said grandly, lifting the bucket from her arm.

"Thank you." She smiled.

"Ignore him," Quin instructed her, frowning. "He's a terrible flirt."

"It's nice to be flirted with," she returned coyly, batting her eyes at him, which made him feel uncomfortable. "It doesn't happen to me very often anymore."

Rafael chuckled. "Then you must be constantly surrounded by idiots. I'm certain by the end of the Season you'll be wishing everyone would leave off so you can garden."

"I actually have an idea about that," Quin returned.

Her expression went from surprise to dismay to distrust so quickly he couldn't be certain he'd actually seen all of them. "About gardening, or about being left alone?"

"I'll explain later."

Rafe raised his hands. "Don't let me stop you. I'll go give the lion something else to roar at." With a jaunty salute he tossed the bucket to a stable hand and strolled toward the house.

Maddie turned to face Quin and folded her arms over her chest. "Well?"

"The art of the insult," he pronounced with satisfaction.

"Beg pardon?"

"The insult. You let Lumley insult you, and you let him get away with it."

"I hit him," she argued, flushing.

"That doesn't count. You can't keep going about doing that, you may run across someone who will hit you back. Not to mention how uncivilized it is. You have to fight them the same way they fight you: with words."

"What am I supposed to say when some . . . man calls me a whore and asks me to be his mistress?"

"That's *exactly* what we need to figure out."

"You're completely insane," she stated, and turned her back.

Quin grinned. "Now you're getting it."

With a heave of her shoulders, she faced him again. "What?"

"You need to have a reply for anything—any insult anyone might choose to fling at you."

"And how am I going to do that, pray tell?"

"We are going to practice. We'll call it . . . anti-rake training." He tried not to laugh at her suspicious expression. "We'll make it into a contest."

"Anti—you *are* insane."

Actually, the more he thought about it, the better it sounded. "No, I'm not. It's brilliant. Once we've come up with an appropriate reply for every inappropriate comment, you'll be invincible—and uninsultable."

"That's not even a word. Leave me alone, Warefield."

Despite her words, he heard the reluctant humor in her tone. "Why should I be the only man in London to do so?" he asked.

Her fist caught him in the shoulder as he dodged. "Stop it!"

Quin grabbed her hand and pulled her up against him. "No hitting allowed," he warned her. "Wound me with your wit, chit."

She pulled free. "And what good will that do?"

"As you know, word travels swiftly here in London. Once the rakes and disreputables learn that they are the ones who end up looking like fools if they bother you, they'll stop insulting you. And they'll begin respecting you. Or at least fearing you."

She narrowed her eyes. "Are you certain of this?"

"Absolutely."

"All right. But I still think it's ridiculous."

It might turn out to be, but at least it gave her something to think about besides how hurt she'd been last night. Quin smiled after her as she headed back inside. If he'd learned one thing about Maddie, it was that she loved a good fight. And hopefully he'd just given her one.

"What a stupid idea," Maddie muttered.

She sat in the drawing room with the duchess, waiting for the Bancroft men to finish their after-dinner discussion and join them. The conversation continued to grow in volume, which would seem to signal either that it was nearly over, or that bloodshed was about to ensue.

"What's a stupid idea, my dear?" Her Grace lowered her book and eyed Maddie over the top of it.

Maddie flushed. "Nothing, Your Grace. I'm sorry; I was talking to myself."

"Not a proper habit for a young lady to have."

"I don't think I have any proper habits at all," Maddie agreed.

The duchess closed her book. "How was Malcolm when you left him? I should have asked sooner."

Maddie didn't quite know how to take Lady Highbarrow's unexpected solicitude, but it seemed the duchess was beginning to tolerate her a little. "He could move his left arm quite well, and he claimed his legs were beginning to tingle. In his last letter, he said he'd actually taken three steps before he fell on Bill Tomkins."

"Who is Bill Tomkins?"

"Mr. Bancroft's footman."

The duchess nodded. "Do you write him? Malcolm, I mean."

Maddie set aside her embroidery, grateful to have someone to talk to. "Yes. Three times a week."

"And what do you tell him?"

"About the weather, how well everything is going, and how much fun I'm having being back in London."

Faint curiosity touched the duchess's dark green eyes, and she moved over to sit on the couch beside Maddie. "So you lie to him."

"Not exactly," Maddie said hesitantly. "He wanted this for me, though, and I don't wish him to worry."

"Wish who to worry?" Quin said from the doorway.

"Your uncle," Her Grace answered, before Maddie could. "Where's Lewis?"

Rafael dropped onto the couch beside his mother. "He said he was going up to his office to write a letter to King George, asking him to have me dismissed from the army before some filthy African native eats me.''

The duchess lifted an eyebrow. ''Lovely thought, dear.''

''His Grace was appalled as well. Until Quin begets a male heir, I am the spare, after all. Wouldn't do for me to end up in some Zulu's belly.''

Maddie wrinkled her nose, torn between alarm and amusement. ''Ooh. Do stop that.''

Rafe grinned. ''Apologies.''

Quin ignored the joking, looking at Maddie until she lowered her eyes and pretended to be distracted by Rafe and the duchess. He always looked at her that way: as though he was trying to see inside her. It didn't exactly make her uneasy, but it unsettled her—because she liked it.

''What are your plans, then, Madeleine?'' the duchess asked.

Quin looked as startled as Maddie at the first genuine expression of interest Lady Highbarrow had shown. ''I'm not certain, Your Grace. I think I've imposed on your kindness for too long.''

The marquis frowned at her, but Her Grace smiled. ''As I recall, the imposition was not entirely your idea.''

''Nearly an abduction, from what I've heard,'' Rafael seconded.

''Even so, without a sponsor I have no reason to remain in London.'' Maddie glanced at Quin, and then away again.

''You have a sponsor,'' he said, bringing his brother a glass of port. ''I spoke with Eloise yesterday. She was thrilled to offer her assistance. We were to meet her today for luncheon, but she sent a note begging off until tomorrow.''

''Eloise?'' Rafe broke in, raising both eyebrows.

"Yes, Eloise. Aren't you tired after your long journey?"

"From Bristol? Not really." Rafael looked at his brother, then stood, offering the duchess his arm. "Catch me up on the gossip, my dear," he said, as she rose. "I hate to laugh at the wrong people."

They exited the room, though the duchess pointedly left the door open. Quin looked after them for a moment, then took a sip of his port and turned to face her. "Well?"

"Well what?"

"You let Rafe get away without a comment on his blatant snobbery, while I can't look at Lord Batton's fourth footman without you expecting me to know his name and whether he has children."

"I'm not that bad," she protested, wondering why it hadn't occurred to her to be angry at Rafael.

"Yes, you are."

"I am not." She stood. "And I'm going to bed. Good night."

He was silent for a moment, looking toward the window. " 'Bed'?" he finally repeated. "I thought the night would just be beginning for you."

Maddie looked at him sideways, her heart skittering again. "What do you mean?"

"Just that I thought you would be receiving most of your callers late in the evening." Obviously reading her puzzled look, he took a step closer. "Your gentlemen callers, that is," he added.

Abruptly she understood. "Stop it, Quin. I've thought about this, and it's a stupid idea."

"I don't think you really have a choice." He reached up and touched her cheek. "I hope I may be your first caller of the evening."

Maddie shivered at his touch, then slapped his hand away. "I mean it, Quin. Leave me alone."

He grabbed her hand and tugged her up against him. "I warned you before about hitting me," he growled. "Insult me instead."

She took a quick breath, angry and exhilarated at the same time. "I wouldn't have taken you for such a Jack-a-dandy, my lord. Apparently I was mistaken in thinking you had scruples."

Quin pursed his lips. "It's a start, I suppose. But you'll have to do better."

He was right; if insult was the only weapon she was allowed to use to defend herself, she would have to come up with something stronger. "I shall attempt to regroup, my lord," she said. "But I am tired tonight."

Quin studied her expression, then sketched a bow. "As you wish. But Maddie, we're not through here. I'm not about to give up."

As she headed upstairs to her bedchamber, Maddie wondered if Quin had been referring to her predicament, or to her—and she didn't know which to hope for.

The Season might have begun badly for Maddie Willits, but it had been even worse for Charles Dunfrey.

Mr. Wheating from the Bank of England had called at Dunfrey House twice, the second time not even bothering to be polite. Dunfrey had the satisfaction of putting the banker out on his backside, but he knew it was a futile gesture of defiance. Unless his luck at the table or in commerce improved, and soon, the bank would own every piece of his property that wasn't entailed.

And so he read the note sent over from Eloise Stokesley with great interest. It didn't explain much, but the simple fact that the daughter of the Earl of Stafford had written him snared his attention. What the "subject of mutual interest" might be he had no idea, but he had every intention of finding out.

He had been planning to call on Lord Walling, to try

to convince the old fool to forgive at least part of the thousand quid gambling note he'd held for the past year. Instead, he donned a conservative gray jacket and waited impatiently for Lady Stokesley's arrival.

Twenty minutes later, the housekeeper showed Eloise Stokesley into his shabby drawing room. He stood and took her hand. "My lady, I must say, this is an unexpected pleasure."

She pulled her fingers free and sat on the end of his couch farthest from where he stood. "Hardly a pleasure for me, Mr. Dunfrey, I assure you."

He leaned one arm on the mantel and eyed his guest speculatively. "Ahh. How may I help you, then, my lady?"

She removed her gloves and folded them neatly on her lap. "I shall be blunt with you, Mr. Dunfrey."

Dunfrey nodded. "Please."

"You at one time were betrothed to a Madeleine Willits."

He frowned, truly startled. "Yes, I was."

"Then you are partly to blame for this fiasco."

"For which fiasco, if I may be so bold?"

"For leaving her to wander about, stealing other people's men and their fortunes."

Dunfrey left the fireplace and sat beside Eloise. "Begging your pardon, my lady, but what in damnation are you talking about? Madeleine Willits is gone, or dead. And good riddance."

"An interesting way to speak of your intended." Eloise fiddled with her gloves, then set them back down again. "She is neither gone nor dead. In fact, she is living at Bancroft House, with the permission of the Duke of Highbarrow."

Dunfrey stared at her, stunned dismay running coldly into his gut. "Highbarrow? Friendly, naive little Maddie climbed as high as that? By Lucifer, life is unfair."

She nodded. "The Marquis of Warefield himself is seeing her reintroduced into society."

Things suddenly began to make sense. "I thought Warefield was to marry you, my lady."

"He is. And he will." She sat back, curving her fine neck to regard him. "It has come to my attention that being a widower is disagreeable to you."

"In what way?"

"To be more precise, you have run through your late wife's money and are now heavily in debt." She looked pointedly at the carpet, threadbare in at least a half dozen spots.

Dunfrey's back stiffened. "I don't believe that's any of your bloody business, Lady Stokesley."

"Mm. A sensitive subject?" she purred. "I assure you, Mr. Dunfrey; you may speak in complete confidence to me."

Dunfrey looked at her assessingly. Business might not be his forte, but he had a good eye for opportunity. And he sensed that something in this unexpected *tête-á-tête* would come out to his benefit. "I am perhaps a little short of ready blunt this spring," he admitted. "But what does that have to do with Madeleine Willits and your Marquis of Warefield?"

"Everything. Quinlan's assisting her as a point of honor. He wants her to be able to marry well, as though she had never been ruined five years ago—or so he says. I'm even hosting the darling for luncheon this afternoon." She sighed distastefully. "If you publicly forgive her for her misbehavior, you will make the eventuality of a good marriage possible for her."

"And?"

"And I will pay you one thousand pounds for your efforts."

Slowly he smiled. "My, you do want Warefield badly. But isn't he worth more than a thousand quid?"

"Yes, but *she* isn't."

Dunfrey sat back and crossed his arms. "She *was*."

Eloise's perfect brow furrowed. "Beg pardon?"

"Her father, Halverston, was ready to give me three thousand quid to take her off five years ago."

"Seems to me that he would have given you even more to marry her *after* she was ruined."

"My thought exactly. Until the damned chit fled into the night."

She looked at him for a long moment, a slow smile spreading across her face. "You did it on purpose."

Dunfrey shrugged. "Odd bird like her, why not squeeze her father for a little more blunt to compensate me for the embarrassment?"

"Except it didn't work," Eloise surmised. "She ran off before you could suggest the solution to Halverston."

"No great loss. Patricia Giles's father gave me a property in York to make her my bride."

"You sold it off eight months ago, as I recall."

She'd obviously been looking into his personal finances. Which meant she knew that a thousand pounds would hold off the hawks for only a month or so, damn her. He needed a good five or six thousand just to make it through the year and give him any sort of foothold on recovering his financial standing. Dunfrey stood and walked over to the window. "I wonder," he mused, half to himself.

"Wonder what?"

"Are her parents in London?"

Eloise shook her head. "I believe they're expected in a week or so. Why—oh, my," she breathed. She pulled her gloves on again and stood. "Whatever you do with her, I don't care. I simply want her away from Warefield. And if you do that, you'll have my gratitude."

"And your thousand quid," he reminded her.

"And my thousand quid. Good hunting, Mr. Dunfrey."

"The same to you, Lady Stokesley."

"I don't want to go."

Quin stood in the doorway of Maddie's bedchamber, where he seemed to be spending a great deal of his time lately. "We were invited."

"You're her betrothed. I'm already having tea this afternoon with Lady Ashton. You go. I'll stay and have luncheon with Rafe."

The marquis frowned. "I'm not her betrothed—yet. And Rafe's going with us." *Whether he wants to or not.* "Be downstairs in five minutes, Maddie, or I'll carry you down."

Quin strode down the hallway to the billiards room, where Rafael was playing a game against himself. The marquis paused watching him for a moment. "Back in London after a year, and you stay in your parents' house and play billiards? Alone? You?"

Rafe glanced up at him, then made another superb shot. "I'm just daft. Ignore me."

"What's wrong?"

"Nothing. Things were just . . . getting a bit sticky in Africa. I needed a rest."

Quin leaned his hands against the billiards table. "What's wrong, Rafael?" he repeated.

His brother shrugged. "Nothing. Really. And I think you have enough to worry about without my adding to the confusion."

"And just what do I have to worry about?"

"Like what excuse you're going to think up this year to delay marrying Eloise."

"I *am* going to marry Eloise this year."

Rafe eyed him distastefully. "Why?"

"Because I gave my word. And because she'll make

a fine wife.'' Quin took a stroll about the room. ''And it wasn't an excuse before; the properties in Cornwall needed to be signed over, and I had to be there.''

''Mm-hm.''

''What?''

Rafael nudged a ball across the table. ''You had the right idea last year,'' he muttered, then looked up again. ''Quin—''

''Oh, shut up.'' Quin frowned at him. ''And go change. You're going with us to luncheon.''

''I most certainly am not.''

''Yes, you are.''

''My memories of Africa are becoming fonder by the moment, you know.''

''Look. Maddie's after any excuse to avoid going back into society. You're her latest. She says you're lonely, and she wants to stay and have luncheon with you. So I told her you were coming with us.''

Rafe leaned on his cue stick, his expression brightening considerably. ''She wants to spend time with me? I'm flattered. Perhaps I'll take her on a picnic.''

''No!'' Quin said, too sharply. ''Just go change, will you?''

His brother tossed the stick onto the table and strolled out the door. ''Fine. I'll attend for Maddie's sake—not for yours.''

Quin looked after him. He and Rafael had always gotten along exceedingly well, probably because not much bothered the easygoing younger Bancroft. At the moment, though, he wished his brother back in Africa—anywhere, in fact, except where Rafe and Maddie could become acquainted.

By the time his two reluctant companions came downstairs, he was ready to wish himself somewhere else as well. While Maddie looked lovely in a dark gray gown, she glowered daggers at him. Rafe, on the other hand, had donned his dress uniform, gold-trimmed red and black, and far too formal for anything less than a grand ball.

"Rafe," he complained.

"You look lovely," Maddie told his brother, obviously recognizing a fellow rebellious spirit.

"Why, thank you, Maddie. I think it brings out my eyes." He fluttered his lashes seductively at her as they went outside.

She laughed. "Oh, definitely. You'll be the belle of the luncheon."

"Get in the damned carriage," Quin growled.

"You don't need to order me about." Maddie glared at him once more, then plunked herself down on the barouche seat.

"Don't expect me to feel guilty," Quin retorted, stepping in front of Rafe to take the seat beside her. "This is for your well-being, not mine."

"I remain unconvinced." She leaned forward and tapped Rafe's polished black Wellington boot with one finger. "You don't actually go into battle looking this splendid, do you?"

"Heavens, no." He sat back in the seat. "The dress uniform is only for surrenders, victories, and parties."

"Then why are you wearing it now?" Quin asked, cutting in on Maddie's pointed admiration.

Rafael shrugged. "I figure I'll be declaring either the first or the second before the afternoon is over."

Quin frowned, disgruntled. "You could at least make an attempt to get along with Eloise. I don't know why you decided to dislike her, anyway."

"I believe the feeling is mutual."

"Why *don't* you like her?" Maddie whispered.

"Oh, no. None of that," Quin protested. "I'm working hard enough to stop the gossip about you without your participating in spreading groundless rumors about other people.''

Maddie folded her arms and scooted as far away from him as she could. ''You are a big bully.''

Quin didn't much like that, but he wasn't certain what to do about it. He realized sitting and conversing with Eloise couldn't be easy for Maddie, and he didn't want her becoming defensive before they'd even arrived.

''We've arrived, my lord,'' Claymore said, from the high driver's perch.

He took a deep breath. ''All right, then.''

This time Rafe was quicker, and he helped Maddie to the ground while Quin stewed behind them. He caught up and took Maddie's other arm. ''Might I have a word with you?''

''What are you going to warn me about now?'' she asked, but released Rafe's arm and stopped to look at him.

''Nothing. I. . . .'' He reached out and straightened a strand of her auburn hair. ''I just want you to like her,'' he said quietly.

She met his gaze. ''Why do you care?''

''Because I do.''

The front doors of Stokesley House opened. The butler emerged, followed by Eloise in a patterned green gown that admirably showed off her tall, slender figure.

''Quin,'' she exclaimed, and held out her hands to him.

He took them. ''Eloise, you remember Miss Willits?''

''Of course.'' Eloise shook Maddie's hand warmly. ''I'm so pleased to be able to help you. And I can't believe Mr. Lumley would dare speak to you that way.''

''Thank you,'' Maddie said, her expression noncommittal.

Quin pointed at his brother, who stood observing an

oak tree with apparent fascination. "And my brother, of course."

Eloise glided past him to lead the way into the house. "Rafael," she said smoothly, barely glancing at him. "You look as though you're dressed for a funeral."

Rafael gave a lazy salute and followed her inside. "You know me, ever hopeful."

Maddie's lips twitched, and she leaned closer to Quin. "Why don't they like one another?" she whispered, her breath soft and warm against his cheek.

"I'm really not certain," he returned in the same tone, relieved and grateful that she seemed to have forgotten her anger at him. "Rafe claims to have reason, but he's never explained it to me. Eloise won't talk about him. Whatever it was, it apparently happened shortly after Rafe returned from Waterloo." He shrugged. "Politics, perhaps."

She looked sideways at him, but at least she didn't disagree with him aloud. In truth, he hadn't a clue. He had merely been hoping that whatever it was, it would go away before the wedding.

"Miss Willits," Eloise said as their party headed through the library and out to the small garden, "did you have any particular friends we might induce to come calling on you, now that you've returned?"

Maddie shook her head. "No."

"Oh, come now," Eloise coaxed with a smile. "Not one?"

"There is no one whose acquaintance I would care to renew," she said flatly. "Or to recall."

Eloise looked at her for a moment. "My goodness." She turned to Quin. "This makes things rather difficult, don't you think?"

Maddie's expression shifted from defiance to humiliation, and Quin stifled an unexpected spark of anger at Eloise. She had to know Maddie might be sensitive about this, and she was generally more tactful than that. "Not really," he answered her, turning from regarding Maddie. "I wouldn't want friends that fickle, either."

Eloise looked as though she wanted to say something, but instead she gestured them to sit at the table settled in the shade of an elm. "We'll need one more place set," she informed a footman, who hurried off.

"You must tell me all about your adventures after you left London," Eloise urged Maddie, as she took her own seat.

"I don't really consider them adventures, Lady Stokesley. I—"

"Oh, please call me Eloise. I feel as though we are practically family."

Maddie looked skeptical, but smiled. "All right, Eloise."

"I'd be happy to tell you all about my adventures in Africa," Rafe broke in, helping himself to a glass of Madeira.

Eloise looked over at him coldly. "Yes, Rafael, how many native girls did you bugg—"

"You know, Maddie," Quin interrupted hurriedly, surprised at the venom in Eloise's voice, "there's no reason we have to do this all at once. We'd be wiser to feel our way slowly, I think."

Maddie looked at him quizzically. "I wish you'd said that before you threw me to the wolves at the opera."

"I didn't thr—"

"You're right, Quin," Eloise agreed. "I thought we might begin with a luncheon, the day after tomorrow. Just a few of my particular friends would be invited. And then a picnic in the country, you know, with a few more friends, yours and mine."

"Yes, that would be excellent," Quin agreed, ignoring Maddie's glare at being excluded from the plans. "I think my mother was being a bit ambitious with the opera last evening.''

''The waters had to be tested.'' Eloise motioned impatiently at the waiting footmen to serve lunch.

''And they were full of sharks,'' Maddie muttered.

Rafe chuckled, lifting an eyebrow at Eloise when she sniffed distastefully. Whatever antagonism was between them had gotten decidedly worse, and Quin had every intention of finding out what was going on.

Then he looked at Maddie, uncharacteristically quiet as she watched Eloise out of the corner of her eye. He might be curious about Rafe and Eloise, but Maddie came first, he decided—not caring to question why her predicament, and her happiness, had become so important to him.

Chapter 11

"Good Lord, that's frightening." Maddie laughed, her voice and expression delighted.

Quin looked up. Rafael leaned around the corner of the stable, a native African mask pulled down over his face, striking in contrast with his blue coat and black breeches.

Rafe took it off. "I believe it's supposed to be the Zulu god of rain. Perhaps he's meant to scare the droplets out of the sky. Quite effective, I imagine." Rafe strolled into the stable and hung the mask on a bridle peg. "You're going riding?"

Quin swung up onto Aristotle before the gelding could escape to greet his former owner. "Yes, we are," he said shortly, tired of his brother's uncanny ability to sense whenever he wanted to spend time alone with Maddie. "See you in a bit."

Maddie looked at him curiously. Not wanting to give away his thoughts, he turned his attention to adjusting Aristotle's reins. She'd been subdued all yesterday afternoon, which had caused him to spend the evening wondering whether he'd done the right thing in turning her over to Eloise. With his mother forbidden from assisting, though, his cousin was the only other choice.

His almost-betrothed certainly knew the correct people, as did he—but once he thought about it, not many of them actually seemed like anyone Maddie would want to be acquainted with. And yesterday Eloise had been sharp-tongued and out of sorts. Perhaps Rafe's presence had rattled her usually calm demeanor, but the whole venture was becoming a damned nuisance. Things had been much simpler before he'd traveled to Langley Hall—before he'd encountered Maddie Willits.

He glanced at her slender figure as his brother helped her into the sidesaddle. "How do you like Honey?" he asked, indicating the spirited chestnut mare.

Maddie smiled "She's wonderful. I'm going to teach her to come when I whistle."

"You're not supposed to whistle," he pointed out, pleased that she approved of the mare.

"Mind if I tag along?" Rafe asked.

Quin, trying to hide his annoyance, turned the restless Aristotle in a circle. "Yes."

"My thanks, brother." Rafe motioned at the head groom. "Wedders? Saddle me a beast, will you? Unless you'll let me ride Aristotle, Quin," he suggested with a sly smile at his brother.

"Absolutely not."

The three of them headed out to Hyde Park, which sparkled with dewdrops in the cool morning sun. Rafael flanked Maddie on one side, while Quin commandeered the other. No doubt they looked ridiculous, like dogs after the same bone. But at this time of day there were few others about who would notice.

After a few moments of silence, Quin cleared his throat. "This early in the morning, I doubt anyone would see if the three of us found a hollow and became acquainted."

Maddie looked startled, then rolled her eyes. "Oh, not that nonsense again."

"*What*?" Rafe roared. "Are you completely jolter-headed? Apologize!"

Quin kept his attention on Maddie. "No."

"Leave me alone," Maddie snapped. "I'm trying to enjoy myself."

"The two of us together would be much more enjoyable."

"Quin!" Rafe bellowed, surprisingly sounding a great deal like their father.

Quin glanced sideways at him. Just about any lady was fair game for Rafe, and it was unlike him to be so protective.

"Don't make me clobber you," Maddie warned, looking as though she very much wanted to.

"You can't go about pummeling everyone who insults you." He leaned closer. "And it *will* happen again—unless you'd rather surrender to the Edward Lumleys of the world," he pressed, knowing she wouldn't be able to ignore the challenge.

"Of course not. But I doubt he'll be insulting me again, anyway."

Rafe looked from one to the other of them. "What the devil is going on?"

"Anti-rake training," Maddie informed him.

"Anti—are you mad, Quin?"

"Oh, shut up," Quin grumbled, attempting to ignore his unhelpful sibling. "Of course Lumley will continue insulting you. Not to your face, perhaps, but any other time he can. And that will hurt you far more than if you'd disposed of him in the proper manner."

"With a pistol?" she suggested.

Rafael burst into laughter, and she grinned back at him. Quin didn't find it amusing at all.

"Rafe, go away," he suggested through clenched teeth.

"Oh, all right," his brother sighed, no doubt sensing

Quin was ready to knock him out of the saddle. He kicked his gray gelding into a trot, heading across the park toward Rotten Row. "Let me know if I need to avenge your honor, Maddie."

She continued to glare at Quin. "That was mean, Warefield."

"Maddie, this is serious. I want you to be able to hold your head up here."

Her expression hurt, she looked away. "I *can* hold my head up here. I didn't do anything wrong."

He reached out and caught Honey's bridle. "I know that."

When he'd planned this anti-rake training, the difficulty had not been in coming up with suggestive situations. Rather it had been in finding ways to word them so as not to give away his feelings toward her. And it wasn't getting any easier.

"You don't have much of a choice about it, darling. You're going to hear stupid, insulting things. You're ruined, remember? So answer me in kind."

She scowled, her eyes glinting. "All right, Warefield. If I were as glib as you seem to think yourself, I would certainly be able to come up with something much more clever than that with which to insult me—*darling*."

Quin nodded. "A passable riposte."

She looked at him sideways, her expression still dark and angry. "I wasn't joking." Maddie wrenched the bridle free of his grip. "And I'd still rather lay you out as flat as Lumley."

"I might let you, if you'd join me there."

She closed her eyes. "I doubt there'd be room for two, what with your swelled head, my lord."

He stifled a grin. "It's not my head that's swelling."

Maddie blushed, then lifted her chin. "You have a better chance of getting acquainted with your horse than you do with me."

She wasn't shy—that was for damned certain. "You can't respond by saying something more suggestive than what I said to you."

"Oh, so now there are rules?"

"Of course there are—"

"Warefield?"

Lord Avery rode toward them, a smile on his doughy face. Unwilling to have poor, dull-witted Peter face to face with Maddie at her most spirited, he wheeled Aristotle around. "I'll be right back. Don't go anywhere."

" 'Don't go anywhere,' " Maddie mimicked imperiously. "As if a lady would wait about for further insults." Immediately she turned her mare to look for Rafael. She spied him after a moment, surrounded by at least a dozen ladies in carriages, and hesitated. "I don't think so," she said to herself, nervous at the crowd, and headed instead for the nearly deserted Ladies' Mile.

Admittedly, their last exchange had been somewhat amusing, but sometimes she absolutely hated Quin Bancroft. He always believed he knew what was best for her, whether she agreed or not. And unbearably self-righteous, he never had anything pleasant, or comforting, or sweet, or romantic to say to her.

Maddie blinked and drew Honey up short. *Romantic?* Where in the world had that come from? Even if she did like him, even if she happened to be desperately fond of him, he would never consider marriage with someone like her. *A ruined chit*—that was what he'd called her—and that was precisely what she was. But Quin. . . .

Despite all her efforts, and even though he was stupidly stubborn and probably took in stray cats and dogs just because he felt sorry for them, all of her dreams and imaginings seemed to center around him. Not even attractive, easygoing, unattached Rafael stirred her pulse and made her heart pound like Quin did.

Maddie looked down at her hands. It was completely

absurd, for her to fall for the Marquis of Warefield simply because he happened to be the first young, handsome gentleman of her own social status who'd been kind to her, both before and after he'd discovered her identity. And when they kissed, the attraction was certainly mutual. But then again, perhaps he was only being polite. If he was one thing, Quinlan Ulysses Bancroft was unfailingly polite.

She sent the chestnut along the quiet track, enjoying the sensation of actually being alone for once. It had been a long time since she'd been able to do much of anything without Quin barking at her heels.

"My . . . my God!"

Maddie yanked hard on the reins, dragging the mare to a halt. All the blood drained from her face, and suddenly she couldn't breathe. She knew that voice—and she'd hoped never to hear it again. Her eyes closed. She couldn't even look.

"Maddie? Maddie Willits? Is it you?"

At the sound of a horse approaching, Maddie took an uneven breath and opened her eyes again. "Charles," she faltered.

Charles Dunfrey looked the same as she remembered—tall, dark-haired, and exceedingly handsome. His brown eyes gazed at her in obvious astonishment, his square, chiseled jaw hanging open. "It *is* you. I can hardly believe it!"

Neither could she. "Ex . . . excuse me," she managed, and yanked the chestnut's reins around with shaking fingers.

"Don't go. Please. Please."

Hesitating, Maddie turned to look at him again, at his hopeful, earnest expression, and tried to ignore the tide of emotions tumbling her about. *He* had turned *her* away five years ago. He hadn't even wanted to hear her explain. She should be angry—not ill and lightheaded with nervousness. "What do you want, Mr. Dunfrey?"

"I thought I'd never see you again." Charles guided his mount a few slow steps closer, as though he were afraid she might bolt.

"That was what you intended, I believe," she said stiffly, groping for anger, indignation, bitterness—anything to bolster her flagging courage.

He shook his head. "No. I was angry—furious. But when you . . . left, I. . . ." Charles looked down, then met her gaze again. "I had a lot of time to think about things, Maddie."

"So did I."

"I. . . ." he began again, then trailed off. "Good Lord, I'm just so surprised to see you, I don't know what to say. Please, tell me you're not still angry. Might . . . might I call on you tomorrow? Are you staying with your parents?"

"No. They . . . I'm staying at Bancroft House, as a guest of the Duchess of Highbarrow. My parents don't know I'm here."

"At Bancroft House?" He reached out as though he wanted to touch her hand where she tightly clutched the reins. At the last moment he stopped himself. "Might I call on you there?"

Again she hesitated, completely unnerved. "Yes. Yes, if you wish."

"Thank you." With a last glance at her, he turned and rode away.

Maddie couldn't stop shaking. She'd dreaded that meeting for so long, and it had been nothing at all like she had imagined. Nothing.

"What in damnation did *he* want?"

Quin looked like a knight ready to charge into battle for his distressed damsel. His green eyes glinting and narrowed, he glared at Charles Dunfrey's retreating back.

Maddie shook herself. "Nothing."

Quin looked sideways at her, his jaw tight and angry. " 'Nothing?' " he repeated. "You spent a long time discussing nothing, then."

"I think he wanted to apologize."

"Apo—" He snapped his mouth shut and looked after Charles again. "And you let him just apologize? After what he did to you? To your reputation?"

A small thrill ran down her spine. He was jealous—over her. "It would make things much easier for me—don't you think?—if Charles and I were to reconcile?"

"Yes . . . I suppose it would," he agreed, with supreme reluctance.

She nodded. "He's going to call on me tomorrow, at Bancroft House."

He glanced at her again, then away, and she could fairly hear his teeth grinding. "Fine. Splendid." Quin wrenched Aristotle around. "Let's go. Where's my damned brother?"

Quin knew his mood had deepened beyond foul when, less than five minutes after their return from Hyde Park, both Maddie and Rafe deserted him to find the duchess and challenge her to a game of piquet.

Damn Charles Dunfrey, anyway. And damn Maddie, for of course being right about a reconciliation between them. He could toil all summer in an attempt to repair the damage to her reputation, yet Dunfrey could smile at her once in public and do the same.

There was no use denying it any longer, though the very idea made him want to smash some very expensive breakables. He didn't just want Maddie to be restored to society; *he* wanted to be the one to do it. He wanted her to be grateful to *him*. He wanted her to need him—and to love him as much as he did her.

His heart pounding, Quin leaned back against the wall

and stared at the closed door to the drawing room where they sat. Where she sat.

Sweet Lucifer, he *loved* her. Of all the idiotic things he'd ever thought or done in his entire life, this was the worst. Even if she hadn't been ruined, Madeleine Willits was no one with whom he could consider anything more serious than an affair. And at the moment, he would have been happy—ecstatic—to have that.

He could hear the three of them in the drawing room, laughing and chatting while they played cards. Even the duchess had warmed to Maddie. Yesterday she'd accompanied Miss Willits to Lady Ashton's, practically daring His Grace to comment. And she'd convinced the duke to delay sending word to Malcolm that they were returning his disgraceful companion to Langley posthaste.

"What are you moping about now?"

Quin jumped, straightening. "I'm not moping," he said stiffly, as the duke emerged from his office, a fistful of papers in one hand. "I'm deciding."

"Deciding what?" His Grace asked skeptically.

Whether to tell Maddie how I feel about her. "Whether I should plan for a summer wedding or an autumn one," he said instead, remembering Eloise and their twenty-three-year agreement with a kind of detached horror. He looked at his father, seeing the swiftly masked surprise on his stern face.

The duke regarded him levelly. "Why not tomorrow, if you're suddenly so eager?"

"Fine by me," Quin snapped, furious and unsettled and trapped. "I'll send a note over to Eloise."

"Don't try to bluff me, Quinlan," Lord Highbarrow warned.

"I'm not," he said shortly, and turned on his heel. "You'd best send a messenger to King George and tell him we'll be needing Westminster Abbey in the morning,'' he continued over his shoulder. ''I don't imagine that will be a problem.''

''So you intend to have the entire peerage thinking you've got Eloise with child and *I* forced a quick marriage? I should say not!'' the duke roared, his expression darkening. ''You haven't been that much a fool, have you?''

Quin faced his father again. ''I thought I was rutting with Miss Willits,'' he snarled, white-faced. ''Make up your mind, Your Grace.''

''Don't you dare speak that way to me, boy, or I'll see you as well liked in London as that red-haired whore!''

That was enough of that. ''You will *not* speak about Maddie in that manner, you pomp—''

''*I'm* not the one—''

The drawing room door opened. ''Lewis,'' the duchess interrupted in a low voice. No doubt the three of them had heard the entire exchange from the drawing room. Quin winced.

''Victoria, stay out—''

''Please,'' she interrupted. ''Lady Finch and Lady DeReese will arrive here any moment. Calm down.''

''Calm down? *You* tell *me* what to do, wife? Bah! I'm going to White's!'' His Grace stalked down the hallway. ''You'll wed Eloise this summer, Quinlan, or when it comes time for a new Duke of Highbarrow, it won't be you! Is that clear?''

Quin didn't answer; he wasn't expected to. His father had given a direct order, and it would be followed. End of argument, end of conversation. He met his mother's concerned, searching gaze, then nodded stiffly at her and turned on his heel.

Aristotle looked annoyed at being taken out twice in one day. Under the circumstances, Quin had little sympathy for him. He rode over to Queen Street and asked if Eloise was in. She wasn't, but the Stokesley butler gave him the direction of the acquaintance she'd gone to visit.

He felt ridiculous chasing Eloise about London. They'd known one another for so long that he could fairly well predict what her reaction would be if he appeared on the Countess Devane's doorstep, looking for her. She was lovely and intelligent and had been groomed from birth to be the future Duchess of Highbarrow—just as he had been schooled to be the future duke. But he wanted to know something that had abruptly become very important for him to discover. He wanted to know what he felt when he was with her.

He knew what he felt when he and Maddie were in the same room: frustrated, antagonized, and exhilarated. In truth, whether he felt anything toward Eloise, it didn't matter. He had always known he would marry her, and so he would. But he continued to Devane's home anyway, climbed the shallow steps, and rapped on the door.

"Lord Warefield." The butler bowed as Quin handed over his calling card and his request. "If you would care to wait in the foyer."

Only a few moments later Eloise appeared from the direction of the upstairs drawing room. "Quin, is something wrong?" she asked, descending the steps toward him.

"No," he said, taking her hand. "I just . . . wanted to make certain I wasn't imposing on you the other day, when I asked you to help me with Maddie."

She smiled warmly. "Of course not. In fact, I was just arranging for Miss Harriet DuChamps and Lady Devane to join us for luncheon tomorrow."

"Good. I appreciate your assistance."

"I'm happy to help." She looked at him for a moment, her perfect brow furrowing just a little. "Was there something else?"

"No. No, of course not." He started to turn away, then stopped again. He had to know. "Eloise, might I . . . make a request of you?"

"Anything, Quin."

Quin glanced up and down the hallway, which was thankfully deserted, and cleared his throat. "Might I kiss you?"

The brief look of puzzlement passed from her face, and she smiled again. "I would like that."

Taking a short breath, Quin stepped closer. He lowered his head as she lifted hers, and he brushed his lips against her soft mouth. For a long moment he lingered there, tasting her mouth, hearing her soft sigh.

Finally he stepped back again. "Thank you."

"Well," she prompted, smiling faintly, "how was it?"

He returned her smile. "Wonderful, Eloise. I just realized I had never kissed you in all this time. I'll see you tomorrow." He bowed and turned away.

"Quin?"

The marquis stopped. "Yes?"

"We need to decide on a date. If we delay much longer, no one will be around to celebrate with us."

"Yes, I know. I'm . . . working out the schedule with His Grace. Soon, though. It will be soon."

He made his way outside, and back to Aristotle. There he stopped, one hand on the gelding's bridle. She'd given him the perfect opportunity to declare himself, and he had done nothing. Well, nothing except admit to himself that he really had no interest at all in his wife-to-be—and a great deal of interest in a woman who could never be his.

"Hm, and what did Lord Warefield want?" Joanna, Lady Devane, curled a strand of her blond hair around and around her finger.

Eloise smiled and resumed her seat. "To kiss me," she murmured, and sipped her tea.

Harriet DuChamps sat forward. "To what?"

"To kiss you?" Joanna repeated skeptically. "He came all this way just for that?"

"We *are* to be married, you know," Eloise pointed out. "And he does dote on me."

"Seems to me he dotes on someone else these days," Lady Devane suggested.

"Quin's always been kind and generous. The poor little ruined bitch had nowhere else to go." She set aside her tea and leaned forward. "And our task, ladies, is to find her somewhere else to go. Posthaste."

Harriet giggled. "They drown unwanted puppies, don't they?"

Joanna and Eloise laughed, and Eloise resumed nibbling at her teacake. "I'll set a large punch bowl at luncheon tomorrow, just in case."

Charles Dunfrey sighed as his coach rattled to a halt. What a blasted nuisance, having to leave London in the middle of the Season. And for a trip to Devonshire, of all places, where there would be absolutely nothing of interest to do, and no one of interest to see.

Half surprised the vehicle had made the journey intact, Dunfrey settled his hat on his head and stood as the door opened. "Good evening, Hoskins," he said, stepping to the ground. "Would the viscount be in this evening?"

The butler stared at him open-mouthed for a moment, astonishment in every line of his thin, dignified countenance. "Mr. . . . Mr. Dunfrey. Yes, he . . . he is. This way, sir."

Hoskins showed him into the drawing room, and in his hurry to leave and inform his employer of their visitor, slammed the door behind him. Dunfrey smiled briefly, then wandered about, looking at the old familiar porcelain miniatures and collection of crystal vases. Little had changed in five years. He turned around as the door opened again.

The tall, silver-haired gentleman standing in the doorway looked poised between shock and dismay as he looked at his houseguest. Dunfrey could little blame him. He'd never thought to set eyes on the viscount again, himself.

Dunfrey bowed. "Good evening, Lord Halverston. I apologize for not sending advance word that I was coming, but I didn't know myself, until this morning." He gave an apologetic, slightly embarrassed smile. "Might I trouble you for a glass of port? I'm . . . a little unsettled."

The viscount nodded warily and motioned at the butler lurking in the hallway behind him. "Hoskins, port." He stepped into the drawing room and closed the door.

For a moment Dunfrey wished he'd asked for Lady Halverston, as she would be easier to deal with, but he didn't want either of them to go running off until he'd had a chance to explain things properly.

"Forgive my directness, Charles," the viscount said, in his dry voice, "but what brings you to Halverston? We did not part well, last time we spoke."

Shaking his head, Dunfrey sat at one end of the couch. "No, we did not," he said earnestly. "And I wish to apologize for that, as well. I . . . well, heat of the moment, you know."

The viscount nodded.

Dunfrey shifted, genuine nervousness augmenting his intentional appearance of agitation. If things went badly this evening, he wouldn't be willing to wager over his ability to avoid debtors' prison. "Well. I don't quite know how to say this. Ah, I—this morning, I saw . . . I saw Madeleine."

Lord Halverston's face went white. "Madeleine? You saw Maddie? My daughter, Maddie?"

Dunfrey hurried to his feet and helped Viscount Halverston into a chair before his knees could buckle, while his own mood continued to lift. Given the circumstances, Robert's continued interest in his daughter's whereabouts could only bode well for him—he hoped. "Yes. Actually, I spoke to her."

"Where is she?" Robert Willits asked, gripping the arms of his chair.

This would be the difficult part. He needed to make himself essential to all this. If Halverston thought himself able to go around outside assistance to get to his daughter, everything would be lost. "In London."

"Lon—where in London?"

"My lord, she seemed none too eager to speak to me, or to speak of you, other than to say that you didn't know she was there. Forgive my curiosity, but I . . . assume that you have not reconciled with her?"

"We haven't been able to find her to do so," Lord Halverston admitted, deep reluctance edging his voice. "Is she well?"

"She is beautiful," he answered truthfully. "Even more so than she was at eighteen." In fact, it had been almost disappointing to see her looking so well. She hadn't pined over him a bit, no doubt.

"Did she say where she's been? Is she—"

"Please, my lord." Dunfrey offered Robert another embarrassed smile. "I spoke to her only briefly. I . . . didn't want to press her tolerance. I have a great deal to make amends for, where she is concerned."

The viscount looked at him assessingly. "You wish to make amends, then?"

Dunfrey nearly smiled at Halverston's hopeful tone. "Yes. Yes, I do. You know that I married after Maddie disappeared. My wife . . . Patricia was dear to me, but she has been gone for over a year now. And when I saw Maddie this morning—well, I realized that she has stolen back into my heart, Robert. Time heals all wounds, they say.''

''So they do, Charles.''

''I am to call on her tomorrow. I thought, though, that you would want to hear my news immediately. And I also wanted your permission to proceed.''

''You still want to marry her, then? Even though you know nothing of her whereabouts for the past five years?''

This was almost too easy. ''My lord, of course I know I'm taking a risk with my reputation. I may very well be censured for my actions if I renew my offer to take Maddie as my wife. And the Lord knows, since Patricia's death, things have not been easy.'' He shrugged. ''But I have come to believe that I owe Maddie another chance.''

The viscount sat forward, his color returning. ''You are a good and understanding man, Charles. I have always thought so.''

''Thank you, Lord Halverston. It is my dearest hope that I shall be able to convince Maddie of the same.''

''Where is she, then?'' the viscount repeated.

Dunfrey had hoped he would forget the question. That, he supposed, would have been too much to hope for. ''I will tell you, but might I suggest a plan of action first? No one wants her to flee again, I'm certain.''

''No, of course not,'' the viscount agreed hastily. ''What's your idea, Dunfrey?''

''Well, she has apparently won the favor of the Duchess of Highbarrow.''

''Highbarrow? My goodness!'' Lord Halverston looked stunned for the third time that evening. ''The Duchess of Highbarrow?''

''Yes. She admitted to me—reluctantly—that she was

staying in the Bancroft household. That is where I'm to call on her tomorrow afternoon.''

For the second time, Viscount Halverston looked hopeful. ''That's an exceedingly good sign, I would say. Please proceed, Charles.''

''Of course,'' Dunfrey agreed, stifling a triumphant smile. He had Halverston now. ''I think you should repair to London, in the—''

''Yes, at once,'' the viscount said eagerly.

''No, no . . . she would know that I had betrayed her trust. You must delay a week or two, and then come to London on some pretext or other. Then we can carefully arrange for you to come across her as if by accident . . . as I did.''

The viscount was nodding. ''I agree. We don't want her upsetting the duchess and taking flight again.''

''Absolutely not. I don't wish to risk losing her again.'' *Or her dowry.* That, though, could be negotiated later, once he had her safely in hand.

Halverston took a breath. ''Nor do I.''

Dunfrey stood. ''Splendid. I should get back to London posthaste. It would never do for me to miss calling on her.''

''You have my deepest gratitude, Charles.''

This time Dunfrey's smile was genuine. ''Thank you, Robert.''

Maddie looked about at her newfound acquaintances. Quin continually reminded her that she was of noble birth, and that she had as much right to hold her head up as anyone else. Rare and appreciated as the compliment had been, he really had no idea what he was talking about.

Even before she'd been ruined, she'd never moved in circles this golden. Daughters, wives, and sisters of this duke, that marquis, and a twelfth-generation viscount surrounded her, gossiping and nibbling daintily on pastries. She'd seen most of them during the short course of her debut Season but had never imagined actually being invited to luncheon with them. She stifled a grimace as a crumb fell from her peach pastry onto the floor. Even less had she thought to be the reason for such a luncheon.

"He actually fell over?"

Lady Margaret Penwide covered her mouth with her hand as she chuckled. "Oh, no. Mrs. Grady stopped his fall."

Eloise, seated beside Maddie, smiled at her and briefly squeezed her hand. The gesture was no doubt meant to be encouraging, but it caused another piece of pastry to break free. This one landed on Maddie's foot.

"She didn't!"

"I suppose it wasn't her fault, for given her girth, she undoubtedly couldn't get out of the way. But she ended up standing there in the middle of Hyde Park with Francis Henning hanging onto her bosom with both hands."

The rest of luncheon went like that, with someone revealing an embarrassing piece of gossip about a mutual acquaintance, and everyone else laughing over it. For Maddie the barbs seemed a little too familiar to be amusing. At the same time, five years ago she hadn't been all that different from Eloise and her friends. She had been a fool.

"Miss Willits?"

She looked up, surprised, as a dark-haired lady sat beside her: Beatrice Densen, she vaguely remembered, a refined lady several years older than Maddie, with a reputation—at least five years ago—for giving elegant salon parties. "Miss Densen," she replied.

"Excuse me a moment, my dear," Eloise said from her other side, and stood. "I need to see to the desserts."

"Of course."

"Miss Willits, if I may be so bold, I have always thought society treated you very cruelly," Beatrice said, taking Maddie's hand.

The abrupt intimacy left her feeling rather uneasy, but she smiled. At least someone was bothering to talk to her instead of simply staring, or worse yet, watching out of the corner of their eye. "Thank you."

"My brother, Gaylord, and I were planning a quiet evening tonight. Could I entice you to join us? Gaylord is a fair whist player."

Maddie smiled. Quin probably wouldn't approve, because it wasn't part of his carefully laid-out plan. "I would love to," she answered.

Beatrice smiled back at her. "I will come around for you myself, at seven, then."

"Thank you."

At half past two, the Warefield coach clattered onto the Stokesleys' short drive to bring her back to Bancroft House. Maddie looked at the red and yellow crest emblazoned on the carriage door in disgust. For someone trying to repair her reputation, Quin certainly had an odd way of going about it.

She'd heard the speculation, carefully out of Eloise's hearing, over why the marquis might be staying with his parents rather than his own perfectly lovely Whiting House. And then she heard her own name as the possible reason.

Still, she decided as she climbed into Quin's coach, at least they had all been kind and polite to her face. She hadn't expected even that much courtesy from them. And she'd handled herself rather well. She hadn't spilled any more than a few crumbs, which she had managed to hide beneath her skirts, and she'd been invited to a dinner. Altogether, she supposed she'd won some sort of victory.

When the coach entered the Bancroft House drive,

though, she changed her mind. Charles Dunfrey's carriage stood there already, waiting. A flutter of nervousness quaked through her. Luncheon had been the easy part.

"Miss Willits, you have a caller," the butler informed her.

"Yes. Thank you, Beeks," she said, her fingers shaking as she removed her hat and shawl, handing them over to his care.

The butler nodded. "You will find him in the drawing room." He hesitated. "Best of luck, Miss Maddie."

She looked at him, surprised. "Thank you."

Her heart pounding, Maddie slowly climbed the stairs. With each step she tried to convince herself that whatever Charles said or thought about her didn't matter. He'd broken off their engagement, and she'd made a life for herself completely independent of him and her parents.

At the top of the stairs, she stopped. Quin stood in the doorway of the library, an open book resting in his hands. He glanced up at her, jade flashing beneath long, black lashes, and then went back to his reading.

"How was luncheon?" he said to the book as she passed by.

"No one called me any terrible names," she returned.

"Did anyone speak to you?"

"It is none of your affair."

"I think it is," he said with more heat, lifting his head again to look at her.

"Then you are wrong."

Before he could reply to that, she opened the drawing room door and stepped inside.

Charles stood as soon as she entered. He looked as uncomfortable as she felt, which actually left her a little more at ease. "Mr. Dunfrey," she said, in as calm a voice as she could manage. "Good afternoon."

"Must we begin with such formality?" he asked. "Please call me Charles."

She nodded. "Very well . . . Charles. Shall I ring for tea?"

He looked at her for another moment, then visibly shook himself and motioned for her to take a seat. "Yes, please."

They were both silent as a footman entered with a tea tray, then vanished again through the open door. Maddie dearly hoped that Quin was not still standing in the library doorway, where he would be able to hear clearly everything that was said. But even if he was, she didn't dare close the door. Here, she most especially needed to behave with propriety. Unnecessary and pointless as she had decided Charles's apology would be, she wanted to prove to him that he had been wrong about her.

"I cannot get over how beautiful you've become," he said into the silence, and she jumped. "And you were a rose among thorns before."

"Thank you. You haven't changed, I don't think."

He chuckled. "You are very kind, my dear."

The mantel clock softly chimed the hour, while Maddie sipped her too hot tea and tried desperately to think of something to say. "I heard that you married," she finally ventured.

"Yes, yes. Patricia Giles. She was several years older than you, I believe. From a good family, though."

"I was sorry to learn of her passing."

Charles nodded. "Thank you. You have a good heart, Maddie. I don't know if I could be so generous, were our positions reversed." He bowed his dark head for a moment. "Maddie, I broke with Spenser the night you . . . I . . . I saw the two of you. He—"

"Charles, I—"

"No, please," he cut across her interruption. "Let me say this. He wrote me several months ago, confessing that he'd been drinking and that his attentions to you had been unwelcome.''

Maddie looked at him for a long moment, a thousand thoughts tumbling through her mind. ''So you know the truth.''

''Yes. Actually, I think I realized it quite a long time ago. When I first saw the two of you, I was so angry . . . jealous and hurt, I think. I wanted to be the only man you'd ever kissed.''

An image of Quin jumped into her head. His warm lips, the light in his eyes when he looked into hers . . . ''I wanted that as well, Charles. But that is an impossibility, and I will not dwell on it.''

He sat forward, taking the teacup and saucer from her hands, and grasping her fingers. ''I do not want you to dwell on it,'' he said earnestly, holding her eyes. ''You have suffered, away from your family and friends, for five years. And not because of your own actions, but because of mine.''

''Charles. . . .''

He knelt at her feet. ''Maddie, do you think, with your generous heart, that you might perhaps—not right away, of course—but do you think eventually you might be able to forgive me?''

She'd dreamed of this, in the first few months after she'd fled London—dreamed of everyone who'd been so awful to her, coming and begging on their hands and knees for her forgiveness. And even five years later, it still felt quite . . . satisfying. ''Yes, Charles. I think I might be able to forgive you.''

He smiled. ''Thank you, Maddie.''

''I—damn it!''

Maddie jumped again, pulling her hands free while Charles swiftly stood. Rafael stumbled into the drawing room with none of his usual grace.

''Rafe, what—''

"Beg pardon, Maddie. Tripped, or something." He turned his attention to Charles. "I say, you're Dunfrey, aren't you?" Rafe strode forward and clasped her former betrothed's hand. "Rafael Bancroft."

Charles looked at him somewhat warily as he retrieved his hand. "I'm pleased to finally meet you, Captain. I've heard a great deal about you."

"Only the good parts are true." Rafe grinned and winked at Maddie. "That your barouche out front?"

"Yes, yes it is. I hope—"

"Fine pair of bays you have there. Wouldn't be interested in selling 'em, would you?"

"My—well—I really hadn't thought about it."

Rafe clapped him on the back, leading him toward the door. "Well, think about it, Dunfrey. I might be willing to part with as much as a hundred quid for the pair, if they're sound."

"A hundred. . . ." Charles looked over his shoulder at Maddie, who sat watching the men's departure with a mixture of relief, disbelief, and amusement. "Maddie— Miss Willits—might I call on you again?"

"Yes, you may."

They disappeared down the hallway. Maddie took a deep breath, and sinking back in the well-cushioned chair, slowly let it out again and closed her eyes. Charles Dunfrey still liked her. Handsome, witty Charles Dunfrey had apologized, and he wished to call on her again.

"The rat's gone, is he?"

Maddie opened one eye to regard the tall, lean figure in the doorway. "As if you didn't know."

"And what do you mean by that, pray tell?" Quin folded his arms across his chest.

The other eye opened as well. "You practically threw poor Rafe in here on his head."

"I did no such thing."

"Well, I really don't care, one way or the other. Miss

Densen invited me to dinner with her and her brother.''
She stood.

"Having dinner with the Densens is not part of the
plan," he said, straightening to block her exit from the
room.

"You're just angry because perhaps you're not quite
so necessary anymore, Warefield," she shot back at him,
shoving against his hard chest with her palm and stalking past him.

Quin looked after her, his eyes narrowed. " 'Not quite
so necessary,' " he mimicked darkly. "Ungrateful
chit.''

Chapter 12

"**Q**uin, I have to admit, your little project is marvelous." Eloise hid the words behind her fine ivory fan. "There's nothing like a diversion to liven up the Season. And you were right, of course: Maddie is actually quite nice, if a bit quiet."

" 'Quiet?' " Grateful for the darkened opera house, Quin lifted an eyebrow in keen curiosity. "How so?"

"Well, perhaps 'quiet' isn't precisely the right word. But you really can't blame her for being reserved. I would be a bit timid myself, not knowing how anyone would react to my presence. I practically had to tie Lady Anne Jeffries to a chair to convince her not to cut poor Madeleine and actually leave the luncheon."

"Maddie seemed to think it went fairly well," Quin said in a low voice. At least the opera below was fairly energetic, so no one was likely to overhear the conversation. "She spoke of a dinner invitation this evening." Actually, she'd thrown it in his face, but he didn't care to go into that.

"Yes. I advised her against it, but I think she was just grateful to have been invited."

Quin straightened. "What do you mean, you 'advised

231

her against it'? Miss Densen is a good friend of yours, is she not?''

''Beatrice is, yes—if a little . . . eccentric. But I would not vouch for Gaylord and his cronies. They—''

'' 'They'?'' Quin repeated sharply, suddenly and absurdly alarmed. ''Maddie said it was to be a private dinner, with just the Densens.''

Eloise rapped him on the arm with her fan. ''You need to spend more time in London.''

''So enlighten me.''

She sighed. ''Gaylord has been holding mixed-gender card parties at his home for better than a year. They began quite modestly—I even attended one myself. But lately—well, very few virtuous ladies attend any longer.'' She shrugged. ''As I said, I tried discreetly to warn her. But Maddie's . . . obstinate nature is what got her into such trouble before, no doubt.''

Densen's mansion was only ten minutes or so from the opera house. Quin stood. ''I should go get her.''

''Don't you dare leave me here to go chasing after Maddie Willits,'' Eloise protested. ''You've already gone far beyond settling any debt. And *I* have listened to enough rumors about why the Bancrofts have been so helpful and generous to a little social insignificant like her.''

Slowly Quin retook his seat. ''I beg your pardon?'' he murmured angrily, even though she was clearly correct.

She reached out to put a hand on his arm. ''It's what everyone is saying, Quin. I wanted you to hear it. Don't be blinded by your wish to do a good deed.''

''I'm not blinded by anything,'' he returned firmly, if not absolutely truthfully.

She sat back and looked at him. ''Very well. I am only concerned. Your first duty is to your family.''

Angrier still at her censure, he took a breath, flexing

his shoulders to try to release some of the tension. "I am aware of that, Eloise."

"We must remain friends, Quin," Eloise said. "I know you are fond of Maddie—you've always taken pity on poor, lost creatures. I only ask that you keep your obligation to help her in perspective."

She was right—again—and he still didn't like hearing it. He still wanted to rush off and rescue Maddie from her own poor judgment. As Eloise had said, though, Maddie's obstinacy in going her own way had likely caused all her troubles in the first place. And he had his own troubles—obligations—to take care of.

"Eloise, might I escort you to Bond Street tomorrow?" he said, by way of answer. "I believe we have something of mutual interest to discuss."

She smiled. "It would be my pleasure, Quin."

Assuming a stolidly stone-faced expression, Maddie stepped past Beeks into Bancroft House's main hallway. They knew only that she'd gone to dinner with the Densens. There was no need for anyone to hear anything further, nor any explanation as to why it had taken her so long to return to her temporary haven. Especially Quin: she'd never hear the end of it if he learned that she'd been to a raucous card party and practically had to bribe the butler to find her a hack so she could leave.

"How was dinner?"

Maddie jumped and whipped around to see Quin exiting the darkened morning room, his expression tense and angry.

"What were you doing in there?"

"Reading," he said shortly. "How was dinner?"

No doubt sensing trouble, Beeks flashed her a sympathetic look and fled downstairs into the kitchen. Maddie put her hands on her hips. "Reading, in the dark? You were spying on me, waiting for me to come back."

"Do you really think I have nothing better to do than sit around and wait for you?"

"Apparently not." Maddie flounced past him, heading up the stairs to her bedchamber.

He followed right behind her. "At least tell me whether you enjoyed Gaylord Densen's company."

A flush reddened her cheeks. "He's very amusing."

A hand snaked around her waist and jerked her sideways with surprising strength. Trying to keep from falling over, Maddie grabbed onto Quin's shoulder and arm as he half-dragged her into the drawing room.

"What in the world are you doing?" she demanded, staggering away from him.

Quin closed and locked the door, then turned to face her. He leaned back against the sturdy oak frame. "We are going to have a little chat."

"More of your stupid rules? How can you possibly have thought up still more of them?"

"Practice."

"I'm very tired. I'd like to go to bed."

"Without telling me about Gaylord Densen's little card party?"

Maddie snapped her mouth shut, any thought of confessing that she'd been misled about the nature of the evening's engagement vanishing. He had no right to act so superior. "What do you wish to know about it, then, my lord?"

He stepped closer to her. "Why didn't you listen to Eloise's advice about going there? She warned you about it."

"She did no such. . . ." Maddie looked at him, then walked over to the writing desk under the window to give herself a moment to think. She couldn't possibly tell Quin; he'd never believe her. "I don't know," she said instead.

"You don't know?"

"Oh, leave me alone."

She tried to push him out of the way, but he didn't budge. Instead, he grabbed her hands and pulled her up against his chest. "You are too bright for me to believe that you don't know why you would attend a card party with a herd of disrespectables. Do you really want that badly to leave here? Or was everyone correct about you encouraging Spenser?"

Her heart wrenched. "How dare you?" she spat, jerking free of his strong grip and stalking back across the room.

"A little less witty tonight, aren't you, dear? Exhausted, no doubt."

When she turned to glare at him, his jade eyes glittered with anger. But fury wasn't the only expression that touched his face. He desired her. He wanted her—and whatever tremors of need and want that triggered in her own soul, it abruptly made several things quite clear. "That's why you dragged me to London in the first place, isn't it?"

His expression darkened further. "What are you talking about?"

"When you kissed me at Langley—you as much as said you wanted me to be your mistress. You still do. You think I really *did* encourage Spenser—so why would I have any objection to the great, grand Marquis of Warefield's attentions?"

He strode toward her, then with obvious effort stopped himself, clenching his fists. "That is absolutely not true, and you know it, Maddie."

"Then why am I here?"

Quin glared at her. "Because Uncle Malcolm asked me to bring you here—and because I behaved poorly and wanted to make amends for it."

She narrowed her eyes. "Oh, really?"

"Yes, really." He jabbed a finger at her. "The least

damned thing you could do is cooperate a little. For God's sake, would it kill you to admit that you're grateful to me?''

She pounced on the word. "Grateful? Grateful? For what? For being able to have stupid, drunken men try to grab my breasts and make idiotic jokes about me?"

"What in damnation are they supposed to think, when you attend gatherings like that? If you behave like a slut, they'll treat you like one!"

The vase was in Maddie's hands almost before she realized she'd snatched it up. With a furious hiss, she dashed the contents into his face. "Self-righteous ass!"

Water dripping down his finely chiseled nose, Quin grabbed her arm. Maddie, more furious than she could ever remember being, wrenched free of his grip. With a loud rip her delicate sleeve tore off in his hand. He glared at it in shock, then flung it to the ground and advanced on her again. "Lightskirt!"

"Oh, now you've hurt me," she taunted, and kicked him in the knee. "Tearing a dress you paid for—you beast!"

"Ow, damn it! That's right—I own almost everything you have on." He yanked off her other sleeve as she gasped in outrage. "And I get nothing in return. You probably gave more to Gaylord and his cronies tonight for fun!"

She grabbed up a porcelain miniature and hurled it at him. "Bastard! You said you didn't *want* anything in return!"

The diminutive Caesar hit his shoulder and fell to the carpet in a hundred pieces. Quin grabbed the room's second vase, and a cascade of cold water and daisies doused Maddie. "I don't anymore!"

She shrieked and flung pillows from the long couch at him. "Liar! I can't even imagine how dull your life must be—no wonder you keep me about!"

"That little error will be remedied tomorrow. And my life is perfectly happy without you in it!" he yelled, throwing a pillow into her face.

She hurled it back at him. "Ha! So that's why I'm all you talk about with your mother and brother—because *you're* so *exciting*."

"Hoyden!"

He grabbed for her again and she spun away, but her skirt came to a sudden stop without her. Ripping free of its stitches, it tangled around her legs and sent her tumbling against the writing desk. Her hair, drenched and coming down from its clips, hung in her face. She swiped it out of the way and spied the brass letter opener engraved with His Grace's initials. "You arrogant, stuffy—" She lifted the letter opener and swung her arm at him.

One of his waistcoat buttons flew off, the threads neatly slashed in two.

"That *is* why you want me about," she panted, her heart beating so furiously she thought it must explode. He backed away warily, looking for an opportunity to grab her weapon away from her. "Because you are so very *dull*."

"I am *not* dull."

Slash went another button to the floor. "Dull!"

He stopped when his back came up against a bookcase.

"Dull!" Through her fury, an odd, fluttering tingle began along her nerves, making her hand shake.

His eyes met hers, his anger deepening into something else entirely. "Damned nuisance," he growled.

The last button came free and rolled beneath the couch. *"Dull,"* she breathed.

Quin grabbed her chin in his fingers and tilted her face up; his mouth closed roughly over hers. He pried the letter opener from her hand and flung it into the corner.

Maddie's pulse raced as her frustrated outrage swept into an equally fierce, wanting desire. She pressed herself against him, pulling his coat and then the buttonless waistcoat from his shoulders. She twined her fingers into his damp honey-colored hair and kissed him hungrily, matching his angry passion with her own.

He took the few threads of dress remaining around her shoulders and ripped them in two. His strength was a little frightening, yet wonderfully exhilarating. "Maddie," he murmured hotly, turning them so that she was the one pinned hard against the bookcase.

She couldn't stop kissing him. She didn't *want* to stop kissing him, and touching him. Her dress was nothing but a tattered rag hanging about her waist until he tore it free and dropped it to the carpet, leaving only her thin, flimsy shift covering her.

He pulled his fine lawn shirt free of his breeches, trailing his mouth along her jawline. What they were doing, she knew distantly in the part of her brain that remained sane, was very, very wrong. And she didn't care. All that mattered was that he didn't stop.

Maddie moved his hands out of the way and tugged the wet shirt over his head. She moaned as his lips found the hollow of her throat, and her fast-beating pulse. Her heart fluttered wildly as he pushed the one remaining strap of the shift from her shoulders, and kissed the bare skin it revealed.

"Oh, God," she murmured, gasping for another unsteady breath as the shift slid down her body to the floor.

He pushed her harder against the bookcase, as though trying to bring them still closer together. Quin covered her mouth with his again, as if to stifle any protest she might make. His hands slipped from her shoulders and down to her breasts, and she drew another ragged breath at his intimate touch.

Maddie ran her hands down his hard, smooth chest, and the muscles jumped beneath his skin. He captured one of her hands and lowered it to the fastenings of his breeches. She could feel his hard, growing arousal, and with fumbling, unsteady fingers undid the fastenings and freed him from confinement.

Twisting, Quin half pushed and half carried her down to the floor. His hot, hungry mouth immediately sought her breasts, and she tangled her hands in his hair and arched against him as her nipples hardened at the caress of his tongue. He must be insane, to want her—and to want her in his parents' own drawing room—and she must be equally mad to encourage him.

His hands swept down her flat belly to her rounded hips, squeezing and kneading her buttocks and pulling her against him. Quin's mouth claimed hers again as he stretched the long, lean length of his body atop hers. His skin against hers was warm and intimate, and when his knee nudged hers apart, she arched her hips again, feeling his throbbing manhood brushing against her thigh.

Moaning as his mouth teased hers open, their tongues caressing, Maddie slid her arms around his strong, muscular shoulders, holding him against her. "Quin," she whispered breathlessly.

He entered her with a growling moan of possession. At her gasp of pain and surprise and wonder, he froze. "Jesus," he muttered raggedly. Burying his face against her shoulder, he held his body very still except for the tremors of tension along his arms. He lifted his head again, his dark green eyes burning into hers. "Jesus," he repeated. "You *were* a virgin."

Before she could gather her wits enough to say that of course she was a virgin, he kissed her again, deeply and roughly. Slowly his hips began to move again, forward and back against her, inside her, and she gasped again. "Oh, Quin, that feels so good," she groaned, lifting her hips to meet his increasing rhythm. "You feel so good."

"God, so do you," he answered, shifting his arms so he could lean down and nibble at her ear. "Hold onto me, Maddie. It gets even better."

Waves of ecstasy made her whole body tremble as he made love to her. She wasn't certain she would live through anything better than this. Her ankles lifted around his hips, as though her body already knew what to do. She threw back her head, half-closing her eyes at the erotic, intimate feeling of him, of Quin, moving inside her.

Another shiver of tension began in her most secret core, and then grew until it exploded into a pulsing, shivering jumble of indescribable delight. Maddie cried out, her entire body arching. Above her Quin thrust deep and fast into her a few more times, and then convulsed against her. Slowly he collapsed on top of her, his weight hard and muscled and welcome.

All of the fight driven out of her, Maddie concentrated on regaining her breath and her senses, and absolutely not on contemplating what she and Quin had just done. And what she already wished he would do again.

Quin closed his eyes, savoring the warm, soft feeling of her body beneath his. Having just made possibly the greatest mistake of his thirty years, he probably should feel considerably worse than he did. The most he could manage, though, was a dim sense that his complicated life had just become much more confused.

The wild pounding of his heart gradually slowed, and with a deep breath he lifted his head to look down at her. "Why didn't you tell me?"

Puzzlement showed briefly in her eyes. "Tell you what?"

"That even after Spenser, in all your five years away from London, you'd managed to remain . . . pure?"

Maddie scowled, then shoved at his shoulders with surprising strength. "Get off me, you big oaf."

Reluctantly he shifted off of her and sat up. Unable to help himself, he let his gaze drift down to her soft, full breasts, heaving with her angry breath. Maddie had a spectacular bosom. "Was it such an idiotic presumption?"

"Only if you know nothing about me," she snapped. "You really *did* believe all those rumors, didn't you?"

"No, of course not."

"Then why did you presume I was a whore?"

He blinked, wishing his brain would hurry up and catch up with his body. That had never been a problem before. "I never did such a thing. It's just that . . . five years is a long time, Maddie." And he'd wanted to make love to her for so long, and then she'd made him so damned angry . . . sweet Lucifer, he *was* an idiot.

Her gray eyes studied his for a long moment, while the excited flush of her cheeks slowly faded. "So you decided that since I was already ruined, you might as well take advantage."

He shifted closer to her, noting that despite her words, she couldn't help dropping her eyes below his waist for a moment. "Now, just a damned minute—I don't recall your trying to stop anything. Just the opposite, I think."

"Well," she began, blushing again, and belatedly covering her lovely chest with her arms, "I simply . . . got a little carried away."

At that his lips twitched in a small grin. "I'll say."

"You stop that!"

"Well, now we're in a spot."

"No, we're not. Go fetch me another dress, and we'll go upstairs to bed. The end."

''To bed together?'' he suggested hopefully, caressing her cheek with the palm of his hand.

For just a moment she shut her eyes, leaning into his embrace. ''This isn't funny, you know.''

He chuckled. ''I know. It's a damned tragedy.'' And one he was rather enjoying. There was a powerful connection between them, and he affected her just as she affected him. And for once, where Maddie was concerned, he actually felt in command of the moment. Still touching her cheek, he rose to his knees and leaned forward to kiss her lightly, at the same time removing her one remaining hairclip and letting her damp auburn hair tumble down her shoulders. ''And in my own, excessively dull way of thinking, I *do* have a solution in mind.''

Slender fingers hesitantly lifted to trace the muscles of his abdomen. ''And what might that be?''

She still desired him, whatever better sense she had. He looked at her face, at the yearning and passion even her renewed anger hadn't been able to drive away. He wondered if she saw a reflection of the same in his own gaze. ''Marry me.''

Pure surprise dilated her eyes. ''What?''

He smiled. ''I said, marry—''

''Why?'' she interrupted. ''Now that I'm truly ruined, why not just keep me as your mistress or something, so that you can still marry Eloise Stokesley like you're supposed to?''

''Don't be ridiculous. At Langley I said I would do right by you, Maddie. I may have . . . stumbled somewhat, but those weren't just words. I meant them.''

''Oh, please.''

Maddie stood and grabbed her shift, the only intact piece of clothing left to her. Looking at the carnage, Quin was surprised he hadn't left bruises on her. For Lucifer's sake, his breeches were still wrapped around one ankle, and he still wore his boots. He'd had mistresses before, but never—*never*—had he been so out of control.

"I can hardly wait for your next 'stumble,' " she continued, pulling the thin garment on over her head and hopelessly disheveled hair. "What will it be? Rendering me naked in the middle of Almack's assembly?"

"Maddie," he protested, standing and yanking his breeches back into place. "I am serious. I'll speak to His Grace in the morning. And we *will* be married. As soon as I can arrange it."

"No, you won't. And no, we won't. It's stupid to throw away two lives, Quin." She hesitated, looking up at him. "Whether this had happened or not, three quarters of London thinks I've done it with someone. Nothing has changed."

Now he was offended. "Something damned well has changed."

"Just listen, won't you?" she said with more heat. "My chances of tricking some gentleman into thinking me respectable and marrying me are zero."

She shrugged, loneliness touching her eyes again, making him want to hold her—even though he half thought she would seriously damage him if he tried.

"They are not," he said.

"They are . . . and they always were. I came here for the sake of your uncle. And once we complete the spectacle at Almack's, I will go back to Langley. I never thought otherwise. I can't believe you did, either."

He stared at her, righteous indignation warring with his desire to take her again, right there on the floor. He'd known she was bright, but he'd had no idea someone so . . . impassioned . . . could be so wise. Too damned wise for her own good. For *his* own good. "But, I—" He stopped the words just in time, just before he said "I love you." If she'd thought him an oaf before, that statement would drop him into irretrievable imbecility.

Maddie bent down to snatch up the tattered remains of her lovely gown. With the bits and pieces gathered in her arms, she unlocked the drawing room door. For a moment she leaned her forehead against the cool, smooth wood, then turned to face him again. "Quin, marry Eloise. Do what you're supposed to do. You don't need me in your life."

Silently she slipped out into the hallway, and a moment later her quiet tread climbed the stairs toward her bedchamber. Quin slowly went about dressing again, and cleaning up the remains of flowers and pillows and broken glass on the carpet. "You're wrong," he whispered, lifting a mangled rose and inhaling the light scent of its broken petals. "I *do* need you in my life."

"Rafe, I think you're just making this up."

The younger Bancroft brother finished a graceful series of turns about the huge ballroom and ended by Maddie's side. "I am not," he protested, his voice echoing in the empty mirrored room. "It's all the rage in Paris, and I have it on the best authority that Lady Beaufort *loves* Paris. She'll be sure to have at least one or two of the latest waltzes, and you don't want to be left out, do you?"

She sighed. "Actually, yes."

He chuckled. "Coward."

Maddie jumped as footsteps echoed into the room behind her, but it was only the duchess. Quin had been absent all morning, and she had to wonder whether he was avoiding her, or if—even worse—he'd gone to set the date for his wedding with Eloise. "Your Grace," she curtsied.

Lady Highbarrow nodded at Maddie. "My husband is in Parliament this morning," she announced, and took the seat at the pianoforte. "And you sound as though you could use some music to cover up the sound of all that awful stomping Rafael is doing.''

"You know how to play a *waltz*, Mother?" Rafe asked in mock amazement.

She lifted an eyebrow at her son. "What your father doesn't know won't hurt us."

"I hope not." He turned and held his hands out to Maddie. "Come, my dear, let me teach you to waltz."

"I know how to waltz."

"Maddie, we've been through this already. Do cooperate a little."

She grinned. "Oh, very well."

The duchess began to play, and Rafe swept an arm about Maddie's waist to swing her into the dance. Like most things from Paris, this waltz seemed more scandalous than its British counterpart. Rafe held her so close to him, they were practically. . . .

She blushed, turning her face so he wouldn't see her sudden discomfiture. She would never forget last night, for it seemed she'd been waiting for Quin to hold her for a lifetime.

"Oh, so now you'll dance with anyone, will you?"

Maddie stiffened at the sound of Quin's voice. Luckily, Rafael held her closely enough that she could regain her composure without stumbling. He looked down at her curiously, but she only smiled. "Anyone but you, my lord."

Rafe nodded approvingly. "Well said. Turned the insult right around, eh, Warefield? And didn't wallop anyone."

"Yes, she did," the marquis admitted grudgingly. At least the admission seemed reluctant to Maddie, for he stayed planted in the doorway, watching her and Rafe twirl about the floor.

Quin looked as impeccably dressed and calm as always, until she glanced at his face. Unless she was mistaken, he'd gotten even less sleep than she had last night.

It would have been so easy, as he held her in his arms. It would have been so simple, to tell him that she loved him. But it wouldn't have changed anything.

Whether he returned her affections, or had simply been guided by animal lust, he had been slated to marry Eloise Stokesley for twenty-three years—since Maddie's birth, and since his seventh year. And her presence could not and would not be allowed to change such an arrangement—not between two families as powerful as the Bancrofts and the Stokesleys.

"Penny for your thoughts, Maddie," Rafe murmured, glancing over her head at his brother. "Quin hasn't frightened you, has he?"

"Why in the world would you say that?"

"Thought I heard the two of you arguing last night."

"We always argue." Maddie blushed again, and Rafe's gaze sharpened a little.

"Yes, you do. I'm surprised Quin hasn't had an apoplexy of his own by now. I thought *I* was the only one who dared argue with the Marquis of Warefield. Except for His Grace, of course."

"Why do you call Lord Highbarrow 'His Grace'? Both you and Quin do it," she asked, to turn the subject.

Rafe shrugged. "He likes it better than being called 'Father.' I heard him once, bellowing at Quin: 'Any damned ass can be a father. *I'm* a duke!' "

Quin strolled over to sit beside his mother at the pianoforte, luckily still out of earshot.

"Might I ask you a question?" she continued carefully.

"Of course, my lady."

"Why do you and Eloise Stokesley not . . . deal well together?"

His expression tightened a little as he shook his head. "It's personal."

"It doesn't concern you that your brother is going to marry her?"

"*You* sound concerned," he replied promptly, obviously trying to put her on the defensive. "Why, do you believe her to be some sort of maniac?"

Maddie forced a smile. "Of course not."

"Rafe, might I have a go at that?" Quin asked, rising again.

"It's a bit modern for you, Quin, don't you think?"

"Very funny," Quin said dryly. "Hand Maddie over, if you please."

She didn't like the way that sounded, as though she was a piece of property. Rafael seemed to sense that, for he hurriedly relinquished her and strolled over to chat with his mother.

"Good morning," Quin said, studying her eyes as he took her in his arms.

"You might have asked me if I *wished* to dance with you," she snapped, trying to keep her attention on her anger rather than on the way her body just wanted to melt into his. It was deuced difficult, being hopelessly attracted to someone and having absolutely no hope of any future with him.

"Grumpy, aren't you? Am I to assume you didn't sleep well?" he continued mildly, far too calm about the whole mess, as far as she was concerned.

"No, I did not."

"Mm," he nodded. "Neither did I. I kept thinking of you."

Despite his lowered voice, Maddie couldn't help glancing at the duchess and Rafe. "Be quiet."

"Aha!" Quin grinned down at her.

"What is it, dear?" Lady Highbarrow asked.

"Nothing, Mother," he answered easily, still gazing at Maddie with an expression of idiotic triumph on his lean, handsome face.

''What 'aha'?'' she muttered, trying not to scowl.

''You wish our liaison to remain a secret.''

''Oh, so now it's a liaison? Last night it was a stumble, I believe,'' she said dryly, wishing he would find an easier topic.

''A tumble, at least,'' he agreed. ''And an exceedingly pleasurable one.''

Before she could kick him, he turned her in his arms and propelled her toward the door leading into the garden.

''We'll be back in a moment,'' he said over his shoulder, as he exited behind her. ''Maddie's feeling faint.''

''I am not feeling faint,'' she hissed, regaining her balance and backing away from him. ''What are you doing?''

He pursued her, not stopping until he had her trapped between himself and a trio of exceedingly thorny rose bushes. ''I didn't want any witnesses if you intended to become violent,'' he answered, and reached past her shoulder to pick a barely blooming red rose, still more a bud than a flower. Slowly he brushed the soft petals along her cheek. ''You see, Maddie, if you truly thought you were ruined beyond hope of redemption, you wouldn't care if I shouted my conquest to the treetops. But you do think there's hope, don't you? Even now.''

''After last night, my lord, I can't believe you're asking me the question. Our . . . our actions *did* ruin me beyond hope of redemption.''

'' 'Our actions'? We made love, Maddie,'' he said softly, brushing the rose along the low neckline of her morning dress, the petals leaving a light, sweet scent on her skin. ''Didn't you enjoy it? You said you did.''

She shivered at the soft caress of the rose, and of his voice. ''It doesn't matter whether I enjoyed it or not.''

''Yes, it does.'' He leaned closer, replacing the rose petals with his lips in a feather-soft touch of his mouth to hers. "Did you enjoy being with me, Maddie?"

She drew a ragged breath, wanting nothing more than to fall to the ground with him and repeat exactly what they had done last night. "Yes."

Quin smiled. "So did I. Very much. Though the next time, I'd like to take more time, to . . . be more thorough."

"The next time?" she repeated, hoping the sudden heat running beneath her skin didn't show on her face. "There will not be a next time. You know that as well as I do."

"I'm fairly stubborn for a dull gentleman, wouldn't you say, my dear?"

"I . . . I didn't mean that, Quin," she said reluctantly. "You made me very angry."

"Even so," he answered softly, gently kissing her once more, and making her pulse begin to flutter all over again, "your point was taken."

Maddie leaned up for another kiss first, in case they should begin another argument, then narrowed her eyes. "What do you mean?"

"Everyone else *has* been running my life since I can remember. I've put up with it because I considered it to be my duty, and because it really wasn't all that difficult to tolerate. Until now."

"Oh, no you don't," she warned, slipping past his shoulder and backing away from him in alarm. "You will *not* use me as an excuse to rebel against your family. Don't be stupid. You have far too much to lose."

She couldn't tell if he was listening or not. He kept nodding, but his expression seemed anything but compliant. Rather, he looked like the idea of making love to her in the garden's soft grass appealed to him as much as it did to her.

"I'm going inside," she stated, holding up a hand to

ward him off. "Charles has invited me to accompany
him on a picnic. I need to change."

He stopped, his expression darkening. "Very well,"
he said stiffly. "Go. I'm to meet Eloise, anyway."

"Very well," she repeated, realizing that she didn't
like Eloise Stokesley at all. "Please be sure to tell her I
thank her for her advice about the Densens. I shall be
more cautious next time." More cautious about Eloise
and her friends, at any rate.

"And so she should be more cautious," Eloise
agreed. She glanced over her shoulder to see Lord and
Lady Pembroke and their daughter Lady Froston walking behind them, and she boldly wrapped her arm
through Quin's. "For heaven's sake, I don't know how
much more clear I could have been."

The marquis nodded at her. "Maddie is in agreement."

Again, though, his tone was rather absent, as though
his mind was elsewhere. Eloise could guess where.
"Good. If she expects me to see her reintroduced into
society, she must at least cooperate with me."

His lips twitched. "She's not very good at that, I'm
afraid."

"Honestly, she isn't good at much, it seems to me."

His arm tensed beneath hers. "I would appreciate if
you didn't repeat that sentiment. We're here to quash
rumors," he said quietly, steel beneath the soft tones,
"not spread them."

So she'd gone too far and insulted the little mopsie.
He didn't seem to care nearly as much about his future
wife's feelings. "Oh, there's Darby's," she cooed, pretending not to hear his censure. "Buy me a new hat,
will you?"

"Another one?"

"I don't believe there's supposed to be a limit, my

dear,'' she chuckled, trying to coax him out of his dol-
drums. ''Come on, I'll let you choose. You do have
excellent taste, for a man.''

''Hm. My thanks.''

She let him choose a pretty green, if rather plain, bonnet, and instructed that it be sent to her address. Something still distracted him, and whatever it was, so far this
morning it had kept him from asking that one particular
question she'd been waiting to hear for five years—since
she'd turned eighteen.

''Is something troubling you, Quin?'' she finally
asked, out of patience.

He shook himself. ''No. My apologies. I suppose my
mind's been elsewhere today.''

''Where has it been?'' she breathed, leaning against
his arm as they strolled along crowded Bond Street. ''On
a certain question you said you needed to ask me today,
I suppose?''

Quin stopped, looking down at her. ''Yes, as a matter
of fact.''

Not liking the hesitant look in his eyes, Eloise forced
a smile. ''Asking it seems so silly. After all, we've
known since . . . forever that we're to be married. If it
makes things any easier on you, your father stopped by
to see me yesterday.''

''He did?''

''Yes. And he informed me that you'd set July the
seventeenth as the date for our wedding. I think that's a
lovely date, and splendid timing, as well.'' She put both
hands on his arm. ''So, what I'm trying to say, dear
Quin, is that you really needn't even ask me. Just know
that I say yes.''

For a long moment he looked down at her, then
slowly shook his head. ''You are better than I deserve.''

She chuckled, relieved. ''Of course I am. Shall we go
ask the duchess to begin compiling a guest list?''

Quin pulled his arm free of her fingers. "Eloise, I can't marry you."

Eloise froze, her relief turning to disbelieving horror. *"What?"*

"Not right now. I need a little time . . . to think."

"About what? Don't be ridiculous, Quin. Your father will cut you off if you delay this wedding for another year." She took a step back. "And so will I. I'm twenty-three, Quin. Most of my friends are already married. Some of them have children. I won't be made a laughingstock."

"That is not my intention," he said stiffly.

Hurriedly Eloise stepped forward again, putting a hand on his arm. "You are a very kind man, Quin; you always have been. If you need to take time to think, then do so. But know that I am here, and know that we both have an obligation to our families." She leaned closer, lowering her voice. "Do you think I haven't met anyone I couldn't fancy myself in love with? But I haven't allowed it to happen. There is too much at stake. You must do the same."

"Don't you think I know that, Eloise?" He took a deep breath. "Just give me a few days. A week. And then I will ask you, properly." Quin smiled a little. "On bended knee."

"A week," she agreed, returning his smile. "Now, take me home. I must choose a gown to wear to the Beauforts' tonight."

He bowed. "Yes, my lady."

Quin strolled ahead to signal his driver, and Eloise stopped to look at her reflection in a shop window. He wanted a week. It might as well have been forever. And something had to be done—before his little slut could ruin the fortunes and futures of two very important families. Apparently Charles Dunfrey wasn't having any effect. She would have to see to that. Immediately.

* * *

Maddie had called him dull. In a sense, she knew what she was talking about. Quin watched her waltzing with Rafe, her natural grace and exuberance rendering the rest of the females at the Beaufort ball pale and awkward by comparison.

Dull. The epithet hit closer than he felt comfortable acknowledging. Well, perhaps he wasn't exactly dull, but he'd certainly taken a great many things for granted. He'd never had to worry about—or even think about—an income, his place in society, or whom he would marry. It had all been taken care of by the time he knew enough to wonder about it.

Maddie laughed at something Rafe said, and a stab of jealousy wrenched Quin's insides unpleasantly. Because of her, because of what had happened to her and what she had accomplished all on her own, he could no longer take anything for granted.

He'd never thought to fall in love with Eloise; they'd known one another so long that a mutual fondness seemed adequate. But since he'd returned to London, even fondness seemed too strong a word.

Certainly Eloise had offered her assistance—or rather, she'd agreed to help him in order to get Maddie out of Bancroft House. To assume otherwise would be absurd. Quin glanced across the room at her, seated between her mother and his own, a charming, poised smile on her lovely face. As always she looked beautiful, her blond hair framing her face with delicate curling tendrils, and the sapphire of her dress matching the blue of her eyes. She looked like a marchioness, and she looked like a stunning future duchess.

And then there was Maddie—who looked like a beautiful wood sprite, captured for a moment before she made her escape into the morning mist. A smile touched his lips. She was certainly an auburn-haired element of nature, and half the gentry present wouldn't even speak to her. They all looked, though, especially the men. There was no doubt about that.

Perhaps she was right about him, after all. With her, he never knew what might happen next. With her, he felt . . . alive. And without her, the past years of his life seemed so lifeless.

"Ah, Warefield."

Quin blinked and turned around. "Mr. Dunfrey." The jealous twinge he'd felt at Rafe expanded into something much darker and angrier.

"Maddie—Miss Willits—has told me of your extraordinary generosity toward her. As her initial . . . predicament was in part my fault, I am exceedingly grateful to you, my lord."

"Don't trouble yourself," Quin said shortly, wishing Dunfrey would go away. "It has nothing to do with you. She was wronged, and I am setting it right."

Dunfrey nodded at him. "Just so. And I hope that I might take a final step in that direction, myself."

So Charles Dunfrey *did* want her again, after all. If Quin had even the least little right to do so, he would have posted a No Trespassing sign right then. Maddie was *his*. But even Dunfrey had more right to Maddie than he did.

And even half ready to strangle the ass for presuming to take away his very favorite person in the world, he knew the choice had to be Maddie's. Even if it killed him. "None of my affair, Dunfrey," he said stiffly. With a nod he turned to find Eloise for the next dance.

As far as his initial—and stupidly naive—plan was concerned, everything was coming together splendidly. Baron Grafford had escorted Maddie out for the quadrille, and her dance card was three-quarters filled. She'd already handed out two perfectly worded set-downs to a pair of overeager gentlemen, and had done no discernible damage to herself—or to them—in the process.

Almack's next assembly was in ten days, and Charles Dunfrey was ready to forgive all and take Maddie as his bride. His debt of honor would be satisfied, and he could go on to marry Eloise a month later, just as the duke had envisioned.

Only one thing was wrong. He'd never expected to fall in love with Maddie Willits—and now that he had, he wasn't certain he could give her up.

Chapter 13

～⌒○⌒～

Charles Dunfrey called on Maddie three times at Bancroft House over the next four days, and he also took her on a picnic and horseback riding at Hyde Park. During that time, with the exception of a few unreadable looks, the Marquis of Warefield seemed to be avoiding her again. She began to think that perhaps Quin had given up on his absurd notion of marrying her, and the idea left her stupidly disappointed and broken-hearted.

After all, the whole idea of his marrying her to restore her honor was completely ridiculous. Even if she had been a paragon of virtue, the future Duke of Highbarrow would have set his gaze much higher than where she stood. It made no sense that she lay awake every night, imagining being with him again, and dreaming of what it would be like actually to marry the man with whom—despite all her intentions to the contrary—she had fallen in love.

Apparently, though, the marquis hadn't given up entirely. The next morning Charles had an appointment, and Quin appeared before she'd finished eating breakfast. "Good morning," he said amiably, taking the seat opposite her.

"Good morning," she answered, wary of his seeming good humor. He was up to something.

He motioned for the platter of fruit, and one of the footmen hurried to bring it to him. "What are your plans for today?"

"I need to write Mr. Bancroft."

Quin sat back and gazed at her. "And tell him what?"

Maddie blushed. As if she could write him about what was actually happening. "I haven't written him yet that Charles Dunfrey has been calling on me, and that he's been quite nice."

"Ah. Considering that his bellowing is what ruined you, I should hope he *would* be quite nice."

"You don't need to be so hostile," she said testily.

"I know, I know," he muttered, half to himself, and sighed. "May I make amends by buying you a new hat?"

"I don't need a new hat."

He paused for a moment, as though she'd said something unexpected. "How about a new dress, then?" His eyes met hers lazily, and a warm, responding tremor went down her spine.

She wished he would quit referring to that night, exciting and intoxicating as it had been. Being reminded of his intimate touch and his passion only reminded her that she would never have that with him again. "A new hat will be more than adequate."

"Splendid. I'll have the phaeton hitched up." With a grin, he rose and snatched a peach from the platter. "Oh, by the way," he continued, "I thought you might want to know: His Grace is taking his breakfast at home this morning." He slipped out the door.

"Egad." Maddie hastily crammed the remaining biscuit in her mouth and washed it down with a gulp of tea. She'd become nearly as adept as the rest of the Bancrofts at evading the duke, thanks to a great deal of luck and a good measure of what Rafe termed her "uncanny nose for trouble."

With a quick and garbled word of thanks to the half dozen footmen awaiting the family's pleasure in the breakfast room, Maddie fled through the kitchen and up the back stairs to her bedchamber. By now even the lofty Bancroft servants were used to her untraditional ways, and her escape warranted a mere nod from the head cook.

After she snatched up her bonnet and gloves from her dressing table, she hurried downstairs by the same route, exiting into the stable yard through the kitchen door.

Quin sat in the driver's seat of the phaeton, waiting for her. "Finished breakfast already?" he asked, offering his hand as she nimbly clambered up beside him.

"You might have warned me earlier," she answered, tying the bonnet under her chin.

"Here, Maddie, let me do that."

She slapped his hand away and turned her shoulder to him. "I can manage, thank you very much."

"Don't you like me to touch you?" he murmured.

Maddie swallowed. "Yes. So don't."

Quin glanced at her, and then snapped the reins. The phaeton started smartly down the short path. They turned out onto the street, and he leaned closer. "You keep telling me you're already ruined. What's the harm—"

She'd been asking herself the same question—repeatedly. "I am not some actress or opera singer, Warefield. I suggest you find one of them to satisfy your baser needs."

For a moment his expression darkened. "You're fitting back into polite society quite well, my dear."

"You make it sound like an insult. My fitting in *is* what *you* wanted, my dear."

"Perhaps. But I wasn't speaking of my 'baser needs,' as you call them. I was talking about desire, Maddie."

She glanced at him, blushing. Everything was so much easier when they were arguing. "Well, stop that, too."

Unexpectedly, he chuckled. "I can stop *talking* about it."

She smiled reluctantly. "Sometimes—just sometimes—I'm glad I rescued you from Mr. Whitmore and Miss Marguerite."

"You rescued *me* from that damned pig?"

"I should say so. If not for me, you—"

"Maddie!"

Startled, she whipped her head around. Standing outside a clothier's shop were Lord and Lady Halverston, gaping at the phaeton as it passed by them.

Quin took one look at her face and pulled up the phaeton. "Who are they?" he snapped.

"My . . . my parents," she choked out.

"Sweet. . . ." he growled, and grabbed hold of her arm before she could jump from the carriage and make an escape.

He needn't have worried. She couldn't move. She couldn't speak. She couldn't utter a word. All she could do was stare at her parents, staring back at her.

"Oh, good heavens," her mother continued, hiking up her skirt and running forward. "It is you. It is you! Maddie!"

The hack driver behind them whistled his annoyance, and Quin maneuvered the phaeton over to the side of the street—even though Maddie would much rather have grabbed the reins and fled. When he gently placed his hand over her clenched one, she jumped again.

"Go say hello," he whispered.

She shook her head tightly. "I can't. Just go."

"Go where?"

"Anywhere."

"I'm here, Maddie," he said quietly, stroking his fingers over hers. "I promised, remember? Nothing will happen to you."

His typical, self-confident arrogance brought her back to herself. "Where were you five years ago?" she muttered, and stood.

Hurriedly Quin tied down the reins and jumped to the ground. Before either of her parents reached them, he had moved to her side of the phaeton and reached up to take her hand. Reading the silent encouragement in his eyes, she grasped his fingers tightly and stepped down to face her parents.

"Mama, Papa," she said, her voice miraculously steady. "You both look well."

They stopped a few feet away, as though afraid she might bolt again if they came nearer. Her mother fluttered a handkerchief. "*We* look well? Where in the world have you been? Do you have any idea how worried we were when you vanished? You simply have no—"

Lord Halverston put a hand on his wife's shoulder. "Please, Julia. There will be time for explanations later. Is this your husband, Maddie?"

Flabbergasted again, Maddie looked at Quin. With a slight grin he pulled free of her grip and stepped forward to hold out his hand. "Quin Bancroft," he said amiably, glancing sideways at Maddie. "A friend."

Lord Halverston shook his hand vigorously. "You are too modest, my lord. Julia, this is the Marquis of Warefield."

Lady Halverston curtsied, her expression stunned and astonished, and her face nearly as white as Maddie's. "My lord."

Quin asked some innocuous question about when the family had arrived in London and Maddie glanced at him, grateful for the reprieve. She stood close beside him while he played the kind, pleasant marquis, and she tried not to shake. Whatever she claimed about being able to stand on her own, she was very glad he was there.

Silently she studied her parents. Except for a little more gray peppering his temples, Robert Willits looked almost unchanged. When he made an effort to be pleasant, as he was doing now for Quin, the viscount could be very charming. What she remembered best about him, though, was the constant barrage of harsh, disapproving words he had for her stubbornness and lack of propriety, and the even worse words he'd bellowed about how she had forever disgraced herself and her family.

Her mother always seconded what her father said, mean and unfair as it frequently seemed. Today, though, Lady Halverston had eyes only for her daughter.

"How long have you been in London?" her mother asked.

She shrugged. "A few weeks."

"A few weeks? Why didn't you write? Why didn't you let us know where you were?"

"I didn't want you to know."

"But you don't mind that everyone else in London knows of your return?" Lord Halverston scowled at her.

She was familiar with the expression. "Coming here was not my idea."

Quin stepped forward, taking her hand again and placing it over his arm. "My mother and my cousin are assisting with Miss Willits's return to society. She was very kind to our family, and we are attempting to repay the favor."

Again Maddie was grateful to the marquis, this time for keeping her past whereabouts a secret. "Your mother will be expecting us," she lied, looking up at him hopefully.

"Yes," he nodded. "I beg your pardon, Halverston, but the duchess hates to be kept waiting."

"Of course," her father hurriedly agreed.

"Perhaps you might wish to call on us this afternoon, at Bancroft House," Quin continued.

"Oh, yes. Bancroft House. We'd be delighted." The viscount nodded at Quin and shook his hand again. "We'll see you at two, then."

Quin turned and helped Maddie back up into the phaeton. When he joined her on the seat she elbowed him hard in the ribs, unable to rein herself in any longer.

"Ouch. What was that for?"

"Traitor," she muttered at him, trying not to stare at her parents.

"Coward," he returned, whispering the word in her ear as he collected the reins. With her mother waving after them, he sent the rig back out into the street.

Maddie sat with her arms crossed over her chest, refusing to look in his direction again. No one could possibly be as annoying as he was and so kind and compassionate at the same time.

"That wasn't so bad, was it?"

"You had no right to invite them to call on me," she snapped. "And I am not a coward."

"I didn't invite them to call on you," he corrected, fleeting humor touching his eyes. "I invited them to call on *me.*"

"Oh, how gracious. I thought you were . . . on my side," she said, searching for the right words. "But you weren't, were you? You were just worried I'd cause a scene and embarrass you."

"No, I—"

"Stop the phaeton. I'm getting out."

"No, you're not." Before she could react, Quin grabbed her arm and yanked her closer. "Maddie, you're upset. That's all right. But please, don't be angry at me for it. I *am* on your side. I'm trying to help, in my own dull, pompous way."

For a moment she let herself lean against his strong, warm shoulder and closed her eyes. It was so absurd that she could be mad enough to spit at him, and at the same time want nothing more than to just melt into his arms.

With a glance at the crowded walkways, she straightened. Melting in the middle of Mayfair would be decidedly unwise. "None of this mess was part of your bargain with Mr. Bancroft, you know."

He grinned. "I didn't bargain for a great deal of this, truth be told, Maddie. But I can't say I'm sorry for any of it."

"Well, that's one of us," she said, with as much sarcasm as she could muster.

"Oh, come now," he chided, obviously not fooled a bit. "If you could reconcile with your parents, wouldn't you want to? Your mother certainly seemed pleased to see you."

So she had. "Don't tell them where I've been, please."

"Your secret is safe with me," he said. Quin drew a long breath. "Maddie?"

She looked at him, watching her with serious green eyes. "Yes?"

He held her gaze for a long moment, then shook himself and faced forward again. "Nothing."

As soon as they returned to Bancroft House, Maddie fled upstairs to change. Just in case, Quin instructed the gardener to let him know if she tried to make an escape out her window. She seemed resigned to speaking with her parents again, but her temperament could be rather mercurial. And he didn't want to risk losing her now. Not until he'd figured things out.

He made his way up to the morning room to inform his mother of the Willitses' impending visit.

"Mama, Maddie's parents are in London," he said, pushing the door open and strolling into the room. "I've invited them. . . ." Belatedly he noticed his mother's guest. "Eloise? I thought you would be visiting Lady Landrey this morning."

Eloise sipped her tea, her blue eyes regarding him warmly. "The poor thing canceled the brunch. Seems her son's been sent down from Cambridge in disgrace."

"I'm surprised Lester was tolerated as long as he was." Quin sat beside her and motioned to a footman for another cup.

"Yes, it's amazing what a healthy endowment will do for one's patience," she smiled. "Sugar?"

"No, thank you."

"What were you saying about Maddie's parents?" The duchess set aside her embroidery and regarded her son.

"We ran across them this morning."

His mother sat forward. "How did they react?"

Quin stifled a smile. Much as she tried to remain aloof, the Duchess of Highbarrow had completely fallen for Maddie's considerable charms. "I'm not certain. Her mother seemed relieved, but her father was apparently more interested in meeting me."

"Can you blame him?" Eloise chuckled. "A ruined bit or the future Duke of Highbarrow?"

"Yes, but the 'ruined bit,' as you call her, is his daughter—whom he hasn't seen in five years." Quin glanced at his second cousin, annoyed. She didn't sound very much like a willing confederate.

"You said you invited them somewhere," his mother broke in. "Here, I presume?"

"Yes. At two this afternoon. I explained that she had done our family a favor and we were repaying her by chaperoning her return to society."

Eloise eyed him coolly. "You didn't mention that you'd kissed her?"

So she'd found out about that. From the duke, no doubt. But he had done a great deal more than kiss Maddie. Quin gazed calmly at Lady Stokesley. "I didn't think it very wise, no. Is something bothering you, Eloise?"

"Only that you haven't kissed me more often, Quin. An oversight I hope you intend to correct soon." She held her cup up, and a footman hurried to refill it. A drop of hot tea splashed on her finger, and she gasped and threw the contents of the cup at the servant's chest. "You idiot! Are you trying to scar me?"

He bowed, wiping frantically at the hot liquid soaking his waistcoat. "No, my lady. Please accept my apologies. I'm terribly sorry. I—"

"Franklin, get out," the duchess ordered.

He bowed again. "Yes, Your Grace. Thank you, Your Grace."

Still bowing, Franklin backed out of the room. His place was immediately taken by another servant, who swiftly cleaned up the mess and provided Eloise with a new cup. Quin watched the incident, disturbed, while his mother glanced at him and calmly added another spoonful of sugar to her tea.

"Eloise tells me you've agreed on July the seventeenth," she said. "Your father will be pleased. In fact, I believe he intended on meeting with the archbishop this morning, to secure Westminster Cathedral." She sipped her tea again, then lifted a finger and set the cup aside. "Oh, and we need to send out invitations immediately. Otherwise, the whole gala will appear to be hastily planned."

"As if you could hastily plan something over twenty-three years in the making," Quin said. Of course His

Grace would be pleased. He'd been the one to choose the date.

"There's no need for sarcasm," Eloise returned, obviously out of countenance with him today.

He really couldn't blame her. In all likelihood, the sooner everything was settled, the better for everyone concerned. Except for him—and except, perhaps, for Maddie. "No. It just seems a great deal of fuss over something everyone's known about for a quarter of a century."

Eloise stood. "Well, I think it's wretched of you," she snapped. "You didn't used to be so cruel and unfeeling."

"Oh, damnation." Reluctantly he stood and walked to the door before her. "My apologies, Eloise. I did not intend to be cruel," he said, feeling distinctly as though he'd enacted the same scene before, and would do so again. Endlessly.

Eloise stopped, looking up at him with her much-praised blue eyes. "I know. Take me riding tomorrow. And buy me something pretty."

Quin forced a smile. "With pleasure."

He escorted her outside and handed her up into her father's carriage. "Until tomorrow, Eloise," he said, kissing her knuckles.

Back in the morning room, his mother had summoned the head cook and was discussing a luncheon menu. He leaned in the doorway, waiting until she finished and dismissed the servant. "For Lord and Lady Halverston, I presume? Thank you, Mother."

"Guests are guests," she said, rising. "And Eloise has actually been quite patient and understanding—for Eloise. Quin, I know Maddie is charming. But—"

He raised a hand. "I know exactly what Maddie is. I don't need everyone between here and Yorkshire reminding me."

She looked at him for a moment. "Good. Now go tell Cook I've decided on the chicken rather than the ham."

More than ready to make his escape before he could hear another lecture about familial duty and obligation, he excused himself. On the way to the kitchen it struck him that his mother hadn't done all that much lecturing lately. Still trying to figure that out, he headed down the back stairs.

In the kitchen doorway, he stopped. A dozen servants gathered around the huge central preparation table, while Franklin, shirtless and grimacing, perched on one edge of it. Maddie stood before him, applying a clean, white bandage to his heat-reddened skin.

"It's not too bad," she comforted, wrapping the bandage about his chest, "though I imagine it hurts quite a bit."

"Just be glad Lady Amiable didn't shoot a bit lower, mate." John, another footman, chuckled.

"Hush now," Cook admonished. "There's a lady present."

John blushed. "Apologies, Miss Maddie."

Quin stifled a smile. Damn it all, now she had his parents' servants calling her that.

"No worries, John. Did you bring Franklin a dry shirt?"

"Aye. Just as you said."

She nodded, smiling up at Franklin. "All right. That should do, then. Take a look in a day or two. If the salve's worked, the redness should be almost gone by then."

The footman hopped down from the table. "My thanks, Miss Maddie."

"My pleasure. And for heaven's sake, duck next time."

He laughed. "I will."

As she turned for the door, Quin swiftly stepped back

around the corner. She passed him, and he grabbed her by the arm. Before she could utter a word, he pushed her up against the wall and bent down to close his mouth over hers. After a moment of stunned surprise, she threw her arms around his shoulders and leaned up into his embrace, kissing him back with rough, hungry passion.

"Quin, stop it," she whispered breathlessly, running her mouth along the line of his jaw. "Someone will see."

"No, they won't." He captured her lips again, teasing her mouth open and kissing her desperately. Heart-pounding arousal ran through him, and he was hard pressed not to lift her skirt right there in the servants' hallway. Good God, he'd completely lost his mind. Finally he pulled one of her hands free and led her toward the back stairs. "Come on," he murmured.

"No," she said, attempting to straighten her disheveled hair and nibbling at his chin at the same time. "I'm mad at you."

"You are?" He kissed her again, both frustrated and amused. "Whatever for?"

She couldn't quite conceal her smile. "For inviting my parents here, of course. I told you that already."

With a determined breath he straightened and took her hands in his. She had such delicate hands. "You're making amends with the rest of London. Do you really want to leave your own mother and father out?"

"It's not that simple, you know," she said quietly, stepping into the circle of his arms.

His heart leaped. Strong as her character was, she'd never seemed to need anyone before—him least of all. Gently he slipped his arms around her shoulders and her slender waist. "I do know," he answered into her auburn hair. "But at least if you make peace with them, you can return to Langley knowing that."

She lifted her head, her gray eyes holding his. "Then

you've accepted that I will return to Langley?''

He shook his head. ''No. I've accepted only that you have the right to return to Langley, if you still wish to—after your debut at Almack's.''

She sighed, still leaning against him. ''Will His Grace be here this afternoon?''

''He's at a meeting fighting for the dwindling rights of the nobility, I believe. Why?''

''For once I wish he was about. I'd like to see my father put in his place.'' Slowly she reached up and traced his lips with her fingers. ''Quin,'' she said softly, ''if you could have lived your life any way you chose, with no promises or obligations or debts, what would you have done?''

''I've never really considered it,'' he mused. ''I suppose I would have liked to have been a professor of literature.''

Maddie lifted an eyebrow. ''Really?''

''Well, yes. You said anything.''

''I know. Go on. You surprise me.''

''And you constantly surprise me,'' he whispered, kissing her once more. ''And of course, I would be married to you.''

She pulled free, scowling again. ''No, you wouldn't, because we would never have met.''

He kept hold of one hand. ''Considering the outlandish way we *did* encounter one another, how can you imagine it could be more unlikely for it to happen in another lifetime?''

A bell rang in the kitchen, corresponding to the pull in one of the rooms upstairs. With a curse Maddie fled past him up the stairs, just as John emerged to answer the bell. ''My lord, do you require something?'' he asked, obviously startled to see the marquis lurking below stairs.

Quin blinked. ''Hm? Oh, just taking a walk. Don't

mind me," he muttered, and turned to follow Maddie. Then he remembered about the chicken. "Damn."

Lord and Lady Halverston arrived promptly at two. Accompanying them were two girls. "I hope you don't mind, my lord," the viscount apologized, gesturing at the young ladies. "They insisted on coming along to see their sister."

Quin nodded. The little minx hadn't told him she had sisters, though he could immediately see the likeness in their light brown hair and high cheekbones. "Of course. Miss Willits is in the drawing room, with the duchess."

The Willits family hurried upstairs behind Beeks, while Franklin took the butler's place at the front door. "Franklin," Quin said, leaving the crowd to go ahead, "are you well?"

"Oh, yes, my lord. No harm done. My own fault, for being so clumsy." He bowed. "My apologies to you, my lord."

"No need. You weren't burned?"

The footman flushed. "I'm quite all right, my lord."

Not wanting to torture the poor fellow further, Quin turned for the stairs. "Very well."

The man wouldn't even admit that he'd been hurt, yet he—or one of the other servants—had actually gone to Maddie for help. Quin paused on the landing as excited giggles and laughter floated down from the drawing room. A year ago, he wouldn't have thought to ask after the footman. He would simply have accepted Eloise's tantrum as a matter of course. It wasn't her first. Nor, he was certain, would it be her last.

He stopped in the doorway. A cacophony of competing voices assaulted his ears, as everyone tried to be heard at once. Uncharacteristically, Maddie was the only one not talking.

Instead, she stood at the far end of the room, one hand gripped by each of her sisters, turning from one to the other as they regaled her with some story. The viscountess stood watching her three daughters with misty eyes, while Lord Halverston was profusely thanking the duchess for her extreme kindness to his willful daughter.

Maddie glanced up. As she saw him, a smile touched her lips, and for the first time a secret passion touched her eyes. Passion for him. "My lord," she said, curtseying.

"Maddie, introduce me to your family," he asked, stepping into the room to join her, and barely able to keep from swinging her in the air and laughing in delight. Sometime over the past few days, he and Maddie, without really even realizing it, seemed to have become a "we."

"This is Polly," she said, lifting the hand of the younger girl, who looked to be twelve or thirteen, with a smattering of freckles across the bridge of her nose. "And this is Claire."

The older of the two curtsied to him politely. She was pretty enough, though not striking as Maddie, her eyes more green than gray, and her face a little rounder. She looked to be sixteen or seventeen, no doubt on the verge of her own debut in society.

"Pleased to make your acquaintance," he said, smiling and taking her hand.

"I've arranged for luncheon," the duchess said, having to raise her voice to be heard over the viscount's continuing protestations of thanks. "This way, if you please."

They trooped into the dining room, where the noise continued unabated throughout the meal. Quin looked on in amazement, wondering how Maddie could have become as independent and witty as she was, in a household of such . . . obtuse silliness.

"Maddie, do you have much to pack?" the viscountess asked.

The comment immediately snared Quin's attention. "To pack for what purpose?"

The room quieted, though his ears were still ringing from the rebounding sound. The viscount cleared his throat. "Willits House is open now, my lord. It wouldn't be seemly for our unmarried daughter to be staying under someone else's roof, elegant as it is."

"My mother is chaperoning her," he replied testily. "There is no impropriety."

"Oh, of course not, my lord," Lord Halverston agreed. "But, well, people will talk, you know."

"They will talk anyway," Maddie said.

"And the more we can minimize it, the better."

Quin looked at Lord Halverston, what remained of his good humor sliding away. She was not leaving. "You might have taken that into consideration five years ago."

"Quin," his mother said sharply. "I believe the decision should be up to Maddie."

Maddie looked about the table, spending the longest moments gazing at Quin and at her father. Finally she turned to the duchess. "Your Grace, I think perhaps I should return to Willits House. Though—"

"No!" Quin snapped, rising.

She swallowed, refusing to meet his furious gaze. "Though I would be extremely grateful if I might continue to call on you—from time to time."

"Of course, my dear. Nothing would please me more."

A great many things would have pleased Quin more, including his never having set eyes on the rest of the damned Willits family. He swallowed the angry retort that came to his lips, and instead nodded and dropped his napkin into his chair. "Very well. I'll summon Mary and have her begin packing your things."

He strode out into the hallway, where he came to a halt, his breathing ragged and hard. He knew precisely what she was doing: because he refused to admit that they would never suit, she was attempting to take the issue out of his hands. Except that he wasn't about to give up. Not yet. Not ever.

Chapter 14

Maddie entered Willits House slowly, fighting the nagging idea that somehow nothing would have changed, even after five years. Everett, the butler, certainly looked the same, despite his expression of stunned surprise.

"Good afternoon, Everett." She smiled, wishing she could feel as easy as she was attempting to act.

"Miss Willits," he stammered, bowing. "Welcome home."

"Thank you." Impulsively she held out her hand. After a startled moment, he shook it. "It's good to see you again."

"And you." A reluctant, admiring smile touched his lips. "You were missed."

The furnishings downstairs hadn't changed, and neither had the paintings nor the burgundy carpeting she'd always detested in the drawing room. Her sisters trailed along behind her, excitedly chatting about their five years of adventures, while she slowly climbed the stairs and tried not to remember the last time she had fled to her bedchamber. She hesitated at the half-closed door, but before she could push it open, Claire stepped forward and barred the way.

"This is my room, now," she said. "Papa said someone might as well have use of it, and you know I never liked the morning sun."

"Claire," her mother called from below, "Maddie may have whichever room she wants."

"Mama," the pretty, brown-haired girl protested, then sighed heavily. "Oh, all right."

"No, Claire, keep it," Maddie replied, turning down the hallway. "I don't especially like my old room, anyway." It had ceased to be a refuge; it had been only a prison, with her locked inside.

Her sisters milled about in the room she chose, then went back downstairs to suggest a trip to the horse auctions to purchase a new mount for Maddie, and horses for each of them. Quin had sent Mary along to Willits House with her, and once she and the luggage arrived upstairs, Maddie was only too happy to stay and help her maid unpack.

"I can manage, Miss Maddie," Mary said, pulling open the mahogany wardrobe three footmen had carried up to the room. "You should be with your family."

"I'm giving them time to adjust." She grimaced. "I'm giving *myself* time to adjust."

For a few moments, she had thought Quin wouldn't let her leave Bancroft House at all. He'd kept himself in check, but his anger showed in every line of his tensed muscles and his tightly clenched jaw. She really hadn't wanted to go, but if she'd stayed she knew she would have given in to him eventually. He was too compelling, his presence too intoxicating. And he was still going to marry Eloise Stokesley in a little over a month.

"Maddie?" her mother said through the half-open door.

"Come in." Self-consciously Maddie brushed at her skirt as she straightened.

The door swung open. "Might I have a word with you?"

Mary curtsied. "Excuse me, Miss Maddie," she said, stepping around Maddie and hurrying out the door.

" 'Miss Maddie?' " Lady Halverston repeated. "Have you given up your place in our family?"

"I thought it was *you* who gave *me* up," she said, without heat. "And I've become used to being called Maddie." She sat on the edge of her bed. This was the moment she had dreaded, when her mother would ask where she'd been, and she would have to decide how much to tell her, and how much of an escape route she wanted to leave herself.

"We began to think you were dead, you know," the viscountess said, sitting at the dressing table. "Being angry and upset is one thing, Madeleine, but you disappeared for five years."

"I wanted to make my own way."

Her mother looked at her. "You say that as though it's nothing," she finally commented. "Your father would have forgiven you eventually, if you'd stayed. You know that."

Maddie kept her temper in check. "I did nothing wrong. I didn't—and I don't—need his forgiveness. And you should know, I am not going to stay. I . . . promised someone I'd remain in London until my debut at Almack's—my second debut at Almack's. I will do so. After that, though, there's no reason for me to be here any longer."

"I see. And to whom did you make this promise?"

"A friend."

"And what about your family?"

"Father told me quite clearly what a burden I was, and how unworthy I was of being a Willits. I haven't forgotten that." She looked down at her hands. "I don't think I ever shall."

"Maddie, the two of you have never been able to go a week without arguing. You never left before."

"Mama, after that, how could I have stayed?"

Lady Halverston looked down for a moment. "Then why did you return?"

"I've already imposed too much on the kindness of the Bancrofts," she said cautiously, not daring to mention anything of the tempest of emotions whirling between her and Quin.

"Lord Warefield seemed quite fond of you," the viscountess noted, examining Maddie's hairbrush and avoiding her gaze.

"Lord Warefield takes his family's obligations very seriously. And he expects people to do as he says. I . . ." She hesitated, trying to avoid saying too much. It would never do if anyone discovered how desperately she loved him. "I don't always agree with him."

"You disagree with the Marquis of Warefield? That seems rather unwise."

Maddie shrugged. "Someone needs to do it."

The viscountess looked at her speculatively. "Maddie—"

"Mama, nothing can be as it was before. I've been on my own for five years, and I liked it—for the most part." Honesty forced her to add the last. "If you wish me to go, I will. But I won't sit about and have Father yell at me, as he did before."

The viscountess stood. "You are still our daughter, however independent you believe yourself to be. The Bancrofts apparently had some hope for you, so we can have no less. But you cannot be allowed to embarrass this family again. Claire has her own debut next year, and I know you would not want to see her chances for a good marriage ruined simply because you have declared yourself independent of everyone and everything around you."

Maddie nodded as her mother left the room. "Very well."

She'd known it wouldn't be easy, coming back, and she had been right. Her mother, however grateful she was to have her daughter again, would bow to her husband's wishes. Maddie sighed. Five years had changed her so much, though she was certain her parents wouldn't think it was for the good. Maddie sank back on the bed, fighting a sudden attack of loneliness and abruptly wondering what Quinlan was up to, now that she was gone.

"What do you mean, 'she's gone'?" Rafe demanded, setting his billiard cue down hard enough to make the balls on the table jump. "And why the hell didn't you tell me when you first came in here?"

Quin glanced at his brother, then went back to chalking his stick. "I didn't feel like it. And I meant just what I said. Her parents came to see her, and she packed up her things and left with them. They all looked quite ecstatic at being together again."

"That's idiotic. They're the reason she left London in the first place. You shouldn't have let her go anywhere."

"Oh, really? And what was I supposed to do? Lock her in her bedchamber? It was my understanding that she didn't like that very much."

"She doesn't belong there," Rafael continued stubbornly.

The marquis eyed his younger brother. He could no longer tell whether he viewed every other male in London through a jealous gaze, but Rafe was certainly upset about something. "They are her family. We are not."

Rafe stalked to the sideboard and poured himself a snifter of brandy. "Yes, they are. The same ones who threw her in Charles Dunfrey's direction before. And now that he's gone and apologized to her, they'll likely do it again.''

"And what's wrong with that?" Quin asked, mostly to have another opinion besides his own.

"Remember when you shoved me into the drawing room and nearly broke my neck? He took me up on my offer."

"What offer?"

"To buy his pair of bays for a hundred quid. I had to backpedal like a madman to keep from getting saddled with 'em.''

"And?"

"Well, aside from the fact that I don't need a pair of coach horses in Africa, they were worth twice that, easily.''

Quin set down his cue, keenly interested now. "Forgive me, Rafe, for not being as brilliant about shady dealings as you, but exactly what about this concerns you?''

His brother shrugged, rolling a billiard ball absently about the table. "It just seems to me that if Dunfrey wanted to sell his bays, he could have gotten a lot more for them than what he was willing to accept.''

Finally Quin began to catch on. "Then you think he wasn't really interested in selling them."

Rafe nodded. "Precisely. He was interested in—"

"The money."

The marquis hefted his cue and returned it to its proper slot along the wall. "Excuse me, Rafe, I have an appointment.''

"With whom?"

Quin turned for the door. "I don't know yet.''

The manager of the Bank of England was quite flustered to see the Marquis of Warefield stroll into the bustling building unaccompanied by accountants or lawyers, and even more so when Quin requested a private audience.

"What may I do for you, Lord Warefield?" he asked solicitously, folding and unfolding his fingers on top of his scratched oak desk.

"I have a rather unusual request to make of you." Quin wondered why he didn't feel a single pang of guilt over what he was about to do.

"Anything, my lord. The Bancroft family's finances are beyond reproach."

"Thank you, Mr. Wheating. That's good to know."

The bank manager loosened his cravat a little. "I meant no offense, my lord. Oh, heavens, no."

"None taken. I don't require a loan, however. I require a little information."

Mr. Wheating's tufted eyebrows furrowed. "Information, my lord? What sort of information?"

Quin tapped his chin. "I'm contemplating something of a business venture with one of my fellows. I'm not terribly well acquainted with him, though, and I wished to know a bit more about his financial stability."

"Oh. Um, well—you know, my lord, information about all of our clients is, well, privileged."

"Of course. I wouldn't want you to break any rules. And I don't need any specifics." Quin leaned forward, smiling confidently, attempting to ignore the tickle in his mind that knew exactly what Maddie would say about his throwing his title around. "Just a general overview. I would be *extremely* grateful."

Mr. Wheating glanced about his empty office. "Who might this fellow be, my lord?"

"Mr. Charles Dunfrey." Quin sat back expectantly.

"Charles Dun—Dunfrey, you say?" Wheating's ruddy features paled. "Oh. Oh, my."

"Could you elaborate?"

"Well, my lord, speaking *generally,* I would have to

say. . . ." Even with the door closed and no one else in the tiny room, he leaned forward across the desk and lowered his voice. "I would have to say that in general, Mr. Dunfrey's finances are a bit shaky."

Quin raised an eyebrow. "A bit shaky?"

The manager cleared his throat. "*Quite* shaky."

"Ah."

"Yes. Into *negative figures*, one might say."

"Oh, dear," Quin said in mock distress, disliking Charles Dunfrey more with every passing moment, "this *is* troubling. I cannot thank you enough, Mr. Wheating." He stood and strolled to the door of the tiny office. "You have saved the Bancrofts a great deal of embarrassment."

Mr. Wheating climbed to his feet and bowed grandly. "My pleasure, my lord, of course."

Quin rode Aristotle back to Grosvenor Square by way of Curzon Street. The avenue was well out of his way, and he knew damned well why he was going that route—the Willitses lived on Curzon Street. He paused outside the wrought-iron gates barring him from Maddie, staring at the curtained windows until the gelding began to fidget.

He contemplated calling on her to inform her of Dunfrey's shaky finances, but for God's sake, she'd been gone from Bancroft House for only three hours. He'd look exactly like what he was—a complete fool, so in love with a ruined chit that he couldn't stand being away from her for more than five minutes.

Besides, just because Dunfrey had called on her once or twice didn't mean either of them was seriously considering marriage again. With Dunfrey's money troubles, it was entirely possible he wouldn't want to be saddled with volatile Maddie Willits for a wife. Marrying into an older, more respected title could do him more good than a few ready quid, if Viscount Halverston even had the kind of blunt that would satisfy him.

Feeling a little better, he kicked Aristotle into a trot and headed toward Bancroft House. They'd already planned to attend the Garrington ball tomorrow evening, and he would be able to see her and dance with her—and perhaps some miracle would occur and he would actually think of a way to get them out of this bloody big hole they'd fallen into. If not, he could always kidnap her and make off to the Orient. No doubt she would be furious, but at least she wouldn't think him dull.

Maddie had barely finished breakfast when Everett entered the room to announce that she had a caller. Her heart leaped. "Who is it?" she asked, trying to hide her excitement and knowing she must be doing a miserable job of it. He'd come to see her, after all!

"Mr. Charles Dunfrey, my lady."

The delight faded from her heart. "Oh."

"My, whatever can Charles want?" her mother asked, looking curiously at her father.

"No idea, I'm sure," he mumbled around his toasted bread.

When he glanced at Maddie, she quickly fixed a smile on her lips. They'd barely spoken since yesterday afternoon, and she had no intention of giving him an excuse to bellow at her again. "I'll go see, I suppose."

Charles turned away from the window as she entered the morning room. "Maddie. I'm so pleased you've returned home."

"Yes, so am I, Charles. Thank you."

"It seems everything has been set right again." He took her hand and brought it to his lips. "Well, almost everything, anyway. Maddie, I need to ask you something. You know I'm not one for speeches, but this has been weighing on me for some time now, and I can't deny it any longer."

Maddie sat in the chair Charles indicated. She had a fair idea of what he wanted to ask, and her own less than pleased reaction didn't surprise her. He'd prefaced his first proposal to her in nearly the same way—and she'd accused *Quin* of being dull.

Back then, she'd been excited and nervous and thrilled, barely able to keep from throwing her arms about him when he'd finally asked the question. And then he'd kissed her, and she *had* thrown her arms about his neck. For a brief two weeks, she'd thought fairy tales really did come true—until she'd been proved very, very wrong.

Charles took her hands and knelt before her. "Maddie, we have been apart for five years, but I believe we were meant to be together. Will you do me the very great honor of becoming my wife?"

For a long time she looked at him, waiting for the thrill, the jangle of nerves, that had accompanied this moment five years earlier. Nothing but a tremor of uneasy nervousness ran through her. Perhaps she was trying too hard—or perhaps it was just that he was no longer the one she dreamed of spending her life with. "May I have some time to consider, Charles?" she asked. "A great deal has changed for me over the past few weeks."

"Of course." He smiled and stood. "But at least allow me one liberty." Slowly he leaned forward and brushed his lips against hers.

Maddie smiled at him, even less moved, if possible, than she had been a moment ago. "Thank you for your patience, Charles. I will give you my answer tomorrow."

He kissed her knuckles again. "I do love you, Maddie. I always have." With a last look, he left the room.

Maddie sat back. Marrying Charles would solve all her problems. It didn't matter that she didn't feel anything toward him. Nothing close to what she felt when Quin merely looked in her direction. But he was marrying someone else. She would never hear Quin laugh again when she insulted him, and she would never feel his arms around her again, holding her, and never—

"Maddie?" Her father stepped into the room. "Where's Charles?"

"He left."

"He—what did he want?"

"To marry me."

"That's splendid!" For a moment he was silent, looking at her expectantly. "Then why did he go?"

She looked up at him. "I told him I would give him my answer tomorrow."

The viscount opened and closed his mouth. "What precisely did you do that for?"

She heard the anger in his voice and tried to answer in a reasonable tone, however tense and uncertain and lonely she might feel. "I wanted a few hours to think about things, Papa."

He folded his arms, his expression darkening even further. "To think about *what* things? He was good enough for you before. And being gone God-knows-where and doing Lucifer-knows-what for five years has hardly elevated your social standing." Lord Halverston narrowed his eyes. "Or is it that you think you're too good for all of us, now that the grand Duchess of Highbarrow has shown you some charity?"

"No! Of course not. Just give me until tomorrow to answer him, Papa. That's all I ask."

"Just so long as you give the correct answer, Madeleine."

When he'd left and closed the door behind him, Maddie shut her eyes. Everything had been so much easier at Langley Hall, where she could be Miss Maddie and spend her evenings playing whist or word puzzles with

Mr. Bancroft and Squire John. But she couldn't deny that she'd been lonely there, too—nor that when John Ramsey asked her to marry him, as she'd sensed he eventually would, she would have said no.

"Miss Willits?" Everett scratched politely at the door.

"Yes?" she asked halfheartedly, sighing.

"Miss, a Mr. Rafael Bancroft is here to see you."

Unexpected tears welled up in her eyes. Perhaps there was still some hope. She wiped at them hurriedly. "Show him in, please."

A moment later the door opened, and Rafe strolled in past Everett. With his usual jaunty grin he bowed, pulling a bright bouquet of flowers from behind his back. "My lady."

She mustered a smile, fighting more tears. "Hello, Rafe."

He looked at her for a moment, and then thrust the bouquet at the butler. "Put these in water, will you?" he asked, and closed the door in Everett's face. "Whatever is wrong? You look like a damned watering pot, Maddie." He dropped into the chair beside her.

"Oh, I don't know," she muttered irritably, wiping at her eyes again. "I'm just glad to see you."

"If I'm so popular with you, then you shouldn't have left Bancroft House or my illustrious company," he commented, reaching out to pluck a hard candy from the dish on the table.

"I had to."

"Mm-hm," he said around the candy, nodding. "Well, you can tell me all your troubles if you like, but it won't do you a bit of good. *I'm* not the one you need to talk to."

She looked at him sideways. "I don't need to talk to anyone."

Rafe sighed heavily. "Suit yourself, Maddie. I am absolutely not going to get pulled into the middle of this mess. I have enough problems of my own.''

''Like what?'' she asked innocently. Something had been bothering him from the moment he'd arrived in London, but as far as she knew, he hadn't confided in anyone.

''Like something I have no intention of telling you about,'' he answered easily. ''But I will tell you this. My brother has had his entire life planned out for him, and he's been perfectly happy with it—until now. He's never had his head twisted around before, Maddie, and you can't expect him to be anything more than a complete idiot about it.'' He patted her on the hand, and stood. ''And that is all I intend to say on the subject.''

She looked at him, amused. ''Is that why you came by? To inform me that you weren't going to say anything?''

''Actually, it was to invite you to go riding with me in Hyde Park tomorrow morning. I believe Quin was supposed to go with you this morning, but he's a bit . . . preoccupied.''

''So you're fulfilling a familial obligation by offering to spend time with me?'' she asked, hurt.

''I'm taking advantage of his stupidity.'' Rafe winked at her. ''I'll come by at seven. Do you have a mount here?''

''No.'' As she was beginning to realize, she had nothing here. Nothing that meant anything, anyway. Not anymore.

''I'll bring Sunny, or whatever her name is.''

Maddie grinned. ''Honey.''

''Honey,'' he repeated, half to himself. ''*Sounds* like something fat old Prinny would own.''

That caught her attention. ''What?''

He squinted one eye. ''Nothing.''

"Rafe," she warned, chuckling. "What did you say?"

The younger Bancroft leaned back against the door. "Well, apparently my daft brother searched all over London for the perfect mount for you—you know how he is—and Prinny—drat, I mean King Georgie—had the exact one Quin wanted."

"So Quin bought Honey from King George, for me?"

"Well, not precisely. Prinny's been after some architect to design a palace somewhere, and—"

"Brighton," she supplied, becoming more intrigued with every disjointed sentence.

"Oh, then you *know* the story."

"Rafe!"

"All right, all right. Prinny's got this architect at Brighton, but he couldn't get Parliament to put up enough blunt to keep him on the job. Quin agreed to make up the difference."

Maddie sat and looked at him in disbelief, a delighted grin tugging at her lips. *"Quin helped King George keep John Nash on salary to renovate Brighton Pavilion, so I could have a horse to ride in London?"*

Rafe nodded. "Mm-hm."

A peal of delighted laughter tumbled from her throat. "Oh, good grief! No wonder he didn't say anything about it to me."

"I say, that's right. I'm not supposed to tell you, you know." He winked again. "Tricked it out of me, you did. Honey and I will be by at seven."

She stood and came forward to rise up and kiss him on the cheek. Before she could complete the gesture, he turned his head and touched his lips to hers. Startled, Maddie rocked back on her heels. "Rafe?"

"I'm not some castrato, you know," he muttered, "and you're quite impressive." He pulled open the door. "Good God, he's an idiot."

"Rafe, this morning Charles Dunfrey asked me to marry him," she blurted, flushing.

He closed the door again. "And?" he asked slowly, his light green eyes sharpening perceptibly.

That was what she liked so much about Rafe: he wasn't nearly as daft as he liked to pretend. She wondered how it must be for him, to be a second son and have the Duke of Highbarrow for a father. "I'm to give him my answer in the morning."

He drummed his fingers against the door for several moments. "You'll be at the Garrington ball tonight, won't you?" he asked finally.

She nodded.

His eyes held hers. "I'll see you there, then."

"Yes, I'll see you there."

After he left, the room seemed quiet and gloomy, and Maddie sat wondering why, precisely, she'd bothered to tell him about Charles. She sighed. Because he would tell Quin, of course. And because no matter what she'd said about wanting the marquis to leave her alone and do his duty by Eloise, she was still in love with him. "Oh, drat it all."

Eloise sat in her coach and watched Rafael Bancroft retrieve his horse and ride away from Willits House. The damned interfering rat couldn't seem to stay out of her affairs. No doubt he'd spent the entire visit with Maddie, trying to convince her to return to Bancroft House before Quin forgot about her.

Well, Maddie was not going to return to Bancroft House. Dunfrey had timed it perfectly, having her parents arrive in London before Quin's stupid sense of honor could ruin everything. How he could possibly think pity was a respectable reason to marry a completely unsatisfactory person she had no idea. But something of that sort had been on his mind; she could see it in his eyes when he looked at Maddie. And she didn't see it in his eyes when he looked at *her*. That didn't matter so much, though, as long as she ended being the one wearing his ring, and his title.

From his brief note of this morning, Dunfrey's plan was working so far—but there were some things she didn't dare leave completely to chance. Not with her future at stake. With a deep breath she lifted her umbrella and rapped on the roof of her coach. The driver started the team and turned into Willits House's short drive. Another coachman jumped down from his perch to open the door and help her to the ground.

"Wait here," she instructed, climbing the shallow steps.

The door swung open just as she reached it. "I am Lady Stokesley," she announced, before the butler could inquire. "I am here to see Miss Willits." She handed over a gilded calling card.

The butler, who had the ill manners to look flustered, showed her into the foyer. "If you'll wait here a moment, my lady."

She had barely enough time to note the inferior artwork lining the hallway before Maddie, accompanied by a plump woman who must have been her mother, appeared. "Maddie," she said warmly, coming forward to take the smaller woman's hands, "how pleased I am to find you here, back with your family. I never expected it."

"We are pleased to have her here," the older woman said. "I am Lady Halverston."

"Oh, yes," Maddie said belatedly, blushing. "Mama, Lady Stokesley. Eloise, my mother, Lady Halverston."

"Charmed," Eloise cooed, gripping the viscountess's fingers. "Your daughter resembles you."

Lady Halverston chuckled with unbecoming amusement. "Thank you for the compliment, Lady Stokesley.

Do come in.'' She led the way into the drab morning room.

It seemed Maddie was a better match for Dunfrey than she'd realized, Eloise thought.''I cannot stay,'' she said hastily, contemplating with horror the idea of actually taking tea with the woman. ''I thought Maddie might wish to accompany me on a picnic.''

Maddie looked at her, something almost suspicious touching her vapidly innocent gaze for a moment. ''Well, thank you, Eloise, but I really don't—''

''Hush, Maddie,'' Lady Halverston interrupted. She put her hand on Eloise's gloved one. ''We've been having a little difficulty adjusting to Maddie's return,'' she confided with a smile. ''I think a bit of fresh air with some friends will be just the thing to restore her spirits.''

Not if I have anything to do with it. Lady Stokesley smiled warmly. ''Say no more. Come with me, Maddie, my dear.''

The girl hesitated again, glancing at her mother, then shrugged. ''I'll get my bonnet,'' she said, and hurried out the door.

''Thank you for your kindness to my daughter,'' the viscountess said. ''We never expected to see her again, and certainly not under such pleasant circumstances.''

''Yes,'' Eloise agreed. ''I have already come to think of her as one of my dearest friends. And Quinlan—that is, Lord Warefield, my betrothed—speaks very highly of her.''

''Lord Warefield *does* seem fond of Maddie. I think he was none too pleased when she left.''

''We're all sorry to see her leave.''

Maddie hurried back into the morning room, her gloves and a pink bonnet clutched in one hand.

''Ah, there you are, my dear. Let's be off, shall we?''

Eloise smiled as she led the way out to her coach. With the extremely helpful friends she had selected to join them, this was going to be so easy, it was almost pitiful. Almost.

Chapter 15

The Duchess of Highbarrow sat in her private room, sewing.

Her favorite chair had been placed before the large window which overlooked the quiet street in front of the mansion, but she had no desire to look outside. She knew very well what was going on out there. A rather annoying clattering and clanging, which had begun below some forty minutes earlier, gave way to a rattling, clopping sound, and then slowly faded away into silence.

Victoria's hands stilled in her lap, and she sighed. She also knew what the absence of sound meant: her sons were gone again.

It made sense. Quin had obviously stayed to keep an eye on Maddie, and Rafael had stayed because of Quin—and Maddie. Once she left, Quin spent an hour stomping about and pretending he wasn't in a black temper. By teatime he had sent for his footmen at Whiting House and moved his things back home. And as he had over the past few years, Rafe went to stay with his brother.

"Victoria?" The bellow echoed up from the hallway, the duke's method of avoiding the necessity of asking the servants for the whereabouts of his wife.

She didn't answer. She didn't need to, for Beeks

would immediately inform his employer that she'd spent the afternoon in her private rooms and had asked not to be disturbed.

A moment later the door opened. "Victoria?"

"Yes?" She picked out her last row of stitches and began them over again. Apparently she hadn't been paying very much attention to her work. She *had* paid attention to several other interesting things in the Bancroft household, though, and for the duke's sake, he had better realize them as well—and soon.

"Where're the randy idiots and their mopsie?"

"If you are referring to our sons and Miss Willits, they are gone."

He closed the door and went to look out the window. "Gone where?"

"Maddie's parents came to see her, and she left with them. Quinlan and Rafael went to Whiting House. You just missed them."

For a moment the duke said nothing as he gazed outside. "Good," he muttered finally.

The duchess set aside her sewing and looked up at her husband. "And why is that good?"

He glanced back at her. "They were too damned noisy. It was like having a flock of geese about."

"And it's much better now—so quiet you can hear the minute hand of the grandfather clock on the landing?"

Slowly His Grace turned around. "Did you like all that nonsense?"

"I liked having my sons home. We don't see them very often, in case you hadn't noticed."

"We're busy folk."

Victoria shook her head. "Not that busy. They don't like coming around, now that they don't have to be here."

"I suppose you're going to blame that on me. Well,

I expect guests under my roof to abide by my laws. Always have.''

"I know," she said quietly.

"And always will. If that's too much for them, then they have no business being here. Glad they're gone." He nodded, as though attempting to convince himself of his own sincerity, and stalked out of the room again.

Occasionally Victoria wondered what would happen if she pushed against his "laws" to the point of open defiance. She'd come close several times, usually with regard to Rafe and his high spirits, but somehow the duke had always managed to deflect or ignore the attack. Lately it had begun to occur to her that his avoidance was no accident—and in a way, that was comforting. He wanted her there, even if the only way he could show it was by ignoring her direct questions and pronouncements.

The duchess picked up her sewing again. Such an obtuse method of rule couldn't last forever, and whether Lewis Bancroft realized it or not, his kingdom had already begun to crumble at the edges. A bright, fiery sprite had entered their lives, and nothing would ever be the same. She glanced out the window toward the light blue, cloud-patched sky. Her sons would certainly never be the same. One of them in particular.

The mutterings began well before Maddie arrived. Quin pretended not to hear them, while carefully tracing their source.

By now they'd spread across the Garrington ballroom, invading nearly every nook and cranny, but the center of the disturbance seemed to be a large group of his most intimate acquaintances. He stopped beside a potted plant and watched them for a moment as they chatted and laughed and managed to exclude all social inferiors by not even noting their presence.

As usual, the main attraction of the group seemed to be his second cousin, and as she leaned sideways to whisper into another intimate's ear, Quin decided he had several rather pointed questions to ask her.

"Eloise?" he said, strolling out from his hiding place and stopping beside her. "I hadn't expected to see you so early in the evening. You look lovely, as always."

She held out her hand for him to take. "It looked to be a sad crush, and I didn't want to have to wade in through the mud and horseshit." Her faithful circle of companions laughed, and she snapped her fan playfully. "Well, it's true, you know."

Quin smiled, unamused, and tucked her hand around his arm. "Might I have a word with you? And a waltz, of course, if you've still one unclaimed."

"I always leave one for you. Excuse me, ladies. My future husband would like to speak to me—in private."

The two of them strolled toward the wide doors that opened out onto the balcony, and with a glance into the half darkness, they stepped outside.

"Ah," Eloise murmured. "Alone at last." With another look around them and down at the darkened garden below, she slipped her hands up on either side of his face, and leaned up to kiss him slowly and deeply.

It was the first time she'd exhibited any kind of passion toward him, and at the moment he wasn't particularly interested. Not in her, anyway. "What was that for?" he asked as they parted.

"Just to remind you that our marriage will be more than a union of names and wealth. I think you'd forgotten that."

Recently his views of what a marriage should be had changed. "When did you decide that?" he asked.

She reached up to touch his cheek again, apparently undaunted by his cool tone. "Oh, Quin, we've known one another for so long. Sometimes I think it would have been better if our parents had kept us apart until it was time for us to marry.''

Quin nodded. ''You favor an element of mystery, I suppose?''

''No, not really. But sometimes I almost believe you think of me as a sister, or something equally awful.''

''I don't, Eloise. But I do think of you as a friend.'' Or rather, he had, until the last few days. Quin lifted her hand away from his face and held it. ''And as a friend, I'd like an explanation.''

Her delicate brow furrowed. ''An explanation of what?''

Quin looked down at her for a moment, wondering when, precisely, he'd ceased to think of her as a potential mate. Probably the moment he had set eyes on Madeleine Willits. ''Did you go somewhere with Maddie today?''

She yanked her hand free. ''I'm trying to seduce you, and you *still* ask me about her?''

''Eloise, she's here in London because of me,'' he returned flatly. ''She's my responsibility. I have an obligation to look—''

''She is *not* your responsibility. She is her own responsibility. You didn't ruin her, Quin. You had nothing to do with it.''

That wasn't exactly true anymore, but as he didn't want to begin a shouting match, he nodded. ''All right. But tell me what happened today.''

''Nothing happened. I invited her on a picnic, as we'd discussed, and—''

''*We* discussed taking her on a picnic,'' Quin agreed. ''With mutual friends attending.''

''Oh, Quin, don't you see? You already spend nearly every day with her. You're not helping her by accompanying her everywhere. Besides, everything was fine. She did very well.''

He continued to watch her, looking for any sign that she could actually be as devious as he had begun to suspect. "Not according to what I've been hearing to-night."

"What have you been hearing?" she asked, meeting his gaze evenly.

She could be telling the truth, he supposed, and truly knew nothing of the widely circulating rumors. But for the first time, he doubted her word. "I heard that she suggested you and your female friends leave so she could enjoy the company of Lord Bramell and Lionel Humphries in private."

Eloise clapped her hand over her mouth, but the expression in her eyes wasn't all that surprised. "Nothing of the sort happened! John and Lionel were there, of course, because you know they always attend such things, but—I mean—when Lady Catherine Prentice arrived, we all went to see her new setter puppy, but Maddie was alone with John and Lionel for only a moment. Two at most."

"You shouldn't have left her alone."

"She wanted to stay behind, Quin. I couldn't drag her across the park, for heaven's sake."

"Damnation," he swore softly. Maddie knew better. Anything she did—anything—whether innocent or not, would be viewed in the worst light possible by her fellows. To stay behind, alone with two single gentlemen, was worse than stupid. And Maddie wasn't stupid. Far from it.

But neither was Eloise. He looked at her speculatively. If his suspicions were correct, Eloise had a great deal of explaining to do. In all fairness, though, his mind didn't exactly work to perfection where Miss Willits was concerned, and he had no proof. Blind in love with Maddie or not, he couldn't accuse Lady Stokesley until he knew for certain that she was guilty of sabotage.

"Just remember, Quin, in a month's time you won't be able to claim poor Maddie as your responsibility any longer." She leaned up against him, her short blond curls tickling his cheek. "That will be me."

"I remember." He wondered why he hadn't always found her so self-centered and cloying. "We'd best go back inside, or we'll be starting some rumors of our own."

He escorted her back to their group of friends and spent the next hour dividing his attention between polite conversation and keeping an eye on the ballroom doorway. Rafe had said Maddie would be attending. He'd also said a few other things, at a rather high volume, and Quin intended to take care of those issues as soon as Miss Willits arrived.

Finally, late enough that she'd likely fought against coming, Maddie and her parents arrived. Quin's breath caught at the sight of her, glorious in green and gray. He watched her take stock of the room and the other guests, and he knew precisely when she decided she didn't want to be there.

"Excuse me for a moment," he said, to whomever happened to be listening, and started across the room toward her. He couldn't help himself. He craved her like he breathed air.

Rafe, obviously making use of his military skills, damn him, reached her first. "Good evening, my dear." He took her hand. "So pleased you could join us this evening."

Quin made a valiant attempt not to break into a full-on charge. It would never do for the Bancroft brothers to begin a tug-of-war over her in the middle of the ballroom. He stopped beside her. "Miss Willits." He smiled, stealing her hand from Rafael's grip and lifting it to his lips. "You look . . . stunning."

"Thank you, my lord," she said, meeting his eyes

and then looking quickly away. "Do let go of my hand."

He complied reluctantly. It seemed like days, rather than hours, since he had seen her last, and he wanted— needed—to touch her. "May I have a waltz with you?"

"I don't think you should," she said, still gazing determinedly at the punch bowl on the refreshment table.

"I do," he answered.

"No."

"Yes." As usual when he argued with her, Quin began to feel as if he was beating his head against a brick wall.

"Better do as he says, Maddie," Rafe put in, for once helpful. "But save one for me as well."

She smiled and looked at him. "Of course I will."

Quin didn't like that. Blast it, now he wanted to pummel people insensible just because she was smiling at them. Somehow, somewhere, he had completely lost control—and the oddest part was, he didn't mind it all that much.

Before he could ask her what in God's name had happened at the picnic, the orchestra began playing again, and he had to excuse himself to dance with his designated partner. For a moment he thought Maddie would have to remain alone beside her parents at the end of the room, but the Duchess of Highbarrow appeared from nowhere and led the Willits family off for a chat.

Whatever orders His Grace had given his wife regarding her assisting Maddie, she seemed to be ignoring them. He would have to call on her tomorrow and thank her: she'd just seen to it that Maddie would have partners for any dance she wished.

And so he danced a quadrille with that young lady, and a country dance with this one, and the entire time he kept his attention on Maddie. When Rafe claimed her hand for the first waltz of the evening, he barely managed to wipe the scowl from his face before he went to fetch Eloise.

"Rafael seems quite fond of Maddie," Eloise purred, as they circled grandly about the crowded room. "Do you think he might offer for her?"

"No," he answered sharply, glancing at the smiling couple again.

"No, I suppose not," she agreed smoothly. "Whatever Rafael's standards might be, your father would never allow such a poor match."

That caught his attention again. "What do you know of Rafe's standards?" he asked.

"Oh, just speculation," she returned. "I have to admit, though, they do look rather good together."

Yes, they did. Tall and muscular, with slightly tousled hair the color of ripened wheat and an easy grin made a little lopsided by the scar on his cheek, Rafe would look good with anyone. And Maddie, tonight wearing Quin's favorite gown because it brought out the gray of her eyes, her auburn hair piled high with curling wisps framing her face, was absolutely mesmerizing.

"So you think her a poor candidate for marriage to a peer?" he pursued, wondering how she would reply.

"Despite your commendable efforts, my dear, how could I think anything else?"

Quin nodded, remembering Eloise throwing tea at a servant, and Maddie slipping down to the kitchen to patch him up. "Then you were being kind to her only for my sake?" he continued.

"I like her, of course," Eloise retorted, her expression exasperated. "I'd like her more if you didn't seem so fond of her."

"Or if she was a social equal," he added.

"You make that sound like a bad thing. We all have standards to uphold, Quin. Especially you."

Quin nodded, wondering if she could sense his growing disgust. "Yes, I do. Thank you for reminding me," he said softly.

She smiled coyly at him. "You're welcome, my love."

By God, Eloise could be a snob. He realized how very much he disliked her, though he wondered how *he* might have reacted to Maddie's unexpected return to London, if he hadn't become acquainted with her first. Quin stifled a completely inappropriate grin. It was more accurate to admit that she'd pummeled him to his senses.

If Eloise had simply stated that she didn't like Maddie, and that she felt threatened by her presence, he could have accepted it. In fact, her honesty would have made him feel an absolute cad. But she'd been devious, and lied, and apparently had set Maddie up for several scandalous episodes. He couldn't help falling in love with Maddie, but he could help how he dealt with it. And Eloise was making the choice a surprisingly easy one.

"May I call on you in the morning?" he asked smoothly, as the music stopped.

"I look forward to it."

Finally he claimed Maddie for the last waltz of the evening, not particularly caring whether she'd already promised it to someone else or not. "I've missed you," he said, sweeping her out onto the dance floor.

"I've been gone for only two days. You *will* have to get used my absence, you know. I'm not your pet hunting dog."

However boldly and carelessly she spoke, Quin felt the tension in her lithe body, and the way her hand shook ever so slightly in his. Though he disliked causing her pain, he couldn't help feeling encouraged: at least she still felt an attraction toward him. Whether it was anything close to the torrent he felt for her, he could only hope.

"You're closer to a wild fox," he agreed, and took a deep breath. "Are you going to marry Charles Dunfrey?"

Gray eyes met his. "Rafe told you?"

"Of course Rafe told me," he snapped. "You knew he would."

"How could I possibly—"

"Are you going to marry him?" he interrupted.

For a long moment she looked up at him, her eyes searching his. "Who did you plan to have me marry when you dragged me back to London?"

"Damnation, Maddie, why won't you ever just answer a blasted question?"

Her lips twitched, humor replacing the somber look in her eyes for just a moment. "Why don't you?"

Quin wanted to be angry at her, but he was keenly aware that his time to converse with her had become severely limited. "All right. I surrender. I . . . hadn't thought that far ahead when I dragged you to London," he admitted. "I merely had a vague idea of saving you."

She actually smiled. "My white knight," she murmured. "Well, I suppose I'm saved."

"Don't marry him, Maddie."

For a moment she looked up at him. "So serious, now. Why are you so stubborn about this?"

Because I love you. "Because I am," he said instead. "I thought that was a character trait you'd admire."

"Quin, I don't want to marry him, really. But—"

"That's all I need to know."

"You are very annoying," Maddie stated. "First you drag me here to marry me off so you won't have to bother with me any longer, and now you tell me not to marry the only man who's asked. I don't—"

"Dunfrey is not the only man who's asked," he reminded her softly. "And he is *not* the man you're going to marry. *I* am."

Maddie looked down at his cravat. "I wish . . ." she said, in a very small voice.

He wanted to take her wan face in his hands and kiss her. "You wish what?"

She met his eyes again, as the music crashed to a halt. "I just wish," she repeated, and stepped back from him amid the applause of the other guests.

"Sometimes wishes come true," he whispered, and escorted her back to her parents.

Charles Dunfrey was there, waiting to take her out onto the floor for the next dance, and Quin's mood immediately soured. He nodded stiffly at his rival, and with a last glance at Maddie, strolled away. Tomorrow he would straighten things out.

Malcolm Bancroft sighed as the coach rattled to a stop. He sat where he was for a few moments, still half wondering what the hell he was doing.

A footman pulled the coach door open, and looked in at him expectantly. "Will you be leaving the coach, sir?" he asked politely.

"Yes, I suppose I will. You'd best call for assistance, though. You're a bit small, and I'm a bit ungainly."

After a moment the footman evidently believed he was serious, for he stepped back and whistled. Another liveried servant appeared, and Malcolm thrust a sturdy cane at each of them. Scooting as close to the door as he could, he heaved himself upright.

"Either catch me, or start running," he warned, and let his weight shift forward.

The footmen grabbed his arms as he half fell out of the coach, and among the three of them they managed to land him feet first on the ground. Taking his canes back, Malcolm began hobbling toward the front steps.

His left leg remained numb to the knee, and he had to keep a constant watch on it to make sure it didn't go wandering off without him. According to his physician, he still tired far too easily and should remain in bed for at least another fortnight. After reading Maddie's last letter, though, he'd decided he couldn't wait that long.

Beeks pulled open the front door as he reached the top step. The butler gaped at him for a moment, then hurried forward to offer his assistance. "Mr. Bancroft. We did not expect you."

Malcolm gave a slight grin. "No, I wouldn't imagine so. Is the old windbag about?"

"His Grace is just preparing to leave for the House of Lords," the butler replied.

"What about Quinlan?"

"Lord Warefield is residing at Whiting House."

Not surprised in the least to hear that, Malcolm headed into the morning room and carefully seated himself on the couch. "Please tell His Eminence I'm here, will you, Beeks?"

The butler nodded. "Of course, Mr. Bancroft."

He'd figured Lewis would make him wait fifteen minutes before he made his appearance, but it was only ten. His brother must have been curious in the extreme to forgo his usual performance.

"Who's watching over Langley?" the duke barked, strolling into the morning room.

"Squire John Ramsey. Who's watching over High-barrow?"

"My estate manager." Lewis glanced at his younger brother, then headed to the window, pulling aside the curtain to look out at the drive. "You've brought luggage. I hope you don't think to stay here; I just cleared that other crowd of fools out."

"I wouldn't stay here if it was the only house left standing in England," Malcolm replied calmly. "I'll stay at Whiting House, with Quinlan."

"Good. What do you want here?"

Mr. Bancroft eyed His Grace for a moment. "To see if you were keeping up your end of the bargain. I can see you're not, though I'm not really surprised."

Lewis faced him. "What bargain?"

"Seeing Maddie Willits back into society."

"That wasn't my damned bargain."

"It is a matter of Bancroft honor."

The duke dropped into the chair opposite his brother. "It's a matter of you and Quin doffing the same girl, and then feeling guilty about it. She doesn't signify, and she's certainly not worth all this trouble."

"She's worth considerably more trouble than you are. You used to have at least a few remnants of usefulness about you. Now you're just loud."

Lewis glared at him. "Get out of my house."

"With pleasure." Using a cane and an arm of the couch for leverage, Malcolm hauled himself to his feet. For a brief moment something uncertain entered the duke's eyes, but it was just as swiftly banished. "I'll be at Whiting House, should you wish to stop by and apologize."

"Not while I'm breathing."

Malcolm smiled. "I can wait."

Quin was on his way out the front door when he saw the coach. He immediately recognized the pair of bays pulling it and couldn't help grinning in relief. Reinforcements had arrived, and it was about damned time.

"What in the world are you doing here?" he asked, striding forward and yanking the coach door open. "And where is your chair?"

"I am walking, thank you very much," Uncle Malcolm returned. "Or a reasonable impression of walking, anyway."

Quin helped his uncle down to the ground and into

the foyer. "Did you stop by Bancroft House? Have you seen Maddie? Did you—"

"Quinlan, what a chatterbox you've become," Malcolm chastised with a grin. "Something on your mind, lad?"

He sat down in the drawing room, while Quin stalked the floor in a circle around him. "You know bloody well something's on my mind," the marquis stated. "It's your fault."

"*My* fault? *What's* my fault?"

"You knew I'd fall in love with her. And I thought you were sending her to London for her own sake." Quin glared at Malcolm. His uncle's smile didn't leave Quin feeling any less agitated; in fact, if he'd been Maddie, he would have been pummeling someone by now. "Well, say something!"

"This *was* for Maddie's sake," Malcolm offered, obviously considering his words. "As soon as I read that it was you Lewis was sending, I knew this would be my last chance to see her restored to her proper place in society. I also knew I'd likely lose her. Sending her away with you was not easy, you know."

"Well, you seemed to forget one rather important fact," Quin snapped at him. "I'm engaged."

Malcolm shrugged. "Obviously this was something I had to throw together rather quickly. You couldn't expect me to take care of all the details."

"The details?" Quin asked skeptically, angered at the idea that he'd somehow been manipulated into this whole disaster, whatever the ultimate reward might turn out to be.

"Yes. As for the part about you falling in love with her, I admit, it crossed my mind, but it wasn't my primary goal. Truly, Quin. I liked you as a youngster—very much—but for all I knew, you'd grown into your father. In which case, Maddie would have drowned you, instead of merely teasing you with the idea.''

"I don't like this," Quin said flatly.

"That's why I hadn't intended to tell you any of it."

Quin sat opposite his uncle. "What changed your mind?"

"This." Malcolm pulled a much-folded piece of parchment out of his pocket and smoothed it open. "Maddie's latest letter."

"Let me see it," Quin demanded.

"Most of it's none of your affair," his uncle replied. "This part, though, I thought you should hear." He lifted the letter again. " 'Charles Dunfrey has been calling on me, and while I doubt he could possibly be as smitten as he once claimed, at least he is polite and respectful. Con—' "

"The bastard," Quin growled, and Malcolm looked up at him.

"Hush. 'Considering that Quin has obligations of his own, and that I don't wish to cause any more trouble for him than I already have, perhaps setting things back the way they were would be the wisest choice, after all.' " He looked up. "It goes on from there, but I found that section particularly alarming."

Shooting to his feet, Quin began pacing again. He'd known she was thinking that, but to hear it worded that way. . . . She sounded so sad, and he had the absurd desire to go to her and snatch her up in his arms. "She won't marry him," he stated.

"What's to stop her?"

Quin looked down at his uncle. "I am." He headed for the door. "I hope you're not too tired to go visiting with me," he said over his shoulder. "I know someone who'd like to see you."

Maddie felt very much in need of an ally. She looked at her father, trying not to glare, trying to be reasonable, and trying very, very hard not to run out the front door and keep running until she reached Quin and Whiting House.

"Are you listening to me?"

"Yes, Father, I'm listening."

"So you will agree to Charles's proposal when he comes by today."

"I haven't decided yet," she said, her calmness edging toward anger. Whatever she'd been through over the past five years, it didn't seem to have changed her father's thinking in the least. And even if she did decide to marry Charles, it would be for her own reasons, and not because of the viscount's bullying and badgering.

"You're too good for him, now?" he asked with scathing sarcasm, folding his arms over his chest and tapping a boot against the floor.

She shrugged. "I don't love him."

"You don't—what in damnation does that matter? Do you think I love your mother?"

Maddie hoped Julia Willits wasn't listening. "I would have hoped so," she said, her voice beginning to shake a little. "She is a good-hearted and kind woman."

"And far too soft on you, obviously."

Maddie's indignant response would no doubt have seen her kicked out of Willits House, but before she could more than open her mouth, Everett scratched at the library door.

"What is it?" the viscount grumbled, obviously displeased at having his tirade interrupted.

Everett opened the door and stuck his head in. "Two callers for Miss Willits," he said.

"Who is it?" Lord Halverston continued to glower.

"A Mr. Bancroft, and the Marquis of Ware—"

"Mr. Bancroft?" Maddie cried, jumping to her feet and pushing past the surprised butler. "Sorry, Everett."

"Quite all right, Miss."

Both men stood in the foyer, and that in itself stopped her. "Mr. Bancroft, *you're standing?*"

"More or less," he grinned. "How are you, my dear?"

Maddie hurried forward and flung her arms about her former employer. "I'm so glad," she whispered, tears running down her face. "I'm *so* glad."

"Now, *that* is a proper greeting," Malcolm said, hugging her back.

"I'd settle for one of those, myself."

Maddie looked up at Quin, who gazed back at her. She smiled tearfully. He *had* come to see her. "Thank you."

"You're welcome," he answered, "but he brought himself to London. I think he's worried you're going to marry the wrong man."

"Ah, Lord Warefield," her father said grandly, emerging from the library and showing no sign at all of his former ill temper. "So kind of you to stop by to see my daughter."

"A pleasure," Quin replied, shaking the viscount's hand. "May I present my uncle, Mr. Bancroft? Malcolm, Viscount Halverston."

Maddie reluctantly relinquished her hold on Mr. Bancroft, and he shook hands with her father as well. "I've heard a great deal about you," Malcolm said noncommittally.

"I wish I could say the same," the viscount answered, looking at his daughter.

Maddie could guess what he was thinking—that she'd had some sort of sordid relationship with Mr. Bancroft. He seemed to think that about every gentleman she mentioned. And she had long ago reached the point that she really didn't care what he thought. She looked up at Quin again.

"How are you today, Miss Willits?" he asked politely.

"Very well, thank you, my lord."

"Might I have a word with you in private?" he continued. "My mother wished me to convey a message to you."

"Of course," she said, trying to cover her sudden excitement, and motioned him to join her in the library.

With her father standing right there in the hallway, they couldn't exactly close the door, but Quin took her hand and led her to a far corner of the room, beneath the high windows. "How are you getting along?" he asked quietly, running his fingers along her cheek.

Maddie closed her eyes as his lips touched hers. She had missed him so much. "As though I never left."

He smiled. "That poorly?"

"Yes." She sighed. "So you came to inquire after my health?"

"Not exactly. I never asked you," he murmured. "What is your dream of an ideal life?"

Unsettled, Maddie turned away. Quin slowly slid his arms about her waist, pulling her back against his chest. "I don't dream," she said. He was making doing the right thing supremely difficult—and he knew it, the bastard.

"Tell me anyway."

She shook her head. "You know." Little by little she let herself relax against him. "It would have been nice."

Quin rested his cheek against her hair. "It *will* be nice," he corrected.

It was too easy—too easy simply to lose herself in the moment, to pretend that it would last forever. Maddie straightened and turned to face him. "Quin, stop—"

His jade eyes held hers, warm and compassionate, looking deeper inside her than anyone had or ever would. And in that moment she knew: she was not going to marry Charles Dunfrey. Thanks to Quin, she knew what it was to love someone. Whatever else happened, she would not marry for anything less.

Slowly he smiled. "What are you thinking?"

Maddie leaned up on her tiptoes and kissed him. "It *is* nice." Her father's voice echoed in from the hallway, and she jumped, taking a step back. "So. Have you been to call on Eloise yet?"

He scowled and shook his head. "I was on my way when Malcolm appeared. I'll go as soon as I see him back to Whiting House. Has Dunfrey been to call on you yet?"

"No."

Quin swallowed, his expression becoming uncertain. "I need to tell you something."

Now she was uneasy. She didn't need another lesson to know that nothing was simple where they were concerned. "I'm listening."

"Even if you decide for some unfathomable reason that you don't want to marry me, there's something you should know about Charles Dunfrey."

"Not spreading rumors, are you?" she asked, only half teasing. He wouldn't dare to stoop so low as to lie about Charles just to convince her not to marry him. Not now.

"This is a fact. Maddie, I discovered something the other day, and considering the circumstances, I don't think I should keep it from you."

"Stop stalling about and tell me, Quin."

"It's Dunfrey's finances. He's—"

"He's what, Warefield?" This was the sort of backbiting behavior she expected from the rest of the nobility; she hadn't expected it of Quin. "He's not as wealthy as you?" she suggested. "I suppose not. But then again, who is?"

"Maddie, you're taking it all wrong. This is not about my pompous snobbery, or your lack thereof."

She put her hands on her hips. "Why don't you explain it to me, then, my lord?"

"I'm trying to explain it, damn it," he snapped. "Dunfrey's one step ahead of the bloody moneylenders, Maddie. Without your dowry, he'll be done for, probably by the end of the Season. I'm worried that—"

"That he's marrying me only for my money? Or for my parents' money, rather?" She shrugged, furious and hurt. "What did you expect? I suppose he couldn't possibly just happen to be poor and simply wish to marry me because he loves me. For heaven's sake, who could be that abysmally stupid?"

"Maddie—"

"Thank you, my lord, you've been a great help. Now, go marry that wretched Eloise, and leave me alone." Tears danced in her eyes, and she lowered her gaze to his chest.

He opened and shut his mouth several times. "Damnation," he cursed. "You are impossible."

"That's what I've been trying to tell you, if you'll recall. Good day, my lord."

She turned on her heel and left the room, pausing only to nod at Malcolm before going upstairs to her bedchamber.

Chapter 16

Quin wanted to strangle her.

He also wanted to kiss the tears from her eyes, and to kiss her sweet, soft lips, and to hold her in his arms again. The thought that he would never do so again wrenched something hard and painful loose in his chest. "Devil a bit," he muttered, stalking out into the hallway. "Let's go, Uncle," he snapped.

"My lord," the viscount said, touching his shoulder, "if my daughter has offended you, please let me apologize. She has no manners, and—"

Quin jabbed a finger at him. "Don't," he snarled, and strode outside.

His dramatic exit was somewhat ruined when it took Malcolm another four minutes to make his way down the stairs and out to the coach, so he sat in the half dark of the vehicle's interior and stewed.

"Another argument?" his uncle grunted, tossing both canes onto the floor.

Quin stood and helped haul him up into the coach and down into a seat. "This is ridiculous. She never listens to me, she misinterprets everything I say, and she is so damned stubborn, I just want to wring her neck."

Malcolm lifted an eyebrow. "And?"

313

"This is all your fault."

"All *I* did was take her in and have an apoplexy. *You're* the one who fell in love," his uncle pointed out. "Don't blame me."

"Why am I doing this?" Quin demanded. "Why am I putting myself through this? No one will appreciate it. I am the bloody future Duke of Highbarrow, for God's sake."

Malcolm just looked at him.

Quin glared right back at him. "Oh, shut up," he finally mumbled. "Love is highly overrated."

"I wouldn't know, Quin."

"Lucky you."

"Do you really mean that, son?"

The marquis sat back and folded his arms across his chest. "No."

Rafael was ecstatic to see Malcolm when they returned to Whiting House. The two of them toddled off together to the morning room, no doubt to gossip the day away about the idiot Marquis of Warefield and his infatuation with a stubborn, impossible . . . lovely, high-spirited, intelligent sprite who was absolutely nothing but trouble. And quite the best thing that had happened to him in his entire life.

By the time he remembered that he'd been heading over to see Eloise, she'd gone out shopping with some friends, and had left word that he was a rude, uncaring beast, and she would see him tomorrow.

"Just as well," Quin informed the Stokesley butler, as he turned on his heel. "I don't feel like another bludgeoning today, anyway."

"Very good, my lord."

He swung back up on Aristotle, intending to return home, until a paralyzing thought occurred to him: Dunfrey was still supposed to call on Maddie today. If he did, and if she was angry enough, there was no telling what she'd do. He kicked Aristotle into a gallop, upsetting the more conservative members of the gentry as they went about their early afternoon visiting.

When he stormed into his morning room, Rafael and Malcolm were playing chess. "Rafe, go visit Maddie," he ordered, ripping off his gloves and tossing them at his brother. "Aristotle's outside."

"Just a damned minute," Rafe said, deftly catching the gloves. "I am a captain in His Majesty's Coldstream Guards. I do *not* go and visit women on command. Nor am I your errand boy." He threw the gloves back. "Go visit her yourself. And don't try to bribe me with my own horse."

"I thought you liked her."

"I do like her. Enough that I'm not going to participate in this silliness any longer."

Quin narrowed his eyes. "What silliness, pray tell?"

Rafe stood. "I don't know what the devil's going on between you," he snapped, all humor for once missing from his light green eyes, "but I do know if you don't take care of it soon, I will." He stomped toward the door.

"What is that supposed to mean?" Quin asked coolly, seething.

Rafe glanced over his shoulder. "Whatever the hell you want it to." He stalked out the front door. A moment later, Quin heard him whistle sharply for a hack.

The marquis took a deep breath and sat in his brother's vacated chair. "Wonderful. Now everyone's angry at me."

"Why did you want Rafe to go see her?" Malcolm asked, calmly removing an opposing knight from the board and setting it with his other captives.

"Dunfrey's going to call on her today. She's supposed to decide whether she's going to marry him or not."

"Ah, that would explain several things." Still looking as though he hadn't a care in the world, Malcolm shifted one of his own pieces sideways and hauled himself to his feet.

"Which things?" Quin asked, following behind him.

"Maddie's being in tears when she saw you this morn—"

"You mean when she saw *you*," Quin amended.

"—When she saw you this morning, and all the colorful names Rafe has been calling you since we returned." Malcolm paused and looked sideways at him. "He was going to see her today, anyway." He smiled. "I think he's half in love with her, too. She has quite a talent for that."

Quin stopped. "For what?"

"For being irresistible to every man who's not terrified of her. Now, don't bother me until dinner is ready. I'm damned tired of limping about."

Rafe didn't return, but sent word that he was spending the night at Bancroft House, along with a heart-lifting "She said no" scrawled on a piece of paper. Staying voluntarily under the same roof as His Grace was a measure of how furious he must have been at his brother.

Actually, even with the good news, Quin was glad Rafael had stayed away—the desire to strangle his brother grew stronger every minute he thought about what Malcolm had said, about Rafe being half in love with Maddie. On the other hand, with Rafe gone, he had no way of knowing why Maddie had turned Dunfrey down.

He spent the night pacing before his bedchamber fireplace, fighting the urge every few minutes to ride off to Willits House and demand to know what had happened. The only thing that stopped him was that he still hadn't broken with Eloise, and that Maddie would know that when she looked at him.

He knew that ultimately she didn't believe he would keep his word to her, or that he would dare brook four hundred years of Bancroft history to marry a social outcast—that he would risk losing his fortune and his title just to be able to wake up each morning and argue with an auburn-haired wood sprite.

So Quin paced until two in the morning, and then he went downstairs to the drawing room and got very, very drunk. Then he thought of something. "Damn," he said, dropping into a chair and toasting himself with another snifter of brandy. "I'm not such an imbecile, after all."

Eloise had clearly decided to make use of deceit and subterfuge to secure his hand. He might as well do the same to prevent it. Quin smiled. With Eloise busy fawning over him, she wouldn't have time to make trouble for Maddie. And after Almack's, all bets were off.

Maddie sat on the edge of her bed, staring at the ivory dress laid out on the quilt. Ten days had gone by so quickly, she could scarcely believe it. And after Almack's tonight, all bets were off.

Rafe had called on her every day for the past week, as had Mr. Bancroft, and, surprisingly enough, the Duchess of Highbarrow. In addition to bolstering her flagging spirits, the Bancrofts' presence inspired her father to allow her to remain at Willits House despite her abysmal stubbornness regarding marriage to Charles Dunfrey. Of Quin Bancroft, though, there was no sign.

She didn't sleep, and she couldn't eat. If she'd been the woman her father wanted her to be, she would have put her feelings and affections aside and graciously informed Charles Dunfrey that she'd changed her mind, that of course she would be his wife.

But marrying for anything but love, and marrying anyone but Quin Bancroft, was unthinkable. After their last argument, though, he'd apparently decided to ignore her existence, instead turning to Eloise and happily carrying on with his stuffy, stupid, maddening engagement. It rendered even daydreaming about their own union completely ridiculous—which didn't stop Maddie from imagining it endlessly. She tried not to listen, but it seemed everyone she encountered had seen Quin just five minutes earlier, and always in the company of Eloise Stokesley.

Rafe hadn't tried to explain his brother's thinking, other than with a cool "Must always keep up appearances, you know." In fact, she knew that he and Quin hadn't been speaking and that Rafe had moved back into Bancroft House, where his mood was so foul, even the duke stayed clear of him.

She hated causing so much pain and anguish. But after tonight it would be over. The Bancrofts would have no more reason to be pleasant to her, and she would have carried out her promise to Mr. Bancroft. Best and worst of all, if she wanted, she would be able to return with him to Langley Hall. The thought wouldn't be so difficult if she could stop thinking of Quin's kisses, and Quin's laugh, and Quin's touch, every moment of every day.

Mary scratched at the door. "Miss Maddie, I need to start getting you ready," she said softly.

"Come in," Maddie said, making an effort to erase the tense, nervous expression from her face. "I may as well get this blasted nuisance over with."

When she came downstairs an hour later, everyone said she looked superb—except for her father, who hadn't said a word to her since she had sent Charles away. She wished she'd realized before how little he cared for her. It would have made the past five years much easier: she could have written her mother or Claire, and told them where she was, and at least they might have corresponded. She wouldn't make the same mistake again, but neither would she stay.

"Are you ready, Maddie?" her mother asked. "Her Grace is to meet us at Almack's."

"Yes, I'm ready. More than ready."

Despite her brave pronouncement, the carriage ride went far too quickly. She would have chosen even the company of her father, cold and stone-faced beside her, over addressing the patronesses of Almack's. It didn't help that she already hated them. How any dozen stodgy women had come to wield such power over their fellows she had no idea, but it couldn't possibly be fair.

Not only was the duchess there waiting for them; so were Rafe and Malcolm. As she glanced across the room at what seemed like hundreds of guests, all ready to second the judgment of the patronesses, her pulse leaped. Quin had come, too. He was dancing with Eloise Stokesley, but at least he had come. She would be able to see him, and perhaps even speak to him, one last time.

She knew she should be angry at him, but the pounding of her heart, the heat in her cheeks, and the way she wanted to kick off her shoes and run across the room to hug and kiss him made one thing very clear: whatever she'd said to him, and however loud she'd yelled and stomped her feet and tried to dislike him, she loved Quin Bancroft.

"Maddie," the duchess murmured, "stop looking at my son."

She jumped. "Was I?" she asked shakily, turning her gaze at once to the white- and ivory-clad girls moving in a shuffling, nervous line before the row of patronesses. Of course, every single one of the stuffy, conceited women seemed to have decided to attend tonight's assembly.

"Yes, you were. I fear, though, that now he seems to

be staring at you as well. He used to know better. You've been a poor influence on him.''

Maddie looked over at her sponsor. Despite her words, she didn't look angry. In fact, she seemed to be rather amused. ''My apologies, Your Grace.''

''Hmm. Well, come on, we'd best get you past the gauntlet.''

''Your Grace?'' Maddie said hesitantly, as she took the older woman's arm. ''Thank you for everything you've done.''

Lady Highbarrow chuckled. ''I think you'd be wise to save your thanks. The evening's not over yet.''

Quin watched. He couldn't help it, because he couldn't keep his eyes off her. He didn't know when he'd stopped looking at this moment as Maddie's triumph and begun looking at it as a death knell to the moments he could spend with her. But as his mother introduced her to each of the Almack patronesses, and as she curtsied politely and received the all-important nod of the head, the tension gnawing at the pit of his stomach grew into a knot of dread and anguish that made even the act of breathing difficult.

After tonight, she could leave. If he made one misstep, if he gave her one more split second to distrust him, he would lose her. And that, he was certain, would kill him.

''Quin, I thought you were over her,'' Eloise murmured, running her fingers along his sleeve.

''I am,'' he replied easily, turning back to face his betrothed. ''Her success is something of a reflection on the Bancrofts, though, don't you think?''

Eloise glanced at Maddie. ''I suppose, but only because you've made it so. You could easily have distanced yourself, and your family, from her anytime you chose.''

''Wouldn't have been much honor in that.'' He risked

another glance as Maddie made it to the end of the gauntlet and emerged triumphant. While he had the overpowering urge to applaud, he also wanted to race over and grab hold of her before she could flee into the night.

The orchestra struck up a waltz. In his dreams, almost from the beginning, he had been the one to dance with her. Instead, Rafe bowed and took her hand to lead her onto the floor.

"He doesn't miss an opportunity to stand up with her, does he?" Eloise noted. "Will you dance with me, my love?"

"Of course," he said.

They danced the waltz, and then he took his mother out for a quadrille. Another entire set followed until the music for another waltz finally began. Seeing several gentlemen heading in Maddie's direction, now that she was accepted again, he quickly excused himself from his circle of cronies.

"This one is mine, I hope," he murmured, as he came up behind her.

She jumped and turned to look up at him. "As you wish, my lord." Her cheeks were flushed from the heat of the room, and her eyes sparkled as he swept her into the dance.

"Congratulations," he said, smiling. "You are a triumph."

"How could I be anything less, with the Duchess of Highbarrow leading the introductions? You should have heard her. She practically threatened those women into accepting me." She chuckled. "It was quite wonderful. Rafe said when Her Grace is determined about something, she's more frightening than a herd of stampeding water buffalo."

"You see Rafe quite a bit these days, don't you?" he asked, unable to keep the jealous edge out of his voice.

Her smile faded. "I see those who come to visit me,"

she answered. "You've been busy elsewhere, apparently." Maddie glanced pointedly at Eloise, dancing with Thomas Danson.

He narrowed his eyes. "Yes, I have, thank you very much."

"Eloise is not *my* fault," she snapped. "You're the one who keeps promising to marry everyone in sight."

"I do not!" he protested.

She looked up at him. "I just wish you would tell me, straight out. You're not hurting anyone, Quin, by doing the right thing and marrying Eloise."

"The right thing is not to marry Eloise," he countered. "Which is exactly why I've been keeping her occupied for the past week."

Maddie's suspicious expression made him want to laugh. "What do you mean, 'keeping her occupied'? She's your betrothed, you big oaf."

"I've recently found that idea very unappealing," he said softly, holding her as closely as he dared in the blasted conservative assembly. "But I decided that while she spends time with me, she can't be making things more difficult for you."

"Oh, so now you're being gallant again?" she said skeptically.

"I thought so."

"Ah. And you'll gallantly stand beside her at Westminster Abbey in two weeks as well, I suppose?"

He heard it then—the jealousy in her voice. Quin smiled. "I don't want to marry Eloise," he whispered, very conscious of the other dancers circling them and how much damage could still be done to her reputation. "Nor do I intend to do so. I love *you*, Maddie."

She actually stumbled, tripping over his foot, and with a grin Quin pulled her against his chest until she could regain her balance.

"Are you all right?" he asked, feeling considerably

more confident than he had a moment before.

"What . . . what did you say?" she asked almost soundlessly, staring up at him white-faced.

"I said that I love you. Is that such a surprise?"

"Well, yes. Quin, you can't love me—you're still betrothed to Eloise."

"Only until tomorrow morning. She can't hurt you now, and I'm not certain I can take another day with her. I'm finding that several of my acquaintances are rather unpleasant to be around—very arrogant, they are."

Maddie grinned, her eyes lighting. "You're an idiot," she whispered.

"I still love you. I'm beginning to think you're impossible not to love."

"Yours is a minority opinion." Maddie took a deep breath. "You shouldn't have told me, anyway—you're only making things more difficult. You're bound to come to your senses soon."

"Be with me tonight, Maddie," he murmured. "We'll figure everything else out tomorrow."

"But Eloise—"

"To hell with Eloise. I want you."

"That's very dishonorable," she said weakly.

He heard the reluctant desire in her voice. It was all he needed. "You're already ruined," he pressed, "thanks to me. Please, Maddie, whatever else happens, I want—"

"Shh," she said. "How in the world do you intend to be with me, Lord Marquis? Are we going to steal into the library and lock the door? Oh, dear me, we've already done that, haven't we?"

He chuckled, delighted. He'd won—at least, for the moment. "That was the drawing room. And when the dance is finished, follow me."

As soon as the waltz ended, people crowded onto the

floor for a country dance. Quin ducked backward, Maddie trailing behind him. As the music started, he slipped out onto the dark balcony. Maddie peeked around the corner, and he pulled her onto the stones. He leaned down to kiss her, but she sidestepped, shoving him away.

"What is it?" he asked, pursuing her toward the railing.

Maddie raised her fist in his direction. "This is what happened before," she hissed, "with that blasted Spenser. I don't want anyone to see you trying to kiss me. Not after I just became respectable again."

"I'll check first, then," he said, and moved past her into the darker shadows. Under the circumstances, he was lucky she hadn't hit him; the only excuse he could give for being so obtuse was that he was having difficulty thinking of anything but feeling the warm, naked slide of her body against his. "All clear," he informed her, returning to her side. "*Now* will you kiss me?"

With another hesitant look around, she lifted up on her toes. Leaning her hands on his chest, she touched her lips to his. Quin shut his eyes at the soft touch, slipping his arms around her slender waist and wondering that she'd ever come this far in trusting him. If he'd been the one betrayed and reviled by his peers, he wasn't certain he'd have been able to do the same.

She sighed. "Oh, my, that's nice." After a moment, she relaxed against him. "What now?" she whispered against his mouth, placing feather-light kisses on his lips and along his jaw and cheek.

White-hot desire blazed through him. "We'd best do something soon," he murmured, "because I am becoming extremely uncomfortable."

"Out here?" she asked skeptically, her breathing uneven.

Quin stepped to the railing and looked down into the

garden. A thick trellis of vines crept up the wall beside the stone abutment. They could climb down, but once there, only the uncertain shadows of the foliage would shield them from curious eyes. And there were plenty of those about. "Devil it." Banging his fist on the railing in growing frustration, he leaned out further and looked up.

"That way." He grinned, pointing to the dark window twenty feet above their heads. "The attic."

"You are completely mad," she declared, unable to stifle a nervous chuckle. "Quin, you're not serious. Almack's attic?"

"Yes, I am. Shall I go first?"

"Quin, I'm not climbing up there. I'll tear my dress."

"Then I suppose we'll have to make love right here." He smiled softly, running his finger along her cheek. "It wouldn't be the first time we've torn one of your lovely gowns, Maddie."

"Oh, damn," she swore, swallowing hard. "If I wasn't already ruined, you would take care of it. Climb the blasted trellis."

He made it up fairly easily. Luckily, the window was unlatched, and he pushed it open and swung his legs over the sill. When he looked down, Maddie had the hem of her gown tucked into her neckline, and she was looking ahead determinedly as she climbed.

"Don't you like heights?" he asked softly, as he guided her into the tall, narrow room.

"I don't believe I'm doing this," she panted, freeing her hem. "I've completely lost my mind. This is so stupid."

Quin lowered his lips over hers, stopping her complaints with a rough, deep kiss. *He* couldn't believe she'd done it, either, and he had no intention of letting her take herself back down the trellis right away.

Everything was covered with dust, but fortunately the

spare furniture was draped with sheets. He released Maddie long enough to uncover an ornate serving table, a long gash across its otherwise smooth surface. Lifting Maddie around the waist, he set her down on the polished oak.

"Quin, we can't do this," she managed, clutching his shoulders and lifting her chin as he trailed his mouth down her soft throat.

"Stop saying that. I want to be with you."

"And I want to be with you. But—"

He backed away just enough to look her in the eye. "You are *not* marrying anyone but me, and I am most certainly not marrying Eloise. Is that clear?"

She scowled. "You can't order me—"

"And *I'm* not marrying Eloise Stokesley," he repeated, before she could manage to turn this into another battle. They didn't have a great deal of time.

Her mouth opened and then closed. "You're not? Truly?"

"Truly." He reached down to grasp her ankles, then slowly slid his hands up along her legs, lifting her skirt as he went.

"Just like that?"

Quin leaned down to brush his lips across her exposed thigh, and the muscles jumped beneath her skin. "Just like that."

"And what about your family?" she pursued raggedly.

"I'll tell them tomorrow." Hungrily he sought her mouth again.

She moaned as his gentle touch found the secret place between her thighs. "But what about—"

"Shh," he murmured. "Don't ask me anything else."

Whether she intended to ask anything or not, she became occupied with nibbling at his lip and then his ear. His heart pounding, Quin tugged her legs around his hips, pulling her close against him. It seemed impossible that such a fiery, passionate woman could have had no lovers before him, but he knew she hadn't. He was her first, and if everything went as he'd planned, as he'd dreamed, he'd be her only lover.

Maddie's hands tugged at his waist, pulling his shirt-tails free of his trousers. With a breathless chuckle, she kissed him, her gray eyes dancing with heat and passion. Her hands fumbled with his fastenings, then freed him from his breeches. Quin moaned as she folded her legs around his hips. He entered her slowly, relishing the feel of her warm, tight flesh around him.

She threw her head back as he pushed into her, twin-ing her hands together behind his neck and holding her-self hard against him. Quin grasped her buttocks, pulling her to him with every thrust of his hips. He wanted to remember everything—the darkness of the night with the half moon rising just over the rooftops, the muffled sound of the country dance below, the lavender scent of Maddie's skin, and the sparkle of her eyes as he looked into them.

They climaxed together, and he buried his face against her shoulder as he shuddered and spilled his seed inside her. Maddie threw her arms about his shoulders, holding tightly to him. After a long time, he lifted his head and gently kissed her again.

"Well, you've ruined me again," she said, still out of breath.

"I seem to be making a habit out of it," he agreed. "I can't help myself. You are irresistible. But one of these days, you and I are going to share an actual bed, with an entire night of nothing but the two of us."

She smiled at him and slowly lifted her hand to stroke his cheek. "That would be very nice," she whispered.

He couldn't help grinning. Maddie hadn't said she loved him, but she did care for him. She'd made that much obvious by the degree of trust she'd shown. Whether or not she would ever be able to tell him so, he had no idea. But he could hope. And he would wait.

"I love you, Maddie. I have since the moment we met."

Her expression sobered. "What do we do now?"

He grinned ruefully. "We climb back down the trellis. Then you and I will go home, to our separate houses. In the morning I will call on my parents, I will call on Eloise, and then I will call on you. You are my heart's desire, Maddie—you make me feel so alive. Nothing else matters but you and me."

"Not your family, or your honor, or your title? What if your father disinherits you?"

He reached up to clasp her hands and brought them around to hold against his chest, over his heart. "I will call on you in the morning," he repeated firmly. "Trust me."

"Do you promise?"

"I promise, my love."

With a last, lingering kiss, Quin helped her down from the table. She wanted him to keep holding her, but a loud laugh from the ballroom below reminded her that they couldn't very well stay hidden in Almack's attic forever—and that was a pity.

He tucked his shirt back into his breeches and attempted to put his hair back in some sort of style, for she'd tousled it rather badly. Maddie self-consciously straightened her skirt and her underthings, feeling rather tousled herself. Pure insanity. That was her only explanation for her behavior since she'd met Quinlan Ulysses Bancroft.

She had heard of men who, once they began, couldn't stop drinking liquor. Day in and day out they craved the stuff, paying attention to nothing else, until finally they drank themselves to death. For the first time she understood the attraction.

She craved Quin with every breath, with every beat of her heart. No one knew her as he did, and certainly no one cared for her as he did. They were completely wrong for one another, but nothing made as much sense as being with him. In the moonlight his hair looked white and silver, and the green of his eyes darkened almost to black.

"What are you looking at?" he asked, as he glanced over at her.

"You," she answered. "I can't figure you out."

He chuckled. "I thought I was being rather obvious, myself."

"Not that." Maddie flushed, though she had to wonder what in the world she had to be embarrassed about. She certainly had no secrets left from him.

Quin flung the old sheet back over the furniture. "What, then?"

"Since you've met me, you've nearly been drowned, shot, attacked by a mad sow, bellowed at by your father, kept—"

"My father bellows all the time," he interrupted. "It has nothing to do with you."

"I just don't understand how, after all that, you could possibly decide that you love me."

Quin looked at her for a long moment, then slowly came forward to fix a straying strand of her hair. "I'm not dull," he said quietly.

"I know that," she agreed. "I was only mad at you before."

Gently he put a finger over her lips. "That's not my point. *I'm* not dull, but my life is. As far back as I can remember, I've known I'd be the Duke of Highbarrow one day. I've known who I am to regard as a friend, and who is an enemy—not because I ever met them, but because of who their great-great ancestors were. I've known whom I'm to marry practically since she was born. You are . . . unexpected. And that's very rare and precious, where I come from.'' He grinned. ''No one's actually ever *attempted* to drown me, before you.''

She searched his eyes, but all she saw was a warmth and passion that matched her own. ''What happens when I become dull and ordinary to you?''

Quin laughed, until she put her hand over his mouth before they heard him downstairs. ''Hush,'' she ordered.

He removed her hand, holding it in his. ''I don't think you could become dull if you wanted to, my dear.'' He chuckled softly, his eyes dancing, and leaned down to kiss her again.

That led to more kissing, until the music stopped below. She looked toward the window. ''Oh, no.''

''It's just the set, Maddie,'' he said, pulling her close against him again, his arms wrapped around her shoulders as if he never intended to let her go. She wouldn't have minded that at all. ''We'll wait until the next one begins, and then we should go.''

She looked up at him dubiously. ''I don't suppose you mean we should sneak out the attic and back downstairs that way.''

''We go down the way we came up,'' he said calmly.

''But I am considerably less motivated to climb down the trellis than I was to climb up,'' Maddie complained, only half joking. ''That's a damned long way down, Quin.''

''I'll go first, so you may fall on me if you feel the need to do so.''

Releasing her, he strolled to the window, peering out carefully. ''The garden appears to be deserted,'' he informed her, and leaned out to look down at the balcony. ''Oops.'' He ducked back inside. ''Apparently we're not the only amorous couple this evening. I must say, Almacks's standards are falling abominably.''

Now that she wasn't quite so . . . involved with Quin, the night air coming in through the window felt chilly against her bare arms. She hugged herself. ''I guess we have to go out the other way, then.''

''No, we don't. We can wait another few minutes.'' He glanced down and then looked at her again. ''Don't you want to know who it is?''

''Absolutely not. Whoever they are, no doubt they want privacy, or they wouldn't be out there.''

Quin straightened and turned back to her. ''Do you want my coat?'' He started to shrug out of it.

''No, I don't want your coat, Sir Galahad,'' she retorted, yanking it back up onto his shoulders. ''You'll have to put it on again in two minutes, anyway.'' He did feel nice and warm, though, so she slipped her arms around his lean waist, under his coat.

He had told her that he loved her, and she wished she could say the words back to him. She felt them, so much that it almost hurt to hold them in, but when she tried, they simply became stuck. Tomorrow, she would tell him. After he told Eloise and his parents that he intended to marry ruined little Maddie Willits.

Once he'd done that, she had the feeling that reality would come crashing down on his head, and he would regret having becoming temporarily mad and said all those wonderful things to her. Until then, she would let everything be a dream. A very pleasant, comforting dream.

''Why did you turn Dunfrey down?'' he murmured into her hair.

She buried her face against his chest. ''I thought about what you said. Charles claimed he loved me, but he sounded just as sincere when he called me a whore in front of all my friends. You were right. I think he just wanted my dowry.''

"Maddie," he said softly.

"It's all right." The music began again, and she started at the sudden noise.

Quin leaned backward and glanced down again. "Hm. Apparently they weren't as amorous as we were. They're gone. In all fairness, though, they didn't remove any clothes."

She chuckled against his hard, well-muscled chest. "Neither did we."

"We rearranged some," he protested. "If you'd like me to be more thorough, I'm quite willing." He shifted. "Exceedingly willing."

She could tell. And if she didn't let go of him now, she never would. "Oh, no you don't," she said, pulling free of his arms. "Get going."

"Minx," he said, turning for the window.

"Oaf."

"Lightskirt." Hopping up onto the sill, he swung his legs outside.

"Blackguard."

"Sprite." Quin disappeared from view.

"Dullard."

His head reappeared. "I say. That last one I handed you was a compliment."

"Oh. Um—hero."

He grinned. "Much better. Come along, my sweet. And you'd best be quick about it." Quin vanished downward again.

He was right. If no one had already discovered their absence, they were luckier than they deserved. Frowning nervously, she hiked her skirts up to her knees and swung her legs out over the garden. Grasping one side of the trellis, she awkwardly stepped onto it.

"Very nice," he murmured from very close below her. "I should have let you lead before."

"Shut up," she snapped quietly, making a game effort

to stomp on his head with her slippered foot. When she'd first seen him, she'd never have thought the Marquis of Warefield could be so very funny and witty and passionate and warm. Thank goodness he'd seen through her anger before she had.

Finally he gripped her about the waist and set her down on the balcony's hard stone. "Do you want to go first, or shall I?" he whispered.

"I will." Someone had left a half-empty glass of Madeira on the railing, and she picked it up, pasted a bored expression on her face, and slowly strolled back into the ballroom.

No one turned immediately to stare at her, and she took that as a good sign. When her mother grabbed her arm, she jumped and nearly spilled the glass down her front.

"Where have you been?" Lady Halverston hissed, her face flushed.

"Getting some air," she replied. "I've been rather nervous tonight."

"Even so, with your reputation, you know better than to go wandering off. People would be more than willing to believe you were up to something. And then all of Lady Highbarrow's efforts would have been for nothing. I could never have explained that to Her Grace."

Maddie tugged her arm free. "Don't worry, Mama. I know what I'm doing. I shan't embarrass you again."

She turned away and caught sight of Rafael. He was in his dress uniform again, splendid and dangerous and handsome. Even the scar across the left side of his face only served to make him look more rakish. He leaned against the wall, a glass of port in each hand, and looked at her. After a long moment, he straightened and made his way around the edge of the ballroom to deliver one of the glasses to his brother.

Maddie took a breath. Rafe, at least, knew something had happened between her and Quin. All she could do was pray that no one else did, and that Quin's optimism about tomorrow would be true. For both their sakes.

Chapter 17

Quin rose early. A year ago—hell, six months ago—he would never have imagined a day like this. And he certainly would never have been looking forward to it. Lately his well-buried adventurous spirit seemed to have emerged, and he knew exactly whom he could thank for it. In fact, he intended to thank her for it as frequently as possible.

Early as it was, Malcolm was up before him, lurking in the upstairs hallway. Today he used only one cane, and unless Quin was mistaken, he looked as though he wanted to wallop his nephew with it.

"Good morning, Uncle." Quin smiled, near enough to whistling that he could easily believe he'd veered off into madness.

"I thought the nobility only rose before noon when residing in the country."

"You sound like Maddie."

"Speaking of whom," Malcolm put in, allowing Quin to help him navigate the stairway, "have you forgotten about her?"

"Forgotten about Maddie? I could as easily forget to breathe."

"Ah. And that is why, I suppose, you've spent prac-

tically every waking moment over the past week with
Eloise Stokesley.''

Quin grinned at him. ''Precisely.''

Malcolm eyed him for a moment. ''Care to explain
that?''

''I do not. I'm going out for a bit. If you wish to go
anywhere, have Claymore drive you.''

''Quinlan.''

He turned around in the doorway. ''Yes, Uncle?''

''What about Maddie?''

''I'm working on it.'' Until everything had been settled, he intended to disclose as little and to as few people
as possible. Even to Maddie's staunchest supporters.

Aristotle glared at him when he went out to the stable,
as the damned horse had done since Rafe had left again.
Quin had him saddled anyway and rode west to Bancroft
House. And then step number one of his carefully laid
plan went awry.

''What do you mean, His Grace went out early?'' he
demanded, frowning at Beeks. ''I sent a note yesterday,
asking for an audience this morning.''

The butler nodded. ''I delivered the note into his hand
myself, my lord. As far as I know, he did read it.''

Quin swore under his breath. ''Did he say where he
was going?''

''No, my lord. He did say, however, that it wouldn't
take long, if you'd care to wait.''

''Blast.'' Little as he liked the idea of sitting about,
which seemed decidedly unheroic, it was the most logical choice. His Grace could be anywhere in London.
''Oh, very well. Is the duchess in?''

''No, my lord. Today is her charitable works day.''

Quin frowned. ''Rafe?'' he asked, though he doubted
he and his brother would have much to say to one another.

''Out riding, my lord.''

"Fine, fine. I'll be in the morning room."

"Ah, my lord?" Beeks said hesitantly.

"What is it?"

"Lady Stokesley is already waiting in the morning room."

Quin looked at the butler for a moment. "Waiting for my father, I presume?"

"That is what she said, my lord."

Narrowing his eyes, Quin gazed down the hallway. That was certainly interesting. "Thank you, Beeks."

The marquis strolled down the long hallway and paused outside the half-open morning room door. The proper thing to do would have been to speak to his father first, but he wouldn't put it past His Grace to have figured out why he had demanded an audience and fled in order to avoid it. And Lucifer knew he was looking forward to a little chat with Eloise, anyway.

He smiled darkly and pushed open the door. "Eloise, good morning! I never would have expected to see you out and about so early."

She jumped, quickly rising. "I could say the same thing about you, Quin. What brings you to Bancroft House?"

Quin waved his hand. "Nothing much. Have you had tea?"

"Well, yes, I—"

"Beeks," he called, leaning out the door again, "have some tea brought in, will you?"

"Right away, my lord."

Studying her face for any sign of what she might be up to this time, Quin took the seat next to her. The *London Times* sat on the end table, but the entire front section was missing, and after a moment he set it aside.

Franklin brought in the tea, and flinched as he caught sight of Eloise. She barely favored him with a glance, obviously not even remembering that she'd scalded the servant with hot tea only a few days before. Quin remembered, though—quite well. Just as he remembered Maddie, below stairs in the kitchen, patching Franklin up again. "Close the door, will you, Franklin?" he asked, as the footman departed.

"Yes, my lord."

As the door shut, Eloise looked at him curiously, then leaned forward to pour them each a cup of tea. "My, my Quin, the two of us, alone?"

"I'd meant to call on you," he said. "You've saved me a trip."

"You have me curious, my love. Please, tell me what is on your mind."

For a moment he sat back, watching as she sipped her tea, a perfect porcelain figurine of impeccable manners and dress. "Eloise, do you believe in love?"

"What?" she asked, lifting an eyebrow. "Is that what you wanted to speak to me about? Of course I do."

He nodded. "Good."

Eloise smiled. "Why is that good?"

"Because it means you'll understand why I'm breaking off our betrothal."

"*What?*" she gasped. The cup of tea fell from her fingers and spilled on the expensive Persian carpet.

"I cannot marry you," he explained calmly.

"Quin, you can't mean that. Not after all this time! We're to be married in a fortnight, for heaven's sake. The invitations have gone out, and the announcement is to be made in the *London Times* tomorrow!"

He shook his head ruefully. "I know. Very poor timing on my part, I suppose."

" 'Poor timing?' Is that all you have to say about it?"

"Well, that's up to you." Quin let the threads of anger that had been pulling at him for the past few weeks begin to twine together. "If you'll get up and leave now, I'm willing to end it at that. If you'd like me to elaborate, believe me, I'll be more than happy to do so.''

Eloise pushed to her feet in a flurry of blue silk. ''It's her, isn't it? That little shrew!''

''No, it's not. Yes, I'm in love with her, but the—''

''It's your damned brother, then!'' she shrieked. ''I'll kill him for this.''

Quin looked at her intently. ''What does Rafael have to do with this?''

''Nothing!'' she snapped, wild-eyed. ''Why, then? Why?''

''The fact is, Eloise, I find you to be a conceited, two-faced, malignant liar, and I really don't want to marry you—regardless of whether anyone else is involved or not.''

Her face went white. ''How *dare* you speak to me that way?'' she hissed. ''If it wasn't for her, you *would* be marrying me.''

Quin stood. ''Don't think,'' he said, in a controlled, quiet voice, ''that because I have been polite to this point, I am some sort of fool. For a long time—for too long, I see now—I was willing to go along with this nonsense because I felt it was my duty to do so.''

''It still is your duty.''

''I have watched you, though,'' he continued, as if she hadn't spoken. ''I have seen you be unfailingly petty and cruel whenever the chance arose, and I have seen you belittle those you thought you could because of the privilege of your rank.''

''What about the privilege of *your* rank? You can't marry her—she's nothing!''

''Eloise, this is about you and me. Leave Maddie out of it.''

''My God, Quin. I can't believe . . . have you told your father?''

''Not yet. I will as soon as he returns.''

She looked at him for a moment, then took a breath

and bent to pick up her teacup and set it back on the tray. "Well, that was nice of you, to tell me first. No one else knows. Nothing is lost." Eloise glanced toward the window, then back at him again. "Listen to me, Quin. I care for you, and I understand. Maddie is the poor, orphaned lamb you've worked very hard to save, and—"

"We were discussing your character," he interrupted.

"—And now you can't let her go. But for God's sake, don't marry her! Make her your mistress. As long as you're discreet, I don't care. Just do something—anything—to get her out of your system, and come to your senses before it's too late!"

"I suggest you never speak of Maddie in that tone again, Eloise. Now get out, before I throw you out."

With great dignity, her hands shaking with suppressed fury, Lady Stokesley turned for the door. "Don't you understand?" she said, as she pulled it open. "Your father will *disown* you when he hears of this. You will have nothing. *Nothing*. And then I won't want you."

He looked into her eyes, fighting the sensation that if she'd had a knife, she would have put it into his back by now. "I will have *her*."

Eloise grabbed her shawl from the butler and stomped down the front steps. Outside her carriage she paused. "No, you won't have her," she vowed, and reentered the house.

The duchess always kept pen, parchment, and ink in the front room, and it only took a moment to scribble out the note. She slipped back out again, and handed the paper to one of her footmen. "Take this to Dunfrey House, and deliver it into Mr. Dunfrey's hand. At once, if you wish to remain in my father's employ."

"Yes, my lady." He doffed his hat and ran off.

The driver helped her up into the coach. She closed the door and sat back. "That should take care of that."

She smiled as the coach rocked into motion.

Fifteen minutes later, as her coach passed Hyde Park—nearly deserted at this time of morning—the door wrenched open.

"Hello, cousin," Rafael Bancroft said with a smile. "Keep going," he barked at the driver, and slipped off his hunter to step inside. His damned horse continued to keep pace with the coach as he slammed the door shut.

"Get out of here," she snapped, kicking at him.

He sat beside her, pushing her body against the wall of the coach. Grabbing her hands, he wrenched her around to face him. "Who was that note for?" he asked, hatred in his light green eyes.

"I don't know what you're talking about. Let go of me and get out, or I'll make certain Quin knows what you've done!"

"I *saw* you hand that note off," he snarled, shaking her. "I've kept my silence, Eloise, to keep my brother. But he doesn't want you anymore, does he? So I can confess our little indiscretion any time I like."

"I'll tell everyone you raped me."

"And will you tell them the same thing about Patrick Oatley? Considering which part of his body your mouth was attached to, I'm not certain anyone would believe it."

"I don't know what you're talking about."

"You did six years ago, when I mentioned that I'd happened to see the two of you together." He smiled, his eyes glinting. "And then, as I recall, you pounced on me, too, to—what was that you said afterward? Oh, yes. To keep me quiet. You're a spirited lover, Eloise, I'll give you that. With lots of practice, I presume. But I'm not going to keep quiet any longer."

She tried to wrench free. "I never wanted you, you pig!"

Rafael grinned. "Liar." He yanked her up against

him. "Now, what did that note say, and to whom did you send it? If you don't tell me, Eloise, I swear, I'll remove every stitch of your clothing and throw you out onto the street."

He meant it. Eloise could see it in his eyes. "I hate you."

"The feeling is mutual, believe me," he answered, in the same tone. "Talk."

She stared at him, her mind racing. Dunfrey should have read the note by now, and if he had any sense, would have moved to act on it. If she could delay Rafael a few more minutes, it would be too late. "It was merely a business proposal," she spat out, fighting against his hard grip.

Shifting so that he held both of her hands pinned beneath one arm, Rafael leaned down and grabbed her leg. Eloise shrieked as he pulled one of her shoes off. He tossed it out the curtained window. "A proposal to whom?" he asked coolly.

"To Charles Dunfrey. Now, leave me alone!"

"Dunfrey?" he repeated, scowling. "What did it say?"

She snapped her jaw shut defiantly, until her other shoe followed the first. "You wouldn't dare."

"Wouldn't I?" Pushing her suddenly forward, he ripped open the back of her expensive dress all the way to her waist. "What did it *say*, damn it?"

Eloise stifled a furious, frightened sob. "I'll kill you for this!"

"You may try." With another wrench her dress came off completely, and he wadded it around one arm. "You're running out of wardrobe, dear."

"It said. . . . " She took a quick breath, trying to decide just how much more defiance he would stand for. As he started to stuff the dress out the window, she shrieked, "It said that I would give him five thousand pounds if he would make Maddie Willits disappear! Now go away, you snake!"

He shoved her away. "You cold-blooded bitch," he growled. "She did nothing to you."

"She took Quin!"

"*You lost him*. Six years ago, when you decided you could shut me up about Oatley by climbing into my bed."

"I did no—"

"Damn it, Eloise, why do you think I took an early leave? If you'd shown the slightest bit of genuine feeling for Quin, I—"

She lunged at him, her nails bared, but he was apparently expecting it, and he shoved her away again. Rafael looked at her coldly for another minute, then jerked her legs out from under her, sending her to the floor of the coach. While she struggled with him to get upright, her shift ripped off in his hands, leaving her in only her stockings.

"You had no right to hurt Maddie," he snarled.

"Then perhaps you should have confessed your sins to your brother before now."

"Bitch." He stood, looking her up and down while she flushed furiously and belatedly tried to cover herself. "Don't bother—I've seen it."

Abruptly mortified that he would throw her out into the street naked, she let her hands drop. "Wouldn't you like to see it again?" she suggested, swiping her disheveled hair out of her face.

He laughed, though his eyes glinted. "This is one snake who's not going near that hole again, dearest."

Shoving the coach door open, he whistled. A moment later, the horse appeared. Dropping her clothes out onto the street, he stepped into the stirrup and swung back into the saddle. "Good-bye, Eloise," he said jauntily, and wrenched the bay around. "And thank you for a lovely time. Again."

Eloise gasped and lurched forward to grab the door shut, but not before several very curious passersby glimpsed her inside.

"My lady?" the driver called, slowing.

"Take me home!" she screamed. *"Now!"*

Maddie looked at Everett in disbelief. "*Who* wants to see me?" she asked, setting her napkin down on the breakfast table, nervous flutters running through her stomach.

"The Duke of Highbarrow, Miss Willits."

Her father, the only other member of the family who'd already risen this morning, pushed away from the table. "Well, don't keep him waiting. Let's go."

"My lord, His Grace requested to see Miss Willits. Alone," the butler stated, and cleared his throat.

"Oh," Viscount Halverston said, and retook his seat. "Go, Maddie. For God's sake."

With a deep breath, Maddie went to find the Duke of Highbarrow in her morning room.

"Shoddy," he noted, turning around.

"Thank you, Your Grace," she answered, grateful he'd begun the conversation—if that's what this was—with an insult.

"How much will it take to convince you to leave London?" he asked, standing by the window and looking at her.

"I believe we've had this conversation before. I will not be bribed."

"What about ten thousand pounds? Is that enough to tear you away from my son?"

She gaped at him. Ten thousand pounds could keep her independent, and in style, for the rest of her life. "Out of consideration for your son, Your Grace," she said stiffly, "I will not repeat this conversation. Now, will you kindly leave?"

"Insolent chit." He flung a folded copy of the *London Times* onto the table in front of her. "You won't get any more out of me."

She glanced down at the page as it slowly fell open— and felt the blood drain from her face. In bold letters half an inch high, a full-page advertisement announced the wedding of the Marquis of Warefield and Lady Stokesley, to be held on Saturday, July the seventeenth. It named the illustrious parents of the illustrious pair, and the time and location of the ceremony. Numbly she noted that the duke had managed to secure Westminster Abbey, after all.

"That," the duke said, jabbing a finger at the paper, "is my son's future. You aren't fit to stand in his shadow, and your continued presence will be nothing but poison to him and to the entire Bancroft family. You are a ruined, inconsequential nothing, and while I might admire your courage at reaching so far beyond your grasp, Quinlan *is,* after all, beyond your grasp."

He stared at her while she continued to look helplessly at the bold, black words on the page. All she could think was that she couldn't have him. His Grace was right. Quin belonged to someone else, and if he tried to change that now, the scandal would be a hundred times worse than what Spenser had done to her. Slowly she sat down on the couch, her legs wobbly and numb.

"Listen, girl," he said in a quieter voice. "All you need to do is call on Bancroft House—at the servants' door. If I see you with packed bags, I'll give you ten thousand pounds, in currency. My offer stands until sunset. After that, you get nothing. Is that clear?"

Maddie didn't answer. After a moment, he stalked out the door. She heard his carriage creak into motion, but she couldn't look away from the announcement. She must have really believed Quin when he'd told her he loved her and that he meant to marry her. She must have believed it, or she wouldn't be feeling as though her heart had been ripped from her breast.

But it didn't matter. Nothing would happen now, except that the duke would have his way, after all. Slowly she stood. She couldn't go to Langley any longer, because with his pride pricked again, Quin might look for her. That much was obvious. Anywhere else in the world would do, so long as she never had to see him again.

From past experience she knew she didn't need much, and at least she had her savings from her employment with Mr. Bancroft this time. Silently she slipped upstairs, hardly noticing the tears wetting her cheeks, and threw a few things into her old, patched valise. She stopped at her dressing table, and quickly wrote out a note to anyone who should care to read it. And for Quin, if he should come to Willits House looking for her.

Hurrying back downstairs before her family could appear, she left the note on top of the newspaper, and her bag just inside the morning room door. "Everett," she said, stepping into the hallway.

"Miss Willits?"

"Would you mind terribly if I asked you to look for my riding gloves? I think I left them in the drawing room yesterday."

The butler smiled and nodded. "My pleasure, Miss Willits." He headed upstairs.

Maddie grabbed her valise and silently slipped out the front door. The nearest stage stop was only a few blocks away, and she set off out down the street at a fast pace.

"Maddie? It *is* you. I was just coming to see you."

She jumped. A coach slowed beside her, and Charles leaned out the half-open door. "I'm sorry, Charles, I'm in something of a hurry," she blurted.

"Randolph, stop," he called to his driver, and hopped to the ground. "Is something wrong?"

"It's . . . a long story, Charles. But no, nothing is wrong. I'm simply on my way to visit someone."

"On foot?"

"I need the fresh air."

She started off again, but he put a hand on her arm to stop her. "Maddie," he said quietly, stepping in front of her. "After what I did to you before, I shouldn't have expected you to agree to marry me." He tilted her chin up with his gloved fingers, his brown eyes holding hers. "But I am yours to command. I owe you at least that. May I take you somewhere?"

She looked up and down the street. People were beginning to stir from their homes, and with every moment the chance that someone would see her, and remember where she'd gone, grew. "Will you take me to the stage?" she asked quickly, before she could change her mind.

"I'll do better than that," he answered, taking her valise and motioning her into the coach. "Where do you want to go?"

With a quick breath she stepped up into the coach. "Anywhere. Dover."

Charles smiled and knocked his cane against the roof. "That's easy enough," he said, as the coach rocked into motion.

"Did you see that?" Polly said, turning away from her sister's bedchamber window.

"See what?" Claire asked sleepily, sitting up in bed and stretching.

"Maddie. She got into a coach and drove off."

"Don't be silly, Polly. She wouldn't do that without telling anyone. Not after the last time."

"But she did. I saw her. I think it was Mr. Dunfrey."

Claire smiled wisely. Polly was such a child sometimes. "Maddie would never get into a carriage with Charles Dunfrey. Never ever."

"Well, you look, then."

Scowling, Claire stood and, pulling on her dressing gown, made her way over to the window. "I don't see—" She stood on her tiptoes. "Oh, it's Rafael Bancroft." She breathed, watching as the gentleman swung down from a magnificent bay horse and ran toward their front door. "Hurry up and help me get dressed."

"What for?"

"Because I want to say good morning to him."

"Do you like him?" Polly asked.

"You're such a baby," Claire chastised. "Everyone likes Rafael Bancroft. He's handsome. And he's a Bancroft."

They could hear him downstairs, talking rather sharply to Papa, so Claire had to settle for combing out her hair and putting on her good slippers before she and Polly hurried down into the breakfast room.

"What do you mean, my father was here?" Rafael snapped, then turned as he saw them enter. "Ladies," he acknowledged, and turned back to the viscount.

"What's going on, Papa?"

"Not now, Claire. Go back to your rooms and get dressed, for heaven's sake."

"But Polly saw Maddie leave," she said, not wanting to miss anything.

"You did?" Rafael asked, turning quickly to Polly. "Where did she go?"

"She didn't go anywhere," Lord Halverston insisted. "She's in the morning room with the Duke of Highbarrow."

Scowling, Rafael turned on his heel and strode out into the hallway. The morning room door was open, and he went inside without asking. At the end table he stopped and picked up a scrap of paper and a section of the morning paper. A moment later he threw them down again, cursing.

''Miss Polly?'' he said urgently. ''Did you see where Maddie went?''

''She got into a coach,'' Polly repeated. ''I think it was Charles Dunfrey's.''

''I told you, that's ridiculous,'' Claire repeated. ''She told him she didn't want to get married. She wouldn't go anywhere with him.''

''Which way were they headed?'' Rafael pursued.

Polly pointed. ''That way.''

''North. Gretna, no doubt.'' He leaned down and kissed her swiftly on the cheek. ''My thanks, my lady,'' he said, and ran past them and back out the door.

Claire glared at her sister. ''You should have let me tell him,'' she snapped. ''That was *my* kiss.''

''Oh, be quiet, girl. What in God's name is going on?'' their father grumbled. He looked at her again. ''And go get dressed!''

''I was about to go looking for you,'' Quin said, as his father stepped into the hallway.

The duke glanced at him for a brief moment, then turned to walk toward the stairs. ''What do you want?''

''I sent over a note yesterday, remember? I wanted to see you this morning.''

''Had something to take care of.''

Quin followed him upstairs to his private office, uneasiness pulling at him. ''Do you have a moment now?''

''Not really.''

The marquis shut the door and leaned back against it. ''This will only take a minute.''

His Grace turned around to face him. ''Don't bother. Do you think I don't know what kind of nonsense you're planning?''

"I hardly consider it nonsense," Quin said, immediately on the defensive, and still trying to maintain a reasonable tone.

"Quinlan Ulysses Bancroft," his father said, in an unexpectedly quiet voice. "You will be the twelfth Duke of Highbarrow. Twelve generations, Quin. Don't you think any of our ancestors ever fancied an unacceptable person? Do you think they married them?"

"I don't give a damn, Father," Quin said shortly. "This generation is in love with Maddie Willits. And I *will* marry her, if she'll have me."

"Hm. And do you know what that would look like? You'd be an embarrassment to the entire family."

Quin folded his arms. "What do you think it looks like for you and Malcolm to be practically spitting at one another in public?"

"That's none of your affair."

He nodded. "And this is none of yours."

"I made an agreement with the Earl of Stafford."

"I didn't." Further argument would likely result only in higher volume, so Quin straightened and turned away. "I just wanted you to know my intentions."

"It doesn't matter, anyway."

Quin stopped and turned around. "What do you mean, it doesn't matter?"

"I've taken care of it."

Sudden alarm tightened the muscles across Quin's back. There had to be a very good reason why his father was so calm about all this. "Just where did you go this morning, Your Grace?"

"You're going to marry Eloise Stokesley. It's settled." The duke sat at his desk and pulled out a stack of ledgers, his usual method of signaling dismissal.

Quin stared at his back. "Sweet Lucifer," he hissed, turning already to grab the door handle and yank it open.

"If you've done anything—*anything*—to hurt Maddie, I'll—"

"You'll *what*, Quinlan?" the duke asked, not bothering to look up.

"I'll show you what a spectacle *I* can make, Father. In spades."

"Quinlan! Don't you dare go after that mopsie!"

Not bothering to respond, Quin strode out the door and down the stairs. The duke had been to see Maddie—he'd wager good blunt on it. And mercurial as her temper was, there was no telling what she might have done in response.

Outside, he stopped, looking around. "Wedders, where is my horse?" he snapped at the groom.

"Begging your lordship's pardon," the groom said, backing away, "but Master Rafe has 'im."

"*What?*"

"Aye, my lord. He took off with old Aristotle right after Lady Stokesley left, my lord. Looked madder 'n piss, if you'll forgive the expression."

"Damnation," he snarled. "Of all the stupid, poorly timed . . . Saddle me another horse. Now!"

"Aye, my lord."

When he burst into the Willitses' front room some moments later, Claire was standing in there, wearing her dressing gown and crying, and there was no sign of Maddie. Lord Halverston sat on the couch, a newspaper in one hand, and shook his head.

"She's ruined it," Claire sobbed. "She's ruined it again! Papa, it's not fair!"

The viscount stood as Quin, immediately sensing that they were discussing Maddie, strode into the room. "Shut up, Claire. Good morning, Lord Warefield. And congratulations."

Quin frowned. "Congratulations for what?"

Maddie's father handed him the front section of the

London Times. "For this, of course, though in truth we did already know. I think everyone does."

Quin snatched the paper out of his hand and perused it quickly. "Blast," he swore. "Damn, damn, damn." His father had seen fit to forestall any argument simply by placing the announcement in the paper a day early. And of course Maddie had seen it. "Where's Maddie?" he demanded, ripping the paper in half and throwing it to the floor.

"I . . . There is some question about that, my lord." The viscount produced a smaller piece of paper.

Quin glanced down at it. " 'Don't look for me,' " he read aloud. He looked up at Halverston again. "What in God's name is going on?"

"I wish I knew, my lord. Today has been completely . . . nonsensical. First His Grace your father very kindly stops by, and then your brother, and now we can't find Maddie, and who knows where—"

"My brother stopped by?" Quin repeated very slowly.

"Just for a moment," the viscount clarified. "And I beg your pardon, my lord, but he wasn't very polite. Demanded to know where my daughter was, and then off he went, without even a 'Good day.' "

"And now you can't find Maddie," Quin said quietly, something very black and angry stirring in his chest.

"Well, she left first, in a coach," Claire said, wiping at her eyes. "At least we think so. Rafael was on a horse."

He nodded. "Yes. He was on *my* horse. Do you by any chance know where they might have been heading?"

"I don't know," she mumbled. "He said something about Gretna."

"Gretna Green, perhaps?" Quin asked calmly, fury tearing through him. Rafe was a dead man. His brother's

message was clear: he'd taken Aristotle, and he'd taken
Maddie. Obviously he didn't intend on coming back.
He'd practically threatened to elope with her once al-
ready.

"Perhaps. He really didn't say."

Quin turned for the door. "So that's how he wants
it," he growled. "All right, Rafe. Let's play."

Chapter 18

$\sim\!\!\!\text{C}\!\!\!\bigcirc\!\!\!\bigcirc\!\!\!\text{C}\!\!\!\sim$

Maddie gazed out the window of Charles Dunfrey's dilapidated coach. Green meadows, stands of trees, and a scattered cottage now and again swept into view and then away again beneath the overcast sky. They were finally out of London, and she tried to relax a little.

She would never see Quin again. He would do his duty and marry Eloise Stokesley, and they would have children, and she would read something about him now and again in a newspaper, and that would be all.

The ache that had begun with the duke's announcement this morning deepened into a hole so black she knew she would never laugh or smile again. Quin would say she was a coward, and she probably was. But finally and ultimately, she hoped he would realize that she'd done it because she loved him—so very much that she would let Eloise marry him, and so much that she wouldn't be able to stand seeing him in the company of his new bride. Ever. Leaving London wasn't a choice, but a necessity.

Maddie shook herself. "Shouldn't we be able to see the coast by now?" she asked, glancing at Charles.

He'd been quiet for the more than two hours they'd

been traveling, and he stirred as though he'd been day-dreaming. "Soon, I'm sure," he said.

"This is really very kind of you," she continued, hoping that talking to him would at least keep her thoughts away from Quin for more than a heartbeat. "I'm sure you must have had other plans for today."

"It's my pleasure, Maddie. Do you mind my asking what happened? You do have a valise with you, after all."

"My aunt is suddenly ill," she improvised. If she could help it, there would be no scandal this time. "In Spain. I need to go tend her, right away."

"Your father's sister?"

She shook her head. "No, my mother's."

The sun broke through the cloud covering, its light shining in her eyes, and she glanced out the window again and frowned.

Just as quickly she wiped the expression from her face. Her heart began to beat at twice its normal rate, and she took a deep breath, trying to calm herself before Charles noticed her discomfiture. As far as she knew, his offer of assistance was completely legitimate. It was merely that the sun wasn't quite where it was supposed to be at this time of morning. "Isn't that odd?" she said, as casually as she could. "I thought the sun would be in front of us."

Charles nodded, yawning. "We're heading a little north, now. In a few minutes we'll turn east again."

"Of course," she agreed, growing more suspicious and uneasy by the moment. "But isn't Dover actually a little south of London?"

He chuckled. "Maddie, I have never doubted your wit and wisdom. Remind me, though, never to have you read a map for me."

Maddie smiled stiffly. "Actually, cartography is something of a hobby of mine."

He looked at her, his gaze sharpening a little. "Is that so?"

"Yes, as a—"

"Hold up there!"

Maddie jumped at the stentorian bellow coming from behind them. "Rafael?" Suddenly she was thankful her escape hadn't gone quite as smoothly as she'd envisioned.

"I say, hold up there, coachman!" came from much closer.

She furrowed her brow and gave Charles her best look of bewildered confusion. "What in the world could Rafael Bancroft want with us?"

Charles leaned forward and rapped his cane against the roof. "I'm sure I have no idea. Keep going, Randolph! We're in a hurry!"

The coach immediately accelerated, rocking precariously on the rutted road.

"I'm not asking again! Stop!"

"Mr. Dunfrey?" The coachman's voice sounded extremely nervous. "Sir, he has a pistol."

"A pistol?" Maddie gasped. Apparently, her hunch had been correct after all, though the realization was not very comforting. "Stop the coach. Something is terribly wrong, I'm sure."

"I thought you needed to be with your aunt as soon as possible," Charles commented, sitting back again. "Ignore him."

"But it must be important!" she insisted, trying to decide if she actually wanted to risk leaping from the carriage while the horses were at a full gallop.

Charles eyed her, clearly annoyed, but she couldn't read anything more than that in his expression. "Oh, very well. Randolph, stop!"

The coach lurched to a halt, nearly sending Maddie

to the floor. She grabbed onto the window frame and hauled herself back onto the seat.

"Maddie!"

Charles pulled the curved handle free from his cane, revealing a very sharp-looking rapier. "Ask him to come in," he said, reaching out to rest the tip of the blade against her throat.

Torn between fury and fright, Maddie clenched her fists and scooted as far back in her seat as she could. The blade followed her. "Rafe? Come in, if you please."

The door opened, followed by a very deadly-looking pistol, and a winded, angry-looking Rafael. "Maddie, come out of—" Rafael began, then swore as he saw the sword. "Sweet Lucifer, Dunfrey. Put it down."

"I believe that's my line," Dunfrey said. "Turn it around slowly, and hand it to me. Randolph! Is he alone?"

"Aye, Mr. Dunfrey."

"Are you all right, Maddie?" Rafe asked, the pistol and his eyes still unwaveringly on Charles.

"Yes, I'm fine, for the moment. What are you doing here?"

"I came to tell you that you're being kidnaped."

"Hmm," Dunfrey sighed, far too calmly. "Dear Lady Stokesley, I suppose?"

"Yes."

"Well, now you're being kidnaped as well, Bancroft. Give me the pistol and sit down."

Still gazing at Dunfrey, Rafe backed off just a little. He whistled sharply.

"What in damnation was that for?" Dunfrey snapped.

Rafael continued to look at him coolly. "Just talking to my horse."

"Well, stop it, and get in here. Slowly."

With a scowl, Rafe turned the weapon and handed it,

butt first, to Charles. "Watch out there," he said, taking the seat beside Maddie. "It's loaded."

"I should hope so. Randolph, go!"

The coach rattled to a start again. Maddie glanced sideways at Rafael, but his attention remained on Charles. "How did you know where I was?" she asked him quietly.

"Convinced Eloise to let me in on the secret," he muttered back, smiling at their captor. "She can be very cooperative, given the correct incentive."

"What does Eloise know about this?"

"Apparently she's been working from the beginning to keep you and Quin apart. I suppose—"

"That's enough of that," Charles interrupted. "You know, Bancroft, you've made this whole thing quite a bit stickier. You won't vanish nearly as easily as Madeleine, I'm afraid."

"No one's vanishing, Dunfrey. Except you, when they send you to the gallows."

"Charles," Maddie put in, trying to keep Dunfrey distracted so that he wouldn't shoot one or the other of them, "why would you do this? You have nothing to gain."

"Except five thousand quid." Rafe folded his arms over his chest and closed his eyes.

Maddie wished she could look so calm. "I don't have five thousand quid."

"Eloise does," Rafe said, already looking half asleep.

Charles smiled and, one-handed, slid the rapier back into the cane. "Actually, it's more than that. By my reckoning, Lord Halverston should be willing to part with at least that much again to get you married respectably."

Abruptly a great many things began to make sense. "You only wanted to marry me for the money?" she asked, anger beginning to edge out her fright. She'd suspected, of course, but this was too much.

"It's the way of the world, Maddie. And be grateful for it. If not for the extra blunt from your father, I would likely throw both you and Bancroft down a well. Now I've only one to worry about."

"I wouldn't count on that," Rafe murmured, so quietly Maddie could barely hear him.

She turned back to the window so Charles wouldn't see the sudden anticipation in her eyes. And she hoped desperately that she would see Quin at least one more time.

When Lady Highbarrow returned home for afternoon tea, a note awaited her. Beeks, looking even more stoic than usual, bowed as he handed it to her.

"From Lord Warefield, Your Grace. A messenger delivered it several hours ago."

"Thank you." Now her sons were reduced to conversing with her via messenger. At the butler's continued dour expression, she paused. "Is something wrong, Beeks?"

"I couldn't say, my lady."

"I see." Curious, she headed up to her private room, where a fresh pot of tea awaited her. Pouring herself a cup, she unfolded the missive—and rose so quickly, she tipped the entire tea tray onto the floor. *"Lewis!"*

The duke appeared a moment later. From his expression, her uncharacteristic shout had completely unsettled him.

"What is it, Victoria?"

"What did you do?" she demanded, stalking up to him, the note clenched in one hand.

He assumed his normal stubborn, imperturbable expression. "I set things to rights."

"Oh, really? Then tell me what you make of this."
She unfolded the note again and read it.

*Rafe and Maddie on their way to Gretna Green.
Am following.*

Q.

The duchess looked up at her husband. "So I repeat,
Lewis, what did you do?"

"That damned fool!" the duke exploded. "Both of
them! We'll be the laughingstock of London. Two Bancrofts chasing after a whore!"

"What concerns me, husband," Victoria said, in a
quiet and controlled voice, "is what will happen when
Quin catches up to them. 'Set everything to rights,' indeed. They'll kill one another."

The Duke of Highbarrow stared at her for a moment,
the color slowly draining from his stern face. "Good
God," he hissed, and turned on his heel. "Damned,
damned fools."

If Maddie had left in a carriage, and Rafael on Aristotle, then logically they intended to meet somewhere
along the way. If Quin had been thinking clearly, he
would have asked Claire whether the coach had any
identifying markings, but he hadn't seemed to be able
to do much but ride at top speed along the north road
and curse his brother in half a dozen languages. It was
easier to focus on Rafael, who had taken her away,
rather than to admit that Maddie had left him.

He had always prided himself on being reasonable and
fair in his dealings, on being in control of his emotions,
and on honoring the responsibilities of his title. As he
traveled the busy road, dodging hay wagons and shep-
herds and stopping every closed carriage he passed, he

didn't give a damn about any of that—or about the ruckus he was causing. Rafael had taken Maddie away, and Rafael would give her back.

It was past noon when he came upon the first clue. Just off the road, a group of young boys surrounded a horse and unsuccessfully tried to grab hold of its dragging reins. Quin looked at the animal more closely, and then sharply pulled up his own mount.

Aristotle dodged nimbly around his would-be captors, at the same time staying within the same small clearing rather than running off, where they would have had no chance of catching him. Quin kneed his gelding toward the group, stopping at the fringe of the trees.

"Aristotle," he called, though the horse had never listened to him before.

To his surprise, the gelding whinnied and trotted up to him. Quin leaned down and picked up the reins.

"He wouldn't leave you behind," he told the horse, his mind racing in a hundred different directions. "Not now. He ordered you to stay here, didn't he? Why would he do that?"

"Hey, milord, that horse yours?" one of the boys called.

"My brother's," he answered. "Have you seen him?"

"That beastie's been here for over an hour. Never seen nobody."

Angry as Quin was, the presence of Aristotle actually made him stop and think for a moment. And when he did, the idea of Rafe and Maddie running off together *and* leaving Aristotle behind to mark their trail made absolutely no sense at all. He looped the bay's reins around the cantle of his saddle and turned north again. Whatever was going on, he was bloody well going to find out what it was.

*   *   *

"You're going to kill that fine pair of horses of yours, if you insist on running them like this," Rafael noted calmly.

"Shut up," Charles snapped.

He'd become increasingly short-tempered all afternoon, and as satisfying as tormenting their captor was, Maddie wished Rafael would let up on him a little. Her own temper was becoming very fragile, and her bottom and legs were cramped from sitting in the ill-sprung coach all day.

"If you're going to kill me," Rafe began again amiably, "you might as well tell me where we're going."

"Rafe," she whispered, looking sideways at him, "do quit reminding him about that."

"No, he's quite right, my dear," Charles countered. "You'll figure it out eventually, anyway. We are going to Gretna Green, so that Maddie and I can be married."

She stared at him. "I am not going to marry you, in Scotland or anywhere else. So you may as well stop the coach right now, and let us—"

"Maddie, Maddie, Maddie," he chastised, shaking his head. "Please understand. I receive five thousand quid for taking you out of London. An additional sum will be mine when *you* are mine. If you make that idea too unpleasant, I will settle for the initial payment, and I'll bury you in the same hole as Bancroft here."

"Kidnaping is one thing," Maddie said, trying to keep her voice steady. "Murder is quite another. I hope you realize that. You're setting a price on the worth of your own life, as well as ours."

"Thank you for your unasked for bits of wisdom, my dear, but allow me some credit." As he had been for the past twenty minutes, he glanced toward the window, pushing the curtains aside with his free hand. "Randolph!" he called in a louder voice. "The eastern road, if you please."

"Aye, Mr. Dunfrey. I see it."

Dunfrey sat back again, the pistol still aimed at Maddie. She supposed that was to discourage Rafe from attempting any sort of rescue or escape, but she wished Charles would stop looking at her as though the idea of shooting her didn't trouble him in the least.

"Once you turned down my proposal, Maddie, I planned this little contingency. Of course, I didn't expect you to run out your front door and into my carriage with your bag all packed, but you have to admit, it did make things a bit easier on me."

The coach lurched as the road beneath them became steadily more rutted. Finally they rocked to a halt, and Randolph jumped down from his perch to pull the door open. Dunfrey gestured with the pistol. "Please follow my coachman, Bancroft. Maddie, you're to stay right behind him."

With a last, angry glance at their captor, Rafe jumped to the ground. Maddie followed, her long skirt catching on the carriage steps and nearly tripping her. The sun was already behind the tall elms to the west, and in both directions the muddy, rutted road was empty of other travelers. Directly before them stood a small inn, a single lantern hanging above a bench by the dark, scarred door.

They seemed to have the inn completely to themselves. The coachman led them into the deserted common room, which at least had a fire going in the stone fireplace. Obviously someone had lit the fire, thank goodness, and Maddie looked about for a friendly innkeeper—or at least, one who could be bribed.

The man who walked in through the kitchen door, though, with a tray of bread and fruit in his arms, didn't look the least bit friendly. He also looked extremely familiar. Maddie blanched, stopping in her tracks, and Dunfrey ran into her from behind, the muzzle of the pistol bruising her spine.

"Ouch! That hurt."

"Sit down," he grumbled.

"But—"

"Sit down in the chair there, Maddie, before I find a more accommodating position for you," Charles said in a darker voice, and pushed her toward the chair set before the fireplace.

Maddie did as he said, her eyes on the tall gentleman setting the food down on the table. He turned to face her and smiled.

"Good evening, Maddie. Haven't seen you for a while. You look more lovely than ever."

"Spenser, that's right, you know Maddie," Charles said more amiably, sitting at the long wooden table, "and this, unfortunately, is Rafael Bancroft. Don't worry, we'll kill him before we move on."

Benjamin Spenser eyed Rafael as the coachman dragged another chair over beside Maddie's. "Bancroft, as in the Duke of Highbarrow's kin?"

"Pleased to meet you," Rafael said, and held out his hand. "You're Benjamin Spenser, I presume? The ass who ruined Maddie?"

"Sit down," he ordered, picking up a coil of rope from the bench. "I've no objection to killing anyone, Dunfrey, but you think splitting a thousand quid is worth the risk of murdering a Bancroft?"

Charles glanced up at him. "It's twice that now."

Rafael snorted. Dunfrey rose and hit him hard across the face with the pistol. Rafael grunted and fell backward into the chair. Charles leaned over him. "I'd kill you for nothing, Bancroft."

"Charles, stop it!" Maddie protested, shooting to her feet. He shoved her back down into the chair.

She looked from her former betrothed to the man who had ruined her. Now that she saw them together, and now that she'd realized how highly Charles valued her dowry, quite a few things made sense.

"Why so sour-faced, Maddie?" Charles cajoled, while Randolph and Spenser tied Rafe to the chair before he could regain his senses.

"You never cared for me at all, did you?" she said quietly, unable to keep the bitterness from her voice. "All you wanted was money for marrying me. As much of it as you could get."

"Why else would I want to marry you?" Dunfrey asked, finally dropping the pistol in one of his coat pockets. "Though I have to admit, if I'd known what you'd end up looking like, I might have been willing to settle for slightly less currency."

"It's a bit late to try flattering me, you ape," she retorted.

Spenser moved behind her with another stout section of rope, and Maddie tensed again. Balling her fist, she surged to her feet and slugged Charles Dunfrey in the chin as hard as she could.

Not expecting the blow, Dunfrey rocked backward and lost his balance. He gripped the edge of the table, blinking. Attempting to take advantage of his momentary surprise, Maddie crashed into him, and they both fell to the floor.

She grabbed for his pocket, trying to recapture the pistol, but he threw her off. She landed hard on her back, the breath knocked out of her. With a curse Dunfrey pounced on her, pinning her by the shoulders with his hands and the weight of his body on top of her.

"This gives me an idea," he snarled, blood welling from a cut lip. Shoving his knee between her legs, he leaned down and kissed her wetly.

"Dunfrey!" Rafael roared, pulling against the ropes that bound him securely to the chair. The coachman gagged him with a rag.

"I warned you not to push me, Maddie," Charles continued. Laying his body harder against her, he kissed her again.

It was foul, wet, and disgusting. And, even worse, she could feel his growing arousal between their bodies. "Get off me," she demanded frantically.

Spenser knelt at her head and grabbed her flailing hands. He grinned down at her. "Share and share alike, I always say," he leered, pinning her arms above her shoulders.

The last of her anger slid into pure fear as Charles, his hands free now, ripped at the front of her dress. "Future husbands first," he said, licking her neck.

The door burst open. "That would be me," Quin snarled, white-faced and disheveled.

"Quin!" Maddie sobbed, relieved.

Quin leaped at Dunfrey. Twisting, Maddie grabbed Spenser's ankle as he scrambled to his feet, sending him sprawling. Dunfrey toppled off of her as Quin plowed into him with a furious growl.

The coachman standing behind Rafe looked as though he didn't know what to do, so Maddie yanked off one of her shoes and hurled it at him. It struck him in the shoulder and he jumped, then broke and ran for the door.

She tried to grab Spenser again, but he regained his feet and dived into the fight. Realizing she wouldn't be of much assistance to Quin against the two big men, Maddie scrambled over to Rafe to untie him. One wrist was already bloody, and the knots were slick and tight. "Stop pulling, or I'll never get you loose," she snapped, and he relaxed his arms a little.

Finally she had him free. He yanked the gag off and slammed into Spenser, knocking him away from Quin and Dunfrey.

Trying to recover her breath, Maddie staggered to her

feet. As she watched in horror, Dunfrey scrambled away from Quin and dug into his coat pocket for the pistol. Her frantic gaze lit on the discarded cane, and she snatched it up.

Dunfrey stood and leveled the pistol at Quin. With a shriek, Maddie pulled the rapier free and stabbed it into Dunfrey's back. *"No!"*

Charles swung around and hit her in the face with the pistol, knocking her hard to the floor. Blurrily, she saw Quin grab the weapon and shove Dunfrey away from her. And then the Duke of Highbarrow, together with a dozen footmen, burst into the room, weapons drawn.

Maddie shut her eyes as the room spun drunkenly. Then someone knelt beside her and lifted her into his arms. "Maddie," Quin breathed, his voice shaking. "Maddie, can you hear me? Open your eyes."

She looked up into his beautiful jade gaze. Breathing a sigh of relief, he pulled her tightly against his chest. Maddie wrapped her arms around his neck, buried her face in his shoulder, and began to sob. "Quin," she said, over and over again. "Oh, Quin."

"Shh," he murmured into her hair. "It's all right. You're all right, Maddie."

"She's not hurt, is she?"

The muscles across Quin's back tensed, and she looked up to see Rafael squatting down beside them, though there seemed to be two or three of him. "No, I'm fine, Rafael. Really."

"Excuse us," Quin said brusquely, and lifted her in his arms. With a warning glance at the Duke of Highbarrow, who actually stepped aside, he carried her outside into the moonlit darkness. He sat on the bench beneath the lantern, and cradled her like a babe. "Why did you leave, Maddie?" he asked quietly. "You said you would wait for me."

She tried to focus her eyes on his lean face. "I've

been enough trouble, Quin. Don't you understand, you and Eloise—''

"Eloise and I are nothing," he interrupted fiercely. "I have already told her my intentions. What about you and Rafael?"

She furrowed her brow. "What about us?"

"You were going with him to Gretna Green."

The muddiness in her head cleared a little. "No, we weren't. Charles was kidnaping me for my dowry. Rafe found out, and came to rescue me."

Quin glanced back toward the open doorway. "Some rescue," he said grudgingly. He looked back at her, holding her gaze for a long time as he stroked her cheek with gentle fingers. "Do you love me, Maddie?" he asked softly.

"Quin, I—"

He shook his head. "Do you love me?"

A tear ran down her cheek. "Of course I love you," she whispered.

Quin closed his eyes for just a moment. "Then marry me."

"I can't. I'm ruined. Twice now."

"At least," he smiled, and leaned down to kiss her softly on the lips. "Marry me."

"You came after me," she said, for the first time realizing exactly what had happened. "You came after me!" The dark, lonely knot in her chest finally broke apart and melted away.

"Of course I did. I love you."

"No, that's not what I mean," she argued, wishing the dull ache in her head would go away so she could speak coherently. "No one came after me the last time." She started crying again. "But you came."

He looked at her for a long time, his expression unreadable, then gathered her up and stood again. "That settles that, Miss Willits."

"Settles what?" she asked, twining her hands in his lapels and wondering that he could lift her so easily.

Quin walked back into the inn, Maddie still in his arms. "Your Grace," he said, and the duke turned from glowering at his captives to eye his son.

"What is it now, boy?"

"Maddie and I are continuing on to Gretna Green."

His Grace's face reddened. "You are not—"

"Do whatever the hell you want with your titles and your land and your heirs," Quin interrupted, and turned on his heel. "Tell mother we'll see her in London next week."

"Quin," Maddie said, "you've gone mad! Put me down!"

"Want company?" Rafe asked, hopping down from the table where he'd been perched.

"No."

"Do you realize what a scandal there'll be?" the duke bellowed, striding after them. "Your wedding to Eloise has already been announced. King George is going to attend!"

Quin stopped and turned around. "Father, I leave it to you to do what you will. In case I haven't made it clear, I don't care. I've been respectable my entire life, and I've discovered something about it."

"And what might that be?" the duke asked, his skeptical expression melting into concern as he realized his son wasn't bluffing.

"It's very dull. I'm tired of it." With a last glance at Rafael, Quin turned and headed them out the door again. "I'll see you in a week," he called over his shoulder.

For once, Maddie didn't know what to say. Quin Bancroft had always been a good-humored, reasonable man—but at the moment, she wouldn't have been surprised if he had decided to travel to Gretna Green on foot, carrying her the entire way. "Quin?" she said quietly.

"Hush. No more arguments. You're far too stubborn, so I'm simply not going to listen to you." He lifted her into Charles's coach. A moment later her valise followed her. A moment after that, Quin himself stepped in, and closed the door.

"Might I ask if anyone is going to drive us, or are we to sit here in the yard all night?" she ventured.

He sat beside her, tugging her close against him so she could rest her aching head on his shoulder. "I recruited Franklin. It seems he's rather fond of you."

"Yes, he's very nice," she agreed, closing her eyes as he wrapped a warm arm about her shoulders. "Remind me to check his bandages tomorrow."

"Yes, love." The coach jolted into motion, and Quin cursed. "You came all this way in this hell-sprung hack?"

"My bottom is sore," she confessed drowsily.

"I'll take care of it at the next town," he murmured into her hair.

"My bottom?"

Quin chuckled. "The coach. And your bottom, if I have anything to say about it."

With a supreme effort, Maddie managed to open one eye. "You can't marry me, Quin."

"I told you that I am not discussing that subject with you," he retorted. "Go to sleep."

"But I'll be an embarrassment," she protested. "You're going to be the Duke of Highbarrow, for heaven's sake."

"I wouldn't wager money on that," he returned, his voice amused. "Maddie, you are more precious to me than anything on this earth, including my title. If I have to be Quin Bancroft to marry you, then I will happily become him. We could raise pigs."

"You can't do that. Everything is planned out for you. You have everything."

"I want only you." He tilted her chin up and kissed her, a feather-light touch of his lips to hers. "Madeleine," he murmured. "Will you marry me?"

"I suppose I have to now," she answered, closing her eyes again, and unable to keep a smile from touching her lips. "This is the third time you've ruined me. Or the fourth. I can't remember."

For a long moment he was silent. "Are you certain it's not Rafe you would rather have here?" he finally asked quietly.

"Rafe?" she asked, surprised, and lifted her head to look up at him. "Why Rafe?"

He shrugged, looking away from her out the window into the darkness. "You seem to get along well."

Maddie relaxed again, comforted by his jealous tone. "We get along too well. I could never argue with him. It would be very dull."

Quin made a sound in his chest that exploded into laughter. "You think," he managed finally, "that *Rafe* is dull?"

They purchased a new, considerably better-sprung carriage in Nottingham, and from there arrived in Gretna Green two days later. Quin kept a close eye on Maddie, worried that once her head cleared she would take to the hills and vanish, but when they entered the quaint little chapel and stood before the extremely surprised priest, she was still beside him.

And five days later, as the coach turned onto King Street in Mayfair, she was seated next to him, though she looked considerably less happy. "You saw the *London Times* yesterday, the same as I did," she said, eyeing him.

"Yes, and I told you not to look at it." Quin grinned and took her hand, stroking her fingers.

"Not looking at it doesn't change anything. And I know you have to care, at least a little bit. 'Highbarrow Heir Elopes to Scotland with Unknown Femme.' Really, Quin. I know you're proud, and I know you didn't like seeing it."

"I am happy," he stated, tugging her across the coach to sit on his lap. "No one can take you away from me now." He touched his lips to hers, thrilling in her quick, passionate response.

She sighed, running her fingers along the line of his jaw. "You may come to regret that. And very soon."

Quin narrowed his eyes. Grabbing her hands in his, he yanked her around to look at him. "Don't say that, Maddie. Ever. You are my life. Without you, I am incomplete. Do you understand?"

Maddie nodded, tears gathering in her eyes. "You say very nice things, you know."

"I mean them," he whispered, kissing her again.

It had been that way since their marriage. He couldn't seem to stop touching her and holding her and kissing her, as though, even with his ring on her finger, he wasn't certain she was real. And in bed, she matched him passion for passion. He'd never delighted in making love as much as he delighted in making love to Maddie. His wild wood sprite would not vanish again.

"Quin?"

"Yes, my sweet?"

"I love you."

Quin kissed each of her fingers, while she smiled happily at him. "I love you, too."

"My lord, my lady, Bancroft House," Franklin called.

"Oh, blast," she grumbled, scooting off his lap. "Are

you certain we couldn't just sail off to Spain or something?''

The carriage rolled to a stop. "Actually, that idea had occurred to me," he confessed. "But I would at least like to say good-bye."

She wrinkled her nose, obviously attempting to put on a brave front. "You're just trying to make me look bad."

He chuckled as Franklin pulled open the door. "As if I could."

Beeks stood at the top of the stairs, waiting for them. "My Lord and Lady Warefield," he nodded. "Welcome."

"Thank you, Beeks."

Maddie smiled at him, and the butler took a step closer. "They've a gauntlet set up for you, I'm afraid," he said in a low voice.

She looked up at Quin. "I told you that we should have arrived a day early," she whispered. "But no, you still insist on being punctual."

"It's good manners. Who's here, Beeks?"

"The duke and duchess, Miss Maddie's parents, Mr. Bancroft, and Mr. Rafael. They've been in the drawing room since breakfast, waiting for you to arrive."

For the moment Quin refrained from pointing out that Maddie was no longer a miss, by any stretch of the imagination. Instead, he held out his hand to the butler. After a startled moment, Beeks smiled and shook it. "My thanks, Beeks."

"Good luck to both of you, my lord."

Quin looked down at Maddie, and took her hand in his. "Ready, my love?"

"May I bring a sword?"

A brief grin touched his lips. "No, you may not."

She sighed. "Then I suppose I'm ready."

The butler preceded them upstairs to the drawing

room. He stepped inside the half open door. "Lord and *Lady* Warefield have arrived," he announced in a very stout voice.

Quin leaned forward. "If you ever lack for employment, Beeks," he murmured, "please see me."

"Yes, my lord."

With Maddie clutching his hand tightly, they stepped past the butler and into the drawing room. Even if he hadn't already known, it was easy to tell the enemies from the allies. Particularly when there seemed to be only one enemy. He'd rehearsed a hundred speeches, but none of them appealed to him as they all stood eyeing one another like dogs trying to decide whether to attack or join together in a pack.

Typically, it was Rafe who moved first.

"You look wonderful, Maddie." He grinned, and strolled forward to kiss her on the cheek. "Even with this old sod. Congratulations to both of you." To Quin's surprise, his younger brother kissed him on the cheek as well.

The Duke of Highbarrow sat by the window and hadn't even glanced in their direction. Rafe shrugged at Quin's look and captured Maddie's hand to drag her over to the room's other occupants. Quin glanced after her, but once Lady Halverston threw her arms around her daughter's neck and began sobbing joyfully, Maddie seemed to recover herself.

"Your Grace," he said quietly, walking over to stand by the window, "shall I begin moving my things out of Warefield?"

"So you did it?" the duke responded, glancing up at his son. "You went and married her?"

"Yes, I did."

"Eloise and her parents went home to Stafford Green. She hasn't been seen in public since you ruined everything. I'll be lucky if Stafford ever speaks to me again."

"I'm sorry for the inconvenience," Quin admitted, sitting in the deep sill. "But I'm not sorry for marrying the woman I love."

"I didn't expect you would apologize."

"So what's it to be, Father?"

Finally the duke turned to look at Maddie, who was standing beside the duchess and watching them. "Bah."

Malcolm released Maddie's hand and hobbled over to his older brother. "Lewis, don't be an ass," he said. "She's ten times the lady Eloise could ever be, and you know it."

"The marriage to Eloise was arranged."

"Because you wanted Stafford's vote in the House. I told you to let it go years ago."

"And I told you to go to hell."

"Well, Langley was as far as I got," Malcolm said calmly.

Quin looked from one to the other. "Just a moment. Do you mean that this not speaking to one another nonsense was because of Eloise and me?"

Malcolm shrugged, a slight grin touching his face. "More or less."

"Good God. You devious bastard." Quin stared at his uncle. "I should—"

"I didn't lie to you, Quin," Malcolm interrupted. "I didn't think of you and Maddie until Lewis's letter."

A warm hand touched Quin's shoulder and slid down his arm to grasp his fingers. "You should have said something, Mr. Bancroft," Maddie chided. "I would have been sure to kill him, then."

His Grace finally stood. "So you think you've won, do you?" he snapped at Maddie.

She looked at him coolly, then released Quin's hand and stepped directly in front of the duke. Quin thought she meant to hit him, and he tensed, ready to leap forward and prevent bloodshed. Instead, though, she raised up on her tiptoes, put a hand on the duke's shoulder, and kissed him on the cheek.

"We began badly, Your Grace. If you wish to continue that way, believe me, I love a good argument. But I would like us to be friends, and I would like my children to know their grandfather."

Maddie was brilliant. She'd hit on Highbarrow's one weakness, and she knew it. Quin slid his arms about her waist and pulled her back against him. "All of your grandchildren," he seconded, kissing Maddie's ear, and fire burning through him at her nearness. "Scores of them."

The duke eyed her for a long moment, then nodded grudgingly. "There'd better be . . . Madeleine."

She nodded. "I shall make a gallant attempt, Your Grace."

"Hurrah!" Rafael shouted, and slapped Quin soundly on the back. "Justice triumphs. May I have my horse back, now, Warefield?"

Quin turned Maddie around and leaned down to kiss her softly. "I love you," he murmured.

"I love you, too," she whispered back, returning his kiss with one of her own. "Now, give Rafe his horse back."

"Anything you wish, my love." He grinned at her. "Stubborn chit."